## PRAISE FOR ANNA BELL



'The perfect laugh-out-loud love story' **Louise Pentland**

'Smart, witty and completely fresh' **Cathy Bramley**

'Romantic and refreshing' **Mhairi McFarlane**

'A fun, bouncy, brilliant tale' ***Heat***

'Funny, relatable and fabulously written' ***Daily Express***

'Perfect for fans of Sophie Kinsella' ***Take a Break***

'Properly funny stuff' ***Fabulous***

'A funny, feel-good read' ***Closer***

'A brilliantly funny, romantic and
effervescent read' ***Frost* magazine**

'Romance, comedy and drama sparkle in this fun, fresh
and frothy concoction' ***Lancashire Evening Post***

'A hilarious and heartwarming story' ***Don't Bend the Spine***

**Anna Bell** lives in the South of France with her young family and energetic Labrador. When not chained to her laptop, Anna can be found basking in the sun in the summer, heading to the ski slopes in the winter (to drink hot chocolate and watch – she can't ski) or having a sneaky treat from the patisserie – all year round! *We Just Clicked* is Anna's eighth novel.

You can find out more about Anna on her website – www.annabellwrites.com or follow her on Twitter @annabell_writes

# We Just Clicked

ANNA
BELL

HQ

ONE PLACE. MANY STORIES

This novel is entirely a work of fiction. The names, characters and incidents portrayed in it are the work of the author's imagination. Any resemblance to actual persons, living or dead, events or localities is entirely coincidental.

HQ
An imprint of HarperCollins*Publishers* Ltd
1 London Bridge Street
London SE1 9GF

This edition 2020

2

First published in Great Britain by
HQ, an imprint of HarperCollins*Publishers* Ltd 2020



Anna Bell asserts the moral right to be identified as the author of this work.
A catalogue record for this book is available from the British Library.

ISBN: 978-0-00-834077-3

MIX
Paper from responsible sources
FSC™ C007454
FSC
www.fsc.org

This book is produced from independently certified FSC™ paper to ensure responsible forest management.

For more information visit: www.harpercollins.co.uk/green

This book is set in 10.3/15 pt. Sabon

Printed and bound in Great Britain by
CPI Group (UK) Ltd, Croydon, CR0 4YY

For Evan, who I become prouder of every day.

# Prologue

If I'd known that the last time I'd see Ben was that unusually hot day in April, I would have made more of an effort to tell him something profound. I would have told him I loved him. Told him I was sorry for all the times I'd fought petty arguments with him. Told him how he was more a part of me than I ever imagined was possible. I certainly wouldn't have told him that he had crappy taste in engagement rings and that his hairline was starting to recede. But I guess in some ways that was better than all the soppy stuff because if I'd known it was the last time, I'd never have let him leave that afternoon at all.

He'd taken me to a high-end jewellery shop whose windows I'd only ever drooled over from the outside. I'd never dared enter it, let alone imagined that I, Izzy Brown, would be allowed to touch one of their exquisite rings.

'Holy shit,' I said, my hand flying up to my mouth in embarrassment of my potty mouth. Luckily the man behind the counter was polite enough to act like he hadn't heard. 'Are you sure the rock's big enough?'

I held the diamond up to the light and it practically blinded me. There was no denying it was a beautiful ring, but it was far too showy.

'It's not that big,' said Ben. Beads of sweat had started to form on his forehead as the magnitude of what was happening hit him. Or maybe he'd caught sight of the price tag. 'I just want it to be special.'

'I think it's too much,' I said, shaking my head and slipping it off. 'I think she'd prefer something more understated.'

'Something like that?' asked Ben, pointing to another equally ostentatious ring.

I shuddered, not because the ring was horrid but because it was exactly the type of ring that I imagined that Cameron would propose with. Not that he'd come here. He'd have flown to Antwerp and bought the perfect diamond first before flying back to have it set. That's what the very few engaged or married traders that he knew had done and Cameron hated to deviate from the pack.

'I think she'd prefer something like...' I walked along to the opposite end of the display cabinet and my eyes fell upon the perfect ring, 'like that.'

I stared at the platinum band with a bright blue sapphire flanked on either side by tiny diamonds. It was elegant and understated, but special none the less. It was exactly what he was looking for.

Ben followed my finger and examined the ring before he looked up at me and a small smile spread across his face.

'Bloody hell, that's the one.'

The man behind the counter pulled it out and rested it on the top and glided it over my finger. It was a little tighter than the first one, but it fit well enough. Ben shook a little as he checked the price tag but relief flooded his face when he saw he could afford it.

'It's an excellent choice,' said the man. He started spieling about the cut and clarity of the diamonds and the pedigree of the sapphire, but I could tell Ben wasn't listening. He'd found the ring and he was happy. As was I – my hand had never looked more beautiful. I fanned my fingers out and stared at it twinkling in the lights. It was entrancing.

The man behind the counter coughed and I looked up a little embarrassed.

'I need to pop it back in the box,' he said.

'Of course, of course,' I said tugging it off. 'It's so beautiful.'

Ben smiled as he handed over his credit card, and just like that, my brother had taken his first step to getting married. Or perhaps it was technically his second step as he'd actually got engaged a few years ago when he'd proposed with a ring from a Christmas cracker. He'd told his fiancée that he'd get her a better ring one day, and after a recent work promotion he'd finally been able to make good on the promise.

'I can't believe you're going to do this,' I said, looping my arm through his as we left the store.

'We've been engaged for three years, it's hardly a shocker.'

'I know, but this is really it, though, isn't it? You've got the proper ring and you're going to set a proper date. This is huge. We should celebrate.'

'I was going to head straight back to the station. I don't really want to be walking round London with it.'

He hugged his backpack tighter to his chest. He looked like such a tourist wearing it over his front.

I pulled out my phone and read a message.

'Cameron's going to the Founder's Arms, it's just over the river from here. Why don't we go and have a quick drink with him before I walk you back to Waterloo?'

Ben looked at his watch and I could tell he was uneasy, but I hadn't seen him in ages. The afternoon had whizzed by and there was still so much to catch up on.

'OK, but the drinks are on you as I don't think I can ever afford to drink again after buying that.'

'Ben, I hope you're not getting into debt for the ring. It's not like the wedding will be cheap and—'

'Izzy, I'm kidding.'

'Good,' I said with relief. 'Of course I'll buy you a celebratory drink anyway. Plus, I can't wait for you to meet Cameron.'

'Oh yes, the famous Cameron. I'm intrigued to meet him too.'

It felt strange that they'd not met before, but my life in London seemed so far removed from my family and friends back home in Basingstoke. The two might only be an hour apart by train but you'd think I was from Timbuktu judging by the reaction I'd get from Cameron when I suggested we visit. I think he expected that he'd turn to dust if he left the Greater London area, like a vampire entering a church.

I stifled a yawn as we weaved through the empty streets. During the week the same ones would be full of City workers bustling about, but at the weekend they were deserted.

'Late night?' asked Ben.

'Kind of, but it's been one of those weeks where every night's been a late one.'

'I don't know how you do it; I can barely manage going out at the weekend now.'

'That's what happens when you're old and settled. You get a mortgage, you get married and next you'll be losing your hair like Dad.'

He rubbed at his hair. 'Oi, I'm only two years older than you and I'm not receding quite yet. Plus I'm not married yet either.'

Ben's been with his fiancée Becca for fifteen years; they met at school, and I think of them as an old married couple. It's been a cruel wait for my mum to splash out on an over-the-top mother-of-the-groom hat and for me who wants to be their bridesmaid.

'So does this mean you're going to have to propose all over again?'

'Oh God, I don't know. Does it? That was the whole point of proposing with the cracker ring. It was supposed to be whimsical.'

'I think that would have been fine if you'd then produced the real ring soon afterwards, but three years… I think you'll have to do it again, and with a ring like that it deserves to be properly romantic.'

He groaned.

'Don't worry, I'll help you think of something.'

By the time we crossed over the river to the pub, we'd come up with a sneaky proposal plan that was both romantic and personal. I'd shed a few happy tears and Ben was once again grateful I'd helped him out.

We arrived at the pub before Cameron and his friends, so we ordered drinks and took them out onto the terrace. We managed to find a recently vacated table on the edge, still covered with empty glasses.

'Will you take my photo?' I said, looking over at the view over the Thames towards St Paul's on the other side.

I didn't bother to wait for a reply; I simply held out my phone to Ben and struck a pose.

'Is this for your Instagram? I see you're doing really well. Over 500 followers?' he said.

'I know. Can you believe it?'

'I told you I had a good feeling about it,' he said, snapping a couple of shots. He checked his work before handing it over with a nod. 'Not bad.'

I had a look myself and was suitably impressed.

'Perfect, I can post that later with all the appropriate hashtags.'

'Move over Zoella,' he said sipping his drink.

'I don't think I'd ever be that big, it's just nice doing something creative again. And you never know, I could perhaps try and make the move into marketing or PR by showing agencies that I understand how to build a brand.'

'Still having no luck on the job front?'

I shook my head. I took a job as a copywriter for an advertising agency that specialised in medical products straight out of university. I thought I was going to have a glittering advertising career and that it would all be cocktails and swanky parties à la *Mad Men*, only the reality was far from glamorous. I didn't mind when I was younger, when it was all about the pay cheque and where the next party was, but as I'd got older I wanted to start focusing on my career. Only five years writing copy about haemorrhoid creams had left me pigeonholed in the medical sector and longing to do work that people didn't read in desperation because they had piles.

'Well, I think you're onto something with the Instagram thing. From what I've seen on your feed, you're a natural. I'm sure you'll be making a living out of it in no time.'

I laughed hard. 'Do you have any idea how hard it would be to get to that stage?'

Ben shrugged. 'I know you could do it. You know, I'm proud of you for giving it a go.' He chinked his glass against mine.

'And I'm proud of you, finally getting married. Can I see the ring again?' I said, clapping my hands together.

He looked around to see if anyone was watching and he leant down into his bag, which he had looped around his leg. He pulled the little ring box out and flipped it open, holding it out to me.

'Oh, it's even more beautiful than I remember it being,' I said, looking at it longingly. 'Can I try it on?'

'I guess so, it's probably safer on your finger than it is in my bag,' he said as I picked it up and slipped it on.

I held my hand out and it felt complete again. The table next to us burst into applause. I looked around to see what they were clapping at and it took me a good few seconds to realise they were all staring at me and Ben.

'Congratulations,' one of them shouted whilst raising their glass.

'What the… Oh no, it's not what it looks like. He's my brother,' I said in slight horror as I tried to slip the ring back off my finger but it didn't want to budge.

The clapping petered out and they all looked a bit embarrassed.

'I was just trying it on,' I said, feeling ridiculous and yanking it even harder, but it wasn't moving in the slightest.

'Well, I hope the actual proposal goes better than that,' said Ben, taking a large sip of his drink.

'Um, that's if I can give you the ring back,' I said, holding up my hand. My finger looked like a plump sausage and it was at least double its normal size.

'You're joking, right?' he said, laughing a little awkwardly before he realised I wasn't laughing back. 'Izzy!'

'I'm sorry,' I said, wincing. 'It won't come off.'

I tried to pull it as hard as I could.

'Don't do that,' he said, screwing up his face. 'You might break it.'

He took an audible deep breath before he stood up.

'Ice, you need to put it in ice. Your hand will shrink,' he said.

'I can put it in my cider,' I said, about to plunge it in.

'Don't you dare, it'll get sticky. Hold tight, I'll get some from the bar.'

Hold tight, I muttered to myself as I sat there looking at my ever-increasing sausage finger.

'Izzy,' shouted a voice and I looked up to see Cameron and a few of his work colleague friends heading across the pub terrace, glasses in hand. 'I didn't realise you'd already be here; I would have got you a drink,' he said as he sat down next to me and gave me a quick kiss on the lips. 'So how did the engagement ring shopping go?'

'Really well,' I said holding my hand up. 'I decided I'd save us the trouble and get the ball rolling.'

I'd been about to laugh, thinking he would too, when his whole face started to crumple.

'Er, Izzy, I don't know what you were thinking but I really don't think we're there, are we? I mean, we only live together because you were living in Balham and I don't go further out than Zone 2. I mean, you know how much I care about you and all—'

'Prosecco on the house,' said a woman, cutting Cameron off mid-flow. 'For the happy couple, I hear you just got engaged!'

Cameron looked up at the barmaid in absolute horror, his face turning pale. I risked a glance at his work colleagues who were all trying to look anywhere but in our direction. All except Tiffany, who was giving me her usual pursed-lipped, narrowed-eye look. I'd long suspected she fancied Cameron, even though he denied it.

'Actually, we didn't,' I said, mortified. 'It was all just a misunderstanding. I was trying on a ring for my brother and it got stuck.'

'Oh well,' said the woman, looking unbothered. 'You might as well have it now anyway, it's been written off by our boss.'

She placed the tray with the bottle and glasses on the table and I muttered a thank you.

'Here's the ice,' said Ben, rushing over and putting it down in front of me.

He grabbed my hand and plunged it into the water.

'Bloody hell, that's cold,' I said, wincing in pain as my hand started to go numb. 'How long have I got to keep it in there?'

'I don't know,' he said, still panicked. 'Until it comes off?'

He turned and noticed Cameron, who was sitting there mute.

'Cameron, this is my brother Ben, Ben this is my boyfriend Cameron, or at least I think he's still my boyfriend, but he's definitely nowhere near being my fiancé,' I said.

They muttered a hello and shook hands, both distracted: Ben by the ring stuck on my finger, Cameron by the conversation we'd just had.

I pulled my hand out of the glass and, much to my and Ben's relief, the ring came off my finger.

Ben cradled it like a newborn baby, wrapping it up in his T-shirt and drying it carefully before depositing it back in the box and in the safety of his backpack.

'So it's *your* ring?' Tiffany said to Ben, with obvious relief.

'Yes, and I think I'd better take it home before anything else happens to it,' he said, downing the rest of his cider. 'Do you mind, Izzy?'

'Of course not,' I said lying.

I got up and gave him a quick hug and he said a quick goodbye to the others before leaving, clutching his bag.

It was the last time I ever saw him.

Two weeks after the pub incident I was on my way to work when my phone rang. My mum's number flashed up and at first I thought she'd phoned me by mistake because it was so early. When I picked up there was a rustling sound on the line, and I was about to hang up when I realised it was Mum sobbing. Eventually my dad took the phone from her, and when he spoke

I barely recognised his voice. It was so quiet and soft, nothing like his usual boom.

'Izzy, are you sitting down? Something awful's happened to Ben.'

I'd immediately started to witter on about an accident and asking if he was in hospital when Dad went quiet. He didn't need to tell me the next bit; I knew from his tone that Ben had died.

The world started to spin and my body and mind seemed to drift away from each other. I could hear Dad telling me details and words jumped out at me – cardiac arrest… arrhythmia… in his sleep – but I couldn't absorb any of it. I was too numb to take it all in, too numb to be able to say anything other than I was coming home.

I was near Paddington, and so I jumped on a train to Reading in the hope of changing from there to Basingstoke. It's not a route I'd usually take going home but I couldn't face travelling across London in rush hour. I went into some sort of a survival mode, putting one foot in front of the other and was amazed to find myself on the right train.

I managed to hold it together until I got to Reading and then it hit me – like slapped me in the face as if a freight train had hit me – and I found myself stranded at the station not knowing how I was going to find my connecting train. All I could think was that Ben was gone and that I'd never see him again.

My legs started to wobble and my phone slid out of my hands, and I couldn't stop myself from falling.

'Whoa, there,' said a man, catching me under my arms and keeping me upright. 'Are you all right?'

My head was throbbing and my legs had gone to jelly.

'Are you all right?' he said again, but it felt like it was coming from somewhere distant.

He continued to hold onto me and I took a moment to look at him. He was dressed in a smart blue shirt that matched his eyes.

'Do you speak English?' he said, elongating every word and speaking very loudly.

'I, um, yes,' I said, confused.

'Sorry, you weren't answering me and I thought… Look, are you OK? Is there someone I could call?'

I shook my head. There really wasn't. Cameron was on a business trip to New York, I'd planned to call him when I got to my parents' house. There was no rush; it was the middle of the night there and it wasn't like he'd be able to do anything from there. I thought back to the one and only time that Cameron had met my brother and my heart started to ache about it – my last afternoon with Ben. 'I'm on my way to my mum and dad's and I… I don't know where the platform is for Basingstoke.'

A breeze whistled through the station and my curls blew into my face. I'd left the house with them wet, I'd planned on putting my hair up at some point on my journey, but I'd forgotten and they'd dried out of control.

'Your mum and dad,' said the man kindly, 'in Basingstoke. OK, OK, we can do that.'

He looked up and scanned the departures board. I couldn't believe that I'd been standing so close and I hadn't noticed it. My mind felt full of fog.

'OK, so Platform 4 at 9.52, you've got ten minutes. I'll take you there,' he said.

I closed my eyes and I was flooded with relief.

'Thank you, I…' I took another deep breath. 'Just thank you.'

'It's no problem, really. Um, OK, can you stand on your own, do you think? You look a bit unsteady.'

'I think so,' I said, focusing on breathing in and out.

He pulled his arms away from me slowly and I successfully proved that I could stand on two feet, much to both our amazement. My hair blew in my face again, and I scraped it out of the way the best I could, but curls kept getting stuck on my tear-stained cheeks.

'Now,' he said, pulling the hair band off my wrist. 'This looks like it's bothering you.'

He scooped my curls up into the messiest topknot ever, but in that split second I was just so grateful that he'd got them away from my face. I stared down at the red ring the band had left on my wrist, wondering why I didn't remember I had it there in the first place.

He bent down and retrieved my phone and wrinkled his face.

'It's a little cracked,' he said, handing it to me. I slipped it into my handbag without looking.

'Least of my worries,' I said, and he nodded.

'Let's get you on that train.'

He steered me by the elbow towards a platform, taking care not to rush me, as I tried desperately to hold the floodgates of emotions shut.

The man walked me halfway along a platform and he continued to hold my elbow until the train arrived, like he was propping me up. It was only when he escorted me onto it that I noticed he wasn't leaving.

'Your train,' I said in protest. 'You don't have to take me to Basingstoke.'

He guided me to a seat, and sat down on the one next to me.

'It's fine, I can catch a later one. I just want to make sure you get there safely. That's all.'

'But really, I'll be fine,' I said, trying to hold back the tears.

'You're not fine, and you don't have to be either,' he said. 'I'll make sure you get to your mum and dad's. Do they live near the station, or do you need a taxi?'

'Taxi,' I just about managed. His kindness was starting to make me choke up.

'OK, then I'll make sure you get in one.'

I stopped protesting and nodded and then the tears started to fall. I cried all over his blue shirt and he sat there patiently passing me napkins that he'd nabbed from the buffet trolley.

I didn't even realise we'd reached our final destination until he gently guided me out of the seat and led me out of the doors. I walked down the stairs into the tunnel to the main entrance, not caring what an absolute state I must have looked like.

I found my ticket and put it into the machine on autopilot and he followed me through the barrier using the ticket he'd purchased on the train. Then he led me to the black cabs waiting outside the station.

'Are you OK from here?' he asked, helping me inside the cab.

I nodded back, 'I am.'

He leant into the front of the cab and handed the driver a £20 note, asking him to take me to where I needed to go.

'She hasn't been drinking, has she? I don't want to clear up any sick,' said the driver.

'No,' he said, shaking his head. 'She's just had a really awful start to the day.'

He turned to me and smiled with his head tilted.

'I'm so sorry for whatever's happened to you,' he practically whispered.

'Thank you. Thank you for everything,' I stuttered. It didn't seem adequate for what he'd done.

He shrugged his shoulders. 'It's what anyone would have done.'

'I don't even know your name.'

'Aidan,' he said softly.

'Thank you, Aidan,' I said.

'You take care,' he said, stepping out of the car and gently closing the door.

'Where to, love?' asked the taxi driver.

I gave him my parents' address and he pulled out into the road. I turned back and looked at Aidan standing there on the pavement. He waved and I waved back. But then I remembered that Ben had gone and the rest of the journey became a blur.

# Two Years Later

Welcome to May
This_Izzy_Loves IGTV
No. followers: 15.3k

*Hello! I'm back. Sorry to those who missed me over the last couple of days. I was away with my family and we chose to stay offline – I know, I KNOW! But I survived and I had lots of time to think up wonderful things that I'm going to put up on my feed this month. Can't wait to share it all with you – including hopefully a great brand collaboration. Keeping all my fingers and toes crossed, and wrapped in plastic – wink.*

# Chapter 1

There are many ridiculous things I have done in the name of 'the Gram'. Walking past restaurants that I know have mouth-wateringly delicious meals only to eat at mediocre places because their food is more photogenic. Standing alone on the South Bank posing like I'm in *Britain's Next Top Model* whilst discreetly pressing the remote for my camera. Maxing out my credit card to bring home an ideal #OutfitOfTheDay wardrobe only to take all the items back after I'd snapped myself in them. But being wrapped up in three 20m rolls of clingfilm in an attempt to snare a lucrative marketing campaign probably takes the biscuit.

'Are we sure this is a good idea?' I ask, staring at the rolls of clingfilm in Marissa's hands like they're a deadly weapon.

'It's a great idea, it's going to be fantastic,' she says. Of course she'd say that; she came up with it. 'It is the perfect Halloween costume and probably the easiest one.'

'Do you think people will get that I'm one of Dexter's victims? Is it too old a TV programme?'

She tuts dismissively and walks closer towards me. She's so keen to get me wrapped up in this plastic that if she wasn't my best friend that I've known for practically my whole life, I'd be worried that she was actually trying to bump me off Dexter-style.

'OK, hold tight,' she says, a glint in her eye.

I know that there's no point in protesting. The only positive I can think of right now is that it might warm me up. I'm standing here in a skin-coloured strapless bra and giant knickers, shivering. I'd turned the heating down thinking that I'd be far too warm when wearing my new plastic fantastic outfit. I hadn't factored in the pre-wrapped stage.

Marissa starts to pass the plastic round and round and it starts to get tighter and tighter.

'Do you think it's actually safe? Are you sure I can't suffocate?'

'Come on, we checked this. Google never lies, right?'

'Did we google that specifically? "Can I die from a clingfilm costume?" Maybe we should have used the American brand name. What do they call it, it's something-wrap isn't it?'

'Saran wrap,' says Marissa, bending down to start wrapping up my waist.

I go to reach for my phone to check and Marissa slaps my hand away.

'It's not like you're going to be covered in it for long. We only need to take a few photos.'

'A *few* photos?' I laugh.

It makes it sound like one or two, but to get the one golden shot we usually take fifty or sixty. Luckily Marissa's a fellow Instagrammer so we go above and beyond classic best friend duties by being each other's stylist, muse, photographer, editor and number one fan.

Our friendship has always been mutually supportive. At fourteen, when I joined the school choir, Marissa did too, despite being tone deaf. At sixteen, when she went all goth I dyed my hair black and boiled all summer long in black velvet dresses. At eighteen, when I wanted a Chinese symbol on the small of my back before I went to university, Marissa not only held my hand but got a matching one on hers too. So when Ben died and I moved back to my hometown of Basingstoke with a serious Instagram addiction, it wasn't long before we fell into our old pattern and she became an addict too.

'OK, here we go,' she says, bending down and wrapping my bum. 'We're getting there. How are you feeling?'

'Like I'm in a straitjacket.'

'Perfect. It's looking great.'

She switches to a new roll.

'We're going through them quickly,' I say. 'Is my bum really that big?'

'It is a lot of plastic, isn't it?' she says.

'Oh crap, do you think I'll get in trouble? Will the brand call me irresponsible?'

Marissa stops and stares at the empty rolls on the floor. 'Shit, I hadn't thought about that.'

We both look down at my costume.

'The thing is, if you stop now and don't post this then we'll have used these rolls anyway and that would be worse,' she says.

'You're right. It's not like I can reuse it,' I say.

'No, you don't want to be covering any more chicken fillets with them,' says Marissa, laughing.

'I'll have you know these are real,' I say, looking down at my chest that's flattened like a pancake and could actually do with something to pad it out.

She carries on and I hope that I don't lose out on the contract because of a misjudgement in green credentials.

Finally she stands back. 'You're all finished,' she says, taking a snap of me on her iPhone to show me.

'Wow, that actually looks pretty good,' I say.

'Now for the blood,' she practically cackles. My eyes widen as she slips on an apron, much too like the real Dexter for my liking.

'What?' she says. 'I don't want to get any on my jeans.'

Marissa signals for me to lie on the plastic sheeting that we've covered my very white lounge with whilst she stirs the lumpy cocoa powder and food dye paste like a witch stirring a cauldron. She bends down and expertly applies the fake blood to my stomach.

'Now the duct tape,' she says, taping my arms above my head. 'And the knife,' she says, whipping one out from her handbag.

'What the—' I shout until I realise there's no glint on it and it's quite clearly plastic.

'Can you believe they still make these?' she says, pushing the fake blade into my stomach, causing the blade to retract into the handle.

'I haven't seen one of those since primary school. I don't think that'd be allowed in the playground anymore.'

'Not likely,' she says, taping the handle to my stomach as discreetly as she can.

'I think you're done,' she says, pulling over the tripod. 'You ready?'

'Uh-huh.'

'OK, pull some scared faces,' she says as she starts clicking.

She takes a couple of shots and then looks down at the camera and pulls it off the tripod.

'I think it looks pretty good. I'm so going to do this for my costume when it's actually Halloween.'

I stare at her emerging bump.

'Erm, you do realise that you're going to be eight months pregnant by then.'

'Oh yeah,' she says, looking down at her stomach. 'I guess that would be way too much plastic.'

'Yep, *that's* the problem with this costume for a pregnant woman.'

'What do you reckon?' she asks, holding the camera above my head so that I can see the photo.

'I love it. But I should have duct tape over my mouth too, don't you think?'

'Are you sure?'

'Yeah, just don't stick it down too hard!'

Receiving a message from an agency representing a well-known supermarket was like a dream come true. They're looking for influencers on Instagram to pitch them ideas for Halloween posts – the caveat being you have to come up with a costume from products you can buy in store. And with a little help from Marissa, who was insanely jealous that I got asked and she didn't, I came up with a killer concept in all sense of the word. I'm just hoping it's enough to win me the campaign. It would be so on brand for me – my theme is all about affordable lifestyle.

My Instagram following has been growing over the last three years and I'm just teetering on the edge of starting to earn good money for sponsored posts. I desperately hope that soon I'll make enough that my monthly earnings go into triple figures. In my wildest dreams I get caught up in fantasies that I'll be able to earn enough to give up the temp job I took when I moved back to Basingstoke or at the very least move out of the little flat I now share with Ben's ex-fiancée Becca and its mouldy bathroom, but right now I'd settle for making more from an ad than the cost of the props involved, which in this case (clingfilm, cocoa powder, food dye and plastic knife) is probably about fifteen quid.

Marissa rips a strip of tape and places it gently over my mouth.

'OK?'

I go to nod but realise that I'm restrained and instead I blink twice, hoping she'll pick up on the new code.

'Right then.'

My phone on the table starts to buzz and ring loudly. Only two people ring my phone: salespeople and my mum.

Marissa peers over at it. 'It's your mum,' she says and without hesitation picks it up.

'Hello, Dawn, I'm afraid Izzy's a bit tied up at the moment and I mean that *literally*… No, unfortunately I'm not being cheeky, it's not a man who's tied her up… No, she's still not dating anyone… No, as far as I know there's been no one since Cameron… I have suggested that… and that… uh-huh, you know what she's like.'

I make a muffled noise through the duct tape to remind her that I'm still here.

'Yes, the bump's fine, thank you… Over the worst of it now, I haven't been sick for a couple of weeks… Yes, December… Yes, Tim is over the moon about being a dad… Yes, Mum said she'd told you at Zumba. OK then, shall I get her to call you when she's free?… uh-huh, uh-huh… right, yes, hopefully see you soon.'

She hangs up the phone and pops it back on the table, as if it was totally normal to have a chat with my mum whilst I lie here constrained by clingfilm.

'Your mum says, can you call her when you're less tied up?'

I blink twice in recognition and Marissa picks up her camera once more. She takes a couple more shots and looks at them, wrinkling her brow at the results.

'It looks a little dark.' She takes the camera off the tripod again and turns it round to face me and I totally agree.

'I'll go and get the standing lamp from your bedroom.'

She leaves me alone and I look up at the ceiling and see there's a cobweb hanging right above my head. I'm scanning it for signs of life – or death in the case of any flies trapped in it – that would signal the existence of a spider. What if there was one right above my head, ready to drop down from its web, and there would be nothing I could do about it? I shiver. There's absolutely no way I could go on *I'm A Celebrity Get Me Out of Here!* I'll have to remember that when they try and lure me onto the show when I'm a huge Instagram star. I might be willing to do crazy things like this whilst I'm a mere wannabe but hopefully the crazy and the ridiculous will stop by the time I become a megastar.

I hear the key in the door and I go to move, but Marissa's done a pretty good job with the duct tape and I'm stuck.

'Don't come in!' I shout. I'm shocked that I can make myself heard through the duct tape; so much for all those Hollywood movies. It doesn't stop Becca though, and I hear her scream before I see her peering over me.

She puts her hand to her chest and takes an over-the-top deep breath.

'What the hell are you doing? You scared the life out of me.'

Becca leans over and rips off the tape, which fortunately wasn't stuck anymore or else I might have had an impromptu waxing session. Her arms are now folded and her nostrils are flaring. And from this angle with her angular bob and straight fringe she looks pretty fierce.

'We were just taking photos,' I stutter.

'Don't tell me this is one of your Instagram photoshoots.'

Marissa walks into the room and Becca points a finger at her. 'You're not going all Sweeney Todd for one of your recipes, are you?'

'No, no. I gave up on the food porn ages ago. Now my feed's more yummy mummy-to-be.'

Becca looks accusingly at me. 'Right, so this is for you then. Bloody Instagram.'

'But this is different, it's for a possible contract – you know, as in *paid*. It's for Halloween.'

'Halloween is months away,' she says, putting her hands on her hips.

'I know but the agency have to pitch it to their client and I guess these things take time to develop,' I say, trailing off.

'Well, a little warning would have been nice.'

'You usually go to the gym on Thursdays. But seeing as you're here we could have a proper girls' night in.'

'Groan,' says Marissa. 'I've got a ticking time bomb in my belly and I've seen what happened to my sister; in a few months' time it'll be like a military operation to even leave the house, let alone see you guys on my own or have the energy to go *out*-out. Let's go for drinks! It *is* Thirsty Thursday.'

Marissa has a name for every day of the week to make it sound like it's a socially acceptable night of the week to go out drinking: Tipsy Tuesday, Wicked Wednesday, Thirsty Thursday, Sunday Funday.

'Tempting as that sounds,' says Becca, 'I've got a date tonight. I just came back for a shower.'

'A date?' says Marissa, arching an eyebrow.

'Uh-huh, with Gareth.'

'Again? Good for you.'

Becca tucks her hair behind her ears and it only highlights how crimson her cheeks have turned.

'Looks like you'll have to make do with Kirsty and Phil and a takeaway,' I say.

Marissa doesn't look pleased. Once she's got a night out in her sights she won't let it go. We'll be out in heels and sequins whether we like it or not.

'We could always go for drinks next weekend,' she replies.

Becca and I exchange glances; we both know we're doomed.

'I'm free on the Friday night,' says Becca, flipping through the post. She pulls a letter out and starts opening it.

'I said I'd go out for drinks with Cleo after work,' I say.

'Ooh I really liked her when we met at your birthday. Why don't Becca and I come and meet you guys? We can get the train to Reading, can't we, Becca? Then it really will be a big night. We can go to one of those cocktail bars and get dressed up all swanky.'

Now it's my turn to groan. The best part of only going for an after-work drink is that I get to leave early because Cleo thinks that Basingstoke is really far from Reading. I've never corrected her that in reality it's only twenty minutes on very frequent trains because my 'long and arduous commute' is an excellent excuse to use when I want to sneak away from work socialising. Unfortunately, Marissa knows when the last trains are and also a cheap cab company that'll drive us home at goodness-knows-what time.

'I'm not sure,' says Becca, wrinkling up her nose. 'I'm old now, I don't know if I can be arsed.'

'You're only two years older than us,' says Marissa. 'And, hello, I'm pregnant if anyone is playing the I'm-not-going-out card, it's me and I'm not. So you have no excuse.'

'Fine,' she says, sighing. She turns her attention back to the letter in her hand. She pulls a face and puts it down on the kitchen island. 'Gas bill.'

I pull the same face. Looks like I won't be drinking that many cocktails whilst we're out next week.

'I better go shower,' says Becca, 'and this place better be less *CSI* when I come out.'

She disappears off and Marissa turns back to me.

'So, she's going out with Gareth again?'

'Uh-huh. I think this must be her third date.'

'Oh right, so it's going well?'

'I guess so. She hasn't really talked to me about it; I think she feels a bit awkward.'

Marissa nods. 'Hmm, I imagine she would. So, should we take more photos?'

'Absolutely. Phil and Kirsty wait for no man,' I say, relieved that Marissa knows when to change the subject.

'But you've got to phone your mum back first.'

I nod as she goes to reapply the tape.

'It didn't sound important – it was something about baking banana bread and some chocolate cake,' she says, shrugging and picking up her camera again.

I wince. 'Oh God, she's baked two cakes?' That's never a good sign. The more she's hit by grief, the more she bakes.

'Yeah, I think so.'

'Oh bugger. Do you mind if we take a raincheck on Kirsty and Phil? I better go and make sure she's OK.'

'Of course, go, go.'

'I might need a little help,' I say, trying and failing to wriggle my arms.

'Oh yeah.' She bends down and helps me out.

'Do you think we'll have got the right shot?'

Marissa's carefully unwrapping me, trying not splatter fake blood all over the flat.

'I'm sure with a little photoshop magic we will have.'

In an ideal world we'd take a few dozen more. As much as I love to escape to Instagram to distract me from the real world, sometimes it's too hard to ignore, like now, when my mum needs me. All I can hope is that we'll have a photo that will be good enough to help elevate me to the next level of influencer – preferably just in time for me to pay the gas bill.

# Chapter 2

I pull my cardigan further round me whilst I wait for my computer to boot up. It's not even warm outside today but for some reason our office has cranked up the air conditioning to Baltic proportions. I dig around in my office drawer and feel triumphant as I pull out a woolly scarf that I haven't needed since last summer.

'Almost time for the fingerless gloves,' says Cleo, her teeth chattering.

I laugh. I love sitting next to Cleo; she makes my job so much more bearable.

After Ben died I wanted to be closer to my parents, so I quit the job in advertising that I hated, moved back to my hometown and started temping at an insurance company in nearby Reading. It was only supposed to be temporary whilst I made the leap into marketing or PR, but like most best-laid plans it hasn't worked out that way and I've been here almost two years now.

Colin is next to arrive at our bank of desks. He walks over to his seat opposite Cleo, looking over his shoulder as he does so for any sign of Mrs Harris. Relieved that she's not in the vicinity he manages to nod a hello to us, which is progress. Last week, after Flamingogate, he wouldn't even acknowledge anyone, choosing only to look at the table.

'Poor Colin,' whispers Cleo.

Someone drops a ream of paper from a box over the other side of the room and we both watch as he flinches.

The poor soul. He'd only gone to touch Mrs Harris's bread flamingo out of admiration, he hadn't intended to break its leg and therefore in her eyes hinder her chances in the Great Office Bake Off competition. Whilst we all love our work colleague Mrs Harris we are all secretly terrified of her, and woe betide anyone who gets on her wrong side.

My computer clearly has that Friday feeling and is slow booting up. I know how it feels. I look at my to-do list, wishing my tasks were a bit more interesting, but temping in the contracts department of an insurance company isn't really the job of my dreams.

My computer *still* hasn't started, so I slip my hand into my bag and I pull out my phone as quietly and unobtrusively as I can. But nothing gets past Cleo.

'Hello, my name is Izzy and I'm an Instagram-aholic,' she says.

'Very funny.' I put my phone face down on the table. 'I wasn't looking at Instagram, actually. I'm waiting for an email. A very important email.'

'Uh-huh. About what?'

'Important things.'

'Important Instagram things?'

I grit my teeth.

'I'm not addicted,' I say, pushing the phone further away from me.

'Sure you're not,' she says, smirking.

'I'm not, honestly.'

'Do I need to remind you of the day that your network went down and you couldn't get online? You nearly went mad.'

'I wouldn't say mad...'

'You went to The Swan to use their WiFi.'

'It's a nice pub,' I say, finding it hard to keep a straight face.

'Um, it's a nice pub if you're touting for business.'

'It's not that bad in there.'

'You got propositioned twice by people wanting your services.'

'Well, they're not that used to having women in there.'

'And you went to McDonald's, multiple times.'

'They do surprisingly good coffee.'

'Uh-huh, and have surprisingly good WiFi.'

I fold my arms defensively. My computer is finally showing signs of life.

'So the fact that you've not been to either establishment since that day…'

'Still doesn't mean to say I'm addicted!'

Cleo's eyebrow is arching – she's not convinced and neither am I.

'I'm just checking my email, that's all,' I protest.

She smiles and turns back to her keyboard with a smug look on her face as if she's older and wiser, when in fact she's only 23 – eight years younger than me. Trust me to sit next to the only millennial who isn't surgically attached to her phone.

I look a little longingly at my overturned phone knowing that I'm going to have to prove her wrong by ignoring it for at least a couple of hours. Despite the fact I'm dying to hear back from the agency about the Halloween campaign. My whole life could change with that one little email! The one that would mean I'd really be an Instagram influencer.

I'm still waiting for my log-in screen to load and I look out across the open-plan floor to see Mrs Harris walking across it clutching a Tupperware box as if her life depended on it. Everyone is giving her a wide berth, and I don't blame them after what happened with Colin.

'Here comes trouble,' I whisper to Cleo, who looks over her computer screen.

'It's not Bake Off day *again*, is it? Surely the competition's nearly finished.'

'They've got another six months left,' whispers Colin.

'*Six months!*' Cleo and I shriek.

'It's once every two weeks over nine months,' he says despondently. 'Which means I've got at least another six months of being in exile.'

'Bloody hell, it feels like they're competing every other day,' sighs Cleo.

'Doesn't it?'

Every six months or so the HR department at McKinley Insurance dream up some crazy scheme to make work more fun. We've had bingo mornings, fancy dress Friday and each of the seven floors competed to have the best Christmas decorations. But this competition takes the biscuit, or cake, or bread – depending on the week. Nothing has united the whole office more than the Great Office Bake Off although nothing has divided it as much, either, thanks to how seriously everyone is taking it.

Poor Colin. I look back over at him and he's plugged in his headphones and his eyes are glued to his computer screen. I'm sure I can see him quivering as Mrs Harris finally reaches our bank of desks.

'Oh, lordy, I did not think I was going to get this here in one piece,' she says, resting the box on the end of the table.

Cleo and I edge out of our seats to take a quick look at what's inside, before she whips two tea towels over the top.

'Oh no, no one is getting a look at this baby until eleven o'clock. I don't want a repeat of bread week,' she says so loudly that the rest of the office falls silent.

'No one wants a repeat of bread week,' I say, feeling for Colin who's gone all pale. He gives me a sheepish look before he grabs his folder and speed marches away.

'So, what's the theme this week, Mrs H?' I ask.

She pauses and purses her lips as if considering the abbreviation I'd accidentally used. Mrs Harris is the only person in the office that doesn't use their first name and instead insists that we address her formally like we've slipped back in time. No one else would get away with doing that but she's so formidable that even our boss, Howard, daren't call her by her first name.

'It's French week,' she says and I breathe a sigh of relief that I've got away with the slip of the tongue. 'So naturally I made a *croquembouche* cake.'

'Naturally,' I say, not having a clue what it is but knowing that it's bound to be delicious. All of Mrs Harris's creations are. It's the reason that I've put on a stone since I started working here.

'Now, I'm going to go and get my coffee. You girls will protect it from everyone else, won't you? I don't want that young whippersnapper from Risk Management coming down here. He's always trying to tempt the ladies with his spicy balls.'

'His what?' I splutter.

'She means his spicy nut balls,' says Cleo, examining her nails. 'I've had them before, they're so overrated.'

'I should have known you'd have tried them,' replies Mrs Harris before she sighs loudly again. 'I've got to go all the way back up the stairs again to get my coffee and with my dodgy ankle, it takes so long.'

I look at the three steps she's referring to that lead up to where the drinks machine is.

'And Colin just got up – he could have at least asked me if I'd wanted a drink. You'd think he'd want to get back in my good books.'

'Do you want me to get you one?' I ask, draining my cup. 'I could do with another one anyway.'

'Ah, Izzy, are you sure?'

'Of course.'

I pick up the mug that Mrs Harris thoughtfully slides towards me. I look at Cleo and she hands me her mug, and I head towards our tea station.

'Don't forget,' Mrs Harris calls after me, 'skimmed milk mocha, two sugars.'

I nod as if she doesn't ask for the same thing every time.

I walk into the little kitchenette area and place the cups down. I pop the tea bags into our mugs and fill them up with hot water, giving them time to brew, only to find that the coffee machine has run out of mocha. Getting coffee for Mrs Harris is like a NASA mission: failure is not an option, or at least it isn't if I want some of her latest Bake Off creation.

I leave our tea brewing and take Mrs Harris's mug down the stairs, grateful for dress-down Friday and the fact that I'm not dicing with death on the shiny stairs like I usually am in heels. I turn the corner to the floor below and I stop as a large selfie stick flies towards me and I have to tilt my head back not to get hit in the face.

'Excuse me,' I tut.

'One sec,' says the man holding the stick before he breaks into the biggest pout I've seen since *Zoolander*.

I fold my arms tightly over my chest and sigh loudly, but he doesn't seem to care that he and his vanity are blocking my way.

With nothing else to do I stare at him and his classical good looks. He almost looks like he's walked out of an Instagram photo, filter and all. His skin is perfect and he's got a strong jaw line, smouldering eyes and full lips. Or at least I think they're full, it's hard to tell with the trout pout.

Dressed in a white linen shirt, sleeves rolled up at the elbows, and a pair of khaki trousers that come to rest at his bare ankles, with expensive-looking loafers on his feet, he looks like he's got lost on his way to a City bankers' retreat.

He shakes his head a little as if he's expecting long, luscious locks to magically appear when in reality his hair is styled into a well-gelled quiff that seems to be frozen in time and space.

He keeps snapping away and I wonder if he's forgotten I'm here, so I cough loudly. He takes at least five more photos before lowering the stick.

'Sorry,' he says, looking up at me for the first time. 'The sunlight in this spot at this exact time makes my skin as glossy as an AR filter. Wanna see the results?'

'I… er…'

He grabs the phone from the end of the stick and without waiting for an answer finds the photos he's just taken and thrusts the phone in my face.

I instantly bite my lip to stop myself from laughing.

'Huh?' he says, looking proud.

'Yeah, it's very um… "Blue Steel",' I say, thinking that surely the pose was a deliberate piss-take.

'"Blue Steel"? What, because of my blue eyes?'

'Um, no. Have you not seen *Zoolander*?'

'No,' he says shaking his head. 'I'm not really into animal things.'

I bite my lip even harder.

'It's about a male model. You should watch it – it might give you some tips.'

His face lights up.

'Thanks. You know you're not the first person to think I should be a model.'

'Well, I didn't actually say that. You know I should be on my—'

I go to walk but he nudges his selfie stick closer to me, pinning me back.

'Yeah, a lot of people think that I look like Channing Tatum. Of course I have better moves than him,' he says with a wink.

'Oh... um...' I picture him grinding like a character from *Magic Mike* and feel my cheeks warming.

He does a bit of a chest ripple with a satisfied smile on his face.

'The likeness is... uncanny. But I better get my coffee or else my colleague will be on the warpath.'

'Yeah, so will my boss, Evil Edward.'

I pull a suitable face of horror. Evil Edward is the Head of Sales and is ferocious. I once heard him shouting at one of the workers he was firing and I work two floors above him.

The man finally removes his selfie stick and folds it away before slipping it into his trousers.

'I'll see you around,' he says, giving me an actual wink before he hurries down the stairs two at a time.

I shake my head in disbelief. And Cleo thinks I'm addicted to Instagram? At least I don't go whipping out my selfie stick at work.

I head down the stairs to the floor below where the vain man works, relieved to find that the coffee machine does have mocha left. I manage to make it back to my floor without being hit in the face with any other selfie sticks and I salvage my tea by pouring in extra milk.

Mrs Harris is unimpressed when I arrive back at my desk. 'Finally, I thought you'd gone to Colombia to get the coffee beans.'

'They were out of mocha on this floor, so just be thankful that you didn't have to walk all the way down to the ground floor to get it.'

'That's the second time this month,' she says, outraged. 'I'll write to the canteen to tell them.'

'I'm sure they'll be delighted,' I say, feeling sorry for the person who's going to receive an all-caps telling-off.

My PC has finally booted up and I log in and check my emails, jotting down notes on the things that need to be done today, before I load up our in-house software.

'So, I ran into this guy in the stairwell,' I say in a low voice to Cleo. I don't want Mrs Harris overhearing; I don't want her accusing me of dilly-dallying when fetching her coffee. 'Tall guy, works in Sales, about our age, brown hair in a neat quiff, dressed to impress, a smile with *all* the teeth.'

Cleo nods. 'I know him. Luke something,' she says, wrinkling up her face. 'Luke Taylor, maybe? He's cute.'

'He's vain. You should have seen the selfie stick that he had down his trousers.'

'*Monsieur*, is that a selfie stick or are you just pleased to see me?' she says in a fake French accent, making me giggle.

Mrs Harris give us a look from the other side of desks and we stop laughing.

'Is he new?' I whisper.

'No, he's been here a while, six months or so. Why all the questions – do you like him? Oh, I bet we could find him on the Link!'

'No!' I say, grabbing her hand away from her mouse. Cleo

tends to use our internal office messaging system as if it's her own personal dating app. 'I just wanted to know who he was.'

'I wonder if he's single?'

'Aren't you seeing that guy from Accounts?'

'Not for me, for you. *You* should totally message him.'

'No, thanks. I make it a rule not to date anyone who takes longer to get ready than me.'

'Yeah but did you check out his bum?'

'Can't say I noticed,' I lie. It was hard to miss in his tight trousers.

'I'd make an exception for that.'

'Uh-oh,' I say, pointing at Jason from Risk Management (aka the young whippersnapper with the spicy balls) who's walking towards us with a pile of papers. Cleo looks over and gasps. 'Mrs Harris!'

'What is it? Can't you see that some of us round here are busy? *Some people* have work to do, you know. We can't all sit around gossiping.'

'Fine, then I won't tell you that there's a bogey at two o'clock on a potential cake raid.'

She looks at her watch and wrinkles her brow.

'Behind you. Jason,' I hiss so that he won't hear me.

She swivels her chair round to face him before jumping up in a more spritely fashion than I've ever seen her move. 'Quick!'

She's waving her arms, motioning for us to get up and join her.

We reluctantly get up and she grabs us, drawing us alongside her desk to create a human shield around her cake.

'Jason,' she says, giving him a hard stare he approaches.

'Mrs Harris,' he says, matching her firm tone. 'I'm just chasing a contract that seems to be stuck with Cleo.'

'And you couldn't send her a message on Link or email her?' she says, raising an eyebrow.

'Sometimes it's quicker to get things done in person.'

He elongates his neck a little in the direction of the Tupperware, and Mrs Harris pulls us in closer towards her to block out his view.

'Cleo will look into it if you give her the details,' she says, sternly.

'Fine,' says Jason, thrusting over a folder.

'Fine,' repeats Mrs Harris.

I've been dragged in so close now that I can practically taste Mrs Harris's Chanel No 5.

Jason turns round on his heels and storms back through the office and Mrs Harris sighs and releases us from her clutches.

'Pesky blighter,' she says. 'He made all that up. Trying to get a look at my cake! These whippersnappers.' She shakes her head.

Dismissed, Cleo and I walk back over to our seats.

'So where were we?' says Cleo as she wheels herself back under her desk. 'Oh yes, Luke Taylor's bum.'

'I think we finished that conversation. I only wanted to know if he'd been here long.'

'Of course you did,' she says with a sarcastic lilt.

I ignore her and turn my attention back to my computer screen. I'm going to knuckle down to my work this morning and I'm not going to stare at my phone. No matter what Cleo says, I'm not addicted.

My phone beeps an email alert as if it knew it was being watched.

My heart starts to beat rapidly as I pick it up and I almost can't breathe when I see that it's the email from the company that I've been waiting for.

*Hi Izzy!*

*Thanks so much for your interest in the campaign we're running. We were super impressed by your ideas but unfortunately we've decided to go another way. We're going to use family bloggers with kids to do cute matching outfit shots. We'd still love to have your support on the campaign, so if you're able to regram or share our posts on your channels we'd be super grateful.*

*Fran x*

My heart sinks as I read the standard rejection spiel that has no doubt been cut and pasted to dozens of other influencer wannabes. This was supposed to be my big break. The one to propel me into triple or quadruple figure earnings that would allow me to quit my job.

'Izzy, Howard's in,' whispers Cleo.

I look up and see our big boss striding across the floor to his desk.

I drop my phone on the desk and pretend to be busy at my computer. The last thing I need is to be let go from here, especially when the Instagram career that I so desperately want seems to be well and truly out of reach.

Welcome to June
This_Izzy_Loves IGTV
No. followers: 15.3k

*How is it the first of June already? This year is racing by. I've got lots to look forward to this month. I'm going out with my besties for a long overdue night out and I'm also only days away from meeting my idol – Small Bubbles!! I am off to a VIP masterclass and I cannot wait to hear all her wisdom and find out exactly how I can rule Insta with her. Can't you just see us as BFFs? Don't you just love her?*

# Chapter 3

I thrust my iPhone back to Cleo, unsatisfied with what I've seen. 'Can you take one more? That person got in the way, and if you could make sure you don't get my feet in that would be ace.'

Cleo sighs but willingly holds up the camera and I walk forward towards it, swishing the skirt of my dress for what feels like the billionth time.

'Is this all for Instagram?'

'Uh-huh. It's partly your fault that I'm all dressed up; you were the one that wanted to go for after-work drinks.'

'Actually, it was Marissa who invoked the dress code,' she says, looking down at her high heels.

'Either way, I've got to make the most of it. Usually at this point on a Friday night I'm chilling in sweatpants.'

Cleo laughs and holds my phone out to me.

I quickly watch back the Boomerang and post it to my stories.

'Can you just hold your foot out for me?' I ask.

'What's wrong with you taking a photo of your own foot?'

I look down at my slightly scuffed Dorothy Perkins shoes that I bought in the sale last year. They're not bad, but they're not her much coveted (by me) Louboutins with their all-important bright red sole. They were a gift from a guy she dated last year.

She has all the luck. The only thing I've ever got from someone I casually dated was my half of the bill.

'Do you really want to compare my shoes to yours?'

She sighs again and holds her foot out and I snap a picture. I put a quick caption, **'These beauties are out with me tonight'** and I post it to stories too.

That's the beauty of Instagram: people don't know that I'm not wearing those shoes. And technically they are coming out with me, so it's not a total lie. They look so beautiful in the picture. I wish that Cleo wasn't two shoe sizes smaller than me.

'So, are we meeting Becca and Marissa outside the station?' she asks.

'Yes, although we should probably get a wriggle on because their train got in a few minutes ago.'

I pop my phone back in my bag and we make our way to the station where we find Marissa scrolling on her phone.

'Hey, sorry we're late,' I say, 'we rushed all the way here from work.'

'Uh-huh,' says Marissa, turning her screen round. I see myself, swishing my skirt in a quick motion.

'Well, with a slight detour,' I say, giving her a quick hug. 'Where's Becca?'

Marissa points at her pacing up and down a few metres away, talking on the phone. She gives us a wave and goes back to her conversation.

'Long time, no see,' says Marissa, turning to Cleo and giving her a hug.

'I know, and look at you.'

Cleo pulls out of the hug and stands back to admire the bump. Marissa pushes it out further and beams.

'I know it's a cliché but you are glowing,' says Cleo.

'That's just from travelling on the trains when the air con's broken,' she replies, laughing.

'So, where are we headed?' I say, hoping that it's somewhere nearby – these heels weren't made for walking.

Marissa's eyes widen and a small smile creeps over her face. 'How about drinks down in Lush and Lime?'

'Won't it be really busy?' I say, groaning. Lush and Lime's where the cool kids hang out. 'It *is* Friday night.'

'Exactly!' she says clapping her hands together. 'It's Friday night and look, we're all out and we're all in heels.'

'We certainly are,' says Cleo, flashing the soles of hers.

'Oh my God, look at those beauties,' says Marissa as she lifts her leg up and examines them from every angle whilst poor Cleo hops about trying to keep her balance.

'Sorry about that,' says Becca, hanging up her phone and giving Cleo and me a quick hug hello. 'So, where are we off to?'

Marissa and I speak at the same time:

'Not decided.'

'Lush and Lime.'

She puts her hand up in front of me in a stop-motion, and turns to Becca.

'Don't listen to her, we're going to Lush and Lime. Anywhere else would be a waste of Cleo's shoes. Plus they have those karaoke pods. We can see if we can get one for later on? Huh, Becca?'

'Not tonight,' she says. 'Let's stick to dancing.'

It's a shame as Becca has the most beautiful voice but she hardly ever sings anymore.

'Good plan, I'm up for a boogie,' says Marissa. 'Let's go.'

When we get to the bar Cleo makes a beeline across the polished wooden floor to get us a drink. Marissa decides to give her a hand and Becca and I wrestle our way to the back, where we're not jostling anyone for elbow space. We manage to find a spot by the window where we can at least dump our jackets and perch our bums on the windowsill.

'So, how was work?' I ask.

'OK. I'm glad the week's over.'

'Me too.' I nod in agreement.

Not that my work is stressful compared to Becca's. She's a probation officer and I honestly don't know how she does it.

'So look at us, out-out,' she says, wriggling to get comfy on the windowsill.

'I know, it's like a modern miracle. Don't tell Marissa, but I'd much rather be sat on our sofa drinking a bottle of Prosecco and watching *The Crown*.'

'I know, me too. We can always watch some when we get home.'

This is why living with Becca has worked out so well. She's my ideal housemate: clean, tidy and loves to stay in as much as I do.

'Great idea. How long do you think we need to stay out?'

'I'm guessing at least two hours, if not three,' says Becca as she slides her feet out of her electric blue peep-toe stilettos. 'Now, that's much better. They're killing me.'

'But they're so pretty.'

'Doesn't make them any less evil.'

'Are they new? I haven't seen them before.'

'I bought them today. To go with the dress I bought last week, for Ascot?'

'Oh,' I say, getting caught off balance. I look down at them again. 'They'll go perfectly.'

She can't hide the smile on her face, it lights her up. I can't remember the last time I saw her this excited about anything and it makes me feel a bit guilty that I haven't talked to her much about Gareth. I still can't think of her being with anyone but Ben.

'Are you excited about Ascot? And about meeting his work colleagues?'

'I'm terrified. It's so soon.'

'It's not that soon. You'll have been dating for a couple of months by then.'

'But what if they don't like me? What if it puts Gareth off?' There's a hint of panic in her voice and I rub her shoulder.

'No one can not like you. Plus, from the sounds of it, Gareth really likes you so I don't think you have anything to worry about.'

I don't mean to emphasise Gareth's name as I say it, but it sticks awkwardly in my throat. I try and think of something else to ask her to show her that I'm not being weird about it, but Marissa appears and thrusts jam jars full of pink liquid at us.

'Do I want to know what it's in it?' I ask, holding up the neon drink to the light.

'I don't think so,' says Cleo, arriving beside Marissa and taking a sip and shuddering.

I take a sip and I shudder even more violently than her. 'Is it me, or are drinks stronger now than when we used to go out?'

'You're just out of practice,' Marissa chides. 'This is exactly why I try and get you to come out more.'

'It's all right for you, yours has no alcohol in it. And it's so loud. Was music always so loud?' I ask, shouting.

'It *is* pretty loud in here,' says Becca. She takes a swig of her drink and her eyes nearly pop out. 'I don't think I'm ever going to sleep again with all these e-numbers.'

'And look how young everyone looks. I feel like I'm at a school disco,' I say.

'Listen to you,' says Marissa, tutting. 'Cleo's going to think that she's out with grandmas.'

Marissa might be the most grown up out of all of us with a mortgage, husband, baby on the way, a dog and a garden shed, but she's showing no signs of slowing down.

'We're not leaving here until you've drunk one too many jam jars and had a boogie.'

I look over at the empty dance floor and wonder if I can have a dance and get it over with. Although with my moves, someone would probably film it and it'd go viral and that's not really how I want to get internet famous.

'One more cocktail, then we dance,' I say, hoping it will have filled up by then.

'I'll get the next ones in then,' says Becca.

I turn and look at her empty glass in horror.

'What? That tasted like Refreshers; so good.' She slides her feet back into her shoes and heads off to the bar.

'Whatever happened to them?' asks Marissa.

'Refreshers? I'm pretty sure you can still buy them,' I say, pulling out my phone to google it and I might just check how many people have viewed my posts whilst I'm there.

'Oh no, you're not looking at your phone whilst we're in the bar,' says Cleo. 'Looking at and talking about Instagram is banned.'

Marissa and I look at each other in horror as it's our favourite topic of conversation.

'What else are we going to talk about – work?' I ask.

'Ew, no,' she says, screwing up her face. 'That's banned too.'

'Then what's left?'

The three of us look around the bar for inspiration.

'How about real life?' says Cleo.

'Real life,' I say, whistling through my teeth, wondering what on earth I have to talk about. 'Um, so what are people up to next week?'

'Ooh, I know, I'm starting a new pregnancy yoga class,' says Marissa, looking at Cleo for approval.

'Nice,' says Cleo. 'I'm sure that'll be really good for the birth.'

'Sod the birth; I'm there to find new friends.'

I laugh. 'Isn't it supposed to be about stretching?'

'Please,' says Marissa, rolling her eyes. 'Anything baby-related is only about finding friends.'

'Don't you meet those at NCT?' chips in Cleo.

'Not anymore. Now you shop for them at yoga, hypnobirthing, Bumps and Burpees and Mum Calm. I've spent a bloody fortune so far and I still haven't found my new BFFs.'

'Luckily for me,' I say, not realising I've been in danger of losing my bestie to a pack of yummy mummies.

'You know what I mean,' she says, blowing me a kiss.

'At least it's all good content for your Insta feed,' I say.

'There is that, and it's good way of finding followers too.'

'Hey, banned,' says Cleo, looking at her watch. 'At least you managed a few minutes without mentioning it.'

'We gave it our best shot. Can you hold this?' asks Marissa, handing me her drink. 'I only need to see liquid and I have to pee these days.'

'So what have you got planned next week, Izzy?' asks Cleo as Becca comes back with a tray of drinks.

'I'm going to watch a charity ice hockey match with my parents.'

The tray starts to wobble and the drinks spill a little over the top.

Cleo reaches over and takes the tray before putting it on the windowsill. She doesn't notice that Becca's gone white as a sheet at the mention of the charity event.

'That sounds good,' says Cleo, dishing out the jam jars.

'Uh-huh and then I'm going to a masterclass next week to hear Small Bubbles talk about becoming an influencer,' I say, quickly moving the conversation on.

'Really? You've kept that quiet,' says Cleo, laughing.

I'm a tad excited about it and I may have mentioned it once or twice or three billion times at work.

'Small Bubbles?' says Becca, the colour feeding back into her cheeks.

'Yeah, you know, Lara McPherson,' I say.

'Any relation to Elle?'

'No,' I say, shaking my head.

'Then, no, I have no idea,' says Becca.

I've probably mentioned her at home before but Becca's not really into social media and the names don't stick.

'She's got millions of followers on YouTube and Instagram? Has a book out? A make-up range?' says Cleo. Becca shakes her head.

'Well, it's going to be good,' I say.

'But technically you can't talk about it as that's Instagram-related,' says Cleo.

'Then I give up. I have nothing else to talk about.'

I'm pretty sure any minute tumbleweed's going to roll past us.

'See, this is why I keep telling you that you need to date more,' Cleo says to me, causing Becca to perk up, nodding.

'Exactly what I've been saying to her too. It's been years since Cameron,' she says.

'Who's Cameron?' asks Cleo and I purse my lips.

Becca looks at me a little guiltily; I guess she assumed that Cleo already knew.

'Just Izzy's last ex,' she says, shrugging it away like it wasn't a big deal; like I hadn't phoned to tell him Ben had died only to discover he was in bed with another woman. 'And it's time for you to move on. If only to give us things to talk about in moments like this.'

'But I haven't got time for a boyfriend. I'm far too busy doing things that you won't let me mention.'

'Faffing about on Instagram is not a good enough reason to stop you from dating,' says Cleo.

Becca looks at me and raises an eyebrow. She knows that Cameron spectacularly breaking my heart is why I haven't exactly been rushing to join Tinder, but even she's started trying to encourage me to meet someone new.

'You should message Luke from work,' says Cleo.

'Who's Luke?' asks Becca.

'An arrogant guy who I will not be messaging.'

'So not Luke, but I agree with Cleo. Why don't you look around tonight?'

Cleo pulls a face. 'People don't really meet in bars anymore. But perhaps we could turn your Instagram addiction into a Hinge one.'

'I just hate the idea; you're trying to find a soulmate, not order a pizza.'

'That's the beauty of Hinge,' says Cleo. 'It's not all about the swiping.'

'Even still. I just don't think that I'm up for meeting someone online.'

'What about that guy?' says Becca, pointing to someone on the other side of the bar.

'He looks about twelve. Plus, I refuse to date anyone who wears skinnier jeans than I do, or anyone who straightens their hair.'

'Urgh, I forgot that you like them grungier than Nirvana,' she says.

'Who's Nirvana?'

Becca and I stare at Cleo. It's times like this when the age gap feels like a chasm.

'I don't like them that grungy, I just like them a little scruffy. That's all.'

'Like him,' says Becca, pointing out the window.

I watch as she points to a little Mexican café across the road. A guy with a faded Led Zeppelin T-shirt and non-skinny jeans is folding up chairs before carrying them inside.

'Now *he* is exactly your type.'

'You can't tell that someone is going to be your type after a split second of looking at them,' I say, staring at the man as he walks back out onto the street.

He looks familiar and it takes a moment for me to place him. And then suddenly I realise – it's *him*. He looks different now than he did that day. Slightly fuller in the face. Slightly longer hair. A bit of stubble where before he was clean-shaven.

My cheeks start to burn and my heart is racing. I cling onto the windowsill to stop my feet from giving out from under me. It's almost like I'm being pulled back to *that day* and all the emotions that went along with it.

I'm vaguely aware that Becca's talking but I have no idea what she's said; I'm too busy staring at the man through the window.

'Izzy, are you OK?' Cleo asks.

Marissa comes back and I can hear them whispering.

'Izzy, what is it?'

Becca puts her arm round me and looks at me before following my gaze to Aidan, who I've been searching for for two years – the guy I never got a chance to thank.

'It's him,' I say in disbelief.

'Him who?' asks Marissa.

'Him, the guy who helped me that day at the station when I'd just got the news about Ben. When I broke down.'

Becca and Marissa look out the window in disbelief.

'Blimey, you never said he was so cute,' says Marissa.

'Funnily enough that wasn't on my mind at the time,' I say, then regret it.

'I didn't mean to—' Marissa starts.

'I know you didn't. It's just…' I stop myself. If I talk about it I don't think I'll be able to stop tears from falling, and this isn't the time or the place.

'So, are you going to thank him?' asks Becca. 'I know you've always wanted to.'

'Not now, I mean I wasn't expecting…' I can't speak to him. Not today. 'I hadn't really thought of what I'd say and he's just finished work; he'll probably want to get home. I'll come back another day.'

We all watch as he takes the sandwich board back inside the café and shuts the door.

'Are you sure you don't want to go over?' asks Marissa.

'No, I'll go another time,' I say, finally finishing my first drink before starting on the second one. The strength and the taste don't seem to bother me now. 'Did you still want to dance?'

'We don't have to if you—' says Marissa.

'Let's go,' I say, firmly.

I look over at the little café just as the lights in the shop go out. I've waited over two years to thank him; a few more days won't hurt.

# Chapter 4

There's something about walking in to the ice rink that always takes me back to my childhood. My dad used to drag Ben and me along to ice hockey matches, then when I was a teenager Marissa and I used to come to the ice disco, trying to pluck up the courage to talk to the boys in their Adidas hoodies.

I spot Mum immediately. She's the only one around here who isn't dressed in team colours. I can see the red Heart2Heart sweatshirt peeking out from under her coat. She wouldn't usually want to come to a match with us – too many memories of us coming with Ben – but this one's special because it's raising money for Heart2Heart, which fundraises to test people for heart defects. A charity we wished we'd known existed a few years ago.

I squeeze past the other fans along the row of bright blue seating to get to her.

'Hello, Izzy love,' she says, standing up from her seat and giving me a big hug.

'Hi, Mum, where's Dad?' I say as she releases me and I sit down next to her.

'Getting snacks, you know him.'

I look out over the crowd to try and spot him.

'You OK?' she asks with concern.

I turn to her and she starts to study my face.

'I'm fine,' I say, pretending. It would be hard being here at the best of times without Ben, but after I saw the guy from the train on Friday night my emotions are all over the place. I felt like a tidal wave of emotions hit me and it's made me relive that day over and over thinking how grateful I was Aidan stepped in when he did. Trust her to pick up on it.

'You don't look fine. Are you taking your vitamins?'

'Yes, Mum.'

'Perhaps you're getting a cold. Or maybe you're getting a chill from the ice,' she says, pressing her hand to my cheek. 'Make sure you keep your coat on.'

'You've got no complaints from me on that front,' I say, zipping it up. I wish I'd worn a warmer sweatshirt underneath.

'Everything OK at work?'

'Yes, no change there.'

Mum's still scrutinising me, she knows I'm hiding something.

She knows all about Aidan and how I've always wished I'd been able to thank him but I don't want to tell her I've seen him. Lately I've seen flickers of her old self. She's smiling more and laughing, even if there is a residual sadness in her eyes. I don't think that will ever leave.

'I had a big night out last week with the girls and I can't do them anymore, takes me ages to recover.'

'Oh yes, I heard about that from Marissa's mum. Fancy her gallivanting around in her condition.'

'She's four months pregnant, Mum, she can still leave the house.'

'Hmm. Well, it was different in my day,' she says, before she starts touching my cheeks with the back of her hand. 'I'll go and get us a hot drink when your dad's back,' she says. 'Speak of the devil.'

I look up to see him squeezing down the aisle, smiling away.

'Hiya,' he says. 'I got you a hot dog on the off chance you were here already.'

'Ooh, thank you,' I say taking one, my stomach rumbling at the sight of it. 'You not having one, Mum?'

'No, they're full of terrible things,' she says, turning her nose up. 'If they don't clog up your arteries they'll probably give you cancer.'

My dad gives me a conspiratorial wink before he bites into his and I follow suit. Over the last couple of years my mum's become paranoid about our health and what we eat.

'I'll get us a cup of tea,' says Mum, getting up. 'Keep you warm.'

'She OK?' I ask Dad as she leaves. 'How's the baking?'

'Not too bad this week. We've only had one lemon drizzle cake.'

'That's not bad,' I say. Baking is like a barometer of Mum's grief: the more cakes she bakes, the worse it is.

'She's getting there. She's finding tonight hard, though. What with it being the first match she's been to without Ben and the whole charity thing. They were talking earlier about how people could get tested for heart conditions and she nearly cut off the circulation in my hand she was squeezing that hard.'

'I get that.'

Dad leans over and puts an arm around me and gives me a squeeze. We never used to be a very tactile family but that all changed two years ago when they phoned to tell me that my brother had died.

Ben was only 31, the same age that I am now. He went to bed one night and never woke up. His fiancée, Becca, found him when she woke up the next morning. He died of sudden arrhythmic death syndrome; he'd had a heart defect which acted like a ticking time bomb, and we'd never known. That's one of the reasons that we try and support Heart2Heart whenever possible.

It might have been two years ago, but it feels like it was yesterday. People tell you that you'll heal in time but they're lying. You learn to cope better but you don't properly heal. How could you?

I just can't get over it. One minute he was in my life and the next he was taken away without any warning. I'd never even told him I loved him. I mean, who tells their brother that? But every day since then I wish I had.

That's all I seem to do. Wish about all the regrets I have. I wish I'd made more effort to come back to Basingstoke to see him. I wish I'd invited him up to stay more. But I mostly I wish that he was still here.

'I got chocolate too,' says Dad as I try to blink back a tear without him noticing.

'The hockey hasn't started yet and we've already gone through most of your snacks,' I point out.

'That's the beauty of a game that has two breaks: plenty of time to run for reinforcements.'

He pulls out a giant packet of Minstrels and, despite having just polished off the hot dog, I'm not shy digging in.

The music starts to blare out as they announce the teams and Mum hurries back and hands us both a steaming cup of tea.

My dad wolf whistles and claps as his team comes in – as does everyone in the rink – and my ears start to ring. The players are all wearing special Heart2Heart jerseys and I feel proud. I hope that thanks to tonight's match more people will be able to be tested for heart defects and other families will be spared our pain.

My parents cheer loudly and I find myself joining in. Whilst it wouldn't be my number one sport to be a spectator at – I prefer ones which have lower risk of a frozen projectile hurtling towards me – I do love the cheesy North American elements of all the music and lights; it's a complete theatrical spectacle. At least thanks to my mum's new aversion to risk since Ben's death, we no longer sit behind the goals. I'm never convinced that those black nets are going to stop anything.

I pull my phone out and hold up my camera to take a video to pop on my stories.

'You're keen,' says Dad.

'It's for Instagram,' I reply, wincing as two players slam into the wall near us. I finish recording and add a few monkeys covering their eyes and horror face emojis to articulate what I'm feeling watching this.

'Right. You still doing that?'

'Uh-huh,' I say, biting my lip a little waiting for the tone of disapproval. My parents think it's a waste of time and that I should get a proper job. They think it's a waste that I'm temping after I had what they thought was a glittering career in London. They don't understand that being an influencer could be a job in its own right. Or that it was the last thing that Ben and I talked about properly and that it was him that had spurred me on.

'I was speaking to Ned the other day and he was saying that they're expanding at White Spot,' says Dad.

I bring up my Insta profile and check the comments and likes.

'That's good for them,' I say, trying to sound uninterested to make him change the subject.

I spent a university summer doing an internship for a family friend's advertising company. It might have looked impressive enough on my CV to get me the copywriting job in London but the only things I learnt that summer were how to make barista-level coffee and that fancy photocopiers are the root of all evil.

'They're recruiting again. I could put a word in. Oooh,' Dad says, gasping when blood spurts out of a player's nose after a collision on the ice. The player continues to skate and I'm slightly mesmerised by the trail of red now following him.

'I'm not actually looking for anything at the moment,' I say.

'I told you not to mention it,' whispers Mum.

'She can't temp forever,' he says as if I'm not here.

'This isn't the time, Si.'

'It never is,' he says, folding his arms.

'I'll tell you what, Dad. I'll take a look at their website and see what they're up to. Thank you,' I say, intervening to stop them from bickering. They've been doing that a lot lately and I hate it.

'Izzy, I bumped into Roger Davenport's mother whilst I was getting the drinks,' says Mum. 'Do you remember Roger? He had such lovely thick hair.'

I almost choke on my tea. I remember Roger Davenport all right. I went to school with him and I used to chat to him sometimes because I thought he was funny. It wasn't until years later that I learnt that Roger had told all his friends that he and his fingers had got very friendly with me one night at a party.

'I remember him,' I say through gritted teeth. I'd love to give him a piece of my mind.

'Apparently he's single, recently divorced, has a nice big house just outside Basingstoke. He runs a call centre.'

She's not exactly selling him to me.

'I'm not really interested in meeting anyone at the moment.'

Dad shakes his head at Mum.

'So it's OK for you to give our daughter life advice, and not me?' she snaps at him.

There's an edge to her voice that I haven't heard before.

'I'm trying to get her to fulfil her potential at work by moving on to a better job, not to get her a boyfriend so she stays in the area.'

'That's not what I was doing,' says Mum, pursing her lips.

'Of course it was.'

'Hey, hey,' I say, thinking that I can't keep up with of all the fighting on the ice, let alone having to keep up with it off it, too. 'Look, I'm fine, really. I'm happy being single and the Instagram account is going well. I'm getting sent free products and I'm really close to getting a paid deal.'

My stomach sinks as I think of the email I got last month but I've got to stay positive – there are plenty of other companies that are looking for micro-influencers like me. Plus I'm off to hear the wisdom of Small Bubbles next week and I'm hoping that I'm going to become instant BFFs so that we can rule Instagram, or at the very least she offers a little nugget of advice that'll make my follower numbers rocket up.

Our team scores and the player who scored does a speedy lap round the ice to cheers and whistles.

'I just don't get why you do all the funny phone stuff and you won't go back to an agency,' says Dad.

'But I'm on the cusp of getting paid for it. This way, I'll get to run my own business.'

Mum and Dad exchange a sceptical look and I'm pleased that they're at least united in something, even if it is that they think I've lost the plot.

'Some influencers make a lot of money and they do it as a full-time job.'

'I just think you should give Ned a call. I bet he'd be pleased to hear from you,' says Dad.

'And Roger's mum gave me his number, just in case you wanted it.' Mum passes me a piece of paper.

I take it, only because now I can send Roger an abusive text whilst drunk telling him where he can shove his fingers. And spoiler alert: it wouldn't be anywhere near me.

Mum smiles like it's a victory and I almost wonder if I should go out with Roger as it's so nice to see her looking happy.

A player slams into the wall before falling back and hitting the ice. 'Holy shit,' I say. 'This is brutal.'

'We've not even made it through the first period yet,' says Dad, laughing. 'More chocolate?'

'Always,' I say, needing a sugar hit.

I thought this evening would be stressful because of the charity connection to Ben, but I hadn't factored in my parents trying to meddle in my life, the underlying tension that's appeared in their marriage or all the fisticuffs on the ice; my nerves are practically shot. If only I could make my Instagram career take off and then my parents would have one less thing to worry about. It would show them that my life's not such a disaster after all.

# Chapter 5

If Marissa doesn't get a move on we're going to be late for the Small Bubbles event. I hastily dial her number and scan the street whilst it's ringing, hoping that I'll see her hurrying along to meet me.

'Hey, don't kill me,' she says as she answers. My stomach sinks. Nothing good can possibly follow that phrase. 'But I was at a Bumps and Burpees class this morning and I pulled a calf muscle and I can't put any weight on it.'

I knew those baby classes were a bad idea.

'Is the baby OK?' I ask in concern.

'The baby is fine seeing as she's nowhere near my calf,' Marissa says, laughing. 'Tim was the same, he wanted to take me to A&E as a precaution. Could you imagine, A&E on a Saturday morning when all the football and rugby injuries are piling in? I'd be there forever.'

'Well, as long as the baby is fine, that's the main thing.'

'Yes, and the calf will heal apparently, might take a bit longer with the weight of the bump. Are you already there?'

'Uh-huh,' I say, looking up at the imposing hotel front, wondering if I'm brave enough to go in by myself.

'Take a selfie with Lara for me! I wanna hear all about it when you get home.'

'Of course,' I say, feeling nervous. 'I hope you get on OK your end.'

'Don't worry about me; Tim's waiting on me and I've got the Amazon Fire Stick controller. Speak to you later,' she says, hanging up.

I'm not usually one to mind going places on my own; I often go to the cinema and I've been to local Ted X talks, but it's not every day I get to go to a masterclass with Lara McPherson, aka Small Bubbles, aka the Queen of Instagram, where there is massive potential for me to totally fangirl. If Marissa was here she'd keep me in check and make sure I didn't do anything stupid to jeopardise the future where Lara and I become BFFs.

I still can't believe I managed to get tickets to the event in the first place; they were limited and sold out within minutes. I'm guessing that we'll get loads of one-on-one time to talk and for me to make a good impression.

I head towards the revolving door and my phone beeps. I look down whilst walking and smack into someone.

'Oh, sorry,' I say, holding up my phone as a way of apology.

The man I bumped into holds up his too and laughs.

'I guess it's inevitable, right? You come to an Insta-event and everyone's walking with their heads down, looking at their phones.' He smiles, and his teeth sparkle with their perfect whiteness.

Hang on. I'd recognise that quiff anywhere.

'Oh wait, it's *you*,' I say, amused.

His eyes light up and he smacks his lips together.

'You know me?' he says in a Joey Tribbiani voice, his eyebrows raised.

'I do,' I confirm.

He gestures for me to walk in front of him through the

revolving door. He's giving me such a deranged look that I'll quite happily go inside where there are people rather than be left outside on the street here alone with him.

'Thanks,' I say, stepping forward.

'I can't believe this has happened. I hoped it would but it's totally unexpected,' he says, following me, his hand clutched over his chest like he's giving an Oscars acceptance speech.

'Because we're both here?' I ask. I always find it weird bumping into colleagues outside of work; I seem to forget they have actual lives too, but if I'd really thought about it I should have guessed Luke and his selfie stick would be here.

'I just never thought I'd get recognised in real life!' Luke says, still gushing.

'What? Oh,' I say as the penny drops. Now it's awkward. He thinks that I know him from Instagram, which is slightly offensive that he doesn't remember who I am at all.

'Do you want a selfie with me?' he says, leaning in closer.

'Have you got a big stick?' I say, unable to resist.

A smile breaks out over his face and he pulls out his telescopic selfie stick from his trouser pocket.

'I never leave home without it,' he says with a wink.

'Perfect,' I say as he slots the phone into the stick. 'Has anyone ever told you you look like Channing Tatum?'

He looks at me again and does the stomach ripple move. 'All the time.'

He holds the stick out and leans into me.

'Shall we do "Blue Steel" pouts?' I say.

His arm drops and he turns to look at me, narrowing his eyes.

'We've met, haven't we?' he says, lowering the stick and taking his phone off.

'Yes, we met in the stairwell at McKinley's a few weeks ago.'

His face falls.

'You look different.'

'More make-up.'

He nods his head. 'You look good. So are you looking forward to this?'

He smiles at me as if there's been no misunderstanding. How does he do that? I'd have been mortified and would have been halfway back to the train station by now. But there's no hint of redness in his cheeks or flash of embarrassment in his eyes.

'I'm Luke,' he says, holding his hand out and I shake it.

'Izzy,' I reply, in disbelief. He has got to be the most self-assured person I have ever met.

'Do you think we should find where this event is, then?' he asks, scanning the lobby.

I glance round too. There are a few people sitting on comfy-looking, egg-shaped chairs reading papers or scrolling through phones. I join the queue to speak to the receptionist, who's busy leaning over the large desk annotating a map for some guests.

'Ah, back there,' Luke says, pointing to a board spelling out the name of the event. 'There it is.'

He holds up the selfie stick and takes a few photos of himself next to the light box.

'Would you mind?' he asks, handing me his phone. He leans his arm over the sign and poses.

'Of course not.'

I snap away, trying not to laugh at his pout, which could give Victoria Beckham a run for her money.

'I guess these will be OK, for stories,' he says, looking through, and I bite my tongue.

We make our way to the queue to get our tickets scanned at the door.

'What kind of content do you post?' I ask.

'Sort of urban male lifestyle – you know fashion, city living, fitness.'

My eyes sweep over his body and a shirtless Channing Tatum with all his ripped muscles pop into my mind.

'Do you blog as well?' I ask, trying to get those kind of thoughts out of my head.

'I vlog on YouTube.'

Of course he does.

Tickets checked, we step into the room and it's not quite the intimate setting I was expecting. It's a huge ballroom with row upon row of seating and nearly every one is filled. I'd have expected a sell-out crowd if we were in London but I hadn't expected it in Reading. Especially when I've paid £65 for the privilege. Maths isn't my strong suit but even I can work out they've made a killing.

'There's two seats together over there. Shall we?' he says, as if it's a given that we're going to sit together.

'Sure, that would be great. I was supposed to be coming with my friend but she's pulled a muscle and she's pregnant,' I say, drifting off.

'Does she Instagram too?'

'Yes, although she can't work out what she wants to do. First she started off with pictures of her dog Bowser, but with his tight black curls it was impossible to tell his bum from his face. So she bought a cat called Molly McMittens and her feed became cute pictures before she found out she was allergic and had to give her away. Then she got married and she focused on weddings,' I say, taking a breath. 'After that she did a food thing – comfort food versus unusual ingredients thing – and now she's pregnant so it's a baby feed.'

'Sounds like she can't settle into her niche. It's hard to find your calling.'

I try hard not to laugh.

We shuffle down a row of chairs where everyone sighs loudly and squeezes in their legs as we pass. None of them make eye contact, they're all too busy on their phones.

'So what's your niche?' he asks.

'Lifestyle with an affordable living slant to it. I felt too many of the influencers have a London bias and the clothes and accessories they feature are too expensive for normal people. So I tend to focus more on high-street brands.'

It still feels weird saying that out loud. It's how I'm now pitching myself to brands – pretending that was always my intention when I started my blog and my Instagram account, when really I'd started going for cheaper products because I couldn't afford the designer price tags.

'How many followers have you got?'

'Just over 15,000,' I say a little proudly.

'Nice,' he says, 'I've got 18,000.'

Of course he has more. He holds his phone above his head and snaps a selfie without flinching in embarrassment like I would.

'I'm working on ways to get it higher,' he says. 'I want to reach 30k by Christmas.'

'That's ambitious,' I say, shocked. That's a huge undertaking.

'I'm hoping Small Bubbles will help.'

'That's why I'm here too,' I say, pretending that it's not to try and make Lara my new BFF.

'So do you get much free stuff?' he asks, taking photos of the room.

'I get a few clothes, mainly from smaller companies, homeware like candles and photo frames and beauty products. I have enough mascaras to last me a lifetime.'

'I see you make good use of it,' he says, laughing for the first time.

I feel a little stupid that I put on extra make-up today like I would for my Insta photoshoots, in the unlikely event that Lara might have seen my feed and recognise me.

'I once read this article about Claudia Winkleman where she said that she's almost unrecognisable without her eye make-up and I thought it was a good idea, you know, so that I can go out incognito without being hounded when I become a mega influencer.'

'Important to prepare for these things. I'm the opposite though. I want to be recognised wherever I go.'

Of course he does. I secretly like that he's more of an Instagram-wanker than I am; it means he doesn't judge me. I remember once trying to explain my eye make-up strategy to Becca and she was not impressed.

'What's your Insta name?'

'This underscore Izzy underscore Loves.'

He types, clicks and swipes.

'I've followed you,' he says, raising an eyebrow.

'Oh right,' I say, pulling my phone out of my pocket. I open up my app and click on the hearts to see that Lukeatmealways has just followed me.

'Luke at Meal Ways? Where's Meal Ways?'

He doesn't look impressed.

'It's Luke at *Me Always,*' he says with added emphasis.

'Oh, right,' I say, wondering if he could be more vain.

I turn my attention back to my phone. I've already mentally pictured what his content will look like. Moody photos of him and his smouldering good looks against beautiful backdrops. I tap 'follow', feeling smug as I scroll through his photos – I was right. I have to hand it to him, though; it's a beautifully curated feed.

There's a sudden ripple of excitement in the audience as the lights start to dim and music starts to play out through the speakers.

'I guess this is what we've been waiting for,' whispers Luke.

I give him a smile and sit on my sweaty hands as I'm beginning to have palpitations. I'm sure Luke would like to think it's because he got so close that his aftershave worked its pheromonal magic, but it's actually because Lara has just glided onto stage. She strikes poses to the beats of the music until it dies down. Everyone whoops and claps and there are camera flashes everywhere. I watch Lara basking in the attention. She's lapping it up like this is what she was made for.

'Thank you, thank you,' she says when the adoration dies down and she steps up to the podium. 'Now, who's ready to become an influencer?'

The whole audience raises their hands. I sit up a little straighter just in case she's going to pluck one of us out of the audience to make our dream come true.

'Well, you're not the only ones. There are over 23 million Instagram users in the UK alone and one billion worldwide. Not everyone is going to become an influencer, and it's certainly not going to happen overnight. It'll take hard work, time and perseverance. But that's how I did it – and now I have over 6 million followers.'

She pauses, and there's an applause that she laps up again.

'So, let me take you on the journey of how I became Small Bubbles...'

'Wow,' I say as the lights go up.

Luke nods next to me. 'That was quite a show.'

'Wasn't it?'

I'm even more in love with my idol now than when I came in. And given the amount of time I spend watching her on Instagram stories, I didn't think that was possible. I might not have the blueprints to Instagram stardom like I'd hoped but I do feel enthused that it is possible to go from zero to hero.

We stand up and we head towards the aisle.

'So are you going to queue up for a selfie?' he asks.

I look at the line already gathering down the aisle. Lara's standing in front of a table, leaning against it and the first audience member goes up and beams away with her as she has her photo taken.

'Well, I thought I might as well, as I'm here. You know, it might boost my followers.' I try and keep my voice casual as if I hadn't given it much thought.

'Me too,' he replies nodding, and we make our way over to the queue.

'So have you been working at McKinley's long?' I ask as we shuffle slowly forward.

'About six months, I was an estate agent before.'

I know I shouldn't stereotype but he lives up to it, being over-confident, over-styled and over-aftershaved.

'I bet you were good at that.'

'Absolutely, I was so good I could have sold an igloo to an eskimo.'

'Yet you still left?'

'The sales weren't fast enough,' he says, shrugging. 'How about you?'

'I've been there two years. It was only supposed to be a stop-gap.'

'Isn't that what everyone says? But let me guess, the dream is to become an influencer, quit your job and live happily ever after.'

'Pretty much,' I say, nodding. I've always known it was a ridiculous dream but seeing a whole ballroom of people trying to do it too has really hammered that point home.

'Me too. The sooner I quit the rat race, the better.'

'I used to work in advertising up in London, I was a copywriter before I… before I joined McKinley's, and I was going to try and move into marketing but then my Instagram started to take off and I thought I'd see where that went. It's a lot easier to have the time and mental head space to run my feed without worrying about work and long hours like I used to.'

'I can imagine. Let's hope we'll both be quitting our jobs before we know it, thanks to that talk,' he says with a wink. 'Did you live up in London too?'

'Uh-huh,' I say, thinking of the shiny flat I shared with Cameron and how quickly I left.

'Isn't it a bit of a comedown living in Reading?'

'Actually, I live in Basingstoke.'

'Bloody hell, that's even worse.'

A surge of hometown pride ripples over me. 'It's actually got a lot going for it.'

He raises a sceptical eyebrow.

'It does. There are couple of cool bars now and a few decent restaurants.'

'Because London doesn't have any of them.'

'And it's got good shops and we've got an ice rink.'

'You're really selling it. Although ice rinks are pretty good places to go on dates; if I take a woman who can't skate she'll be clinging onto me all night.'

'Is that the only way to get a woman to touch you?' I say, laughing.

'Oh believe me, women are always touching me. I'm like one of those guys from the Lynx adverts.'

I think of the adverts with the guys dousing themselves in aftershave only to be surrounded by dozens of beautiful women pawing at them. The only thing that I can imagine Luke having in common with that scenario is the dousing himself in aftershave.

We're edging closer to the front of the queue and my heart is starting to race. I'm thinking what I'm going to say to Lara. The queue moves forward every thirty seconds or so, which means I've got thirty seconds to convince her to become my new BFF.

'Wow, look. That girl's dressed in Lara white,' says Luke, pointing at the woman at the front of the queue.

Lara's always dressed top-to-toe in white and the young woman is following suit. She's wearing a white summer dress, which was either an optimistic outfit choice on a cold day, or she wanted to colour co-ordinate with Lara and it was the only white thing she owned.

'So try-hard,' he says, slipping off his jacket to reveal a tight white T-shirt.

I look up and down the queue and I notice everyone is dressed in fifty shades of white.

I look over at Lara standing in her top, fluffy cardigan, stone-washed jeans and brogues, all of which are white. I'm going to totally clash. I've worn the trendiest thing I own which is a pretty, vintage-style tea dress that a local designer sent me, and I've teamed it with black biker boots and a leather jacket to hide the safety pins I use to hold the dress together as I can't get the zip done up. I thought it would make me look super on-trend, but it's so bright compared to her – I might as well be wearing neon. How did I not think about that?

'Izzy? Are you OK? You've gone all pale.'

'Have I?' I say, pleased. At least my face might match her style.

'OK, so are you two having your photo taken together or singularly?' says a bored-looking PR woman as we reach the front.

'Oh, I think—'

'Together,' says Luke.

'Great. Gets us through quicker. So you'll get two photos taken but with the same device. No touching Lara,' she says in a stern voice, her eyes narrowing on mine as if she knows I'm a super-fan who won't be able to control myself. 'If you want to make it look like you've got your arm around her you can balance your hand on the table behind like so.'

She demonstrates with the same tired enthusiasm as cabin crew pointing out emergency exits.

The PR woman drifts off to prise away the girl having her photo taken with Lara and it's our turn. I'm so excited. Luke has to give me a little nudge as my feet don't appear to be working and we're directed to stand on either side of Lara.

'Hi,' she says, beaming. 'You two a couple?'

'Oh, no, we're colleagues,' I say with a high-pitched squeal.

'Oh, that's a shame. You look like you'd make a cute couple and couples always do really well with brands on Insta,' she says with a hint of sneer. 'There's always so much content for them – first they have the big wedding, then they do the house renovation, then they have babies. Anyway, are you ready for the photo?'

The PR woman stares at me so I make sure that I leave a safe distance between me and Lara when I balance my hand on the table. My hand makes contact with another hand and I immediately jump. At first I think in horror that it's Lara and that I might get ejected before I get my selfie, but it's only Luke. I'm about to breathe a sigh of relief when his hand tries to hold mine. I snatch my hand away, grazing Lara's fluffy cardigan in the process.

'Smile,' says another PR woman, who snaps a photo on Luke's phone.

'Thanks for coming,' says Lara. She moves forward, only I go with her. I look down in horror and see that my watch is stuck on her cardigan.

'Come on, Izzy,' says Luke, going to grab my other arm before he gasps.

'What's going on?' asks the PR woman, surging forward.

Lara bends down to get a bottle of water off the floor and I go along for the ride, not wanting to rip her expensive-looking cardigan.

'Oh my God. Is she touching me?' she screams.

'I'm not touching you,' I say, flustered. I'm aware the whole room is watching me. 'It's just my watch. Look, my hand is here.'

I do a wave but it's fruitless as Lara can't actually see my hand behind her.

'A watch? Who in this day and age wears a watch? Why would you when you have a phone!' she shrieks.

'I've always worn one,' I stammer. 'I've never got one stuck before.'

Of course the first time had to be now.

I turn to Luke for help, but he's holding up his phone – he's actually *filming* this.

'Hey!' I shriek in a tone to rival Lara's.

He shrugs and puts his phone down.

'Get her off me. I can feel her touching me,' says Lara.

The two PR women push me out the way so that I'm as far away as I could be without dislocating my shoulder. They examine the stuck watch in such a way that anyone would think that they were performing open heart surgery.

'There's a thread that's wrapped right around it. We could cut it,' says the woman who took the photo.

Lara gasps in a way that lets them know that's not an option.

'If I could just—' says one of the women twisting my arm round impossible angles, 'aha, got it.'

My arm falls and I rub my aching shoulder.

Lara turns and glares at me, before her hand flies up to her forehead.

'I need a moment,' she says loudly. She storms up the stage stairs and into the wings.

'I told you not to touch her,' the PR woman hisses and I start to back away. 'God knows how long she'll be. Do you remember when the woman touched her arm in Birmingham? She didn't come back for 40 minutes.'

The other PR woman nods her head and, along with all the people in the queue, gives me a frosty stare.

'Thanks, sorry, I'll leave,' I stutter. I hurry out of the room in fear, only stopping to catch my breath when I reach the safety of the lobby.

'That was intense,' says Luke, who did his best to distance himself when Watchgate was going down.

'Not quite to plan,' I concede.

By now Lara was supposed to have followed me on Instagram and we'd be meeting after the event for cocktails to cement our new-found friendship. I fear the only reason she'd want to know my name right now would be to take out a restraining order against me.

‘Photo looks good though,’ he says, showing me.

He clearly means of him and Lara, who look in perfect harmony in their white outfits and perfect smiles. I, on the other hand, stick out like a sore thumb with my bright dress and my goofy star-struck grin plastered on my face.

‘Hmm,’ I say, thinking that it doesn’t really matter what I look like, ‘I can’t post that now.’

‘Come on, she didn’t even look at you and I reckon after all those pictures she won’t even remember who the person with the watch was.’

‘You think?’ I ask, hopefully.

‘Of course. I’ll even promise I won’t put the footage on YouTube.’

‘You’ll delete it instead?’

‘OK, I barely got anything before you shouted at me anyway.’

We walk back out of the revolving doors and we stop on the pavement and I’m about to say goodbye when he leans close to me and holds up his camera. ‘Say, “Cheese”.’

I automatically smile before I realise what’s happening.

‘Huh,’ he says looking at it. ‘Look, she was right, we do make a good-looking couple.’

I look at the photo and whilst Luke is so far from my type, you’d never know that from that photo. We do look good together.

‘So this has been fun, we should meet up again,’ he says.

‘We should?’

‘Definitely,’ he says, fixing his eyes on mine. I almost get the impression that he’s coming on to me. Although my non-existent love life is testament to the fact that this isn’t really my area of expertise.

‘Right, well, I better go and catch a train,’ I say before I turn and hurry towards the station in an attempt to diffuse the situation.

‘I’ll see you soon,’ he shouts down the street and I turn and give him a half-hearted wave.

It takes until I get seated on the train until I feel brave enough to pull out my phone to check if Watchgate has gone viral, only to see a picture of Luke and me pop up on my feed. He must have posted whilst he was walking.

Lukeatmealways
What a night. Not only did I get to meet the gorgeous @small_bubbles but I got to meet the equally gorgeous @This_Izzy_Loves too. Our eyes met across a crowded room of Instagrammers #instalove #smallbubbles #instaconference

Hashtag Instalove? So he was being flirty.

I could not imagine a man that I’d want to date less. Let’s just hope he forgets me like the first time I met him. I don’t really have a whole heap of experience of letting men down gently and something tells me Luke and his giant ego doesn’t have a whole lot of experience of being on the receiving end of it.

# Chapter 6

I scroll through a contract template on my computer, trying to ignore the fact that Mrs Harris has being trying to catch my eye for the last ten minutes. I start to fill in the details of the new client when Mrs Harris clears her throat loudly.

I notice Colin's face is mere inches away from the paper on his desk as he tries to keep his head down, quite literally.

'What do you need, Mrs Harris?' asks Cleo.

'Ah, Cleo love. What a poppet you are. I didn't want to disturb you when you were so busy. Plus, I need Izzy and her skills for this job.'

'What skills does she have that I don't?'

Mrs Harris sighs. 'The ability to not get too distracted. I need Izzy because she'll stay mission-focused and won't start flirting with the first stud muffin she sees.'

'Stud muffin,' says Cleo, giggling.

'What would my mission be?' I ask, looking up over my screen.

'I just need you to pop down to Adjustments. I've heard some rumours that they've got muffins today.'

'Stud ones?' I say, setting Cleo off again and earning a tut from Mrs Harris. 'There are biscuits over in Accounts; I could grab you one of those instead?'

That would save me a set of stairs to walk down.

'No, no, I think the muffins downstairs are supposed to be very good. Be a poppet, get me one or two. I'm a bit hungry, forgot my lunch today.'

'Right,' I say, knowing she buys her lunch in the canteen. 'So this has nothing to do with the rumour that Jason is testing out a recipe for the next stage in the competition?'

'Izzy, however could you think that of me? That I could resort to such – such *underhand* espionage? All I want is to not waste away at my desk.'

'We wouldn't want that now, would we?'

I could probably do with stretching my legs, so I pick a folder out of my in-tray to give myself a cover story for my walk around.

'And whilst you're there, stop at the second floor and see if Mary in Billing has baked anything or Miles, he's on that floor too?'

I mock-salute and head off on my mission. I walk down the stairs thinking of Luke posing here before and it makes me nervous that I'm going to bump into him. Not that he'd be here now: it's raining, making the light in here terrible.

I still can't get over that photo he posted the other night. We work in the same office block so the odds of bumping into each other are statistically quite high. I've started walking round the office with a nervous feeling in the pit of my stomach, reminding me of when I moved between lessons at school, hoping I'd bump into one of my crushes. Only this time, it's the opposite. I'm trying *not* to bump into him. I've never been very good with unwanted advances from the opposite sex although luckily for me it doesn't happen very often. I'm just hoping that I won't see him for a few weeks and he forgets who I am, again.

I push the door open to Claims Adjustments. Their floor has got an identical layout to ours and I'm always freaked out seeing the wrong people sitting at the desks.

I spot Jason and make a discreet beeline for him, pretending I'm searching for someone else.

There are a couple of people at the end of his desk hovering over some tin foil containers and the scent of cinnamon is wafting through the air. But before I can reach it, Jason leaps into my path and folds his arm like a bouncer.

'Can I help you?'

'Oh yes,' I say, looking down at my folder as if hoping it'll give me some magical answers. 'I'm looking for Sarah.'

Every department has a Sarah, right?

He looks at me suspiciously.

'She's not in today. She'll be back tomorrow.'

'Right,' I say relieved that my cover story has held up.

'Do you want to leave a note?'

'No, no, I'll come back,' I say, trying and failing to see over the side of the silver container. 'Boy, something smells good.'

'Tell Mrs Harris I said hello,' he says, glaring at me.

'Will do,' I mutter sheepishly.

I hurry out of their floor. I'd make a terrible spy. I'm slightly scared of going back to Mrs Harris empty-handed, so I make my way to the next floor down to see if I can find Mary or Miles.

I push open the door, it's so noisy. There are long rows of desks and everyone's wearing headsets with microphones and it's impossible to tell who's talking on the phone and who's talking to each other.

I try to look purposeful with my red folder as I walk briskly along, sniffing the air for baking scents. I notice a collection of biscuit tins on a central table and people seem to be swooping in and grabbing mini cupcakes on their way to and from the giant printer. I try and keep my heart rate steady whilst I make my way to the printer, reaching into the tin as I pass. And just like that, I've taken one brazenly. I'm chuffed I got away with it until I come face to face with a woman who I recognise from a health and safety training course I had to go on.

'Aren't you going to eat that?' asks Brenda.

'Oh, I was saving it for a cup of tea,' I bluster.

'We haven't seen you on this floor before,' she says, not taking her eyes off the cupcake I'm holding.

I suddenly feel like I've edged into the wrong side of town and I hastily shove it into my mouth.

I'm hit with a burst of something boozy and citrusy and usually I'd savour every single second of it, but I'm too scared so instead I wolf it down.

'I recognise you,' says Brenda, 'Don't you work in Contracts?'

I watch her turn and wave at Mary – whose cupcakes they are – and her face looks like thunder.

'I – er, I'm here to find someone,' I lie.

'She's with me,' says a voice and I look up and see Luke. I'd forgotten that Billing and Sales were on the same floor; so much for trying to avoid him.

He flashes Brenda, and Mary who's joined us, one of his winning smiles and they relax.

'Ah, Luke, have you had a mini cupcake? They're mojito-flavoured,' says Mary slipping into cougar mode.

'Thanks, but I'm watching my figure,' he says, patting his stomach.

Mary and Brenda titter with laughter and he grabs my elbow and guides me down to the other end of the office in case the spell he's cast wears off.

'What are you doing?' he says. 'It's savage down here at the moment! This Bake Off is bringing out the worst in people.'

'Thanks for rescuing me.'

'You're just lucky it wasn't Miles,' he says, nodding across to a man who almost snarls at us for looking in his direction. He must have witnessed the exchange with Brenda and Mary because he's clutching his tin of baked goods close to his chest. 'Now, open that folder and I'll pretend to look at it. I don't think we're out of the woods yet.'

I hastily open the folder and he starts nodding.

'I'll point at this, and you nod.'

I play along.

'I had fun the other night. Turn the page.'

'Umm-hmm,' I say, pretending I'm fascinated with the piece of paper in front of me.

'I was going to send you a message using Link but I didn't know your surname.'

'Oh,' I say, shutting the folder and then regretting it as my name is written in large letters on the front.

'Izzy Brown, got it,' he says with a firm nod. 'I'll send you a message when I resolve the situation.'

He speaks loudly and gestures for me to go.

I have one last look at Brenda and Mary who are standing with their hands on their hips, shooting me daggers.

'Oh right. Thanks for your help,' I mutter. MI6 really aren't going to come knocking on my door anytime soon.

By the time I make it back to my desk I'm exhausted and in desperate need of a cup of tea.

'Well?' says Mrs Harris, lowering her glasses onto the tip of her nose and looking over them.

'Jason wouldn't let me get within three metres of his creation, but it smelled of cinnamon.'

'Just cinnamon?'

'Like a cin-a-bon concession.'

'Got it,' she says, writing it down on her notepad. 'Go on.'

'And then I swung past Mary's desk and her mini cupcakes were mojito-flavoured. And oh my God they were soooo—' I stop abruptly when I see Mrs Harris's nostrils flaring. 'They were OK. You know, the sponge was all melt-in-your-mouth-fluffy and the frosting was all creamy and the lime was zingy on my tongue then the rum gave it an unexpected kick—' I can still taste it on the tip of my tongue. 'They were just OK, though. And, you know, so unimaginative. I bet if you'd have made them they'd have tasted heaps better.'

'You weren't supposed to taste it, that was *my* job. I'm the one with the sophisticated palate.'

'Sorry, I couldn't help it, Brenda from Sales was coming for me.'

'And Miles?' she says arching her eyebrow.

'He saw me get rumbled by Mary.'

Mrs Harris tuts loudly and turns her attention to her screen. I think I'm in the dog house.

Colin gives me a little smile in solidarity.

My computer beeps and I see I've got a new message on Link. I click on it and read it.

Luke Taylor:
I've got something I want to talk to you about. Do you want to meet me for lunch today?

Blimey, I didn't expect to hear from him so quickly. Does this mean he's super keen? I'm so out of the loop with dating. How do I tell him I'm not interested in that way?

Izzy Brown:
I'm a bit busy today. Snowed under. Could we do it another time?

I'm hoping he'll take the hint. I'd actually been planning to phone my mum during my break to see how she's getting on. Going to see the ice hockey has set her back and I've been trying to phone her daily.

Luke Taylor:
Yes, you seemed busy walking round our floor trying to steal baking secrets.

I don't know what to write. He'll be seeing the dots to indicate that I'm typing and unless I respond smartish he'll expect an essay. Think, Izzy, *think*. What subtly says 'I'm not interested in you' but is still very polite?

Luke Taylor:
Just come along and hear what I have to say. Meet you outside the main block at 1pm?

He isn't giving me much room to get out of it and I get the impression that he's going to be persistent.

Izzy Brown:
1pm is fine. See you then.

'How are you so flushed in this ice box of an office?' says Cleo, wheeling her chair next to mine. She touches her cold hands to my cheeks. I didn't know they were burning.

'Oh, I don't know. Maybe it was the rum in those cupcakes.'

'Or maybe it's because Luke Taylor just sent you a message,' she says, her eyes lighting up. I turn back to my screen to see that he's sent a message saying, See you then.

'What's all that about?' she asks.

'Nothing! I saw him the other night at that Instagram event—'

'Oh, you did, did you?' She's doing a patronising head tilt and overemphasising all her words.

'I did. And now he wants to meet me for lunch.'

'Lunch,' she parrots back, eyebrow raised.

'Yes, *just* lunch. He has something he wants to discuss, apparently.'

'Uh-huh,' she says, smirking. 'You've got a date, it's about time.'

'It's not a date,' I say firmly.

'Whatever,' she says, winking.

I give up. She's never going to believe me. It's absolutely and categorically not a date and not because I'm afraid of having my heart broken again but because he's not my type in the slightest.

# Chapter 7

I dodge through the mass exodus that always happens during lunch hour scanning for Luke. I spot him channelling James Dean, leaning with his back against a wall, dressed in a leather jacket with large aviator sunglasses on.

'You came,' he says, walking forward to meet me.

'Well, I figured you knew where I worked if I didn't.'

'Yeah and I could have totally dobbed you into Mary and Brenda.'

I mock gasp, 'You wouldn't dare.'

'Never underestimate me just because of my extremely pretty face.'

I shake my head, he really is intolerable.

'So, you hungry?' he says, starting to walk.

'Starving.'

'Great, I've got somewhere in mind,' he says, without running it past me for approval. 'So did you manage to stay out of trouble for the rest of the morning? Brenda and Mary have been watching the doors to the floor ever since you left.'

'They'll be pleased to know that apart from the coffee machine, I didn't leave my desk and I actually knuckled down and did some work.'

'Huh? Work at work. Interesting.'

'Well, that's what they pay me to do so I figure that I should do it every so often.'

'Wise plan,' he says. We walk through one of the back streets on the edge of the high street. 'I thought we could go to this new little café,' he says, leading me towards it. I recognise it, and it takes me a moment to place it as the Mexican café I saw from the window of the bar when I was out with the girls.

My skin prickles at the thought of the Aidan in his Led Zeppelin T-shirt. I'd promised myself I'd come back to talk to him but I hadn't built up the courage. I wonder if he'll be inside and if he'll recognise me. I start to panic. I don't want to thank him in front of Luke, but if he does recognise me then it would be rude not to say anything.

'Oh, is that Mexican food?' I say with an over-the-top wince, pretending that it's not one of my favourite type of foods.

'Mostly, but I think they do other cuisines, too.'

We're close enough to see in through the windows. I can only see two women behind the counter; no sign of him.

'Let's give it a try,' says Luke, pushing open the door. 'The lighting's great in here and the food's vibrant so it works for my feed.'

I'm beginning to realise that he's not the kind of guy who takes no for an answer.

The café's bigger on the inside than it looks, and there are a few free tables at the back.

'This is cute,' I say, loving the bright yellow-painted walls and the multicoloured sombreros lining it.

'Yeah, a selfie against these walls really sets off my tan,' says Luke.

We queue at the counter waiting for our turn to order, and I stare at the menu. It all looks so good.

‘I think I might get a spicy pulled pork and cheese burrito,’ I say, struggling to choose.

‘Brave choice for someone who doesn’t like Mexican,’ Luke says, raising a neat and tidy eyebrow. I can’t help staring at it, wondering if he plucks them.

‘Well, if I’m not going to like it, might as well go the whole hog. Get it? Hog – pulled pork.’

He smiles but I don’t think he gets it. Perhaps I can put him off with my bad jokes.

‘What can I get you?’ asks the woman behind the counter. She’s got long dark brown hair and sun-kissed skin and she smiles warmly at us. I fully expect Luke to swoop in and start flirting madly with her, and I’m a little surprised when he orders his lunch without any fuss.

I order my burrito, loving the fact that the woman lets me choose all the different elements of it. It looks mammoth by the time it’s all rolled up.

‘How are you going to get that in your mouth?’ asks Luke.

‘You’d be surprised what I can get in my mouth,’ I say.

Luke’s face lights up and I wish I could take it back.

‘Sounds like a challenge.’

I ignore him and pick up the cutlery from the table and start to cut into it instead. ‘So what did you want to speak to me about so urgently?’ I say.

I watch with jealousy as he bites straight into his whilst I’m forced to eat teeny tiny forkfuls trying to keep it from coming unravelled. ‘No beating around the bush, I like it,’ he says, after he finishes what he’s chewing. ‘Are you single?’

I choke on the tiny mouthful I’m eating.

‘Um, I’m technically single, but not really single, single.’

He narrows his eyes.

'You mean you're seeing someone but it's not Facebook official?'

'No, I mean I'm not seeing anyone and I don't want to at the moment. I'm happy just being me and alone.'

He wrinkles his face before he relaxes it again.

'My Instagram post of us two was really popular.'

'Was it?' I'd not looked it again as I'd been trying to block it out.

'It had over 8,000 likes.'

Blimey. Despite having over 15,000 followers the most amount of likes for a single post of mine was 3,000.

'Bloody hell, did it? You must have really dedicated followers.'

'I don't think it's just to do with me; it's more our story.'

'*Our* story?'

'Yeah, you know people are suckers for romance. Everyone's been eating it up. You should have read the comments. They kept asking if I was going to ask you out and it got me thinking.'

He pulls out his phone and shows me the picture again. 'We look great together and I thought we could have an old-school classic romance. You know, we could be the Romeo and Juliet of the Instagram world.'

'Er, you know they died at the end, right?'

'OK, then,' he says, waving a hand. 'Antony and Cleopatra.'

'Um, they died too.'

He sighs loudly. 'OK, perhaps not classic romance, but how about Brad and Angelina.'

'They got divorced, years ago.'

'Bloody hell. Isn't there one shining example of romance?'

'No, because it's inevitable that where there's love there's heartbreak.'

I give up with my knife and fork and bite into the burrito whilst holding it with my hands.

'I'm sensing issues here, but the point is, we could be that shining example.'

'Um,' I say, screwing up my face. 'It's really not a good time for me. I'm at a point in my life where I need to focus on me and what makes me happy as well as concentrating on my Instagram and—'

'Izzy, you don't think I'm hitting on you for real, do you?' he says, cutting me off with a little laugh.

'Um, no of course not,' I say, trying to hide the fact I'm a bit miffed. I know I didn't want to date him but it was flattering thinking that he was interested. 'Although, I'll have you know I'm a pretty good catch.'

'I'm sure you are – perhaps if you weren't carrying round so much emotional baggage. Let me guess, your ex cheated on you and broke your heart?'

I'm stunned that he was able to guess so easily. Although my heartbreak isn't simply as a result of Cameron cheating. It was more to do with the timing in relation to Ben's death, which magnified it all.

'How did you know?'

'I've been a shoulder to cry on many a time. I'm an excellent rebound, but not for you. I actually like you.'

'I don't know if I should be pleased or offended. But wait, I'm confused, if you're not asking me out, what are you asking me?'

'You know how Lara was saying that brands like Instagram couples? There's a lot of cross pollination for couples. Sharing each other's followers, boosting each other's likes. Big brands like it as it stretches their reach.'

'I imagine they do,' I say, sipping my drink, totally lost as to where this conversation's leading.

'Yeah, and my followers actually liked that I'd met someone. I thought they'd all be jealous as hell.'

'This might be news to you, but not everyone follows someone on Instagram because they want to hook up with them.'

He chuckles a little before seeing my face is deadpan.

'Oh, Izzy, you should read my inbox.'

'What, is it like mine? Full of bots trying to scam you by pretending they fancy you.'

'I feel like we're going off topic... I think we should date. Everyone would love us on Instagram.'

I blink a couple of times trying to process what he's just said.

'You want to date me, for Instagram?'

'Exactly. Like fake date,' he says nodding and tucking into his burrito like he's just suggested something totally normal.

I look at my Coke and wish it were something stronger. 'Fake date? What does that even mean?'

'It's exactly like it sounds,' he says through a mouthful of burrito. 'We'd make it look on Instagram like we were dating. You're already in the habit of planning and staging photos. This is no different. We'd take photos of us on our first date, second date and so on – we both share the photos, add cute hashtags and hopefully we'll grow our number of followers and move up a level as Influencers.'

It takes me a moment to fully digest what he's saying and then I start to laugh.

'Now that was funny,' I say. 'You had me going for a minute.'

I pick up my burrito to start eating again.

'I'm not kidding,' he says.

My jaw drops open and I put down my food.

'Luke, we can't fake a relationship.'

'Why not? Everyone fakes everything on Instagram. How would it be any different?'

'Not everything on Instagram is fake.'

'Come on, almost everything on it is manipulated somehow. When was the last time you posted a photo of yourself without a filter?'

'That's different,' I protest.

'Why is it?'

'Because it just is,' I say, folding my arms over my chest.

'OK,' he says, shrugging. 'It was just an idea. A way for us to get to that 30k mark by Christmas. You know, that's when people start making money.'

I try to comprehend what he's proposing. It wouldn't be the most ridiculous thing I'd have done for my feed – we all know that involved two rolls of clingfilm and some corn starch and red food dye – but it would certainly be up there amongst them.

'How would you see it working?' I say with a huff. It might be a terrible idea but I'm slightly intrigued nonetheless.

'Well,' he says with a smug smile.

I raise my eyebrow in a warning. 'I haven't said I'll do it.'

'Your eyes have. Look, it wouldn't have to be much. We'd maintain our individual feeds but we'd go on dates and post photos of us on them. We wouldn't necessarily have to meet up a lot, we could take photos in a few different outfits at a time – or one outside then one indoor but post them on different days so that people think they've been taken at different times.'

'And that's it? We go out a few times and take a few selfies?'

'Yep. We'll do it for a little bit to try and get the numbers up. Hopefully we'll catch the attention of some companies who'll pay us to advertise their products on our feed.'

It's almost making sense.

'But how will it end? We couldn't be like those couples that Lara was talking about – we're not buying a house to do up, or having a baby.'

'I guess at some point we've got to break up. Mutually, of course. We'll probably decide that we're better off friends or something to make sure we don't alienate our joint followers.'

He's got it all worked out. The annoying thing is that I think his idea could work. I've been scratching my head for ways to bump up my followers and this could be it.

'I don't know. This feels wrong.'

I finally admit defeat with my burrito and push it to one side.

'Look, we're not doing any harm, we're both single, we're not cheating on anyone. All we're doing is a few photos. No big deal. Do you have many family and close friends that follow you?'

'Only a few close friends.'

When I set up my Instagram I deliberately wanted it keep it separate from my real life and didn't advertise it on my personal Facebook account. I love the anonymity of it and the fact that no one on there knows the real me.

'Then I suggest you tell them the truth so that they don't ruin it in the comments, and we keep it a secret from everyone else.'

'That would make sense.'

If I did it, it's not the kind of thing I'd want everyone to know.

The bell goes over the café door and I look up and see Aidan. He's even better-looking up close, despite being dressed in scruffy jeans and another faded band T-shirt.

He walks in carrying a cardboard box overflowing with fresh vegetables. I'm terrified he's going to look over and I don't want to talk to him in front of Luke, it's too personal.

But he doesn't look my way, he only has eyes for the woman behind the counter, and I can't blame him, she's gorgeous. She's midway through serving a customer and when he smiles at her she beams back and blows him an over-the-top kiss in a way that makes me sure that they're together.

'Hello...' says Luke, staring at me. 'Earth to Izzy.'

'Huh?'

Aidan disappears through the kitchen door. As it swings shut behind him, I let out a deep breath.

'So, are you in?' asks Luke.

'Can I think about it?'

'OK, but an offer like this,' he says, waving his hands down his face and torso, 'doesn't come along every day.'

'It certainly doesn't,' I say, trying to rein in my sarcasm.

The woman from behind the counter swings through the door into the kitchen and I almost immediately hear her laugh echo back.

'Did you want to head back to the office?' I say, looking at Luke's empty plate. I suddenly don't want to be here when Aidan walks back through. He seems to stir up so many emotions in me that I'm not ready to confront.

'Sure,' says Luke. 'I can tell you more about my masterplan en route.'

I guess it couldn't hurt to hear more about his plan. I know in my heart of hearts that it's a dishonest thing to do, but seeing Aidan only serves as a reminder of how much my life has changed since the day I met him. Then I was working at an advertising agency, living in a swanky flat with my boyfriend; now I'm living in a shared flat in my hometown and temping. My Instagram account is the one thing in my life that I've really got going for me. It's the one thing that my brother Ben would be super proud of me for.

Perhaps it wouldn't be the worst thing in the world to take a little short cut to boost my followers. And who knows, perhaps a relationship with Luke could be the perfect kind, the kind where no one gets hurt.

# Chapter 8

Every man and his dog seems to have descended on Basingstoke's shopping centre thanks to the torrential rain outside, meaning that it's extra specially busy for a Saturday, yet in telling Becca about Luke I've come up with a canny tactic to part the crowds.

'He said *what*?' screams Becca, causing fellow shoppers around to give us a wide berth.

'Oh, you heard me right. He wants to fake date me.'

'*Fake* date you?'

'Yep, he wants to pretend that we're in a relationship.'

'Why?'

'To grow our Instagram accounts and get the attention of brands.'

Becca scoffs.

'How on earth did he come up with that?'

'Lara McPherson said at her talk that couples do really well on Instagram because their content is widened by the lifestyle choices they can make together. You know, they buy and renovate houses, get married and have babies.'

Becca opens her mouth so wide I can see her tonsils.

'Don't worry, we're not going that far. It'll be more the story of us getting together. Luke wants to share our story on Instagram and he wants to talk about it in his vlogs.'

Becca still hasn't shut her mouth.

'I really have heard everything now,' she says eventually. 'You're not seriously going to do it, are you?'

'That is the million-dollar question,' I say. I stop as we reach H&M. 'Hang on, I've got to take this stuff back.'

'You know, it would be a whole lot simpler if you shopped online and sent everything back.'

'Have you seen the queue at the post office at the weekend? Plus, I'd have to order double the amount as not all of it would fit. This way I get to try it on first to make sure it fits before I buy it.'

Becca sighs and follows me into the shop. I waddle along with my bags to queue up for the tills.

'I thought you were going to keep the mustard shirt,' she says, peering into my bag.

'I know, but I really couldn't justify it. I'll have to do my next haul from Primark and then I might be able to keep some.'

'Next,' shouts a bored-looking teenage girl.

She flicks her long hair over her shoulder and eyes the bag in my arms suspiciously.

'I'd like to return these please,' I say, sliding the bags across the counter before retrieving the receipt from my own bag.

She looks straight into my eyes before she studies the receipt.

'All of them?'

I nod. 'Uh-huh. They just didn't suit me when I got home. Do you use special lighting in the fitting rooms?' I say, looking over at them.

She purses her lips and grabs the items out of the bag, rotating each one and making sure the tags are still firmly attached.

I start to get a bit nervous. In all my returning history I've never had this much scrutiny.

'This, here,' she says, pointing to a mark on one of the shirts that looks like make-up.

'That must have been there when I bought it – someone must have tried it on in the shop,' I say, looking at the stain in horror. How did I not notice that before? Was it in the photos that I took? 'I swear that I only tried them on and look – that shade of foundation is nothing like my skin tone.'

The girl gives me another suspicious look before picking up the next item. I try to relax but my heart is still racing. I know that it wasn't me who caused the stain; I am so careful. That's why most of my #OutfitOfTheDay ensembles are button-down shirts or dresses – nothing that goes over my head and therefore nothing that can get make-up-stained.

'Have you got your original payment card?'

'Uh-huh,' I say, and she motions for me to put it into the card reader.

She makes me sign some receipts and she gives me one more scowl before I'm allowed to go.

'I think next time I will order online,' I whisper to Becca as we head out the shop.

'Good move. Coffee?'

We start walking towards our usual coffee shop.

'So what's this Luke like then?' asks Becca.

'I've never met anyone as confident or as egotistical. He's so sure of himself.'

'If you don't like him then why are you considering faking a relationship with him?'

I look down at my blistered hands. 'Because I don't want to cut my hands to ribbons every Saturday to take clothes back. I want to take the next step up as an influencer.'

'Then why don't you do it?' says Becca after a pause.

I'm shocked because she's usually the sensible one. I've been counting on her to be outraged; for her to be my moral compass and to tell me it's a terrible idea. When I first told her that I wanted to become an influencer she thought it was crazy that I'd want to lead such a public life.

'I'm just not sure people would believe that I was actually going out with someone so attractive.'

Becca tuts. 'Do not make me do the whole "you're gorgeous" speech.'

'I wasn't. I just meant I wonder if anyone would believe it.'

'Why wouldn't they? Look at all the fake news out there – if people want to believe it they will.'

'So you think I should do it?'

'If it's going to give you both of you a bit of a boost and it's not hurting anyone, is it? There's so much bad news that a little love story like this might be quite nice. People like to watch a love story develop.'

We reach the coffee shop and I make a beeline for a tiny table in the corner where we always sit.

'Plus, you lie all the time on your feed,' she says, sitting down.

'Um, I do not.'

'You just took back £200 worth of clothes that you'll be "wearing" as your #OutfitOfTheDay for the next month.'

'Yeah, but I wore them once, didn't I?'

'And when was the last time you took a natural selfie?'

'I took one of me slobbing in PJs on the sofa last week.'

'You straightened your hair, put on clean PJs and reapplied a full face of make-up beforehand. Think about it, it's all fake.'

Becca really doesn't get Instagram.

'But that's just little stuff, isn't it? I mean, this is huge. This is a big life event.'

'You're dating the guy, not marrying him. You said that the

plan isn't to do it forever. Plus, you never know, you might get to know him and you might like him.'

I give her a hard stare.

'Sometimes these things creep up on you when you least expect it,' she says.

'Like you and Gareth?' I blurt out and then I feel guilty.

'Exactly.' She blushes a little and pushes the sugar bowl round the table. 'I wasn't thinking that I was going to meet anyone, certainly not so soon.'

For so long Becca was my partner-in-crime nursing a broken heart and swearing off men, but ever since she started seeing Gareth she keeps nudging me back towards the dating game.

'Look, this isn't going to be *To All the Boys I've Loved Before,*' I say thinking of our recent Netflix watch.

'I love that movie so much,' she says, swooning.

'Luke is no Peter Kavinsky, that's for sure.'

'But he could be. Isn't that the point? You don't know him well enough not to know that. I wasn't sure about Gareth at first.'

'That's different. For starters, from what you've told me about Gareth, he's not a self-obsessed arsehole.'

Becca laughs. 'He definitely isn't.'

'I am almost willing to bet my life's savings on the fact that mine and Luke Taylor's relationship is going to be purely business.'

'You don't have any life savings.'

'Very funny,' I say, even though it's woefully true. I take a deep breath. 'Are you sure that I should do this?'

Becca's always been the older sister I've never had and I've always looked up to her for advice.

'I think that it might be fun for you to do it. You haven't had the best few years and maybe it's time for something good to happen. I know you're not interested in him romantically, but you've worked so hard to get your Instagram following off the ground and if this is a little shortcut to get you there a bit quicker, then I say, why not?'

It has been a crappy few years, not just for me but for both of us. I moved in with Becca when Ben died, at a time when she needed me as much as I needed; her only now she's starting to move on, and I guess it's time for me to do the same.

'You know what, you're right,' I say decisively. 'I think I'm going to do it.'

'So, when are you going to tell him?'

'No time like the present,' I say, feeling like I should strike whilst the iron's hot before I get a chance to chicken out. I pull my phone out of my bag to send him a Whatsapp to tell him I'm in.

My phone beeps back immediately.

Luke Taylor:
Great! I'll make it official.

'Looks like it's on,' I say to Becca as the waitress comes over and takes our order.

My phone beeps again and it's a message from Luke telling me to check my Instagram.

I open it up and see that I've been tagged in a photo. It's a side-profile photo with the Mexican café as the backdrop. He must have taken it when I was in my dream world watching Aidan.

I hold it out for Becca to see.

'Wow, that's such a gorgeous photo, so natural. And that caption,' she says, whistling through her teeth.

'I know, isn't that something?'

I take my phone back from her and re-read it.

Lukeatmealways
To the beautiful @This_Izzy_loves who's captured my heart – Please go out with me!
#pleasesayyes #fingerscrossed #romance
#WeMetOnInstagram

The post is punctuated with love heart emojis. It's only been up a few minutes but it's already racking up the likes. Luke was right, people are eating this stuff up.

I take a snapshot of Luke's post asking me out and click to add a new photo to go alongside it. I tip the wrapped sugar cubes out onto the table and arrange them into letters. It takes a surprising amount to form the word yes.

'Can you put your torch on on your phone,' I ask Becca, checking the light levels with a test shot.

Becca obliges and when the cubes are illuminated in the right way I take my photo. I tag Luke and add a couple holding hands emoji hoping that people on my feed will scroll across to see his original question.

I put my phone down face down on the table, my cheeks feeling flushed. There's no going back now – I'm officially fake dating Luke Taylor.

Welcome to July
This_Izzy_Loves IGTV
No. followers: 15.8k

*Hey, guys. What a month June was, huh? From getting to meet Small Bubbles who was every bit as lovely as she appears to meeting fellow Instagrammer Luke. I can't believe how many messages you've been sending me about him. I'm sure you're more excited than I am about my first date with him. And no, for all those of you that have asked, I have absolutely no idea what he's got planned! I adore surprises so can't wait to find out. For those who want to be super involved I'm really stuck with what to wear so I've thrown a couple of outfits on my Insta stories with a poll. Please vote to tell me which one you like better. What would I do without you all to guide me?*

# Chapter 9

I give my hair one last brush and lean forward into the mirror to double-check my eye make-up.

'What am I doing?' I mutter to myself, before turning and walking out of the toilets at work. I make my way out of the building to meet Luke. He's leaning against the wall again perfecting his model pose.

'Right on time. You look good,' he says.

'Thanks.'

We have one of those moments where it's slightly awkward and neither of us knows whether we should hug or kiss each other on the cheek.

I'm not really down with what the etiquette is for fake boyfriends so in the end I plump for patting him on the arm like he's an elderly relative.

'So, ready to go?'

'I guess so.'

'You sound about as excited as if you were going to the dentist. Come on, Izzy, this might be purely business but that doesn't mean it can't be fun, right? Didn't you see the number of new followers you had after you posted "yes"? Everyone else is excited.'

'Yes, I know. I'll try to be more enthusiastic. Maybe if I knew what we're doing.'

'All in good time. Let's go.'

He hands me a large reusable shopping bag. I don't expect it to be so heavy.

'Whoa, don't drop it,' he says, catching it before it makes impact with the ground. 'That's got glasses in it. Here.'

He swaps the bag for a picnic basket.

'That's just as heavy.'

'But its contents are less breakable. Come on.'

He trots off and I notice he's wearing a large backpack.

'How far have I got to take this?' I ask.

'Not far, only to the park by the old abbey ruins.'

At least it's only a five-minute walk from here so my arms probably won't drop off by then.

'What's in the bags then?' I ask.

'Props.'

'Is there at least some food?' I ate an early lunch and I'm starving.

'There is, but you can't eat any of it as I've put dyes in it so that it looks better on camera.'

I stop walking, my poor stomach rebelling.

'I'm kidding. There is edible food. I promised you dinner, there will be dinner.'

'Good, I'm bloody famished.'

I start walking again and it isn't long before we've made it to the park.

It wouldn't be my first choice of picnic location; it's hemmed in on two sides by a busy road and despite the trees surrounding it, it still feels like you're bang in the middle of the city.

'Where do you want to sit?' I ask, looking round for somewhere close by so that I can dive into that picnic basket as soon as possible.

'I've got a spot under a tree in mind,' he says, frogmarching me along.

I look over at the entrance to the abbey ruins. There's a big sign over the closed gates advertising a cinema screening for this evening. There are a few people waiting nearby, presumably for the gates to open.

'Oh look, they're showing an outdoor film here later on,' I say, squinting to read the sign. '*Dirty Dancing*. How predictable.'

'I would have thought you'd love *Dirty Dancing*.'

'Why, because I'm a woman? It's not that I don't like it,' I say with a sigh. 'I mean, it's an all right film and the Swayze is pretty hot, it's just I wish they'd branch out and show movies that you might not have seen. I mean, it's like when all the winter ones just show *Love Actually* and *Elf*.

'Are we going to walk much further? My arms are aching.'

'Not too far. You see that tree?'

'That one that's miles away in the distance?'

'This park isn't even a mile long. It's a hundred metres, max. You'll be grateful when we get there that it's a bit more secluded. I'm guessing you're not going to like the next part of the plan as much as I thought.'

'As long as you weren't kidding about the food we'll be fine.'

We finally reach the tree, and I carefully lower the basket I'm carrying onto the floor. Luke quickly gets to work, spreading a large picnic blanket on the ground, before delicately unpacking the crockery and glassware from the shopping bag I nearly dropped. Finally he opens the wicker basket.

'Now,' he says a little sternly. 'You can't eat until after the photos or else it'll spoil it.'

He starts opening containers of yummy food and scooping

them into nice bowls to make them look more homemade and less supermarket bought and I start to drool.

'Oh good God, have a falafel,' he says, handing me over the almost empty packet.

'Do I get to dip it in the hummus?'

'Only if you smooth it over after.'

I dip it in, taking the biggest chunk of hummus possible.

'Oh God, that's good,' I say, biting into it. 'So, so good.'

He hands me over a little samosa bite and I eat it greedily.

'Also amazing. Have you got anything to drink?'

He pulls out a bottle of expensive-looking elderflower cordial and I do an involuntary nose wrinkle.

'Do you not like it?' he asks.

'I'm sure it's very nice. I just always buy cloudy lemonade when I have a picnic, you can't beat it.'

'Noted for next time,' he says.

I sneak in another falafel causing him to give me a hard stare.

'So if you were in charge of the outdoor cinema, what would you show?'

He slaps my hand away from taking another samosa from the pyramid he's just built.

'Definitely *The Princess Bride*. Have you seen it?'

'I don't think so.'

'Ah, my brother and I used to watch it all the time.' I smile at the memory.

'Who's in it?'

'Mandy Patinkin. You know, Saul from *Homeland*.'

He shakes his head.

'Well, you're missing out. In fact, it's playing in Newbury in a few weeks, if you wanted to come? It's got some epic sword battles in it and it's hilarious.'

'Tempting, but I'm busy.'

'But you don't know when it is.'

'No, I don't, but we don't want to overload our feeds with classic films. We should probably do as many different things as we can.'

I shrug my shoulders. 'Your loss, it truly is the best.'

'Why don't you take your brother?'

'Oh… he died,' I mutter.

'He died? Oh, Izzy, I'm sorry for putting my foot in it.'

'You weren't to know. He had a problem with his heart. He died in his sleep.'

Luke's eyes soften and he stops taking things out of boxes. He reaches for a falafel and dips it in the hummus before handing it to me.

'I'm sorry,' he says.

I shrug my shoulders and eat the falafel. 'You know, a few more of these would make me feel better.'

He pulls the bowl away again and smiles.

'Nice try. You can eat properly soon.'

He reaches into another bag and pulls out a string of fairy lights.

'Oh no,' I say groaning. 'Fairy lights, really?'

He starts untangling them.

'Everyone loves fairy lights.'

'I love them, too, at Christmas. This is just cheesy, and it's not even dark.'

'I can make it look dark in Photoshop. Can you grab that end for me?'

He twists them round the wide trunk of the tree and then jumps to throw them over a long, overhanging branch.

He switches them on and steps back to admire his handwork.

'What do you think?' he says, clearly happy with his efforts judging by the smile on his face.

I walk back to him where he's now erecting a tripod. It's so pretentious; it's so Instagram.

'I don't know how much of the fairy lights you'll get in though if we're sitting down on the rug.'

'Who said we were going to be sitting down?'

He screws his camera onto the tripod and then starts to fiddle with its position.

'So you're going to make us pose up against the tree,' I say, trying to work out what I'm missing. There are people walking through the park and I'm going to feel like a bit of dick posing up here.

'Not exactly, but I'll be standing, at least.'

'Right, you better tell me what's going on now, or I'm going to eat all the sausage rolls.'

I lunge at them and he pulls my arm back.

'OK. I saw that they had the outdoor film here tonight and I thought it would be perfect. I mean, all women love *Dirty Dancing*. Well, all except you.'

'So we're pretending we're having a picnic at the movies. I guess we're lying about everything else…'

'We're not going to pretend; we're going to go watch the movie and take photos of the screen. I've got friends saving us a spot.'

'What? This isn't what I signed up for,' I protest.

'It's exactly what you signed up for. But wait, it gets better.'

'I somehow doubt that.'

'Well, everyone there will be taking photos of the same thing, right? The screen, their picnic.'

I point down at the picnic. 'So far, so cliché.'

'Exactly, but I thought it would be fun to re-enact a bit from your favourite movie.'

‘What, have a sword fight from *The Princess Bride*?’

‘Very funny. But think of your Insta feed – *Dirty Dancing* would totally be in keeping as being one of your favourite films.’

‘So now I’m lying about our relationship *and* my favourite films.’

‘Yes, keep up,’ he says matter-of-factly.

‘So when you say “re-enact” you want us to dance, here, by the tree.’ I look around the park. At least he’s found a part that’s mostly secluded, bar a man walking his dog.

‘Not dance. Think, what’s the most iconic part of the movie?’

‘Oh no,’ I say, my heart sinking. ‘I am *not* doing the lift.’

‘But look at it, it’ll be amazing. I’ll stand there,’ he says, pointing, and then you’ll be up there, which is just where the fairy lights are.’

He shows me how he’s framed the shot on the camera.

‘It would look really good,’ I agree. ‘There’s just one teeny tiny problem: I’m not doing it. Can’t we just have a picnic like normal people?’

‘Of course we could,’ says Luke, exasperated. ‘We could do all the things that normal people do, but that totally misses the point. We’re trying to do something different. To get noticed. To get brands to want to pay us.’

I purse my lips together. ‘I just better not break my bloody neck.’

‘I watched a YouTube tutorial at lunchtime; it seems very straightforward.’

‘Didn’t seem that straightforward in the film, that’s why they had to do it in the water.’

Luke sighs. ‘Come on, let’s do a couple of practice runs before I start the timer. You’ll need to take your cardigan off.’

I unbutton my cardigan, and it clicks into place. That’s why he wanted me to wear a white button-down shirt and light blue jeans – it's in homage to the kind of outfits that Baby wore in the movie. 'If I'd known I wouldn't have straightened my hair, it's naturally curly.'

'Now you tell me!' he says. 'OK, so all you have to do is keep running at me OK, and when you get to me I'll lift you straight up. Then you use all your stomach muscles to hold yourself upright and your arms out.'

'What stomach muscles? Are you sure this is going to be safe?'

'Of course, as long as you don't knock me unconscious or my back doesn't give way,' he says. 'Or you don't fall head-first to the ground. Just don't put your weight too far forward.'

'So, all in all foolproof? Look, couldn't we do another scene from the movie? You running your finger down my waist and me laughing?'

'Not quite the blockbuster moment. Come on, nothing ventured, nothing gained.'

He really is stubborn when he gets an idea in his head.

I walk backwards until he tells me to stop. I loosen up, rolling my neck from side to side and shrugging my shoulders to limber up.

'Now the key is to run, and keep running. Don't stop.'

'Don't stop,' I mutter to myself. 'Got it.'

I look over my shoulder, double-checking there's no one in the immediate vicinity, before I take a deep breath. I start to run, concentrating on giving myself enough momentum.

'Bloody hell, this isn't *Braveheart*!' he says as I crash into him. 'That face – you look like you're doing a battle cry. Come on, you've got to look like you're falling in love.'

I mutter some swear words under my breath whilst walking back to my starting line.

'Look lustful.'

I do my best sexy look.

'Lustful not constipated,' he shouts.

I sigh loudly. 'Are you sure we can't just do a standing pose?'

'No, we're going to nail this.' He pulls out the remote control for his camera and presses the button.

'OK,' I say, taking another deep breath; anyone would think I'm preparing to run the hundred metres at the Olympics.

'Three, two, one, run!' shouts Luke, holding his hands out ready.

I run towards him with all my might. I feel his hands make contact with my waist and he thrusts me into the air and I throw my arms out as I get higher and higher, and I actually think we're going to make it. My legs have swung out backwards, and I'm determined that I'm not going to dive head-first into the knobbly-looking tree roots below. I have the biggest smile on my face that we've only gone and done it, when Luke starts to wobble and my legs, which seemed to have risen so elegantly into the air, are being pulled back by gravity, like a pendulum swinging.

'Fuck,' shouts Luke as my feet kick him in the balls.

He drops me and I hit the ground stumbling to stay upright.

He cups his crotch and hops about doubled over; it is absolutely not a laughing matter and I try desperately to suppress the giggle that's escaping my lips.

'I'm so sorry, but you never told me how to land.'

He ignores me and alternates between swearing and yelping as he hops around.

'I was trying so hard not to dive-bomb over the top that I didn't think about the momentum in my legs and…' He's looking so pale. 'Do you want me to have a look?'

'I think you've done enough damage,' he says, the pain audible in his voice. 'I don't want you to come near my balls ever again.'

He turns away from me and moves further apart.

'That's absolutely fine by me.'

Whilst his back's turned, I help myself to a sausage roll.

'I saw that,' he says, his voice sounding more normal.

I take another and shove it in my mouth, capitalising on the fact that he's not in a position to do anything about it.

He does a low whistle and hobbles over to the camera. I'd almost forgotten about it.

He takes it off the tripod and I walk over to see what it's captured.

'Am I too close to your balls here, do I need to step back?'

He scowls at me before he starts to scroll through the pictures. They show me doing a slo-mo run up to him; he must have had the camera on burst mode, capturing one photo every split second. I gasp when we get to the lift.

'Oh my God, we actually got it,' I say in disbelief. There's a photo of me full-on in the air, before it all went so horribly wrong. My line might look a little off, but with the trees behind us and the picnic in the foreground, the picture's more than good enough to impress even the most discerning of browsers.

'With a little Photoshop magic, this will look pretty cool,' Luke says.

'What's art without a little bit of pain, huh?'

He gives me a look to let me know that it's too early to make jokes about it.

He carries on scrolling and we watch the look of horror on both of our faces in the photos when we get to the fall. Luke stops scrolling; I don't think he wants to relive that again just yet.

'So now do we get to eat?'

Luke looks at his watch. 'We can eat a little bit, but we should pack up to get ready for the film.'

'Oh, that's right. I forgot we actually have to watch the movie.'

'Now, now, where's your enthusiasm? My friends are saving us the best seats at the front.'

'Bloody hell, and there was me hoping I could sneak out from the back with nobody watching me.'

'You probably still could. I imagine there'll be a lot of Prosecco drinking going on and a lot of people heading to the loo.'

'And you wouldn't mind?'

'No, I might leave early too. Means I can get home and edit the photos so we can post it before the movie's over. Help fuel the myth that we didn't Photoshop it.'

I sit down at the picnic blanket and start to devour the food. Luke winces as he joins me, still in pain, and we both laugh a little at the ridiculousness.

'It's certainly been a memorable first date,' I say to him.

'One to tell the grandkids.'

'We're not going that far, remember,' I say, trying to remind him that this will be over long before that. 'So what are you going to caption the photo? Let me guess: "No one puts Izzy in a corner."'

I laugh, thinking that he wouldn't be that predictable, but I notice that he looks crestfallen.

'What would you caption it, then?'

'I don't know, if I had bigger boobs you could have had: "She was carrying some watermelons."'

'And that's not cheesy? Didn't you used to be a copywriter?' he says laughing.

'All right, all right. Not a very good one.'

The sun is starting to set and I can see a steady stream of people in the distance going into the ruins.

'You seem to have put this picnic together pretty well. And battery-powered fairy lights, too – have you done this before?' I ask.

He gives me a wink. 'I have. The money that went on those lights was the best £20 I've ever spent. I've had a pretty good return on it, if you know what I mean.'

I suddenly feel less guilty for kicking him in the balls, maybe it was karmic payback.

'So, do you think it's that easy with women? A few fairy lights, a picnic?'

He pops an olive in his mouth. 'The key with any woman is to make them feel like they're special and that you've made an effort. A quick trip to M&S, chuck things into Tupperware, bring a blanket and string up some fairy lights. It's cheap but the results are certainly cheerful.'

My nostrils flare. I knew there was a reason I wasn't into clichéd romantic tropes – because they're easily exploited.

'Aren't you eating any more?' he says, hoovering up the last of the sausage rolls. 'I thought you were starving.'

'I think I've had enough,' I say, wondering if I'm only speaking about the food.

'Cool, OK, well, let's pack this up and we get onto phase two of the evening.'

'Can't wait,' I say, hoping we see a spike in our Instagram feed and it makes this all worthwhile.

# Chapter 10

The heavens open and I look up at the black sky wondering what happened to the summer.

'Bloody hell,' says Marissa, linking her arm through mine to keep herself steady. 'These are not shoes for running in.'

I look down at her sandals and my flip-flops. Neither are made for running or rain.

'It's only a bit of water,' I say, trying to make her slow down. 'It'll be better to get there in one piece.'

We're only fifty metres away from the shopping centre but with the speed we're travelling at, we could probably set the world's slowest record over that distance. By the time we get there we're drenched from head to toe.

I pull my now very frizzy hair back into a ponytail and slip on the cardigan that had been round my waist.

'I must look like a drowned rat,' I say, laughing.

'You don't look that bad, but I wouldn't be taking any selfies at the moment.'

'Luckily my Instagram is buzzing from my *Dirty Dancing* date with Luke.'

'It looked amazing from the photos.'

'It was really fun, despite the fact that I had to put up with Luke.'

Marissa laughs. 'I still don't believe he can be that bad.'

'He is, really. But, it's working. I've had over 7,000 likes already.'

'Bloody hell. I remember when I had Molly McMittens I was pleased I'd had almost 700 likes.'

'Poor Molly McMittens,' I say.

'There is nothing poor about her – do you know that her new owner still has that feed? She gets double the amounts of likes than I do. I told you that cat was the way forward.'

'You couldn't have kept her, you know that. Your face.'

She strokes it in memory, but it was at least double the size when she'd owned Molly. She'd persevered at first, thinking she had hay fever, but the pharmacist was pretty keen to point out that hay fever in the middle of winter isn't very common. She was describing the amount of black mould she had in her bathroom when the pharmacist saw a cat hair on her coat and in a few Sherlock moves he deduced that Molly McMittens was to blame.

Being Marissa and desperate to grow her Instagram, she powered on for a few weeks, hoping he was wrong, but eventually no filter could hide her puffy-looking eyes and she had to rehome Molly. Luckily she had a colleague at work whose daughter was desperate for a cat, so at least there was a happy ending.

'I know. It's just a shame that Bowser is so unphotogenic. If only Tim would let me get another puppy.'

'A puppy is for life, not just for Instagram,' I say in a stern tone.

We walk further into the shopping centre, when Marissa points. 'Look, it's Becca. *Becca!*' she shouts, waving.

Becca turns round and her eyes almost pop out of her head. Her hands are entwined with a man's and I realise why she's feeling uncomfortable.

'Hi,' says Becca, walking over. 'How are you two?'

'Fine, thanks,' says Marissa, grinning straight at Gareth. 'Hello.'

'Oh, right, guys, this is Gareth, Gareth this is Marissa and um, Izzy.'

'Oh, wow. Great to meet you both,' he says, leaning forward to shake our hands. 'I was beginning to think that Bec made you up.'

Becca laughs nervously and I notice that she won't look me in the eye.

'We were just on our way to grab a drink. Do you want to join us?' he asks.

Becca looks horrified, but before I can make an excuse Marissa pipes up.

'We'd love to,' she says before she looks at me and she clocks my expression.

'It'll only be a quick one,' says Becca. 'We've got a dinner reservation.'

'We're early and it's Sunday night and it's pretty quiet,' says Gareth. 'I'm sure they won't mind if we're not bang on time. I want to hear all about you from your friends.'

He leans over and gives her a kiss on her forehead and I feel like I've been winded.

'Come on,' says Gareth, leading the way.

Marissa loops her arm through mine again, this time to steady me, and we walk behind Gareth and Becca.

'Are you OK?' she whispers to me as we walk along. 'I wasn't thinking. I was so excited to meet him and—'

'I'm fine. I've got to meet him some time,' I say, wishing that I'd been prepared for it.

We push open the doors to the bar and Marissa makes a beeline for the toilet.

'Can you get me a glass of fizzy water?' she asks before she leaves.

'I'll get the drinks, you ladies get a table. What are we drinking?'

'I'll have a Coke,' I say.

'A Coke, OK, are you sure?'

'Yeah, school night and all. Marissa wanted a fizzy water.'

'Cheap round, and you, Bec?'

'I'll have a glass of Malbec, thanks.'

We find a table near the window and sit down.

'So, he seems nice,' I say.

I watch him at the bar, gesturing politely to the barman and smiling as he orders. He looks like an accountant, even though it's the weekend. He's got neat-looking jeans on and fitted V-neck jumper. He seems nice and safe and stable, which is probably exactly what Becca needs.

'He is, he's really nice. I just wasn't expecting you to meet him just yet.'

'We had to meet him sometime.'

'I know, I know,' she says in an almost whisper before leaning across the table. She keeps looking over her shoulder at Gareth. 'It's just I didn't expect it to be now and he doesn't exactly know… everything.'

'What do you mean?'

She looks sheepish. 'I told him that I was in a serious relationship and living with someone before, but that's it.'

'He doesn't know about Ben?' I say, gasping.

She closes her eyes for a second before she looks straight at me. 'No. I sort of missed my chance. Bringing up the fact that your fiancé died isn't really the kind of thing that goes down well on a first date. I tried that once before with that Tinder guy, do you remember?'

I nod. I remember cuddling her as she cried when he didn't

want to see her anymore because she had 'too much emotional baggage'.

But whilst I can understand that it might not be the first thing she told him, I would have thought they'd have talked about it by now.

'So in the whole time you've been dating there hasn't been a good time to tell him?'

She shakes her head.

'I've tried to so many times, but I just couldn't. The stupid thing is that I know he'll be really good about it, but it still doesn't make it any easier. Most people have an ex out of choice or because of something went wrong, but Ben and I, well, you know...'

'You were meant to be,' I say, a lump catching in my throat.

'You know when I'm staying at Gareth's, I often wake up in a panic and have to check he's breathing, and then I'm wide awake just watching him sleep.'

'Becca,' I say, my heart breaking for her. It must have been so awful for her to have woken up and found Ben.

I reach out and take her hand across the table and give her a quick squeeze.

'It's probably all the more reason for me to tell him. I'm terrified that one of these days he's going to wake up in the night when I'm watching him and it'll freak him out.'

I smile before I look up at see that Gareth is coming back with the drinks and I do a subtle cough. She dabs at her eyes and plants a big smile on her face.

'Here you go,' he says, sliding our drinks to us.

'Thanks,' I say, trying to get used to him sitting so close to Becca. 'So, I hear you're an accountant?'

'For my sins,' he says with a little bit of canned laughter.

'And you enjoy it?'

'I do. It's actually a lot more interesting than people think. It's quite amazing what some of my clients try to get away with.'

'I can imagine. I work in insurance and some of the claims that people put in are ridiculous. At Christmas the claims department sends out a round-up of the best ones.'

He chuckles again.

'It must be so great for you two living together, two old school friends.'

'Hmm,' I say, realising how awkward him not knowing about Ben is. It's the foundation of mine and Becca's friendship. It's how I met her, even though she was two years above me at school and it's how I ended up living with her now. There were too many memories for her in the house she shared with Ben, so she sold it and we rented a flat together. At the time I thought I'd done it to be there for her, but looking back it was just as much about me needing to grieve with her.

'So what was Becca like at school?' he asks.

'We don't have to talk about this,' she says awkwardly.

'Of course we do, I want to hear all about you,' he says.

'Um, she was like she is now,' I say. 'Pretty. She had all the boys after her, of course.' Although there was only one that captured her heart. 'She was always the lead in the school play with her voice. Has she sung for you yet?'

'Izzy.' Becca shoots me a filthy look.

'She's got a great voice and she doesn't sing enough anymore.'

Becca hasn't really sung much since Ben died. We've all got our coping mechanisms: mine's Instagram, my mum's is baking and Becca's stopped singing because Ben was her biggest fan.

He turns to her and smiles. 'I am looking forward to hearing that.' He kisses her on the top of her head and my heart burns in sadness. My hands start to shake a little and I sit on them. I hadn't realised that seeing Becca with someone else would make me feel this way. I knew it would be a little weird but I wasn't prepared to feel so sad.

'So what are you guys doing in town?' asks Gareth.

I try and pull myself together for Becca's sake. I really want to be happy for her.

'Marissa and I went to the cinema to see the new Marvel movie earlier and then we went for a cup of tea at the top of town.'

'How was the film?'

'It was OK, but I'm not really into them like Marissa is.'

'No, I don't really like them either. I can't think of the last time I went to the cinema; there never seems to be anything on,' says Gareth.

'I haven't been either,' says Becca.

'I'm going to the cult cinema club in Newbury next month to see *The Princess Bride*. They're doing a run of Eighties and Nineties films.'

'Is that the one with the sword fighting?' asks Gareth.

'Uh-huh,' says Becca.

'Huh, I never got that movie. Thought it was a bit over-the-top.'

'It's not everyone's cup of tea,' I say, 'but I love it.'

And so did Ben. I'm not expecting Becca to have picked a carbon copy of him to date but it's surprising how different they are.

'So, what have I missed?' says Marissa, arriving at our table and pulling out the chair next to me. 'I'm sure you'll have covered all the usual things: day jobs, hobbies et cetera,' she says, waving her hand around. 'Let's get down to the nitty gritty. What are your intentions with Becca?'

'Marissa!' Becca gasps in horror.

Gareth starts to stutter, but before he can get a chance to reply, Becca drains her drink.

'Don't you think we better go?' she asks him, pointedly. 'Our table was booked for seven and it's almost quarter to.'

'It's not going to take us fifteen minutes to walk to the top of town,' he says, chuckling. 'Let's see, my intentions. Well, I guess that depends on Becca. I'm hoping that this time next year she'll be living with me.'

I knock my Coke over the table. I'd been reaching for it, but the shock of hearing that made my hand spasm. Becca's staring at him and she doesn't notice at first that the Coke's in danger of dripping on her.

'I'm so sorry,' I babble, 'did I get you?' I grab some napkins out of the dispenser and start blotting it.

'No, don't worry, it missed,' says Becca. 'I think we should take it as a sign that we should be leaving.'

'OK then,' says Gareth, finishing his wine. 'But I want to do this again so I can meet you both properly. It's been a pleasure, ladies.'

'Likewise,' I say, smiling. I'm still trying to mop up the Coke.

Becca gives me a little wave over her shoulder as they leave.

'I can't believe that they left like that when I've only just come back,' Marissa complains. 'I barely got to ask any questions.'

'Don't take it personally. I think Becca wanted to get him away from you as quickly as possible.'

'How am I not supposed to take that personally?'

'She didn't have an opportunity to brief you like she did me when he went to the bar. She hasn't told him about Ben.'

'What?' Marissa says, her jaw nearly hitting the table as it flies open. 'Not at all?'

'She told him she'd been engaged, but not that he'd died.'

'Bloody hell. So he doesn't know that you were his sister?'

I shake my head. I can feel tears prickling behind my eyes and I will myself not to cry.

'He thinks that we were school friends.'

'Oh, well I guess that's partly true. You *did* know each other at school.'

'Yes, but only because she was Ben's girlfriend. It just feels weird rewriting the past.'

'I'm sure she'll tell him.'

'I know, I'm sure she will. It was just a bit of shock that she hadn't. Ben was such a huge part of her life.'

I look over at the bar wishing I'd picked something stronger to drink than Coke.

'So, what's he like?' asks Marissa.

'He seems… he's really nice.'

'But…?'

'How did you know there was a but?'

'Because you've got that look on your face.'

I take a deep breath. 'He's nothing like Ben. I know that sounds absolutely ridiculous as I guess in some ways it would have been harder if she'd picked someone exactly like him. But he's nothing like him at all. I mean he doesn't get *The Princess Bride*.'

'Izzy, I hate to break it to you, but not a lot of people do. Me included.'

I half smile.

'Becca really likes him,' says Marissa. 'I'm sure once you get to know him…'

'I know, I know. It's just I can't imagine us all hanging out like we used to and I think it just hit me that that's gone forever.'

A tear rolls down my cheek and I wipe it away.

'It's OK not to be OK about this you know.'

'I just feel like an awful friend.'

'You're not, it's grief. It's a bitch and it's unpredictable.'

I blink my eyes rapidly so that I don't cry.

'Can we change the subject?' I ask.

'If you want to.'

I nod my head.

'How many more likes has your Instagram post had since you last checked?'

I pull my phone out and see that it's gone up by a hundred since I last checked. I turn it round and show her.

'Holy moly – that figure.'

I smile and it makes me feel a teeny, tiny bit better. Looking back over the last couple of years I don't know what I would have done without Instagram. If only I could live in the virtual life I present and not have to think about what happens in the real world, and then my life would be perfect.

# Chapter 11

It might be Monday morning, but I've got no hint of back-to-work blues today as the *Dirty Dancing* post on Instagram has been huge. People have been going crazy for it – I've had over 8,500 likes for it. Eight and a half thousand! That's a 50 per cent engagement rate from my followers, which is amazing in the land of metrics.

I haven't even had any time to dwell on meeting Gareth yesterday because I've been so busy responding to comments and monitoring the rising figures.

'There's your coffee, Mrs Harris,' I say, handing her a steaming cup from my tray before delivering one to Colin, who nods in thanks (he's still not verbal), and Cleo, who thanks me before carrying on with her work.

'What were you up to at the weekend?' asks Mrs Harris, narrowing her eyes. 'You've got a look about you.'

'I got more Instagram followers.' I can't help the grin spreading over my face.

'That's what the spring in your step is about? You be careful, Izzy. They don't call it "spinstergram" for nothing.'

'No one calls it that.'

'Well, they should and they will if you spend more time on it than with real men. It's like that Kinder app.'

'Tinder,' I correct. 'Kinder are the chocolate eggs.'

'See, it's all going so horribly wrong with you young folk. You need everything sweet. I saw chocolate pizza in the supermarket the other day.'

'You can't call us "you young folk", you're not that old.'

She smiles and for a minute I think she's going to accept the compliment.

'I'm old enough to be a grandmother; some of my friends already are,' she says instead.

'At 31 I'm hypothetically old enough to be a grandmother too. You know, if I'd been less into books and more into boys when I was an early teen.'

Mrs Harris scoffs and goes back to her work.

I sip my coffee and try to focus on my screen. I'm already getting a surprising amount done today; it's amazing how efficient I'm being when all I want to do is shove my phone in people's faces and say, 'Looooooook at how popular I am!'

A message from Luke pops up on Link.

Luke Taylor:
Did you see? I had over 9k likes on my photo!!! 48% reach!!!

I type back immediately.

Izzy Brown:
I got 8.5k :) Your idea of posting photos on both of our accounts totally worked. I know that we won't get that type of engagement every time, but still :)

Luke Taylor:
I know. Brands have surely got to start noticing us after that. Meet me for lunch? We can plan strategy.

Izzy Brown:
Are we taking over Westeros next?

Luke Taylor:
WTF????

Izzy Brown:
Game of Thrones? Ah, never mind.

Luke Taylor:
Quick tip – men in tights = no-no from me

Izzy Brown:
Not sure they wear tights…

Luke Taylor:
There are dragons in it. Also a no from me. Lunch?

Izzy Brown:
I've got sandwiches. Wanna eat in the park?

Luke Taylor:
Fine. See you at 1, usual place.

Look at us having a usual place. It's like we really are dating.

'You haven't even looked at your phone and you're smiling,' Mrs Harris says and I try to make my face neutral. I don't want her to think I'm happy because I'm meeting Luke for lunch. 'Have you been forwarded a funny email from Claims? Has someone tried to claim for hoover-related injuries again?'

'Don't mention that,' I say, wincing. 'Anytime the cleaners bring a Henry Hoover in the office I flinch – what those poor painted-on eyes of his have to see.'

'Then what? Don't tell me you're taking a leaf out of Cleo's book and dipping your pen in the company ink?'

'Hey,' says Cleo.

'For the record I am not dating anyone,' I say. 'Not that it would matter if I was.'

'Exactly,' says Cleo. 'We work in a massive office, Mrs Harris. It's not like I'm dating Colin.'

Poor Colin goes beetroot red at the mention.

'Lucky you're not,' she says. 'You wouldn't trust him around your buns.'

It's all too much for Colin. He grabs a folder and walks off across the office.

'So what are you doing then, young Izzy? You're not applying for work in another department, are you?'

Mrs Harris doesn't like change. She'd be upset if she knew that I'd leave in a heartbeat if my influencer career was financially viable. I'll have to start reminding her that I'm only a temp and this was only ever supposed to be a stop-gap, no matter how much fun we have when we're supposed to be working.

'Is it that Jason in Risk Management? Is he trying to poach you? He may only be doing it to get to me, you know.'

'Gee, thanks for doubting my professional abilities,' I say, 'but no, I'm not being poached. A guy from Sales is helping me with my Instagram stuff. He's just a friend.'

'Again, this is what's wrong with you young people. You're all "friends with benefits". Well, let me give you some advice: there won't be many friends wanting to give you benefits when you hit a certain age and gravity takes hold.'

'Thanks for your wise words, Mrs H.'

'You're welcome,' she says, giving me a smile.

And with that, I slip in my earphones and get back to work.

I'm first to make it outside our building at 1 p.m. While I'm waiting I do a quick Instagram story post, featuring my watch with lots of party poppers going off around it and the caption, **'Lunchtime!'**

'Hey, you're on time.' Luke appears in front of me, and I put my phone away.

'Sometimes I manage it.'

We start walking towards the park that we took the *Dirty Dancing* photos in.

'So, did you have a good weekend?' I ask.

'Pretty good.'

'What did you do?'

'You know, hung out.'

'Wow, thanks, I'm so much the wiser,' I say mock-rolling my eyes at him. 'Who did you hang out with?'

'People.'

'Pretty sure that's a given. Mates? Dates?' I say, shrugging my shoulder and looking for some elaboration.

'You sound like an actual girlfriend. I hung out with my mates Tom and Jack on Saturday, we went to the pub to watch the footie and then we went back to Tom's and watched the boxing on Saturday night. Then on Sunday I did a bit of gaming until I met a group of friends for brunch. Happy now?'

'Kind of. "Brunch with friends" is quite vague...'

'But it does exactly what it says on the tin.'

He goes quiet and I'm guessing that's all the information I'm going to get.

'Don't you want to know what I did?' I ask.

'When?'

'At the weekend?'

He sighs.

'You know, the up-side of having a fake relationship rather than a real one is that you don't have to make small talk. Or learn about your partner's friends who you don't care about.'

'I bet Instagram Luke would care.'

'And that's why he's only a fantasy,' he says.

We walk along for a bit in silence and eventually I can't take it.

'I actually went to the cinema and then we bumped into my friend and her new boyfriend Gareth. He's an accountant.'

'You're right, I *was* missing out by not knowing that,' he says sarcastically as we arrive at the park.

Of course he doesn't understand the subtext of what I said but he doesn't want to find out either. He really isn't interested in anything but himself. I give him a little shove through the gateway to the park and he turns and gives me a smile.

'Let's get down to business then,' I say, sitting down on an empty bench and pulling out a notepad. Evidently no point in wasting any more of my lunch break on small talk.

'I've come up with a few ideas for dates,' he says, sitting down next to me and pulling up a list on his phone.

'Are you actually telling me what they are?' I say, thinking back to his big surprises last time.

'I don't see why not.'

'Do I get a veto?'

'You're not going to need it.'

'Really? Well, as long as none of it involves me dressed in underwear or swimwear.'

His face falls. 'Trip to the lido's out, then?'

'Yep, I had far too many creepy messages the last time I wore a bikini on Insta.'

'Too bad. I always get pretty good comments on photos of me topless,' he says with a grin.

'What's next?'

'Rowing at Henley,' he says, scrolling down his list.

'Veto.'

'Why?'

'It's so *Bridget Jones* and so cliché.'

'But women love romantic clichés.'

'Not all women. Don't you think we shouldn't just copy movies?'

'OK,' he says, swiping up and down with his finger.

'Have you got anything else?'

'Not really.'

I shake my head at the lack of imagination.

'Why don't we keep it simple – go to a restaurant,' I suggest. 'We might be able to wangle a free meal.'

'I like that. There's a fancy new Italian that might be up for it. Hey, we could do that thing with spaghetti like in—'

'*Lady and the Tramp?* Last time I looked, that was a movie. We could go on a wine tour at the vineyard in Twyford.'

'Like that. Bet it would make a great actual date. Bit sophisticated. Bit boozy.'

He makes a note in his phone and I'm not sure if it's for us or his real-life dating repertoire.

'So dinner, wine tasting,' he says, nodding. 'What about one of those aerial climbing parks?'

'The ones where you have those harnesses on that give you a giant wedgie, and the helmets flatten your hair?'

'Oh yeah, couldn't flatten this big boy,' he says, patting his quiff. 'I feel like we should do something active. Are you sure we couldn't do the rowing? It's not the *most* iconic *Bridget Jones* moment, is it? It's not like I'm asking you to wear a bunny costume.'

'Bet that was on your original list.'

He purses his lips to stop himself laughing. 'Maybe but perhaps I guessed it would share the same fate as anything in a swimsuit.'

'Damn straight. Get you, knowing *Bridget Jones* back-to-front.'

'You might not like chick flicks but I do.'

'I don't believe you,' I say, pulling my sandwich out of my bag and tucking in.

'Fine. I get my ideas for dates from them,' he says, shrugging.

'You know women would like it if you did things from the heart too – things that they might actually like rather than what Hollywood thinks they should like.'

He looks at me like I've just imparted great wisdom.

'Do you think that's something you'll try?' I ask. Perhaps I'm going to be able to change him for the better.

'Yeah, well, I'm going to copy what we do on our dates. You know I've gone to all the effort with you, might as well get some use out of it. I bet I could have a date straight after when it's all set up.'

'Why don't you just invite them along on our date? They could take the photos,' I say, joking.

'That's not a bad idea,' he says.

I close my eyes and take a deep breath. My mum was right: a leopard never changes his spots.

‘So, can we put rowing back on the table?’

‘Fine,’ I say, sighing. He seems so keen on it.

‘Right, I’ll link our Google calendars together and then we can come up with a schedule.’

‘I don’t have a Google calendar,’ I say.

‘OK, then what do you use?’

I pull my trusty paper diary out of my handbag.

‘You cannot be serious,’ he says, groaning. ‘You are far too old-school for your own good. Don’t you remember how much trouble your watch got us in?’

‘I haven’t had many diary-related incidents.’

He eyes it suspiciously just in case.

‘I’ll set you up with a Google calendar and send you the link. Ideally we should do something this week.’

‘I’m free any night but Saturday. I’m off to see *The Princess Bride* – you’re still welcome to join me if you like, I’m going by myself.’

‘I wonder why,’ he mutters. ‘Wish I could, but I’m busy.’

‘I’ll know if you’re lying with the shared calendar.’

He laughs. ‘No tights, remember. How about tomorrow night after work? Let’s get dinner so we can strike whilst the iron is hot. I think we’ll aim for posting once or twice a week to make it believable at first and then we can ramp up posts as we get more serious.’

I must look alarmed because then he says, ‘Don’t look so horrified; we can do multiple dates in one session with outfit changes. You won’t actually have to go out with me three times a week.’

I try not to sigh too loudly with relief.

‘I’m busy this weekend,’ he says, scrolling through his phone. ‘So how about Henley a week on Sunday. Are you free?’

‘Uh-huh,’ I say, making a note of it.

'All sorted then. Now, in the meantime, don't forget to respond to your comments. Brands love that.'

'I know,' I say, remembering the wisdom of Small Bubbles. 'I'll keep plugging away. It's hard when there are so many.'

'Just think what it'll be like when we get even bigger.'

His eyes widen and I think his head starts to swell.

Whereas I want to become an influencer to change my life and to make Ben proud, I think that Luke is all about the fame. I guess it doesn't matter why we're both doing it, as long as it works and we get to where we both want to be.

# Chapter 12

I arrive at *The Princess Bride* so early that the pre-film adverts are on and the lights are still up. I really wish I'd been able to find someone to come with me to see it as being here, alone I'm thinking about how much Ben would have loved this. I miss him so much.

I pull my phone out of my bag to pop it on silent and I see that I've got a new Whatsapp message from Luke.

> Luke:
> See if you can nab someone to stage a photo with you and we can use it at a later date.

I wrinkle my nose up. I see a major flaw in his plan.

> Me:
> Won't people know it's not you?

> Luke:
> Make a heart with your hands and someone else's. Against a dark background no one will know. But make sure they're big hands, OK? – I've got a reputation to protect.

I send an eye-rolling emoji to him.

Me:
Are you at least quoting *Grease 2*?

Luke:
Never seen it.

Me:
Come on… have you not seen any of the classics?

Luke:
I've seen *Dirty Dancing*.

Me:
I'm turning my phone off now…

Luke:
Don't forget to take the photo.

Me:
Yes, Luke of the BIG hands, got it.

I'm actually scanning the people walking in to see how big their hands are.

Luke:
Good, we'll save it to use next week. Have you seen that people loved the restaurant photos?

Ah, yes, the restaurant photos. They were lovely, unlike the dinner itself which was stone cold by the time we got to eat it after the mammoth photoshoot. I'd talked Luke out of bringing his tripod, encouraging him to use his iPhone instead, only to die of embarrassment when he extended his selfie stick until it was hanging over the middle of the next couple's table. In the end the guy was so pissed off with Luke that he offered to take the photos of us himself, probably so he didn't end up with a phone in his face.

Me:
I saw. Better go. Lights are going down and my chances of finding a man with the right hand-girth are dwindling.

He replies with a thumbs-up, oblivious to my sarcasm. I wonder how I'm going to take this bloody photo; I'm obviously not going to ask a random stranger. I wonder if I could make an optical illusion with my own hands, holding one closer to the screen so it looked bigger. I balance my popcorn between my legs and after setting my camera to timer, I hold it under my chin and hope for the best.

The phone slips and it flashes right in my eye as it takes the photo mid-flight. I go to grab it before it tumbles to the floor and I spray popcorn everywhere.

'Are you OK?' asks a man.

In all the commotion I didn't notice that a man has sat down a couple of seats away from me.

I turn to tell him in a very British way that I'm absolutely fine, despite the fact I'm mourning two-thirds of my tub of popcorn, when I catch sight of who it is. It's Aidan from the train station. I stare at him open-mouthed for a second, but he shows no sign of recognising me.

'I'm fine, thank you,' I say. 'I was trying to take a photo of my hands and it all went a bit pear-shaped.'

'A photo of your hands?' he says, raising an eyebrow.

'Uh-huh.' I feel like a ginormous dick and wish I hadn't explained what I was doing.

'Don't tell me, Facebook photo?' he says, sounding unimpressed.

'It's for a friend. I said I'd take a photo of my hands in a heart shape.'

'As you do. Did you want me to take it for you?'

'I couldn't ask you to do that...' I want to add that he's done so much already, but I don't because he doesn't seem to realise that we've already met. It's so hard to pluck up the courage to thank him because I know it's going to catapult me back to the emotions of that day.

'Really, what else am I going to do waiting for the film? I've already memorised the number of the fast-food shops from the adverts,' he says, pointing at the screen.

I smile. Aidan is literally the nicest guy in the world, and I look down at his hands which are a size that I imagine Luke will be happy with.

'So what are we going to do?' he asks, sliding across to sit next to me.

'I'll make half a heart with one hand and you make the other with your hand.'

He gives me a look.

'I know it's cheesy. But I promised my friend.'

He gives me a quizzical look before he holds his hand out.

'Like this,' he says, making a claw shape. I laugh and go to reshape it and I feel a jolt when my fingers touch his. I look at him to see if he noticed and he's looking straight at me.

'Sorry, a heart is more like this.'

I bend his fingers round before I get my phone ready and make the mirror image with my left hand.

My hand is shaking with nerves and I take the photo quickly. The flash goes off and I immediately take my hand out of the pose and pull up the photo on my phone. I'm amazed it's worked. Our hands are perfectly silhouetted in a heart with the screen as our backdrop. I turn it for Aidan to see.

'Nice,' he says.

I'm about to reply when a torch is flashed in my face.

'Excuse me, we have a no-filming policy,' says a cross-sounding usher.

'I was just taking a photo,' I say, holding up my phone, terrified that I'm going to be ejected.

'Look, no filming,' says the usher. 'We don't want any video piracy here.'

'Video piracy?' says Aidan. 'You do realise this film is over thirty years old, don't you?'

'It doesn't make it any less of a crime.'

'But it hasn't even started yet,' I protest.

The usher sighs loudly.

'Just put your phone away. If we see it out again we'll confiscate it and you'll both be removed.'

'Me as well?' says Aidan.

'We're not together,' I splutter. 'I don't know him!' I don't want him to get kicked out because of me.

'Is he bothering you? Was your flash a cry for help?' The usher points the torch in Aidan's face.

Aidan puts his hand over his eyes to block out the torch beam.

'No, no, he wasn't bothering me. I asked him to help me with a photo, which on reflection was a very silly thing to do. Look, I'm putting my phone down,' I say, lowering it like it's a loaded weapon. 'I'll just put it in my bag.'

When the usher's satisfied my phone is safely put away, he lowers the torch.

The lights start to fade and the first trailer starts to play.

'No more or else you're out, right?' says the usher before he marches off.

'I'm so sorry. Can I at least offer you some popcorn to apologise?'

I hold out my tub only to remember I spilt most of it on the floor.

'Tempting, but I'm all right with my pick 'n' mix,' he says, holding up his bag. 'That was a bit intense, wasn't it?'

'Just slightly. I can't remember if I put my phone on silent and I'm too scared now to check.'

He laughs at me.

'No, I'm deadly serious. What if it goes off in the movie and he chucks me out?'

I bend down and peek at my phone in my bag and I'm relieved when I see the silent symbol on the top.

'You're not touching that phone again, are you?' The usher's voice comes booming before the torch beam shines on my bag.

'No,' I say, holding my hands up. 'I was just collecting some of the popcorn I'd spilt.'

I pick up a couple of bits off the floor and I cringe as I put them back in my tub.

Satisfied, he turns and walks away again.

'I've never known a cinema trip to be so stressful,' says Aidan.

I look into my tub of popcorn, there's no way I can eat it now. I could barely see on the floor, God knows what I put into there.

'I know, stressful and I've lost most of my food.'

'You can share some pick 'n' mix, if you like?'

'Thank you, but I couldn't. I think I've got some mints in my bag. I'll make do with those.'

'Are you really going to reach into your bag again?'

I look over in the corner where the usher is eyeballing us.

'Perhaps not.'

Aidan opens up the paper bag he's holding and puts it under my nose.

'Thank you,' I say, pulling out a jelly snake.

'You're welcome.'

'Sssh,' whispers a voice from two rows back, making us giggle.

'I should have asked, did you want me to move back across,' he says, leaning in closer to whisper. 'I don't want us to get in any more trouble. Or for you to think that I'm "bothering you",' he says.

'I absolutely don't think you're bothering me. You and your pick 'n' mix can stay right there.'

It's a bittersweet experience watching the film; it brings back so many memories of watching it with Ben, and it makes me wish more than ever that he was here with me. I manage to keep it together for the whole film but when the credits start to roll a rogue tear escapes and I hastily wipe it away.

'You know, every time I watch the film I get sad too,' says Aidan. 'I always wanted Miracle Max to actually fully restore Westley. I always feel it's so unjust that he's left partly paralysed.'

I laugh and wipe my eyes. 'At least he got the girl at the end.'

'I guess so.'

The lights come back on and the rest of the cinema-goers stand up and start shuffling out.

'You OK?' he asks in a serious tone.

'Yes and no,' I say, taking a deep breath. 'It's just, it always reminds me of watching it when I was a kid. Brings back memories.'

'Painful ones?'

'Happy ones, which is almost worse,' I say, looking him in the eye.

'I'm sorry, this is going to sound a little nuts,' he says, screwing his face up. 'But have me met before? God, that sounds like such a line. It's not a line, I'm not trying to hit on you or anything. Not that I wouldn't want to hit on you, there's nothing wrong with you, you know, looks-wise, it's just – oh crap. Have we met before?'

He's cute when he's flustered but I put him out of his misery and nod.

'It was a couple of years ago. You helped me at the station to catch a train, I—'

'That was you? You look so different – your hair.'

'Yeah, it's straight now. I mean, it's still curly, but I straighten it.'

'Those curls were cool. Not that your straight hair isn't nice. It's all glossy and shiny… but I meant, the curly hair's a bit more fun and…' He looks pained. 'I'm not usually like this. I'm usually quite articulate.'

'I'm really glad I ran into you, actually. I've been wanting to thank you for that day.'

I feel bad lying that I haven't seen him since then, but I don't know how I would explain not thanking him on those occasions. It didn't feel right then, but it does now.

'I always wished I'd been able to check afterwards that you were OK,' he says. 'I wish I'd gone with you in that taxi to make you sure you'd got to your mum's.'

'You did so much,' I say, letting out a small breath. This was always going to make me feel emotional. 'Thank you.'

'I did what anyone would have done.'

'Ha, I think most people were running in the opposite direction. But seriously, I wouldn't have made it without you.'

He's smiling and his cheeks are reddening.

'So, what are you doing in Newbury? I thought you lived in London?'

'After the day I met you, the day my brother... died, I moved back to Basingstoke to be closer to my parents. And Newbury's not that far of a drive, you know, to see a film like this.'

'Your brother?' I see his shoulders sag, like the enormity of what happened that day hits him. 'That's what happened. I'm so sorry. I couldn't imagine.'

'Nor could I,' I say, blinking back the tears that want to fall. 'That's why this film made me happy sad. It was our film.'

'Shit,' says Aidan.

'We used to watch the film over and over as kids. And we'd act out the sword fight scenes and pretend we were running away from Humperdinck.'

'Sounds fun.'

'It was. I know I should feel grateful that I have good memories to look back on, but it doesn't make up for the fact that I can't reminisce with him about them. Like the time we pretended to be Buttercup and Westley and I pushed him off the end of the sofa and he did an over-the-top fall knocking over one of my mum's expensive china figurines. We spent weeks trying to hide the fact that we'd snapped the arm right off. It was one of those you-had-to-be there moments, but whenever we talked about it we'd end up in hysterics.'

Aidan nods.

'I can imagine. As much as my younger brother is a pain in the bum, I'd really miss him if he wasn't around.'

'Do you get on well?'

'Well enough. We were always at each other's throats when we were kids, though. He's quite a bit younger and had terrible taste in movies. He was obsessed with the *Teenage Mutant Ninja Turtle* movies.'

I pull a face.

'Yeah, his taste isn't much better now, his favourite franchise is *The Fast and the Furious*.'

'Ohhhhh, that's rough.'

'Tell me about it. I mean, the first couple weren't that bad, but if, like me, you're not into fast cars, it all gets a bit same-same.'

I try and keep the sadness out of my smile, but I can't. It's this film and seeing Aidan. So many emotions are swilling round me.

'I'm sorry, I'm upsetting you,' he says softly.

'No, you're not. It's actually refreshing to talk about it. So many people either change the subject or go to great lengths to avoid talking about their siblings around me. It's nice that you're being so normal about it.'

'Not many people call me normal; makes a nice change.'

He smiles and dimples appear in his cheeks. I didn't get to see his smile the day that Ben died, but it lights up his whole face.

'It's rare to find another fan of *The Princess Bride*,' I say.

'It's an underrated classic. Have you read the book?'

'I think I tried to when I was younger, Ben must have had a copy.'

'It's definitely worth a re-read if you get a chance.'

Everyone else has left the room and the usher is glaring at us again and I take it as our cue to leave.

I stand up and Aidan does the same and he follows me out of the cinema.

The usher gives us a look as we pass and I keep my bag close to my chest in case he's still got designs on my phone. We quickly walk through the lobby and out into the fresh air.

catches my eye.
say, pointing at it. 'Now *that*
in ages.'

It's next month's cult classic movie, on for one night only.

'I haven't either.. I never thought they'd beat *The Princess Bride*,' he says.

'Perhaps we could watch it together?' The words tumble out my mouth before I can stop them. 'I mean watch it as friends, not as in a date. I don't *do* dating.'

I want the ground to open up and swallow me.

'Dating too good for you?' he says, looking amused.

'No, it's just, I'm single through choice at the moment and that's how I want to stay.'

Much better way to protect my heart.

'Fair enough. *Goonies* it is then, as friends.' He looks at his watch and frowns. 'I've actually got to go. I've got a train to get.'

'Back to Reading?' I say then realise that he hasn't told me where he lives.

He looks at me like I've caught him off guard.

'Is it that obvious that I don't come from Newbury? Do I not look posh enough?'

'I um, no, it's just I met you that time in Reading, so I assumed that was where you were from,' I say, thinking on my feet.

drove?'

'I did, but my … he direction of the car park. …

I desperately just want to run …

'Thanks again for that day on the tra…

'I'm so pleased to know that you're OK. I'll … for *The Goonies*,' he says.

'Indeed,' I say, giving him a goodbye wave.

I'm about to turn and walk away when he steps forward and wraps me up in a hug. My head instinctively comes to a rest on his chest. It's so intimate, yet it feels completely normal. When he pulls away it feels like we've been standing there for ages when in reality it can only have been seconds.

'I still don't even know your name,' he says.

'Izzy.'

'I'm Aidan. Take care, Izzy, and I'll see you next month.'

I turn and walk away.

Seeing *The Princess Bride* without Ben was always going to be emotional, but meeting Aidan properly and being able to thank him made it even more so. Yet, instead of feeling sad I'm happy because I feel I might have found a new friend.

Welcome to August
This_Izzy_Loves IGTV
No. followers: 17.3k

*Ah, you guys! You're making me blush with all the love you're sending mine and Luke's way. I absolutely cannot hide how smitten I am with him, isn't he great? I'm trying not to post too many photos of us but you know what it's like when you're falling head over heels and you lose all sense of proportion. Welcome, new followers, there are so many of you, do come and say hello! This month I'll be making the most of the weather and making sure that I get as much wear out of my summer dresses as humanly possible. And Lukey, babe, if you're watching this I am getting ready for our date, I promise. Mwah!*

# Chapter 13

'I can't believe he turned up to a date with another woman,' says Marissa, almost crying with laughter as I recount the story of my latest date with Luke to her and Becca. We went rowing in Henley and it was the perfect date, or at least it was for him and his date Meredith. She was less than impressed that I tagged along.

'I know. When he said he was going to copy our staged dates for his own, I thought he meant after we'd finished, but he turned her into our unofficial photographer and made her take all our photos, pretending to her that we were doing a work project,' I say.

We're making our way towards the quieter end of Basingstoke town centre to go for lunch.

'I'm surprised she didn't push him overboard,' says Becca, giggling.

I open the door to the restaurant and we wait to be seated.

'But that's the ridiculous thing, she was mad at me for coming and it was me that was in danger. She kept giving me these hard stares and rocking the boat whenever I moved around.'

'So the big question is, was it worth it?' asks Becca.

A smile breaks out over my face.

'As of this morning, our latest photo had 10,000 likes and I've got heaps of new followers.'

'That's amazing. I really hope this little one helps me reach those crazy numbers,' says Marissa, tapping her belly.

'I'm sure he or she will,' I laugh.

A waiter walks over to us. 'Table for three?'

'Yes, please,' I say. He picks up menus from a pile and leads us across the restaurant.

'Oh, hello!' says Marissa in surprise, and I turn to see my parents, sitting on a table of two. I don't know how I missed them.

'Marissa!' says my mum, shoving some magazines off their table and leaping up to give her a hug, before she spots me and Becca. She gives me a quick squeeze before wrapping Becca up in a warm embrace. 'And so nice to see you, we haven't seen you for ages.'

'I know, I've been meaning to come round with Izzy, but work's been so crazy lately,' she says and I can see her cringing. I know that she feels awkward going round to see my parents since she started dating Gareth.

'Of course, of course,' says Mum, sitting back down at the table. 'It's just nice to see you today. And you two, also, of course.'

'Thanks, Mum, I feel so loved,' I say, but I'm only joking and my mum knows it.

I know how much seeing Becca means to them; they still feel like she's a link to Ben. Even if the dynamic is beginning to change the more that Becca is starting to piece her life back together and move on, in a way they'll never be able to do.

'Did you want to join us?' Dad asks. 'We've only just ordered.'

'I'm sure the girls would like to talk amongst themselves,' says Mum. 'You don't want two oldies cramping your style.'

I see Becca looking a little relieved and I'm about to tell them that I'll pop round to theirs later on, when Marissa jumps in.

'Don't be silly, we'd love to eat with you. Is that OK?' she asks the waiter.

'Um, sure, I can move a table across to make it big enough for five,' he says.

I look at Mum, she doesn't looked thrilled at the prospect, and neither am I, but both of us are so polite and British that we don't say anything because the waiter's already moving the table.

I wouldn't normally have any objection to it, but this is the first time that my friends have seen my parents since I started fake dating Luke and I never thought to brief them to not mention him should this occasion arise.

'Can you just move your brochures?' asks the manager.

'Oh, yes.' My mum bends down and picks them up and the waiter slides in the new table.

Mum rolls up the brochures and tries to shove them into her handbag but they don't fit and they slide across the floor to my feet. I go to help her and one unrolls in my hand.

'Southeast Asia?' I say, my brow wrinkling at the travel brochure. It's a bit of a departure from their usual spot somewhere along the Portuguese coast.

'Hmm,' says Mum taking an extra-long sip on her water.

'Oh lovely,' says Marissa. 'Are you thinking of going?'

'Well, we're—' starts Dad.

'Just an idea,' says Mum. 'Sue down the road went recently and said how wonderful it was and we were passing the travel agent's. Gosh, it's hot in here, isn't it?'

She starts fanning herself with the menu.

'It's quite warm,' says Marissa, slipping off her cardigan. 'But then I'm hot all the time these days.'

She waves her hand across her bump that's getting ever bigger.

'But you look wonderful,' says Mum. 'Positively glowing.'

I sit down next to Dad and flick through a few pages. The

brochures advertise group trips that seem to range from one week to two months.

'When are you thinking of going?' I ask.

'In the new year,' he says.

'For a holiday? Or one of these longer trips?' I feel the anxiety rise at the thought of them going away for a long time.

'We thought—' starts my dad.

'We haven't even decided we're going yet,' says Mum, firmly. 'I mean, I need to look into whether it's sanitary. You hear about people going to these places and getting awful tummy bugs, don't you?'

For once, I'm relieved by my mum's health paranoia. I know that I'm 31 and I should be old enough for my parents to go off on a trip, but I guess, like Mum, Ben's death has affected me in ways I don't always acknowledge. I may only see my parents once a week or so, but I take extreme comfort in knowing that they are only five minutes away if I need them.

'I think if you're careful about where you go and where you eat, I'm sure you'd be fine,' says Becca. 'I think it sounds like a great thing to do. Might be just the kind of break you both need.'

She takes my mum's hand and gives it a squeeze like an unspoken nod to the pain they both still feel and the encouragement they need to take a step forward.

'Told you,' says Dad to Mum.

'What are you going to get, Izzy?' asks Mum, deliberately ignoring Dad's comments. 'I've ordered the butternut squash ravioli. Full of good minerals and vitamins.'

I look down at the menu. I was going to have a very cheesy, heart-attack inducing, meat feast pizza, but maybe I'll go for a goat's cheese salad instead.

'I used a lot of squash when I was doing my food blog,' says Marissa. 'I did this really good squash cake with maple syrup and cream cheese frosting.'

'Oh, I'll have to get the recipe,' says Mum, 'I'm always baking cakes to take into work.'

'Which is lucky,' says my dad, tapping his belly. 'With all the baking you do, I'd be as big as a house if I had to eat it all.'

Mum smiles at him and he smiles back and I take that and the holiday brochures as a sign that the brief moment of bickering was nothing to worry about.

'So how's your internet thing going?' Dad says to me.

'Oh, it's good, thanks,' I say, surprised that he's asked.

'It's better than good,' says Marissa, not looking up from her menu and therefore not seeing the looks I'm giving to try and get her to be quiet. 'The post Izzy did with Luke has blown up.'

'Who's Luke?' asks Mum.

'Um, he's a guy at work who's been helping me with the photos.'

'Single, is he?' she says with a hint of a hope.

'Not exactly,' says Marissa, laughing.

'Hmm, well you know your father was with someone else when I met him.'

I look between my parents, horrified and unsure what I'm supposed to do with this nugget of information, so I grunt like a disgruntled teenager and choose to ignore it.

'Is he good-looking?' Mum asks Marissa.

'Very. He looks like a model.'

Mum turns back to me and raises an eyebrow. 'Sounds promising.'

'No, Mum. It's not at all. He's very attractive but that's about all he has going for him. Trust me, you wouldn't want me to go out with him.'

'I've still got Roger Davenport's number if you need it,' she says.

Marissa splutters the water she was drinking.

'Roger Davenport?' she says. 'As in, *Roger Davenport*?'

She holds up her hands and wiggles her fingers forcing me to clench my jaw.

'That would be him,' I say. 'Mum ran into his mum and she wants to set me up with him.'

'Bloody hell,' Marissa says. 'Sorry, Dawn, but I can't really see Izzy with Roger.'

'Well, could you see her with this Luke?' Mum asks.

'No, she can't,' I say, answering for her. 'But luckily I'm absolutely fine being by myself.'

'Do you want to order drinks?' asks the waiter materialising by our table.

'Yes, please,' I say, 'a large glass of white wine for me.'

Becca and Marissa order drinks too.

'So Becca,' says my Dad, 'how are things with you? Work OK?'

I breathe a sigh of relief that the conversation has moved away from me and my fake love life.

'Work's fine, thanks, Simon.'

'I saw your parents the other day,' says Mum, 'and they said you were seeing someone.'

A look of panic spread across Becca's face.

'Yes, um, his name's Gareth. Nice guy. An accountant,' she says, folding the corners of her napkin over.

Mum nods and gives a weak smile. If it had been anyone else talking she'd have turned to me and made a dig about hoping I'd meet a nice accountant too. I imagine it's hard for them to picture her with anyone else too; I guess we're always all going to be guilty of thinking of her as Ben's fiancée, but she can't be frozen in time forever, not like Ben.

‘So Marissa’s trying to decide whether she should find out if she’s having a girl or a boy,’ I say, jumping in to avoid the awkwardness that’s descended on the table. Becca looks grateful.

‘Oh really, it’s all so different these days,’ says Mum. ‘We weren’t given the choice; we just got presented the baby, like the scene in *The Lion King* where they hold it up.’

Marissa laughs. ‘I love that idea of a *Lion King* moment, but I’m such an impatient person. Plus I quite like the idea of doing a big gender reveal.’

My parents’ faces are blank.

‘It’s when you do a big announcement on social media revealing to everyone what you’re having,’ Marissa explains.

‘Very different these days,’ says Mum again. ‘It’s like these baby showers, will you have one of those too?’

‘I don’t know,’ says Marissa. ‘Usually they’re organised as a surprise by your friends.’

She looks at Becca and I with a small smile on her face.

‘Well, you know, they’re supposed to be a surprise,’ I say with a forced laugh, thinking that I’m an awful friend for not realising I’d need to do this. I throw Becca a WTF look and she looks similarly concerned. I start mentally calculating her due date to work out if we’ve got time to organise one.

The waiter takes the heat off me by bringing us our drinks and taking our food order.

‘Your mum’s so excited about the baby,’ Mum says. ‘She was wearing an “Expectant Grandma” T-shirt at Zumba the other night.’

‘Hmm,’ says Marissa, unimpressed. ‘She’s been wearing that since we told her, even before we’d announced it officially.’

‘I guess she’s trying to get her money’s worth,’ I joke.

Marissa doesn’t look so sure.

'How much maternity leave are you taking?' asks Mum.

'I want to take off the full year, but I think we'll have to wait and see how it goes with money,' she says shrugging, trying to make it seem like less of a big deal than it is.

Marissa's a recruitment consultant and a lot of her money comes from commission. I know she's worried that they won't be able to afford for her not to work. The only saving grace is that her mother lives nearby and she's offered to help out with some of the childcare.

Mum gives Marissa a sympathetic nod.

'It's hard these days. You mothers are under a lot more pressure than we were. It's a shame though, as I do think you should spend every second you can with them. It goes so quick.' She takes a large sip of wine and I know that I've got to distract her from thoughts of Ben as a baby.

'So they're playing *The Goonies* at the classic cinema in Newbury in a couple of weeks, if any of you fancy coming with me?'

'Is that that one with the sword-fighting that you and Ben always watched as kids?' asks Dad.

'No, it's the other one we saw loads with the kids and the pirates.'

'Don't look at me,' says Marissa, 'I never got that movie either.'

'Becca, are you in?' I ask.

'When is it?'

'Two weeks today.'

She pulls up the calendar on her phone.

'Oh, I can't, sorry. I'm going to a wedding.'

'That's exciting,' says Marissa. 'Whose?'

She pauses and then swipes on her phone again.

'Just someone,' she says with a shrug.

'You know you haven't said anything to me about it; sounds to me like you're making an excuse,' I say, laughing. 'Are you sure you're really going to a wedding?'

'Actually, it's one of Gareth's cousins, I'm going as his plus one.'

'Oh,' I say. 'That's big, going to a wedding.'

She nods and takes a sip of her wine.

I feel awful that I can't get any excitement into my voice. It's a huge milestone in a relationship and I desperately want to be a supportive friend like I would with anyone else. We've grown even closer over the last two years yet all of a sudden a chasm seems to have opened up between us and I can't breach it.

'I'll bet it will be lovely,' says Mum; she's putting on a brave face too.

'Thanks,' she says. 'I'm so nervous, it'll be the first time I've met most of his family.'

'Don't be nervous, they'll love you,' says Mum, taking Becca's hand and giving it a squeeze. 'Any family would.'

'Thanks, Dawn,' she says and I see her blink back a tear.

'Oh my God,' says Marissa suddenly, pushing her seat back and clasping her little bump.

'What's wrong?' I say.

A huge smile breaks out over her face.

'I felt it kick, the baby actually kicked,' she says, and I can see her eyes sparkling as she moves her hands over her bump.

We've been so distracted during Marissa's pregnancy talking about the outfits that she can dress him or her up in and how it will make her Insta blow up, but seeing the look of utter contentment and wonder on her face it really hits me that she's going to be a mum.

It almost moves me to tears. I look around the table and it seems I'm not the only one.

'He or she is moving!' Marissa says. 'This shit just got real.'

I lean over and give her a hug. 'It certainly did.'

Not only is Marissa's baby the exact thing that this table needs as a distraction from all the awkward undercurrents, she or he will remind us of how life goes on and at times how wonderful it can be.

# Chapter 14

I stare at my computer screen and the words start to blur in front me. I've been reading and re-reading the same paragraph for the past ten minutes, unable to concentrate.

I keep thinking about the meal with my parents. Everyone seems to be moving on with their lives, Becca with Gareth, my parents and their trip to Asia, Marissa and her baby. It's made me realise how much my life has stagnated.

I'm really behind on my work today. Not only has my mind been elsewhere, we also had another round of the Great Office Bake Off this morning. It was 'free-from' week, so bakers were challenged to come up with a cake that was either gluten free, dairy free or vegan. Mrs Harris created a rose and pistachio masterpiece that tasted wickedly indulgent and a little bit exotic. She sailed through to the next round with flying colours which means she should be happy, but she's done nothing but moan and groan since.

'I think I've got food poisoning,' says Mrs Harris, clutching at her stomach. 'It was that vegan cake that Sandra in Legal made. It's made me feel proper queasy.'

'Are you sure it's not the fact that you sampled so many cakes?' says Cleo, in my opinion, quite bravely.

'It's important to sample the competition.'

'There are fifteen of you left; did you eat fifteen pieces of cake?' says Cleo, aghast.

'They were only small pieces,' Mrs Harris says with a groan. 'At least there'll only be fourteen in the next round. I was surprised that Marco from Statistical went out. I thought his Italian flair would see him further.'

'Yes, that was a disappointing loss for the competition all right, I'm going to miss him,' says Cleo, fanning her cheeks and making it obvious it's his looks and not his baking abilities she's going to miss.

'You can always wander through his floor,' I say to Cleo.

'Oh no,' she says, shivering. 'You have to walk through the underwriters to get there and there's something creepy about them.'

'You do know they're underwriters, not undertakers?'

'I know but in my head they're all those Mr Burns types creaking their fingers and trying to swindle everyone out of everything. They're the ones who never want to pay up.'

I laugh and turn back to Mrs Harris.

'What's the brief for next week then?' I ask, changing the subject.

The only people taking this Bake Off more seriously than the bakers are the HR department that dreamt up the idea. After the contestants make it through to the next round they get handed a gold envelope with next week's baking challenge.

'Next week it's unleavened bread.'

She gives Colin a look and I see him visibly turn purple as the 'b' word is mentioned.

'You better not even *look* in the bread's direction,' she says to him stroppily. 'Even if it's as flat as a pancake, I'm sure you'd still be able to break it.'

Colin carries on typing, but even from here I can see that he's typing nonsense.

'You know, I think Colin's more than said he's sorry,' I snap. It's hard enough to concentrate on my work as it is without this unnecessary drama.

Cleo gasps and Mrs Harris gives me a dirty look as if I'd been the one to break the leg of the bread flamingo. We all find Mrs Harris amusing but this joke has gone too long.

'I'm just saying that it's been at least two months, if not more, and I don't think he should be ostracised anymore.'

'Are you making a bird pun to remind me of the hurt he inflicted?' she says, folding her arms over her chest.

I stand firm. 'Bad choice of words, but come on, it was an accident that any one of us could have had. You and Colin are going to be sitting next to each other for the foreseeable future and this is not a very healthy work environment. This has gone too far, Mrs Harris.'

Now it's her turn to gasp.

My cheeks are flushed and my heart is racing. I'm not known for my confrontation skills, but I've got too much on my mind and I'm not feeling very tolerant today.

I take a deep breath, feeling bad that I'm taking out my mood on other people and I'm about to apologise when the unthinkable happens. Mrs Harris looks over at Colin with her lips pursed.

'You promise you won't touch my baps again, or anything else I bake?'

Colin looks too scared to speak.

'Promise?' asks Mrs Harris.

He nods slowly whilst still averting his gaze.

'OK then,' she says. 'I won't mention bread week again. Or flamingos.'

She turns back to her screen and I look over at Colin, who's just staring at her, shell-shocked.

Cleo looks over at me and we exchange WTF? looks. She turns back to her computer and a second later I get a ping on my work Link.

Cleo Dawson:
Go you! Look what you just did.

Izzy Brown:
Did I actually make things better, though? Is this the calm before the storm?

Mrs Harris stands up and I hold my breath.

'Anyone want a drink?' she asks, picking up her cup.

I'm too stunned to reply.

Cleo Dawson:
Quick, look, out the window, there's a flying pig.

I hold up my mug and Mrs Harris takes it. She even takes Colin's. I feel like my outburst might have upset the space-time continuum or at the very least our office dynamics and I can't imagine how this is going to pan out.

My phone vibrates with an email. I open it and see that it's from a marketing agency. My heart had only just started beating at a normal speed after the confrontation and now it's racing again.

*Hi Izzy!*

*We love your Instagram feed and your budding romance*

*with Luke (@Lukeatmealways). We are working on a social media campaign for a well-known gin company and we're looking for influencers to take part.*

*The brand wants to build relationships and would like to work on sponsored content that would be an agreed number of photos on yours and Luke's main feeds, plus mentions on your stories.*

*Obviously we'd work with you in developing the creative as we'd want the brand to fit in with your content seamlessly. We're thinking that it would be a behind-the-scenes tour of the company's distillery and then some photos of you enjoying some gin at home – or perhaps out and about on one of your fantastic dates!*

*Let me know if you'd be interested and I'll send you some further information. Also, if you and Luke have a press pack then please send it over and from there we can discuss your fees for the sponsored ads.*

*All the very best,*
*Amelia xx*

Oh. My. God. I tap a quick message to Luke and tell him to meet me on the stairwell where we first met and I hurry across the floor towards the stairs.

On the way I pass Mrs Harris carrying the tray of mugs.

'Oh, I see. I go to all the effort to get you a hot drink and now you're rushing off and you're not even going to drink it. Bloody typical. Remind me never to make you another one.'

And she's back. Phew. For a minute there I thought I'd broken Mrs Harris.

I race across the office and down a flight of stairs until I reach what I now think of as 'the selfie spot'. I pace up and down the little landing, wondering how long it will take him to get here.

'Where's the fire?' says Luke as he saunters up the stairs.

'You would not *believe* the email I just got.'

'Let me guess, they've decided to do a remake of *The Princess Bride*?'

'Why would you say something so mean?' I say, putting my hand over my heart. 'Like they would ever do such a thing.'

'They remade *Dirty Dancing*.'

'Yeah and look how that turned out.'

'Look, we're going off-topic. Who emailed you?'

'A marketing agency who represents a gin brand. They want us to go to a distillery and do a behind-the-scenes tour and then to drink gin on our dates.'

'And they're paying us?'

'Uh-huh. She didn't say how much, but they're going to pay us. She said to send them our press pack and register our interest and then she'd send out the particulars.'

'Bloody hell,' says Luke, running his fingers through his hair. I'm worried that they're going to get stuck in his perfect quiff but they appear out the other side unscathed.

'I know, right?'

'And a gin company. There are pretty good hashtags for gin,' he says.

'I really hate gin, but you can drink mine on the tour.'

Luke pulls a face.

'I hate it, too.'

'What? We can't both hate it. Are you sure you don't like it a tiny bit?'

'Are you sure *you* don't? Is this like your "I don't like Mexican food"? And then you'll have it and really like it?' he says.

My cheeks flush a little at my lie.

'No, and I've actually conducted many tastings of gin to make sure, and I really hate it.'

'But if they're paying us, I'm sure we could keep it down long enough for a photo?' Luke looks hopeful but my stomach is lurching at the thought.

'Or perhaps it's like wine tasting when you can spit it out?'

'Who actually spits the wine out though?' he says. 'Surely that's the point of those tastings – to get drunk?'

'True. You know this is probably the only thing we've got in common: our mutual dislike of gin,' I say, and he looks a little taken aback. 'Just think: our first sponsored post.'

'Let's hope it's the first of many,' says Luke, holding out his hand for me to high five him. 'You know, I was also thinking that it might be good to do something for charity too. It would raise our profile.'

'And help out the charity?' As per usual he's missing the point.

'Of course, that too. We could do a run or something.'

'Or something is definitely preferable,' I say, thinking that I keep starting Couch to 5k and not making it past the first week's training.

'I see that you always like Heart2Heart's post, I guess because of your brother, so I thought I'd approach them.'

I know his motives aren't exactly saintly, but I'd be over the moon to help them out.

'Yeah, that would be good.'

'I'll look into it,' he says.

We hear a door open and the clip-clop of a pair of heels on the stairs.

'Meet me at the usual place after work and we can reply to her?' I say.

'OK,' he says as I hurry back up the stairs practically jumping for joy.

When I make it back to my desk I'm positively beaming.

'Your tea's nearly cold now,' says Mrs Harris before I've had a chance to sit down. 'I would make you another but you know I've got my dodgy ankle.'

'Still warm,' I say, taking a sip. It's a bloody good cup of tea. Perhaps I should stand up to her more often.

I turn my attention back to my computer. It was hard enough focusing on my work before but now thoughts of sponsored posts are buzzing round my mind. A brand wants to work with us – *us!* It wasn't one of those standard emails either; the marketing contact knew about our relationship and everything.

I always felt that becoming an influencer was a pipe dream, but all of a sudden it doesn't feel so out of my reach. All of a sudden it feels like it might just happen and maybe my life might be getting back on track along with everyone else's.

# Chapter 15

I pull at the hem of my sweatshirt, wondering if it's too much to go to see *The Goonies* with 'Truffle shuffle' emblazoned on the front. It was a Christmas present from Ben and Becca but I know Ben would have chosen it.

I practically lived it in it after he died. Some people mourn in black but I mourned in the novelty T-shirts and sweatshirts he'd bought me over the years. I don't know when I stopped wearing them, but it feels like the right time to dig it out again.

Between that and my hair that I let dry naturally curly this morning, I feel really self-conscious. I'd gone to dry it straight as I usually would, and then I thought about Aidan complimenting my curls and I ended up leaving it. I'm trying not to worry that he'll think I did it just for him. It's a ridiculous thing to think when a) I've made it clear I'm not interested in dating and therefore I shouldn't care what he thinks, b) he mentioned he had a girlfriend and c) he's a man so probably wouldn't overthink the significance like I am. Even still, I've tied my hair up in a ponytail to make the curls less obvious.

I walk towards the entrance of the cinema and groan when I see that the usher on the door is the one that threatened to kick me out last time.

I keep my head down in the small queue, wishing I'd left my

hair down for a disguise, and when I reach the door I hold out my ticket without looking at him.

'Thank you,' he says taking it and tearing off the stub before he hands it back to me.

'Thanks,' I mutter and I'm just about to shuffle past when he holds his arm out to block my path.

'It's you,' he says, narrowing his eyes. 'Can I check your bag, please? For security reasons.'

'But you haven't asked anyone else.'

'Well, you were acting suspiciously last time. We have the right to ask,' he says, pointing to a sign which says as much.

'Fine,' I say, pulling open my handbag for him to have a look.

It's quite a big handbag that I keep everything in, from snacks to hair accessories to kitchen utensils. Once something goes in the bag it never seems to come out and it's in a right muddle.

'What's this?' he says, pulling out a selfie stick.

'So I have a selfie stick,' I say, folding my arms. 'It's not like I'm going to use that to film, is it? Hardly discreet.'

His eyes widen.

'Not that I would film discreetly either. I'm not going to film.'

He looks in my bag again and points at a portable tripod.

'Again, that's hardly discreet. Look there's nothing in there for filming, only accessories.'

'Other than your phone,' he says.

'Yes, just like everyone else.'

I look at the queue that's getting longer behind me.

He sighs loudly and has one more rifle through and I guess he's disappointed that there's no hidden compartment with filming equipment stashed inside.

'Can I take my seat now or do I need to be frisked first?'

He gives me a look and I hope I haven't just given him an idea.

He offers my handbag back and I snatch it and walk into the auditorium feeling flustered.

It's already busy inside despite the movie not starting for another twenty minutes. It's a popular film and the tickets sold out quickly. I scan the rows looking for Aidan and worrying that he might not have bought a ticket in time.

I find a seat in a row near the middle that has a few empty places.

I sit down and go to open my box of Maltesers. My hands are still shaking from the confrontation with the usher and I tug at the cardboard divider under the lid a little too forcefully and the chocolates go flying.

'Shit,' I mumble, trying to recover the rogue Maltesers rolling away from me. I'm hunting around on my hands and knees when I see a pair of Vans trainers in front of me. I look up and there, smiling down at me, is Aidan.

'Do you always throw your food?' he says, laughing.

'Always,' I say, scrambling to my feet.

He leans over to give me a hug and my heart starts to pound. I put my arms out to hug him back realising that I'm still clutching my rapidly melting chocolates.

We pull away and he looks down at my sweatshirt and points at it.

'Holy shit, Truffle Shuffle! That was what people used to chant at me when I was a kid. Brings back painful memories,' he says.

'I'm so sorry, if I'd known…' I mutter, my cheeks flushing.

'Just kidding,' he says, laughing. 'It was only my brother who used to chant it. Not exactly scarring. I had a bit of a jelly belly when I was young.'

I look down at his stomach, which looks all taut and toned under his T-shirt.

'I see you don't have that problem now,' I say, trying to stop my mind from imagining the six pack that I suspect he's got under there. 'Sorry, not that I was looking. It's just your T-shirt is quite tight…'

Stop talking, Izzy. Stop talking right now.

Aidan smiles and his dimples appear.

'I'm not that toned. It's just I find it difficult to put on weight,' he says, patting his stomach, my eyes following.

What is wrong with me? I've got to get a grip of myself, he has a girlfriend.

'I wish I had that problem.'

'I cycle about a hundred miles a week.'

'Bloody hell, that's exactly why I will never have that problem. I think I'll stick with my Maltesers. Although I usually try and eat them rather than just smear them over my hands.'

'Excuse me,' says a voice and we look up and see the usher standing at the end of the row pointing at us. 'Will you sit down, people behind you can't see.'

I look behind to see that everyone is staring at us talking; I'd forgotten there was anyone else here.

We sit down hastily and the usher groans and moves closer towards us.

'I should have known it would be you two. I thought you said you didn't know each other last time. Was it all some elaborate cover story?'

'We didn't know each other,' I say. 'Well, we had met before, but Aidan didn't recognise me, and anyway, we met again last time, so we weren't lying.'

The usher gives us a hard stare. 'No filming and no funny business.'

He walks off leaving Aidan and me to snigger.

'Did you hear him? No funny business.'

'Well, that's scuppered all my plans. Might as well leave now,' he says.

I feel my cheeks aching with all the smiling. There's something so easy about being in Aidan's company. I can't remember the last time I was this relaxed with a man that I hardly knew.

I look down at my hands and realise they're still covered in a chocolate mess.

'You couldn't reach into my bag and grab a tissue, could you?'

Aidan looks horrified.

'I promise you it won't bite. It's either that or I have to go and wash my hands and then I have to go past our friend again and he gave me such a hard time getting in the first time.'

'OK,' he says lifting it up off the floor and breathing out. 'I'm going in.'

He puts his hand in and rummages around. It doesn't help that the lights have dimmed and the rotating slideshow adverts for local businesses has started.

'What the bloody hell is this?' he says, pulling out a spoon.

'I take it everywhere, then I don't have to use plastic stirrers. I'm saving the environment.'

'Very commendable,' he says putting it back in and pulls out the selfie stick.

'Oh, don't get that out here,' I whisper. 'Our friend over there nearly banned me for having that.'

'For once I'm with him. I hate those bloody things.'

I'm glad the lights are dim and he can't see my rosy cheeks.

'It's not mine. Well, it is, but it's for a work thing. I'm not a vain selfie taker,' I say, lying heavily. I take selfies all the time.

'Phew,' says Aidan, 'I didn't want you to belong to the dark side.'

'The dark side?' I say gulping.

'Yeah. I'm not big into social media, I sort of hate what it represents. My ex, Zoe, was obsessed, she was all like "me, my selfie and I". There almost wasn't room in our relationship for me.'

I squeak in reply. Perhaps I might wait a bit before I tell him about my Instagram aspirations.

'Sorry, I didn't mean to sound so bitter,' he says, finding the packet of tissues. He pulls one out and reaches over and takes my hands in his and wipes the chocolate away. The electricity is crackling and I wonder if he can feel it too. Not that it matters; even if he didn't have a girlfriend, it sounds like he'd hate my Instagramming.

'Don't be silly,' I say, trying to ignore the fact that he's finished wiping and yet he's still holding my hands.

'Things like that always sound so petty after a break-up. You look back and wonder how such minor things could bother you. Of course there were big things too.'

'Yep, unfortunately there usually are in my experience.'

We don't say anything for a second and it begins to feel very wrong that we're holding hands still and I pull away. It's almost like we were teetering on the edge of something more than friendship and it's not what I want, especially with Aidan having a girlfriend. I'm not being that woman.

He coughs as if he's embarrassed that he hadn't noticed about the hands.

'So, *The Goonies*,' he says, steering us onto safer ground.

'Yep,' I say. 'So the question is, are you going to show me your Truffle Shuffle?'

He goes to lift up his T-shirt. So much for safer ground. Luckily for me he drops his hand again.

'I don't do a Truffle Shuffle for just anyone, you know. And you have to earn it.'

'How does one earn a Truffle Shuffle?'

*Stop flirting, Izzy.*

'Ah, now that would be telling.'

The lights go down at exactly the right moment so he can't see that my cheeks are burning.

'Seeing as you've lost most your chocolates, do you want a pick 'n' mix?'

'I thought you'd never ask,' I say, reaching into the bag and we settle into watching the trailers and munching on sweets.

When the film finishes we find ourselves on the same spot on the pavement outside the cinema, trying to stay dry from the rain under the awning.

'Do you, um, fancy getting a drink?' says Aidan. 'A quick one?'

'Yeah, I'd like that, I mean, if you don't have to rush off for your train?'

'No, no,' he says checking his watch. 'I'm good for a bit, as long as I don't miss the last one home.'

He gestures towards the pub across the road and we start walking towards it.

'Ah, would you be in trouble,' I say, thinking that he's probably going home to Saskia.

'Yeah, the boss would kill me. He has to have a carrot to eat before he goes to bed or else he's up in the middle of the night starving hungry.'

I wrinkle my forehead in confusion.

'Haven't I mentioned Barney before?'

'No,' I say, shaking my head.

'My dog, Barney?'

He holds the door open of the pub and we wander over to the bar.

'What kind of a dog is he?'

'A big, dopey chocolate Labrador.'

'Ah, I bet he's cute.'

Aidan pulls his phone out of his pocket and swipes before showing me a photo.

'Bloody hell, he's adorable.'

'Yep, and he knows it too. Gets away with murder.'

'My nan used to have a collie when I was growing up,' I say. 'I used to love going to her house as he always made such a fuss. It must be nice always having someone excited to see you.'

'I was excited to see you today,' he says before he groans. 'Sorry, I didn't mean that to sound like such a line. Saskia's always telling me that I come out with the cheesiest things.'

I try not to be disappointed that he's mentioned his girlfriend.

'Doesn't she like classic films?' I ask and he looks at me a little strangely.

'Not really. She's more of an art-house, indie film type of girl.'

Of course she is. All sophisticated to go with her Amazonian looks.

'I'm always exhausted after going to the cinema with her as everything's got subtitles and it's such an effort to concentrate.'

'Yeah, I have to be in the mood to watch subtitled films,' I say, like I watch them frequently when in reality I watch them if I'm having trouble sleeping as no matter how good they are I always fall asleep.

We get our drinks and take them over to a table in the corner.

'So have you had Barney long?'

'About a year and a half, I guess? I got him when I bought my house. I felt I needed company and I guessed it would be less intrusive than having a lodger. I was wrong; I can't even go to the loo without him budging the door open to see what's going on.'

I laugh. I can just imagine how naughty Barney is.

'Do you have any pets?' he asks.

'No, my friend and I live in a flat and we're at work all day, it wouldn't be fair.'

'Yeah, they enjoy company,' he says, sitting down at the table. 'So do you like being back in Basingstoke?'

'Most of the time. Growing up I couldn't wait to escape it, but it all changed when Ben died. I guess I worked out what and who I really cared about and I moved back. Perhaps if it hadn't happened that way I still would have moved back, but it would have taken longer.'

'Sounds familiar. I went to uni in Bristol and lived there for a few years after.'

'How come you moved back?'

He shrugs a little. 'Most of my friends moved on and then I got back in touch with a girl I knew from home – Zoe, the one I mentioned earlier – and we started seeing each other.' He starts to shift a little uncomfortably in his chair. 'It seemed like the easiest thing to do, move back to be closer to her, plus I already knew people in the area. It's surprising how many people I knew from school are back too.'

'Tell me about it,' I say. 'It seems like everyone I know had some sort of homing beacon activated when it was time to settle down. I'm always bumping into people I haven't seen for years pushing prams around.'

'It's weird, isn't it? I don't feel any older than I did when I was at school and then all of a sudden I see someone from back then and they've got grey hair or a bald patch and it makes me realise I'm old.'

'Personally I don't think you look a day over 17.'

'Thanks, I usually go for 22,' he says, laughing.

I look at him trying to work out how old he is. He's got little laughter lines on his face but his beard is making it harder to age him.

'You're trying to guess how old I am, aren't you?'

'No, I'm not,' I say, knowing I'm a rubbish liar.

'You are, I can see it on your face. You're looking at my crow's feet.'

'You don't have crow's feet.'

'So you *have* looked,' he says in mock horror. 'I'm 36.'

'Sheesh. I didn't think you were under 40.' I laugh to let him know I'm kidding.

'Forty's the new 30 you know.'

'That's what I've heard, Grandad.'

'So how old are you? Or should I guess?'

I do a sharp intake of breath.

'You should never guess a woman's age – it will never end well.'

'Neither does going through her handbag,' he says, laughing.

'I'll put you out of your misery, I'm 31.'

'That's what I was going to say.'

'Sure you were,' I say, nodding.

He drinks his drink and gives me a playful smile.

'So what do you do for work?' I ask him. 'I know you said you had a café?'

'I'm an app designer,' he says.

'Ooh, that's interesting.'

He shrugs his shoulders.

'It can be. I work for non-profits mainly, so making companion apps for museum exhibitions and that kind of thing. It's good, though, as I get to work from home.'

'I bet Barney likes that.'

‘Oh yes, he has a bed next to my desk and he nudges me every few hours to remind me to get up and either feed or walk him. Who needs a FitBit to remind you to move when you’ve got a dog?’

I laugh.

‘So tell me about your work,’ he says.

‘It’s kind of boring,’ I say, wrinkling up my nose. ‘But the people I work with more than make up for it,’ I say.

‘Then tell me about them.’

‘OK,’ I say, wondering how on earth I’m going to describe Mrs Harris. I begin to explain my colleagues and the Great Office Bake Off and Aidan can’t stop laughing. By the time I’ve finished filling him in on the inter-office politics we’ve both finished our drinks.

‘Do you want another one?’

He looks at his watch and winces.

‘I would love to, but I better go and get the train.’

‘Of course,’ I say, trying to hide my disappointment.

I slip my sweatshirt back on and stand up.

We walk out of the pub and at last it’s stopped raining. I love that smell you get after summer rain when it’s all warm and humid.

‘It was really nice to see you again,’ he says. ‘Although it always seems rushed. So why don’t we get a bite to eat before the movie next month?’

‘Oh,’ I say, getting a bit flustered. ‘Next month?’

‘Sorry, I just assumed. *Drop Dead Fred*,’ he says.

‘I love that film. Yes, that sounds great.’ Dinner for me always sounds like a date but I guess there’s no reason why two friends can’t go for dinner. ‘Let’s meet up before.’

‘Great, say Ted’s at seven o’clock?’

'Sounds good to me. Hadn't you better get going? Or you'll miss your train.'

He leans over and gives me a quick hug goodbye. Not the long drawn-out emotional one we had last time, but the kind you'd give your mate.

'I'm so glad we've become friends, Izzy. I'll see you next month,' he says before walking away.

'Me too,' I say more to myself than him.

There's something between Aidan and me, and the more time I spend with him the harder it is to ignore, but with neither of us in a place to date, I can't do anything about it.

Welcome to September
This_Izzy_Loves IGTV
No. followers: 18.8k

*How is it the end of summer already? I desperately didn't want this one to end. All those long summer nights spent al fresco cuddling up to Luke, and trips to the lido. Let's hope we have an Indian Summer!*
*I'm thrilled you all enjoyed seeing me at the gym with Luke. I totally agree that it's always good to let your other half see you at your worst and you only saw the 'before' pictures so believe me I was a frizzy and sweaty mess by the end. I also can't move my arms above my head – will the feeling ever come back? I think Luke and I will be sticking to gentler things in the future – Netflix and chill is much more my cup of tea!*

# Chapter 16

I'm surprised when I arrive at Luke's place. It's an old Victorian semi-detached redbrick house with large protruding bay windows at the front and a latticed iron porch. It's beautiful but I'd always imagined him in a modern penthouse flat in one of the more glamorous areas of the city, whereas his house screams 'suburban family'.

I knock on the door and he answers with a smile on his face.

'Nice digs,' I say.

He shrugs. 'I've lived in worse. Come on in.'

I follow him down a long corridor; I peek into the lounge as we pass with its wooden floors and duck egg walls. It's immaculately tidy and completely unlike any shared house that I've ever visited.

'Who do you live with, professional cleaners?'

'Very funny. We're just not slobs. Which is handy as women hate coming back to messy houses.'

Who says men can't multitask? Luke never only thinks with his brain.

We walk into the large, square kitchen and I spot a big box on the table; I still can't believe it represents the start of what could be a paid career. Ben would be so proud.

'Are you OK?' he says, looking over at the box.

'It's just such a big thing, isn't it? Not only are we getting sent free clothes, we're getting paid for it too,' I say, turning my attention back to the box, 'and Macchiato is such an up-and-coming designer.'

'Macchiato is a type of coffee. *Mak-eay-to* is the designer.'

I fail to hear the difference in his pronunciation but nod along anyway.

'Either way, I'm excited to see what's inside. Are we still going to do a big unboxing video?'

'Yeah,' he says, 'I've got the tripod out so we can both do it. Do you want a drink or anything before we start? I got you in some of that cloudy lemonade you like.'

'That's really thoughtful of you,' I say, taken aback.

He shrugs, and for a moment I wonder if I've got him wrong.

'It's habit, I've found that it pays to remember the little details, makes a woman feel special.'

I close my eyes and take a deep breath; I haven't got him wrong after all.

'I'm not thirsty. Shall we just do it?'

He goes over and screws his phone to the tripod and comes back with a little remote control.

'Right, are you ready? Have you ever done an unboxing video before?'

'No, have you?'

'No,' he says.

'Right, well we just open it, don't we?'

'Yeah,' he says, nodding. 'Do you think we need a knife?'

'Perhaps. I guess if we'd thought ahead, we could have had one of those special letter openers that YouTubers have.'

'The one that says, *look at me I get sent so much free stuff that I need an opener*.'

'That's the one.'

He leans over to the kitchen drawer. 'We'll use a steak knife.'

'Steak knife. Fancy.'

He gives me a look and I shut my mouth.

'Ready?'

'Yep.'

'And we're rolling,' he says and I bite my lip to stop laughing. 'Here we are in my kitchen. That's right, ladies and gents, This_Izzy_Loves is in my kitchen, it's the morning after the night before, wink.'

'OK, start again. What was that about, *wink*?'

'People want to know if we've... you know.'

'No one wants to know that.'

'Come on, of course they do. Look how popular *Love Island* is.'

'Well, we're not in Casa Amor,' I say, crossing my arms over my chest.

'Fine, no mentioning our sex life. Take two.'

He presses the button again and this time I take the reins.

'I have just literally arrived at Luke's house,' I say, giving him a definite stare, 'and we've been sent this very exciting box.'

'And we're really looking forward to opening it, aren't we, Baby Girl?' he says, slipping his arm around me.

'We certainly are, Snookums.'

He throws me a look and I flutter my eyelashes. Two can play at the ridiculous pet names game.

'Let's open it, shall we?' I say.

He pauses and smiles at the camera before taking the steak knife and slicing through the packaging.

'Ooh, look at the beautiful tissue paper and there's a note. "Dear Izzy and Luke, can't wait to see you wearing our designs. Lots and love from M x."'

'And for those of you wondering who M is – it's *Mak-eay-to*,' he says with another wink.

'OK,' I say, rustling through the tissue and finding the items and whipping them out: 'Ta-d-ahhh – *oooh*.'

'What the bloody hell is *that*?' says Luke.

'I have no idea.'

I hold the scratchy feeling silver fabric out and try and work out which way round it goes. Eventually I find what looks like the top.

'What the... are they dungarees?' I say.

I'm genuinely puzzled having never seen anything quite like it before.

'Shit, we're still recording,' says Luke fumbling for the remote control.

'Well, we can't use that, our faces weren't exactly complimentary.'

'We'll have to film it again and try and look happy about it. Do you think this is your piece or mine?'

'Hopefully yours,' I say, throwing it at him and pulling the next one out of the box. 'I think there's been a mistake; they seem to have sent that one twice.'

'They can't have made two of those things, could they? It's hideous.'

He grabs it out of my hands and examines it. 'This one is smaller. Oh no, it can't be.'

'What?'

'I think they're his and hers.'

My jaw drops open.

'Didn't it say something in the email about it – that they were going to be gender fluid or gender neutral or something,' he says.

'We've got to send them back, I'll look like a sack of potatoes.'

I furiously examine it, hoping to find at least one redeeming feature.

'What about me? At least you could try and make it look sexy.'

'Since when have dungarees been sexy?'

'If you wore it without a top…'

'If I wore it without a top it would violate YouTube rules.'

'We could always try. Aren't YouTube more liberal with nudity these days?'

He looks so hopeful.

'Is there anything else in the box, you know like a bin liner to put over our heads?'

Luke fishes round the box and pulls out two bits of mesh.

'Oh,' he says, his brow furrowed. 'I think this buttons onto the dungaree straps. There you go, happy now? Your modesty will be all covered up.'

'Bloody hell, I think I'd rather no top,' I say, sighing.

A smile forms on Luke's face.

'I didn't mean that literally,' I say.

'I didn't even say anything,' says Luke.

'Yeah, but you were thinking it, weren't you?'

He doesn't answer, he doesn't need to.

'So, are you ready to unbox it again?' he asks.

'Can't we say it got lost in the post?' I say, wincing.

'And risk them sending anything worse?'

'You're right. I'll put them back. Have you got any tape for the box?'

Luke digs around in a kitchen drawer whilst I wrap the items back up, hoping they miraculously transform into something better when I pull them out again.

'Got some,' he says,waving a roll of tape. 'Do you think we should write a script?'

'I don't know, won't that come out a little staged?'

'I guess we can't all be natural actors like myself,' he says.

'No, Channing, we're not all double threats.'

'I like to think I'm a triple threat,' he says with a knowing look. 'I'm extremely talented in the—'

'Yes, yes, I walked into that one. Let's just be spontaneous, OK?'

'Fine, more smiles than shock.'

He presses the button on the remote control.

'Here we are with an unboxing video. I can hardly believe that *Mak-eay-to* have sent us some outfits,' says Luke.

'Yay,' I say, doing jazz hands.

'What the hell are those?' he says, turning to me with a look of disgust.

I look down at my hands. 'I'm trying to show enthusiasm.'

'It seems sarcastic.'

'Perhaps I'm trying to keep the attention away from my face.'

Luke presses stop on the video.

'OK, I've got it, how about we keep the original introduction and we can just re-film us opening the box. I'll do a close up of your hands when you undo the box and then it'll make it more seamless in the edit.'

'That could work,' I say, nodding.

'You're going to have to keep talking whilst I zoom in on the box. Just be upbeat and talk about how you can't wait to get into it.'

'OK,' I say, taking a calming breath.

'And then you can use the knife to open it. Do you think you'll be able to do that?'

'I think I can handle that,' I snap as he zooms in.

He gives a thumbs up and I start to witter on about the package.

'I cannot believe we get to see what's in here. We are so blessed to have this opportunity.'

I take the knife and plunge it into the box and zip it along.

'Good,' says Luke. He readjusts the camera so it's pointing at us again. 'Let's open it up.'

He opens the box. Both of us are reluctant to dive in.

'You go,' I say to him and he smiles at me.

'Ladies first, I insist.'

I groan but one of us needs to be brave. I pull out the first pair of dungarees and hold them up to the camera – and try to conceal my gasp as I spot the massive rip down the back. I must have slashed the knife right down it.

'Um, Luke,' I say, interrupting his spiel about the shiny fabric. I hold the back towards him.

'Bloody hell, Izzy. You had one job! One!'

'I know, I'm sorry. I guess the tape wasn't that thick and I hadn't wrapped the clothes up enough in the tissue.'

He points the remote control at the camera and presses the button with more force than necessary.

'Good job we didn't do this as a live video,' I say, trying to lighten the mood. Luke glares at me.

'It's not funny, Izzy. What are we going to do?'

'It's fine. No one has to see it, it's at the back. I end up pinning most of the clothes I get sent to me as they don't fit. We'll just photograph them from the front and no one will be any the wiser.'

'But we have to take photos of us wearing this outside. We're going to look ridiculous as it is, let alone with our backs hanging out.'

'It's only one that's ripped.'

Luke digs in the box and pulls out the identical piece to see whose I destroyed. He audibly sighs with relief when he realises it's mine. 'At least you're used to it.'

'Yes,' I say, gritting my teeth at his chivalry. 'Do we need to film the rest?'

'Yeah, we'll put it back in the box and then we'll go from there.'

This time we make it all the way through with an Oscar-worthy performance. We manage to pull everything out of the boxes whilst smiling, concealing the giant rip.

'I thought we'd never finish,' says Luke when he finally turns off the camera.

'Me neither. Good luck with the editing.'

'Thanks, I'm going to need it,' he says, laughing.

'Where on earth are we going to wear these?' I say, pulling out the press release information from the box. '*The new gender fluid collection is designed to transition easily from office to the bar. So on trend. So Makayto.*'

'Could you imagine wearing it to work?' he says.

'It is casual Friday next week.' Last Friday of the month, always a highlight.

'You're not serious, I'd never live it down.'

'Of course I'm not serious. Not with the Arctic air conditioning. Maybe in the middle of winter when I wear all my summer dresses to work.'

'I can never tell if you're joking or not.'

'Of course I'm joking. The only place this would be acceptable to wear would be a spa – it looks like one of those special suits you wear to sweat yourself thin.'

'So where *are* we going to wear it?' Luke asks. 'It's going to look a bit weird if we only model it in the house.'

'I know, I know. But in the press release they mention the office and the bar, so ideally we want a photo of us in both types of location.'

'OK, what about us sitting at a desk, to make it look like an office? My roommate upstairs is a PhD student and has a desk. I'm sure we could use that.'

'Has your other roommate got a bar in his room too?'

'Unfortunately not.'

'So we will have to go out into the actual world for that one?' I say, raising an eyebrow.

'Maybe they won't be so bad when we put them on,' he says, holding it up again and wincing.

'Are you kidding me? They are going to look hideous.'

'There's only one way to find out,' he says.

Five minutes later and I'm standing on the cold tiles of Luke's bathroom trying to see what I look like from the vanity mirror mounted on the wall. At least the modesty panel seems to be keeping my boobs covered, even if it does look rubbish at the back with my bra exposed and the giant rip.

'Well?' shouts Luke through the door.

'I'm not sure I can come out.'

'Come on, it can't look worse than mine.'

'Wanna bet?'

I take a deep breath and unbolt the door.

I look him up and down and he does the same, before both of us burst out laughing.

'Maybe this his and hers thing is what's been missing from all my relationships,' he says.

I put my hand on my hip causing the fabric to stretch, and the results are definitely not flattering.

'Do you think there's a filter on earth that's going to make this look any better?' I ask, knowing the answer already.

'Think of the money.'

I close my eyes and do exactly that. But this isn't just about the money for me. This is validation that I'm not wasting my time on a pipe dream. Ben believed I could do this and I feel like I'm doing it for him as well as me.

'Six photos and a few posts on stories,' says Luke.

'OK.' I need to concentrate on the big picture and what this represents. 'Let's get this over with.'

# Chapter 17

My belly's churning like a washing machine walking into Ted's restaurant. I wish my belly would understand that this is categorically not a date.

I push open the door at ten to seven and a whoosh of lively chatter greets me. It's already really busy with families and groups of people.

I try not to draw too much attention to myself standing at the front looking for Aidan, but it's so busy that he could be here and I wouldn't know it.

'Can I help?' asks the waitress.

'I'm meeting a… friend,' I say.

'Oh, a *friend*,' she says. 'Gotcha. Have you booked?'

'I think so.'

'Great, what's the name?'

'Um, Aidan. Well, mine's not, but the table might be under that. Table for two?'

She scans down her list.

'Can't see an Aidan. Would it be under his surname?'

'Possibly,' I say, looking over her shoulder and hoping he's already sat here. 'I don't know it.'

'You're going on a date with someone and you haven't googled them first?' she says with a look of horror.

'No, I haven't, but I met him in real life when I was at the cinema.'

'You picked up a guy at the cinema? How did you know he wasn't a weirdo?'

'I didn't pick him up, we're just friends. And I'd sort of met him before… Shall I wait for him at the bar?'

'Yeah, of course, sorry,' she says, scuttling off.

I walk over to the bar and climb up onto a very tall high stool with some difficulty, and order an elderflower mocktail.

'Hey,' says Aidan, appearing next to me before I even take my first sip. 'How are you?'

'Good, good,' I say far too enthusiastically. 'And you?'

'Yes, good. And you?'

'Good…'

We seem to have forgotten the art of conversation.

'Shall we get our table? I didn't know what name it would be under,' I say.

'Great, table, yeah,' he says, nodding. He seems to be as nervous as I am.

I manage to shimmy down off the stool and follow him over to the waitress.

'He found you then? Doesn't look like a weirdo,' she says in a whisper to me as she scrutinises him. 'What name's the table booked under?'

'Simmons,' says Aidan.

'Ah, there you go,' says the waitress, giving me a wink. 'You'll be able to find him on Facebook now and properly vet him.' My cheeks start to burn and I try to ignore the look of confusion on Aidan's face. 'Your table will be ready in about five or ten minutes, if you take a seat at the bar.'

She hands Aidan a pager and I look back at the high stool

that's fast becoming my new nemesis. Aidan seems to mount his in a single motion whereas I have to use the little step all the while clinging onto the bar to make sure the stool doesn't swing away from me.

'You OK there?' he asks, reaching out to help me.

'Yeah, fine,' I say when I finally plant my bum on the seat. I pick up my drink and sip it to demonstrate.

'You look different,' I say, trying to work out what it is. 'Your beard is gone.'

'Not entirely,' he says, rubbing at the stubble that stands in its place. 'It got so hot in August that it had to come off, though. Now I'll grow it again to keep me warm until winter. By the time they play *It's a Wonderful Life* on TV I'll be like a yeti.'

'Interesting,' I say, nodding whilst trying to picture him with a full-on big beard.

'And you're wearing your hair curly again.'

'Felt like a change,' I say, lying. My numbers on Instagram have been creeping up and I don't really want to be seen out on a 'non-date' with a man who isn't Luke so I figured I'd look as different as I could from This_Izzy_Loves. I know it's lame, but the curls are my version of Clark Kent's glasses.

'Your table's ready.'

I mutter under my breath as now I've got to get off this bloody stool again. If I'd have known it was going to be so quick I would have stood against it in a casual lean.

We're escorted across to a table in the middle of the restaurant. At least the seats are at normal height and don't require any athletic training.

'Have you eaten here before?' I ask, picking up the menu.

'No, but I walk past it on the way to the train and it's always looked nice. Have you?'

'No, but I've heard the burgers are good.'

'I'm going to have the Mexican burger. Saskia's been talking about doing one at the café so I might as well check out the competition.'

'That's a good boyfriend thing to do,' I say.

'Boyfriend?' he says, looking over the top of the overly large menu.

'Yeah, you know, Saskia's your girlfriend?'

I'm still debating between the aoili burger and the stilton one and it takes me a minute to notice that Aidan's staring at me.

'Saskia's my partner.'

'Ooh, sorry, I didn't mean to offend you with the semantics. I always think of partner and girlfriend as being a bit same, same. But I'll try harder.'

Aidan laughs. 'That's not what I meant. Saskia's my business partner.'

'Your *business* partner,' I say slowly.

'Uh-huh. She's an old friend who needed someone to invest in her café idea and I'd developed an app for fun that had done well and I had some money in the bank.'

He laughs like it's really funny, and I want to tell him that it wasn't *that* ludicrous a theory as I'd seen her blowing that kiss to him, but I can't as then he'd know I'd seen him and ignored him.

'There's absolutely nothing between me and Saskia. We're purely platonic,' he says, picking up his beer.

I don't mean to look up but I do and I find myself staring him straight in the eye.

'Right, OK. So just like us.'

He chokes on the beer he's sipping. 'Um, I guess so. Yeah, absolutely. I mean we're the epitome of platonic friendship.'

The waitress comes up to our table at that exact moment and she gives us a look.

'I could come back?' she says, retreating slowly.

'No, don't worry. We're only discussing how we're just good friends,' I say, getting flustered.

'Always good to get those things out in the open,' says the waitress with a hint of pity in her smile. 'So, did you want to order or should I come back?'

'Let's order,' says Aidan. 'I'll go for the Mexican burger. And a large Peroni to drink.'

'OK, and you?'

'I'll go for the loaded burger with aioli.'

'You know that has garlic on, right?'

'Uh-huh.'

'OK, then, guess it's just as well that you're just friends,' she says with a wink, before taking our menus and walking off.

'That was weird, wasn't it?' says Aidan, looking over his shoulder at the waitress with a confused look on his face.

'We were having a chat before you arrived… never mind,' I say, stirring my cocktail with the metal stirrer. 'So, Saskia's your business partner. Does that mean you have any other… partner in your life?'

Not that it should matter whether he does or he doesn't, seeing as we've discovered that we're platonic friends and all that.

'No, no other partners, business or otherwise,' he says. 'I don't want one either.'

'Wow. That's pretty certain.' He sounds so much like me.

He shrugs his shoulders.

'My ex, Zoe, so much shit went down when we broke up and the only way I found to convince myself to get through it was to not put myself through it again. I mean, I'm not talking about forever, but I can't imagine that it would be for a long, long time.'

'I absolutely get that,' I say, copying the waitress's pitying nod.

'You said you didn't date, either,' he says.

'Have you seen the men available on Tinder?' I say with a joke.

'I've seen them all right,' he says, idly picking up his cutlery.

'*Oh*,' I say. I might have got this whole thing very wrong indeed. 'So you like men?'

'What? No,' he says, shaking his head. 'I saw the men on Tinder because Zoe showed me. Right near the end we had this fight and she showed me all the men that had swiped right for her as if to show me all the men that were potentially better than me.'

'What?' I say loud enough that the people at the next table all turn and look at us. I lean in and lower my voice. 'What an absolute bitch.'

He half smiles.

'I don't often call people names but you're right, she was. And that wasn't even the worst thing she did.'

'What could possibly be worse?'

'She ended up flirting with an ex on Facebook and getting back together with him. Although she dated both of us for a few months just to make sure she was making the right decision.'

'Shit, that is worse. I stand by my earlier comments, what a bitch.'

Aidan smiles weakly.

'You know, I can beat your story though. My ex was worse,' I say, sipping my drink.

He pulls a face. 'I really don't think that's possible.'

'Wanna bet?'

'I always like a bet. Loser buys the sweets at the cinema?' he says. 'And I hope you do lose, not because I don't want to buy the sweets but because I'd hate to think you were with someone more awful than Zoe.'

'Unfortunately he was,' I say, confident I'm going to win. 'I was living with my now-ex, Cameron, up in London. I thought we were happy and in love. Cameron was in New York on business the day that Ben died, and I phoned him when I got back to my parents' house. It was the middle of the night for him and at first when his work colleague Tiffany picked up, I thought reception had put me through to the wrong room, but it turned out they hadn't.'

'Bloody hell.'

'Yep. I guess there's never a good time to find out that your boyfriend's been cheating on you. Apparently, they'd been sleeping together for years but dated other people as inter-office dating was against the rules.'

I take hold of my drink and wish it was something stronger. Elderflower doesn't really have the kind of edge I need right now.

'Pick 'n' mix on me then,' he says, whistling through his teeth.

We sit in silence for a minute and I'm furious. Not only at Cameron but at Zoe too for treating someone as nice as Aidan so badly.

'I don't know what's worse: the fact they did those awful things or the fact that they've left us not wanting to risk another relationship,' he says.

'Bet you're glad we came for the burger first.'

'I think next time we should stick to having a drink after the film and we only discuss that.'

'Might be a safer plan,' I say with a sigh.

The waitress brings over our amazing-looking burgers and pops them down in front of us. Usually I'd take a photo for my Instagram stories, but knowing how much that would remind Aidan of his ex, all I do this time is squirt some ketchup on my plate and tuck in.

'Bloody hell, those chips are hot,' I say, dropping it fast and drinking quickly to soothe my poor burnt tongue. I'm not used to hot food anymore, by the time I take a couple of sips, it's a lot cooler. I wait for a moment before taking a bite of my burger and the waitress was right, it's super garlicky. I might have to get mints instead of my usual Maltesers. I reckon that everyone else in the cinema is going to be able to smell me.

The film was exactly what we needed after our meal. A little light relief. Yes, there were sad moments in it, but it was also heart-warming and funny and absolutely what we needed. Aidan and I have been waxing lyrical about the genius that was Rik Mayall in the pub for the best part of an hour.

'Bugger, it's train o'clock, I'm afraid,' he says, draining his pint. 'I'm glad we had dinner after all or else this would have felt too short.'

'I know, time's really flown,' I say, finishing my drink and standing up to go.

I shuffle out of the comfy booth and we head outside.

'I've had a really good time tonight,' says Aidan.

'Me too.'

'It was nice to talk about the heavy stuff as well,' he says.

'It was. You know you can talk to me about it, anytime. You know, if you need to.'

'Thanks, I appreciate that,' he says. He rocks back on his heels and puts his hands in his pockets. 'You know, I'm over my ex. I realise I probably made it sound like I wasn't when I talked about her.'

'It's OK, you don't need to explain,' I say, noticing that we're standing pretty close to each other on the street and I'm starting to regret the choice of burger.

'I want to,' he says, putting his hands in his pockets. 'I'm not angry at her, I'm angry at myself that I let her treat me the way she did. I've spent the last year and a half becoming me again and it's great, and I don't want to change who I am.'

'But maybe you wouldn't need to,' I say, stopping before we go through the door to the pub. We shuffle away from smokers and end up on the pavement alone, still standing far too close to each other. 'If you met the right person they wouldn't want to change you. They'd accept you for your crow's feet, your slightly too much stubble and your wardrobe that only seems to consist of band T-shirts.' I pause for a second. 'And for the fact that you like those awful spaceship sweets. That person wouldn't care because they would know that you're one of the most caring and thoughtful people and that you have excellent taste in films and do fantastic impressions and you have what look like pretty rock star abs…' I stop, suddenly realising what I'm saying. Aidan's looking at me with intensity and I can't figure out what he's thinking...

'Is that what they'll think?' he says, a small smile appearing over his lips.

'Well, you know, *something* like that.'

He leans towards me and my stomach starts to flip. My heart is racing and I tilt my head and move towards him.

And then a guy drunkenly knocks into Aidan. 'Sorry, mate,' he says, staggering off again.

I'm sure Aidan was going to kiss me. My lips are still tingling in anticipation, but whatever spell had fallen over us has been broken and Aidan coughs and backs away.

'I guess that I should be getting that train.'

I breathe out, trying to get over what almost happened. My legs are trembling and my heart is going nineteen to the dozen, but I pretend I'm fine and plant a fake smile on my face.

He gives me an arm's length hug then mutters a quick goodbye before he goes. He must have been relieved that we got interrupted as he couldn't get away from me quick enough.

But that's not how I feel. I'm glued to the spot watching him go.

I've never wanted to kiss anyone as much as I want to kiss him right now but as usual when it comes to my love, life all I'm left with is the familiar pang of heartbreak.

Welcome to October
This_Izzy_Loves IGTV
No. followers: 19.6k

*Hurrah, it's officially autumn! Luke and I went for a walk through crunchy leaves today and he decided we should have a leaf fight and I'm still picking bits out of my hair. Did you see the meal we had afterwards on my stories? I'm still full from that sticky toffee pudding – it was every bit as good as it looked! Luckily we've just got a chilled night planned. I think we'll crack open some more of the gin we got from our tour last month. If you didn't see our distillery visit, the link's in my bio to the video. The recipe for our new signature cocktail 'The Luzy' is on there and it's fantastic, if not a little strong – you have been warned!*

# Chapter 18

Marissa's become even easier to spot in the crowded shopping centre with her ever-increasing baby bump. She sees me and heads toward me carrying a large cardboard cake box.

'Hello, you,' she says, giving me a quick hug. It makes me wince with pain. 'What's with you?'

'Gin hangover,' I say, shuddering. Luke and I spent last night trying to recreate the cocktail recipe from our distillery tour. We'd planned to use water instead of alcohol but we had been gifted so much gin that it seemed a shame to waste it. And it hadn't tasted that bad on the tour when it was in a cocktail. I was about to call myself a gin convert, until I woke up in agony this morning thinking that someone was trying to smash through my head with a pneumonic drill.

'Oh bless you. Hangover food it is then.'

'Yes, let's go to McDonald's or Burger King,' I say, wincing in the sunlight. Since when has it been so sunny in October?

'We're not eating fast food. I'm about to give birth to a tiny human, which means I'm going to have a lifetime of eating in places like that. Let's go somewhere less child-friendly like the Boozy Goose. They do those amazing chicken wings.'

I like that bar and the lights aren't too bright.

'OK,' I say, nodding.

We start walking towards the bar and I loop my arm through Marissa's. You'd think I was the heavily pregnant one at the speed I'm insisting we walk.

'I thought you were going to fake your gin photos?'

'We were going to,' I say, groaning at the memory, 'but then we figured we might as well have one.'

'Or ten, I'm guessing by the state of you.'

'I sort of lost track...'

'So, drinking with Luke on a Friday night, huh?'

I see her not-so-subtle eyebrow raising.

'It was a nice night,' I say, shrugging. 'I wouldn't say we're becoming friends, but we're definitely getting used to spending time with each other and it's not totally awful.'

'High praise indeed,' says Marissa, pushing open the door. We climb up the stairs to where the bar is located. 'So is it still just a showmance, or is it turning into something more? The way he looks at you in those pictures...'

We round the top of the stairs and I pull a face before I head over to the sofas in the corner.

'There is nothing in the way he looks at me other than the pound signs in front of his eyes. I'm merely a way of him making money, nothing more.'

She raises a sceptical eyebrow and I choose to ignore it.

'Although he did surprise me by contacting Heart2Heart. I thought he'd want to do a fun run or something, but he wants to do a proper fundraiser.'

'Right, so he organised for you to do a fundraiser for a charity that's really special to you and you really think he's only in it for the money?' asks Marissa, placing the white cardboard box she's carrying on the table.

'He said it was to raise our profile.'

'Then why not pick a better-known charity?'

I sigh. Occasionally Luke can do nice things and it's hard to reconcile those with the normal selfish things he does.

'What's in the box?' I ask, changing the subject.

'It's a cake,' she says far too loudly and perkily for my hung-over state. 'It's for the gender reveal.'

'You've decided to do one?'

'Uh-huh,' she says, clapping her hands together. 'Tim finally agreed to it. We're going to stream it via Instagram Live tomorrow. I haven't dared tell my mum; she's going to be well pissed off she won't have the opportunity to announce our news to the world first like she usually does.'

I laugh. Marissa's mum does like to be the centre of attention.

'I can't believe you're going to keep that cake until tomorrow.'

'There's no point streaming it on a Saturday night.'

I open the box's flap and peer inside.

'Could I just scrape off a little bit of the icing and look?'

'No,' screams Marissa. 'That's cheating. You'll find out tomorrow, just like my thousand other followers.'

'I can't believe you haven't looked.'

'People would know. I'm so crap at faking anything.'

'Yeah, I get that,' I say, thinking back to the awful Makayto unboxing.

'I'm dying to know though,' she says, rubbing her belly. 'It seems so weird that all that's standing in my way of knowing if it's a boy or a girl is a centimetre of frosting.'

I push the cardboard box gently in her direction to tempt her.

'No,' she says. 'It wouldn't be right. Not without Tim.'

'And the rest of your followers?' I can't even copy one of her sceptical eyebrow-raises. It's too much effort today.

'Let's change the subject,' she says. 'How was dinner and

a movie with your *friend* Aidan?' she asks, sounding a little too like that waitress for my liking. I've told Marissa about the cinema trips with him, although I've made it clear that we're just good friends. I definitely haven't told her we almost kissed and that I've regretted the fact that we didn't ever since.

'I told you on the phone, dinner and a movie was good, thank you.'

'So, when are you seeing him next?'

'I'm not sure. We usually meet at the monthly cult cinema, but this month is *The Exorcist* and there's no way I can go and see that in the cinema. I saw it once on a grainy VHS and it scared the shit out of me. So I won't see him until November.'

'I guess that isn't a problem if he's just a mate, is it?'

I look up from my menu and she's staring at me with a knowing smile on her face.

'You know, you could ring him,' she says. 'Arrange to see another film. There are other cinemas.'

'I don't have his number.'

'What?' She shakes her head at me. 'Such a rookie mistake. Well then, send him a message on Facebook. And don't tell me that you haven't looked him up on there as I know you have.'

My cheeks flush a little. Of course I have. It's the first thing I did when I got home after I'd found out his surname.

'Do you know what you want to eat?' I ask, slowly rising to my feet. I need food and I need it quickly.

'I'll have the big nachos and don't think you're escaping this conversation by going to the bar. It'll be waiting for you when you get back.'

'Great,' I mutter.

Marissa's true to her word as, no sooner have I returned to the sofa with the drinks, she launches straight back into it.

'I don't want to hear that you don't like Aidan or that you're just friends, because we've been friends for twenty-one years and that look in your eyes only means one thing. You have it bad for him.'

'I wouldn't say I have it bad exactly ...'

'Ah-ha,' she says, a smile exploding on her face. 'I knew it.'

'You just said as much,' I say, confused.

'I thought it, but I didn't know. And now you've confirmed it,' she says, looking far too pleased with herself.

This is why I should have cancelled today. My guard has been well and truly lowered by my hangover.

'So, what are you going to do about it?' she asks.

'I'm not going to do anything about it.'

'Because of his girlfriend?'

I shift uncomfortably on the sofa. I haven't updated Marissa yet on the Saskia conversation.

'What? Has he dumped his girlfriend?' She's edging so far forward on the sofa that I'm worried that she'll topple over any minute from the weight of the baby.

'He never had a girlfriend,' I say, realising I'm too weak to not divulge everything today. 'She was his *business* partner.'

'Bloody hell, so he's single. And you're single. And you have the horn, I can see it in your eyes.'

I tut at her.

'It doesn't change anything.'

'It changes *everything*. You've got to ask him out.'

'I can't. I'm dating Luke.'

'Fake dating,' she says, rolling her eyes. 'You're not honestly letting that stop you. Look what Aidan did the day that Ben died. You should totally ask him out.'

'But he's not even interested. He sounds like he was hurt by an ex.'

'Like you,' she says, gesturing at me.

'Exactly. And like me, he's not ready to date yet.'

Marissa humphs. She looks over to a pile of leaflets in the corner before leaping up in a eureka moment.

'This is what you should do,' she says, walking back and handing a glossy booklet to me.

'What is it?' I say, taking it.

'It's for the theatre.'

'I don't get it.' I flick through the pages and wonder what I'm missing.

'You pick something that's only on for a night or two, message him and tell him you've got no one to go with and voilà. It's one friend helping out another friend and hopefully you'll end up smooching at the end of the night.'

I think of our near kiss and I'm tempted.

'That sounds ridiculous. And I bet there's nothing on.'

I land on a page and prove myself wrong.

'Huh, *Salome* by Oscar Wilde. Do you remember doing one of his plays at school?'

'No,' she says, wrinkling her nose up.

'You do, we did *The Importance of Being Earnest*. We all dressed up in big Victorian dresses.'

She looks at me blankly.

'Don't remember. But to be fair all I can remember from drama class was Jimmy Marsden.'

I lose Marissa for a minute whilst she thinks about her teenage crush.

'That'll be perfect,' she says eventually.

'You have no idea what it is.'

'It doesn't really matter. You just need an excuse.'

She picks up my phone and hands it to me.

'Do it now.'

I take it and slip it into my hoodie pocket.

'Even if I was going to do it, I couldn't do it when I was this hungover; my brain is barely functioning.'

'Promise when you do it later you'll tell me?'

'I promise, *if* I do it and it's a big if.'

'You'll do it,' she says, wriggling her bum back into the sofa, seemingly content.

'I can't believe you're going on a date with him, it's so exciting. I'm so pleased, Izzy, that everything's coming together for you. You're getting a boyfriend, and also... I think I've found you your dream job!'

'Steady on, he's nowhere near my boyfriend. And hang on, I'm not looking to move jobs!'

'You might be if it was your dream one. I have a client who's looking for a digital marketing manager. It's a really dynamic company and the salary's pretty good and they've got good healthcare and benefits,' she says.

'Has this got anything to do with your commission and that expensive pram you want?'

'Absolutely not,' she says far too unconvincingly. 'But I did think that it might be good for you. You always said that that's why you started doing your Instagram – so that you could move into a digital marketing role.'

'I know, but it's quite a leap from being a copywriter and I've had time off. I think I really should build up my influencer brand a bit more so I could really impress people.'

'I'm sure they wouldn't mind,' she says. I notice she's not looking me in the eye.

'Have you already spoken to them about me?'

'I might have done, informally, and they seemed really positive.'

'Marissa,' I say, sighing.

'I know, I'm sorry, it's just it seemed like you'd be a perfect fit and I thought it would be really good for you.'

'But my feed, I feel like I'm getting somewhere. If it keeps growing at the rate that it is, I might be making decent money soon.'

'Yeah, but it's a gamble, isn't it?' she says. I can tell she's choosing her words carefully. 'This could give you proper job security. You might be able to save enough to get a deposit for your own place.'

'You're starting to sound like Becca,' I say, trying to laugh it off.

The barman plonks two steaming plates of food down in front of us and I greedily reach for my chicken wings and start nibbling straight away. I'm getting into this whole eating food whilst it's hot.

'Why don't I send you over the job spec and you can see? I know you're doing really well with your Instagram and I am of course insanely jealous as I'm never going to reach those heights, but I just think that this is such a good opportunity. I mean, wasn't this what it was all supposed to be for?'

I put down my first chicken bone, gnawed clean.

'It was at one point,' I say, taking a deep breath. Marissa's my best friend and I can usually talk to her about everything, but I'm embarrassed to talk to her about this. I want her to understand why it means so much to me, though. 'I was talking to Ben about it when he came up to London to buy Becca's engagement ring and he told me that I shouldn't just set my sights on changing jobs but that I should try and make it as an influencer. It seemed like such a silly dream, but the closer I've come to achieving it, the more I want to, for him. He'd have been so proud.'

'Ah, Izzy,' she says, inching forward and grabbing my hand. 'Why ever didn't you tell me?'

I shrug my shoulders. 'After Ben died I found Instagram such an escape from all the grief. I liked the fact that people didn't know about me or my problems and they didn't all treat me like I was broken or do the sympathetic head tilt. It almost made me think that it was him nudging me in the right direction.' I take a sip of my drink. 'I sound stupid.'

'No, you don't,' says Marissa. 'But you know he'd be pleased and proud of you whatever you did.'

'I know, and if it doesn't work out then I will definitely start looking at a more stable career. But right now, I've got to at least try. For him.'

Marissa's silent for a minute before she takes a bite of her nachos.

'I can't believe you didn't tell me though,' she says. 'Does this mean that you have other secrets from me? Are you and Luke really a couple?'

'Er, no, we're definitely not. And I don't have any other secrets from you. I was just a bit embarrassed talking about that with you. Damn the hangover, it's like taking a freaking honesty pill.'

'You know you can always talk to me about the Ben stuff, don't you? I know that you and Becca talk about it a lot, but I am always here.'

'I know you are,' I say, nodding and blinking back a tear. 'And thanks, I haven't been talking to Becca as much as I used to about this stuff.'

I feel sad that I haven't told Becca. When Ben died we used to talk about everything but since she's started dating Gareth, things have changed between us. I miss how we used to be.

'I'm glad you told me,' she says, squeezing my hand that she's still holding. 'You can always talk to me. Even when you become a jet-setting mega influencer.'

'I don't think that's going to happen,' I say. 'Perhaps you should send me over that job spec.'

'No, follow your dream,' she says. 'But don't just do it for Ben, Izzy, do it for you too.'

A tear runs down my cheek and I wipe it away and smile. I don't know what I did to deserve such a lovely friend. I lean over the table to give her a hug and Marissa stands up slightly to meet me in the middle. We pull out of the hug and as she sits down her bump catches the corner of the cake box.

I look down in horror as the bottom of the box catapults up.

'No!' I shout, reaching out to grab it but I'm too late. The box tumbles to the ground and the cake splats all over the wooden floor.

We both stare in horror. There's a mass of white icing poking out from the underside of the box, and what looks to be pink sponge cake.

'Oh my God, oh my God, oh my God. I'm having a little girl,' she screams, leaping up and narrowly avoiding tipping over her nachos this time. 'This bump is a bloody liability.'

'It is. But you're having a girl!'

I give her yet another hug and we do a lot of squealing.

'I'm having a little girl, Izzy,' says Marissa, finally sitting down, wiping away the tears.

'I know,' I say, beaming. I have no doubt that we'd have been doing the same dance had the sponge been blue but just knowing what it's going to be is so magical.

'I'm terrified of having a little girl. How will I keep her safe? What if people are mean to her? What if—'

'She'll be fine. She's got you as her mum.'

That sets Marissa off crying again and I don't know whether

it's the post-alcohol blues or the fact that this lunch has been bloody emotional, but I start bawling too.

The barman walks over with a dustpan and brush to clear up the cake, but he looks between the mess on the floor and our blubbing and thinks better of it. He leaves us the dustpan and a bin bag and creeps away.

We just about get the tears under control and I stand up to clear up the cake.

'I still can't believe it,' Marissa says. 'Just think, you're going to have a goddaughter.'

I look at Marissa for confirmation that I haven't misheard and she grins manically at me.

I whoop loudly, my hangover forgotten, and the happy tears start again and it's a long time before they stop.

# Chapter 19

I slip a tight-fitting cardigan over my blouse and I walk into the kitchen where Becca's making a cup of tea.

'What do you think? Do I look OK? Not too casual?'

I walk into the bedroom to peruse my outfit again in the full-length mirror before Becca can answer.

'You look great,' she says, following me into my room and leaning on the door frame. 'Your hair.'

I put my hand up to my curls and push them up and they spring down again.

'Does it look too big?'

'No, I love it.'

Becca's holding her tea in her hand and looking at me.

'I don't look too smart, do I? It's been a long time since I've been to the theatre; I'm not too sure what to wear anymore.'

'Yeah, like that's the reason you're fussing over what you're wearing. Nothing to do with the fact you're meeting Aidan.'

I don't want to admit she might be right. It should be no different from meeting up with him at the cinema, but it is. Now that I know he's single and I want to kiss him.

I should never have followed Marissa's advice, but Facebook makes it far too easy. It might have taken me a couple of hours to craft the perfect message and pluck up the courage to send it, but once I had, we'd arranged to meet up within minutes.

'Whatever,' I say, going all teenager.

Becca smiles; she can't seem to understand why I don't want to date him. I can think of lots of reasons, the fake dating, bad timing, but it mainly boils down to me being scared of getting hurt again.

I'm about to run out the door when my phone rings. My heart sinks, thinking that it's him phoning to cancel, so I'm relieved when I dig it out of my bag and realise that it's only Luke.

'Hiya,' I answer.

'Hey, guess what?' he says. I can hear the excitement in his voice.

'Channing Tatum has pulled a muscle and he wants you to take over from him in the next *Magic Mike* film?'

Becca gives me a WTF look and I shake my head at her.

'Very funny,' he says. 'Maybe not as exciting as that, but pretty close. We got approached by a big country hotel – they want us to feature in their ad campaign. They're not only going to give us a free stay, but they're going to pay us £2,000 as well.'

'Holy shit!' I say, stunned.

'I know! All we've got to do is post some videos and photos on our feed during the weekend stay, and pose for some pictures their photographer will take and they'll put them in their brochures and ads.'

'Bloody hell, that's amazing. That would pay my rent for the next two months,' I say, the reality hitting me as to what the money could do.

'And this is only one company. Imagine if we had two or three of those a month.'

'Imagine,' I say feeling a little light-headed.

'Anyway, I'll send you through the details. I just wanted to let you know before you went out.'

'How did you know I was going out?'

'Uh, our Google calendars are synced, remember? By the way, didn't have you down as the kind of girl that got a Brazilian wax,' he says, laughing.

'The "B" in a "B Wax" could mean a lot of things. I'm hanging up now.'

I've got quite into using the calendar on my phone. Although I'd been posting everything to my personal calendar, I'll need to check that.

I say goodbye to Becca and hurry out of the flat towards the station where we're meeting.

*We're just friends, just friends,* I repeat in my head to calm my nerves. Aidan doesn't want a relationship and neither do I. He doesn't know that I've got a crush on him and it's not like I'm going to act on it, so really I should have nothing to be nervous about.

When I get to the station he's already standing there. I do a little run to get to him. I wish I hadn't because I'm not the most athletic person and instead of jogging like a *Baywatch* babe I'm thundering along like an elephant.

'Sorry, have you been here long?'

'No, I literally just arrived.'

He leans over to give me what I think is a hug but when his lips graze my ear I realise he was going for a kiss on the cheek and we're left in a weird moment where I'm trying to lean into the hug and he's trying to withdraw from the kiss. FML. Why did I listen to Marissa?

'Shall we get going?' I say.

'Sure, yes, it's been a long time since I've been to Basingstoke, so I'll let you lead the way.'

I don't dwell on the fact that we stood on this very spot the day Ben died, before he bundled me into a taxi and instead we walk down the steps towards the town centre.

'Do you know anything about this play we're going to see?'

'Only a little, but I love Oscar Wilde's plays and so I imagine it'll be good. Apparently it has a sexy topless dance in it.'

I see Aidan's cheeks colour and I wish I'd not mentioned it.

'Oh, that'll be something to look forward to, I guess.'

I wish I hadn't googled the play this afternoon. Sitting next to him whilst he's watching a scantily dressed woman do the sexy dance of the seven veils isn't really what I had in mind. It's awkward enough with me trying to ignore the chemistry between us, let alone seeing a steamy performance. I shove my hands into my coat pockets in a bid to stop my palms from getting any more clammy.

'At least it's supposed to be a short play,' I say, trying to put the dance from my mind. 'We can go to the pub after.'

'Great,' he says, nodding. 'Pubs are always good. So, how's your month been? Done anything interesting?'

I pause before I speak. I'm so used to doing my monthly round-ups that I almost go into my upbeat Instagram voice before I check myself.

'It's been quite quiet,' I say, thinking that being in a fake relationship with Luke takes up a ridiculous amount of time. Not only do we have to do our fake dates but we also have to comment on each other's posts with sickening little in-jokes and public emoji-filled conversations. 'My best friend Marissa's having a baby so I'm trying to spend a lot of time with her before she gives birth in December, and I've also been planning a surprise baby shower for her with my friend and flatmate, Becca.'

'Baby shower? Is that a thing? I thought they only did it in America.'

'No, they do them here now too. I'm excited. I think it's going to be a hen do Part II, just without the sambuca and perhaps fewer strippers, thank goodness. I'm not really into oiled-up naked men gyrating in front of me.'

'Isn't that covered by law of the hen, that you're not supposed to talk about it?'

'Oh yeah, I guess so. There was this one with a stubbly bum and—'

'Law of the hen.'

'That's supposed to protect me and my secrets, not you.'

'I think it works both ways,' he says, making me laugh.

There's something about talking with Aidan that's so easy.

'So here we are,' I say, looking up at the theatre. In hindsight we should have arranged to get here earlier to have a quick drink first. I could have done with calming the nerves I didn't realise I was going to have. We head straight inside and after scanning our tickets we get directed to our seats.

'Looks like we've got a good view,' I say as we show our tickets again before the inner doors. 'Right at the front.'

'I guess we'll have a good view of the special dance,' he says, raising an eyebrow and I instantly regret booking tickets.

'There are lots of men here,' I say, looking around at how busy it is, 'now there's a surprise. Reckon they're all here for the boobs?'

Aidan looks around too before he looks back at me.

'I don't think so, somehow. How much do you know about this interpretation of the play?'

I follow his eyes around the theatre and I start to notice that the men are being quite tactile with each other. The penny slowly drops that we might be the only straight people in the audience and it makes me wonder about the play we're about to see.

'Um,' says Aidan, straining to see the programme of the guy

next to us. The front cover has a topless man on the front holding a veil. 'So you know that sexy dance you promised me?'

'The one with the seven veils,' I say, cringing.

'Better hope the man isn't oiled up as he does his dance,' he says laughing and I can't help joining him and then we can't stop. It seems the more men that pour into the little theatre, the more it makes us giggle.

'And to think we could have gone to see *The Exorcist*,' he says finally.

I wipe the tears away from my eyes, my cheeks aching.

'We've probably got time to escape before it starts,' I whisper.

'Nah, come on. I'm sure it won't be that graphic. We're in Basingstoke, after all. It'll give us something to talk about in the pub after.'

'I'm sure it will. So,' I say, having finally recovered from my bout of hysterics, 'what have you been up to today?'

'I went and met Saskia for lunch.'

'Oh, Saskia, how's she?'

'Good. Very loved up with her girlfriend.'

Of course she is, making me feel even more like an idiot for misconstruing their relationship.

'How's the café going? It's been open a few months now, hasn't it?'

'Yeah,' he says, nodding. 'It's going OK. We've had a few teething problems and I don't think it'll make money anytime soon, but I'm kind of in it for the long haul.'

'I hope it does really well.'

'I hope so too, because I did put pretty much my entire savings into it. Plus I keep getting roped into doing runs to the wholesalers or to the greengrocer's to get more stock and it would be great if we could afford to employ more staff.'

'So that you can hide away in your house and not have to see anyone.'

'Exactly. I like to go to work in my pants and it's been a right drag having to get dressed when they call me.'

*Don't picture him in his pants. Don't picture him in his pants.*

'Sometimes I think I'd like to work from home and escape the drama of our office.'

'Your office sounds great though. Have there been any more Bake Off antics?'

'Oh my goodness. There have,' I say, and I quickly fill him in on the latest goings-on, not leaving out the fact that Colin has now resumed his role of chief taster of Mrs Harris's wares, although she spoon-feeds him as he's not allowed to touch them.

I've just finished telling him about Jason from Risk Management being knocked out of the competition when the lights dim and an excited ripple of chatter goes through the audience before it goes silent and the play starts.

When the play finishes, Aidan bolts like a horse and I have to run to keep up with him.

'You know I think it would have been less scary to watch *The Exorcist*,' he says, shaking out his arms.

'I'm really sorry. I didn't realise that he was going to be stark bollock naked.'

'Do you have to mention the word bollocks. I'm trying to cleanse my mind of images.'

I think this has been the only time I've been to the theatre where I wish I'd had worse seats. It would have been much better up in the Gods where we would have been unable to see that level of anatomical detail.

'It was like right there, practically in my face,' he says, shuddering.

'I feel your pain. Why are men's bits so unpretty? And that other guy, the one with the tights on.'

'Oh,' he says, raising his hand to stop me. 'I'm hoping that was an unfortunate wardrobe malfunction or else he was in all sorts of trouble.'

I can't help but giggle and he starts too.

'The play was good though, don't you think?'

It only makes him laugh harder.

'It was different, I'll give you that, but as much as I enjoyed elements of it, I think in the future we should stick to Eighties and Nineties films.'

'Yes, at least we'd have seen them before and they'd be properly vetted.'

'Vetted, exactly. Now can you take me to the pub to buy me a quick drink before I catch the train home.'

'Of course.'

We head to the quietest pub we can find on a Saturday night.

'What do you want to drink?'

'Just a beer, thanks.'

I go over to the bar and he heads off to the toilets.

'Oh my God, it's Izzy, isn't it?' says a woman, coming up to me.

I turn to look at her and I can't place her. This happens every so often, someone from school that I don't recognise. The perils of living in your hometown.

'Izzy and Luke?' she says, her smile widening.

'Oh no,' I say in what comes out in a Scottish accent and I go with it. 'That's not me. Sorry, lassie.'

Lassie? I think it's a step too far but she buys the accent.

'Oh, sorry. I've had a lot to drink tonight. But you look a bit like her. She's in this Instagram couple I follow.'

'Sounds delightful,' I say my accent turning slightly Irish, but the woman doesn't seem to notice.

'What can I get you?' asks a man behind the bar.

The woman is still next to me so I order Aidan a beer and myself a single malt whisky to keep in character, but as the barman puts it down, the smell of it turns my stomach, and I order a Coke too.

I'm just getting my change when Aidan comes back from the toilet.

'Have a good night,' says the woman as I go to leave.

'Thanks, lassie,' I say.

Aidan stares at me with amusement.

'Did you get yourself a wee dram?' he says in an accent that reminds me of David Tennant.

'I did indeed.'

We make our way to a quiet table.

'Do I want to know what that was about?' he asks in his normal accent.

'Someone who thought they knew me from school,' I say. 'I couldn't be arsed to do all the small talk to find out if we did know each other or not; I'm sure I'd remember her if we'd been close.'

'Oh, if I'd known I'd have joined in, although I do a better Irish accent,' he says, demonstrating.

'Ooh, tell me more.'

We spend the next half an hour trying and mostly failing to talk using different accents. The more whisky and Coke I drink, the more convincing I think I sound. By the time Aidan's walking me home an hour later, my facial muscles are aching where I've been laughing so much.

He insists on walking me to my block of flats and, seeing as it's at the end of the approach to the station, I let him, as it's not too far out of his way.

'Well, Izzy, thank you for the most uncomfortable yet one of the funniest nights of my life.'

'An evening out with me is never dull,' I say.

'I'm starting to realise that,' he says, nodding.

A train rattles past slowly as it pulls into the station, reminding me that Aidan's got to go.

'Thanks for walking me back and for being such good company.'

'You're welcome. So, *Flight of the Navigator* then, next month.'

'Hmmm, yes, I guess I'll see you in five weeks' time.'

It suddenly seems like a very long time away.

'You know, sometimes I get lonely on dog walks.'

'Isn't that why you've got Barney?'

Aidan bites his lip.

'Yes, but sometimes his conversation isn't up to much.'

'I've heard that about Labradors. Well, I like to walk, as long as it's not too cold, or wet.'

'Great, I'll give you a shout in the spring then.'

I laugh and wish I'd worn a warmer coat; the whisky's wearing off and it's cold out.

'Perhaps I could dig out some gloves and waterproof jacket and come with you.' I want another excuse to see him and I don't think I'll be able to convince him to see another play.

'That would be lovely. One weekend?'

I nod.

'OK, I'll send you a message then.'

'I'd like that.'

'Right, I'll be going then,' he says. He doesn't move. He's so close to me that I could reach out and touch him, only I don't.

Even if he hadn't sworn off relationships, now is not a good time for me to be looking for love. The hotel campaign only goes to show how on the cusp I am of my life seriously changing. My influencer dreams are starting to become a reality and I don't want to mess up the opportunity.

He leans over and kisses me on the cheek and I try and ignore the crackle of electricity.

'I've got to get my train,' he says in almost a whisper.

'Yes, you go,' I say, ignoring the voice in my head that wants me to beg him to stay.

'I'll see you soon, for the dog walk?'

'Absolutely,' I say a little too enthusiastically.

I watch him go and realise that I'm in trouble as the more time I spend with him, the more I fall for him and that can't happen when I'm so close to living my dream.

Welcome to November
This_Izzy_Loves IGTV
No. followers: 19.9k

*It's November – hurrah! One of my favourite months as it's starting to get properly cold out and I can layer up in all my scarves and coats. Thanks for all of your Halloween love. Yes, it did take me a long time to make the costume and for all of you concerned about wasting the clingfilm, that's the second time I've now worn that outfit and I'm hoping to use it again. Didn't Luke look hot as Dexter?*

*There's also been a lot of love for our Makayto-sponsored pics. So much so that the discount code stopped working as they'd sold out. But I have good news on that front: it's now back in stock! I'll pop a link in the comments and you too can match your other half – imagine wearing those outfits on Christmas Day!*

*I am such a lucky lady to have Luke in my life. You would not believe the things that come out of his mouth, he's a true catch. He's also a massive zapper of time as between keeping up my Insta feed, working and seeing him, I have zero opportunity for anything else. Not that I'm complaining, I wish I could be with him 24/7. Yes, I know it's sickening, but I don't care.*

# Chapter 20

'Bloody traffic,' I say as we inch closer to the outskirts of the city only to be halted by yet another red light.

'That's Friday night for you,' says Luke.

'I'm itching to get onto the open road and try this baby out.'

I stroke the steering wheel of the electric car we've been loaned for the weekend.

'Do you think we're ever going to get there, I'm starving.' My stomach starts to growl to illustrate the point.

'I've got some food,' he says, reaching down into his satchel and pulling out a Tupperware tub. 'Miles at work was trying out some Bake Off recipes. It's Asian week next week and he made me extra spring rolls because he knows how much I love them.'

'I love them too, give me one,' I say, holding out a hand and Luke passes me one.

'Do you think they're a bit messy to eat in here?'

'This car's so hi-tech it'll probably clean itself,' I say, biting into the flaky pastry and spilling crumbs everywhere. 'Oh my God, that is so good. The standard of the last few contestants is so high. I don't know how they're going to pick a winner.'

'We'll soon find out. Have you heard that they're announcing the winner at the Christmas party?'

'Yes, Mrs Harris has already bought her dress for when she goes up on stage.'

'Let's hope she at least makes it through the last two rounds then,' says Luke.

'She'd better do, or that's all we'll hear about forever more.'

He hands me over another one and I stuff it in my mouth.

'What's in them? Is it chicken?'

'Prawns, I think. You've got to try his samosas too.'

He hands me one and I almost miss the light turning green. Luckily for me the car behind me beeps and I shove the rest of a samosa into my mouth before I pull away. I make it onto the main road and the traffic is flowing and I finally get the car to go over 20 mph for the first time since we pulled out of the garage.

'This car is amazing,' I say, the speedometer ramping up.

'Can you drive it a bit slower?' I watch him searching to find something to cling onto. 'Why doesn't this one have handles?'

'Maybe if you say "handles" loud enough one will appear like they did on the outside. I feel like I'm James Bond,' I say.

'Well, you don't have to drive like him.'

'Calm down, grandma, I'm hardly going that fast – just feels it because we were stop-start in traffic before.'

'You're going fast enough,' he says, clearly having palpitations.

'Look, there's nothing wrong with my driving but if you'd prefer we could let the car drive itself,' I say, flicking a lever. 'Look, no hands.'

I wiggle my fingers and Luke actually looks like he's going to lose it.

'Put your hands back on the wheel. Put them on now! You're not supposed to be doing that. The woman said that even when self-driving you have to keep your hands on the wheel; it'll sense you don't have them on.'

I groan like he's a killjoy before I put my hands back on the steering wheel, but to be honest I was shitting my pants. As cool as this car is, I'm not sure if I like it being in control.

'OK, I'll put it back onto manual drive.'

'Actually, I think I felt safer with the robot.'

'Hey,' I say. 'I'll have you know that I'm a good driver. At least I have my licence.'

'So do I, it's only been suspended temporarily.'

'And you're the one telling me off for speeding and that's how you lost yours.'

He grips onto the side of seat.

'I got done by the same bloody speed camera in a thirty.'

'Four times.'

'Yeah, but three of them were in the same week and I just thought the lights were bright down that road. Anyway, there's a difference between going fast and being reckless.'

I start to giggle. No one has ever called me reckless before. I'm not even exceeding the speed limit.

'I still don't know why you agreed to test drive a car for the weekend if you couldn't drive,' I say.

'It said it was a driverless car and I read it quickly. I just thought it would look better than arriving at the hotel in your little Micra. No offence.'

'None taken. Have you got any more of those spring rolls?'

Luke hands me another and I gobble it down and by the time we make it to our turning we've eaten the whole tub.

'Take a left here,' says Luke, just as the onboard computer tells me the same thing.

I pull off the main road and follow the sat nav. A few minutes later, we pass the sign for Ingleford Manor and we head down a long driveway to an imposing-looking country hotel.

'Wow, this place is beautiful.' We drive around the large fountain in the middle of the turning circle and follow the signs for the car park. 'That rain's really coming down now.'

I spot a space close to the entrance and I slow down to pull in.

'Whoa, what are you doing?' gasps Luke.

'Parking.'

'Um, that space might be big enough for your Micra, but it isn't big enough for this car. Why don't you let it park itself?'

'I'm perfectly capable of doing it.'

'What's the point of barking if you have a dog? Come on, put the auto park on.'

I want to make a point but, even though I'm convinced that that space is big enough, I don't really want to take the car back to the shiny showroom with a massive scratch down it.

I set the car into auto park mode and fold my arms for a moment before Luke gives me the stare of death and I place my hands back on the wheel.

'Told you that space was too small,' says Luke as the car drives past it.

'Maybe, but it's just driven past that one and it was massive.'

The car eventually finds us a space at the end of a row of cars and reverses with a precision that amazes me.

'Now that was impressive,' says Luke.

'Would have been more impressive if it had been closer to the door.'

'At least you don't have to worry about your hair like I do,' he says, touching his quiff.

I beg to differ on both counts because my hair's going to turn into a frizzy mess the moment the humidity hits it and his hair has been gelled into oblivion and I'm pretty sure that quiff will be as waterproof as Gore-Tex.

I open the door and I plunge my foot into a puddle and the water seeps into my ankle boot. I walk around to the front of the car, shaking my foot.

'Trust you to find a puddle,' he says in a such a smug way and I hope that I'm wrong about his quiff and that it flattens like a pancake.

He walks round to the boot and opens it. I reach to get my bag but he holds my hand back. 'Oh no, sweetie, I've got these.'

I roll my eyes. I'd forgotten that the act starts all over again. The car ride here wasn't too bad, but mainly because I didn't have to act like I was in love with him.

I look up at the redbrick hotel and the ivy creeping up over it. It looks beautiful highlighted by the warm yellow lights, even in the pouring rain. It's so romantic and I wish I was with someone that I cared about. Aidan pops into my mind and I try to push him out again.

We walk up the steps and push open the heavy door and Luke takes my hand. We're instantly greeted by the staff at the front desk with a warm, welcoming smile.

'Good evening,' smiles the receptionist.

'Hello, I'm Luke Taylor and this is Izzy.'

'Izzy and Luke,' says a guy running out of the office. 'You're here.'

He claps his hands together before holding them out to us.

'I'm the manager, Grant. I was the one who asked Russell to contact you.'

'Nice to meet you,' I say, offering my hand which he shakes.

'So I've given you lovebirds our most romantic suite. You're going to love it – it was redone in the spring. All our honeymooners go mad for it, especially the amazing baths.'

'Ooh, I love a good soak,' I say, thinking that I can hide in the bath to get away from Luke for an hour or two.

'I'll take you up there personally, I want to see your faces,' he says, leading us upstairs.

'This staircase is gorgeous.'

I run my hand along the wooden banister. I love the way that it bends round. It's the type that you can imagine a princess gliding down.

'Everyone loves this staircase, especially brides,' he says with a not-so-subtle wink.

Luke had better not be listening. I take a look over and luckily he's swiping on his phone oblivious.

'You know, we're not only an extremely popular wedding venue but proposal venue too. There aren't many couples that come here for a romantic weekend away and leave without a ring on a finger, eh, Luke?'

He looks up from his phone and Grant repeats himself.

'Did you hear that, honey?' he says, much to Grant's delight.

I've only just met him but I can imagine what he's thinking: if we got engaged here it would be an advertiser's dream.

I look at Luke's giant case and hope that it's not hiding a very tiny ring box.

We head into a lift to the top floor and find ourselves in a corridor with only one door.

'And here's your suite.'

He flings the door open and we walk into an amazingly opulent room where everything vies for my attention: the modern four-poster bed, the ornate fireplace, the large sash windows that I bet when it's light will reveal sweeping views across the countryside, and the his and her bathtubs in front of the window right in the middle of the main room.

'Nice, huh?' says Grant. 'The bathtubs are such a hit with everyone who stays here.'

Luke is nodding. 'I'm sure we're going to love those, aren't we, honey?'

I nod, disappointed that I'm not going to have my lazy soak after all. I pan round the room until I get to the bathroom.

'Whoa,' I say, unable to find the words. Instead I point at the glass wall that separates the bathroom from the bedroom. The toilet is parallel to the bed and the shower faces it.

My stomach starts to pinch in revulsion.

'We find it transforms the bathroom space, makes it so light,' says Grant.

'Clever idea,' says Luke, seemingly unfazed.

'It's quite a bold statement, isn't it?' I say, almost hyperventilating. 'I mean what happens if you're in the early stages of your relationship?'

*Or not even in one?*

'I'm sure that isn't an issue for you two lovebirds,' says Grant, dismissing my concerns.

'And the bed,' I say, 'that looks a little small for double.'

When he said we had a suite, I'd imagined some super-duper king-size bed that would have felt like Luke and I were sleeping in different postcodes. Or maybe even a sofa that one of us could escape to, but there's only a small chaise longue that would leave your legs hanging off the end.

'We did initially test the room with super-king beds but the feedback was that couples wanted to come together on their break and they felt they were getting lost in the beds.'

'That's perfect for us, we love to cuddle,' says Luke and I try not to outwardly cringe.

'Perfect. I knew you guys were going to love it. Now, I've got a whole list of activities for you to try tomorrow, but tonight we can offer you a table in the restaurant or perhaps you'd like room service instead?'

He's hinting at every turn that all we're going to do is have sex in this room. It's making me want to escape.

'Restaurant,' I say and Luke nods.

'Great choice. I'll leave you to freshen up. I'll book you a table, for what, 8 p.m.?'

'That would be great,' says Luke.

'I'll leave you the details of what you can do tomorrow and we'll chat again in the morning and you can tell me your picks,' he says, clapping his hands. 'The photographer will be on site from eleven.'

He hands me the printout and I look down at it: clay-pigeon shooting, falconry, yoga, spa, horse riding. Looks like we won't have to be trapped alone in our room trying not to watch each other go to the toilet. Hurrah.

Grant closes the door and Luke's about to jump on the bed, but I manage to stop him.

'We've got to take a photo of the rose petals on the bed first,' I say, holding his arm back and pulling out my phone. There's a red heart made of petals on the crisp white sheets.

'How many roses do you reckon it took to make those – one, two? That's pretty cheap but effective.'

I don't even bother to roll my eyes anymore; I've become immune to him mining every romantic trope for exploitative purposes.

My stomach pinches again and I rub my belly.

'You OK?' asks Luke. 'You're wincing.'

'My tummy feels a little bit weird.'

I'm hit again by a pain that's sharp and sudden. I look over to the toilet. Oh no. Do not do this. Not yet. I was hoping that I could hold off going to the loo until I went down to dinner, but my stomach growls angrily and I doubt I could even make it down to the lobby.

I run into the toilet and panic washes over me. I hastily grab a towel and hold it up with one hand whilst pulling my pants down with the other, in a mad scramble to get on the toilet. What happens next isn't pretty and I look behind my towel to see Luke lying on the bed. Oh God. He must have heard every little noise. I'm not sure if it's a blessing or a curse that we're not a real couple. I'm guessing this particular scenario would be a pretty embarrassing moment in any couple's relationship, perhaps I should be grateful I already feel slightly ashamed when I look at him.

My arms holding the towel start to shake and I feel beads of sweat forming on my forehead. My stomach lurches again only this time it's different – I'm going to be sick. With no time to think about it, I wrap the towel round my waist, flush the toilet and immediately vomit.

When the wave of vomiting finishes, my head starts to throb and I shuffle backwards so that I'm leaning back against the cold hard wall tiles.

There's a knock on the glass. I look up expecting it to be Luke checking on me but I spot his green face and I know what he needs to do. I flush the loo again and pick up the bin before crawling towards the door.

'Holy shit,' he says.

'Uh-huh,' I say as I shut him in. Luckily he's got the TV on and it's up loud so I don't hear anything. Instead I sit huddled on the floor hugging the bin, trying to ignore my stomach pains.

When eventually it becomes unbearable I crawl towards the bathroom.

I shield my eyes with my hand before knocking on the glass.

'Hang on,' shouts Luke and I hear the flush going. 'Can you wait?'

'Nope,' I say, reaching up for the door handle.

'OK, come in,' he shouts.

He barely makes it out of the bathroom when I reach the toilet.

It's a long time before I get back up again and I put the towel round my waist and splash water on my face at the sink, before I sink down onto the floor. It feels safer to stay within reach.

Luke taps on the glass and comes in and washes water on his face too.

'Bloody hell, those spring rolls,' I say, my stomach churning. 'I'm guessing eating prawn spring rolls that have sat out of the fridge in Tupperware all day wasn't the best idea.'

My body goes into spasm as my stomach cramps.

Luke hands me a cold, wet flannel and I pop it on my clammy forehead.

'What are we going to tell Grant? We can't tell them we've got the shits.'

'He did drop enough hints about us being curled up in our love den. I'll ring down and tell them we'll order room service for dinner. We can take photos of it and he'll never know we didn't eat it.'

'But what about the photos on Insta stories?'

'We'll fake them. It's not like we don't anyway. We'll run the baths and put loads of bubbles in, and we could have another photo of us in robes and face masks,' I say. I feel too rough to worry about all the deceit.

'Did you bring face masks?'

'No, but we can put that moisturiser on our face,' I say pointing at the decanter on the side. 'Oh hang on. Get out, get out, get out.'

Luke moves like lightning. I no longer seem to care that I'm flashing my bits through the glass as I scramble back onto the loo.

When I eventually make it out, Luke's on the phone.

'Uh-huh, yeah, room service. No, it's OK, I don't think the chef needs to do that,' he says going greener, presumably at the mention of food. 'OK, if you insist. And could we also get some fizzy water? Uh-huh, of course Prosecco,' he says, wincing. 'Great. Thanks.'

He puts the phone down and rolls over on the bed.

'Oh bloody hell, here I go again,' he says, dashing to the bathroom.

I close my eyes and wonder if this is karma for what we're doing.

# Chapter 21

Spending the night in the world's smallest double bed with Luke was always going to be testing, but throw stomach issues and a glass-walled toilet into the mix and we truly had the night from hell. Any time one of us got to sleep, the other one would have to go to the loo. There only seems to be one setting on the bathroom light, which is extremely bright, and thanks to the wonderful glass doors it was on, it lit up the whole room like Blackpool Illuminations. We did try at one point to only use our phone torches but given that the room is pitch black and our bellies gave us approximately twenty seconds of warning, there wasn't time.

My alarm goes off and I roll over to see how Luke's feeling. Only instead of seeing him on the other side of the bed, I find myself staring at him naked in the shower. I quickly roll over to face the windows. At least I only saw his bum.

I pick up my phone and check out my metrics to see how we got on yesterday. We've had lots of views and people like our smug hotel selfie that we took in our matching robes. If only they'd seen us simultaneously throwing up ten minutes later.

I also see that I've got a message from Aidan on Whatsapp.

Aidan:
Hiya. Hope all is well with you. Do you fancy coming with me to walk Barney this afternoon?

My heart sinks. I wish I could. I type quickly back.

Me:
I'd have loved to, but I'm on a work thing this weekend. I'm free next Sunday?

Aidan:
Next Sunday works for me. Look forward to entertaining stories from what happened with your colleagues!

I hate the fact that I've lied to him, but at least the one up-side of this food poisoning is that I can honestly tell him I spent the whole time holed up in the room.

Me:
;)

Luke comes out of the bathroom with a tiny towel wrapped around his waist.

'Why have you got a goofy smile on your face?' he asks.

I put the phone down on the bedside table and try to make my face look normal.

'Just texting a friend.'

'Oh,' he says, nodding. 'I have those types of friends.'

I want to tell him that Aidan's not a friend with benefits, but I can't even bring myself to talk about him in front of Luke.

'Just make sure you don't get too friendly; we don't want to blow this thing,' he says.

'I know,' I say, thinking back to the moment of our near kiss. 'How was your shower?'

'It really helped. I'm starting to feel a lot better, mainly because I don't think I can possibly have anything left to come out of me.'

'Tell me about it.'

There's a knock at the door and Luke saunters over to open it.

I pull up my sheets, not for modesty, but to conceal the fact that I'm wearing button-down flannel pyjamas. I brought my least sexy PJs with me.

'Ah, thanks,' says Luke as a waiter wheels in a little trolley of food.

'Compliments of Grant,' says the waiter. He actually bows his head and walks back out of the room.

The smell of fresh coffee wafts over and it doesn't make me want to heave.

Luke pulls up the silver dish lids and reveals a platter of smoked salmon and eggs and one of fresh fruit.

'Cover the salmon,' I say, putting my hand over my mouth.

'How about fizzy water for breakfast?' he says, pouring me a glass.

'Perfect,' I say. 'What a bloody waste this is. It's all free and we're drinking water.'

'Maybe we'll get better as the day goes on.'

'Maybe.'

'So,' he says, going over to pick up the list of suggested activities. 'What are we going to do today? Clay-pigeon shooting?'

'I don't know if I've got the energy to wield a shotgun over my head. How about the falconry? We'll just stand there and the bird will do all the work.'

Luke winces.

'I hate birds.'

'You hate birds?'

'Uh-huh. I don't want one flying round my head. What if it landed in my hair?'

'Because it would mistake your quiff for a perch?'

'Very funny. Because I don't like them. They're like rats with wings. And those beaks and the pecking. No, I don't like them at all.'

'OK,' I say, thinking if we were a real couple how much I'd be finding out about him this weekend. 'No birds. What else is on the list?'

'Archery.'

'Too physical.'

'Yoga.'

'Too physical.'

'I'll save myself time: tennis, horse riding and cycling are all out then.'

'Is there anything left?'

'Spa.'

'Now you're talking.'

'Spa it is. I'll phone Grant and let him know.'

'I'm so delighted to show you both our new spa,' says Grant, walking us through the area. 'We upgraded it last year and it has wonderful reviews now. You're going to come out feeling like new people.'

Being a Saturday, the large pool area is full of people, relaxing in their robes on sun loungers, swimming and lazing around in the pool. I'm looking forward to lying down and indulging in one of the glossy magazines that are stocked around the room.

'Now, here's Bill, the photographer,' he says, introducing us to a middle-aged man. He shakes our hands and we all mutter a few pleasantries.

'The exciting news is, I've managed to squeeze you in for a couple's mud session,' says Grant.

'Mud?' I squeak. 'I thought we were just going to spa.'

'You are, but you simply must try the mud, it's unlike anything you will have experienced. I'll introduce you to Jacinda who'll be looking after you. Bill will come along and take photos in the middle too,' he says, bundling us into a room where there's a tall thin woman smiling at us.

'Hello, I'm Jacinda, so lovely to meet you. I'm going to be guiding you on this journey today.

'First of all you're going to get into the bath and once you're settled, I'll come in and apply the mud to your face and shoulders. I'll come back in again and press a hot towel on your face. And then once you're ready to get out, you'll shower and then I'll transfer you into the nap room.'

'Nap room,' I say, homing in on the one part of this that sounds good.

'Yes, you'll be so relaxed that you'll need it. Now, I'll leave you to get in yourselves. The best thing to do is to sit on the edge of the bath and lower yourself in gently. You'll probably need to help each other.'

'Is it going to be OK to go to the spa after if my bikini's all muddy?' I ask.

Jacinda tinkles with laughter. 'Oh no, you need to be naked in the mud. It'll stain your clothes.

'Don't worry,' she says, reacting to my look of horror. 'I'll make sure you're decent before the photographer comes along.'

Jacinda bows much like the waiter and leaves us alone in the room.

'I've always wanted to go mudding since I watched *Suits*,' says Luke.

'Me too,' I say, staring at the mud. It's much thicker and gloopier than the glossy mud from the baths in the TV programme.

'You know it's funny that people say that I'm like Harvey Specter.'

'What – because of his arrogance?' I say, thinking of the main character.

'More because of his looks.'

'If you say so,' I say, sniggering.

He gives me a hard stare before he turns back to the mud.

'I don't think I can do this,' he says.

'Thank God, I thought I was being a prude.'

'Not the getting naked part,' he says, dismissing my body insecurities with a shrug. 'It's that mud, it reminds me of…'

He doesn't need to finish that sentence.

'Tell me about it, and that smell.'

'How long did Jacinda say we'd be in here, twenty minutes?'

'That doesn't sound like a long time but I reckon it would be. What happens if we've got to go to the toilet whilst we're in there?'

We stare even harder at the mud.

'She's going to be back in a minute,' I say, not believing that I'm actually going to go through with this. 'And the photographer is coming.'

'You're right,' says Luke. He rolls his head to the sides and breathes out deeply. 'OK, I'm going in.'

He pulls his swimming trunks off and I barely have time to close my eyes before he scrambles up onto the side of the baths.

I hear lots of squelching and a couple of groans.

'It's not that bad,' he says. 'Just don't breathe in.'

I open my eyes and see he's mostly submerged. I curse like a trooper and I peel off my bikini.

'Close your eyes,' I say to Luke.

'What? You might need help.'

'You managed it, I'm sure I'll be fine. Close your eyes.'

He sighs loudly and I take that as confirmation that he has.

I climb up onto the side of the bath, practically bent over double clinging onto my boobs. I lower a foot into the mud thinking that I'm going to sink but it sort of floats and I realise that it's not going to be a graceful glide into the mud that I imagined it would be. I force myself in, inch by inch, with the poise of a beached whale.

'This is so weird. It feels like I'm floating.'

'I know, I think we are.'

'It's hot. Are you hot?'

'I'm hot,' he replies in a much calmer voice than mine.

I can feel beads of sweat forming on my forehead and I'm starting to panic. Mainly because I don't think I'd be able to get out in a hurry if I needed to.

Jacinda glides into the room just in time. She has such an air of serenity about her that I start to relax.

'How are you finding it?' she says, rubbing mud into my shoulders.

'It's lovely…' Apart from the fact I'm lying naked next to my fake boyfriend, sweating out of every pore and trying not to panic about the fact that I won't be able to escape if nature calls.

'Great. I'll send the photographer in for a few snaps. I'll make sure he doesn't stay too long as you need to have proper alone time. Such a special gift, isn't it? Time like this away from devices when you're suspended in mud unable to move and with each other's undivided attention.'

She opens the door and Bill breezes in with a large camera round his neck.

'Look at each other lovingly,' he says whilst he snaps away from all different angles.

I don't think we've ever had to hold up the pretence so long and he finally seems happy with his photos and leaves us to it. Jacinda follows behind him.

'This is pretty intense,' says Luke. 'How's your belly holding up?'

'It's OK for the moment.'

'Ten minutes left,' he says.

'Bloody hell. I'm not going to make it.'

'Sure you are. Let's talk.'

'Great. Now you want to talk. Weren't you the one that said that the up-side of our relationship was that we didn't have to?'

'Do you want sit here in silence for the next ten minutes and think about your stomach?'

'No,' I say, breathing out. 'What should we talk about?'

'How about today's football? Reading have got a good shot.'

'Anything but football,' I say groaning. I'd rather think about my belly.

'OK, do you think I should dye my hair? Go a bit blonder?'

'I think your hair's already quite blond.'

'Oh no, I don't mean on my head. I mean—'

'Stop talking. I've changed my mind about the talking.'

'Whatever.'

Another thirty seconds tick by but I realise that I can't take the silence.

'Did you always want to be an influencer?' I ask.

Since I spoke with Marissa I've been thinking a lot about why I started and why I keep going.

'Not really. I joined Insta as I thought it would get me more women.'

'Deep,' I say.

'What were you expecting me to say? That I did it because I was woefully unconfident and online I could be someone that people actually liked?'

He says it quietly and I wonder if there's any truth in it. I'm convinced he thinks mainly with his dick, but every so often I get glimpses that there's more to him. In those tiny moments, like when he passed me a flannel for my forehead when I was sick, or when he reached out to a charity close to my heart, I see flashes of who he could be.

'Of course I only did it for the women and the fame,' he says in a slightly less confident way than usual.

'Do you think you'll ever settle down?' I ask him.

'I dunno. If I met the right woman. That's the cliché, right?'

'It only takes one woman to change a man,' I say, thinking it would take one hell of a woman in Luke's case.

'It's hard, though, isn't it, to think that you'd be enough for one person. I mean, how do you know that they wouldn't get bored or see through you?'

He looks at me and it's like I see the real him for the first time. The door bursts open and Jacinda breezes in with towels on a tray and by the time I look back at Luke, the vulnerability on his face is gone.

'All OK?' she asks, defusing the mood.

'Fine,' we mumble.

'Good,' she says, rubbing a flannel over our faces. 'Just a little longer and then you can get out and shower.'

'Do you mind if I get out now?' I ask. The heat is getting to me and I don't feel quite right. Plus I want to shower without Luke.

'Sure, I'll get a wrap.'

She holds out a long cloth and helps to pull me out. It's so slippy underfoot, but she wraps me up like a mummy and leads me over to the shower.

'Are you staying in, Luke?' calls Jacinda.

'Yeah, I'm fine.'

'OK, Izzy, there are fresh towels for when you've finished and after you can lie down in the room on the left.'

I thank her and start scrubbing away at the mud. It feels quite therapeutic to get it all off. Any other day I'd take my time, but today I'm under pressure; I need to get to the bathroom.

I manage to get as much off as possible and find the nearest loo. Bloody spring rolls.

By the time that I make it back into the relaxing room, Luke is flat out on one of the beds, fast asleep.

Jacinda follows me in.

'He didn't get a lot of sleep last night,' I say before realising how awful that sounds. She gives me a little smile.

'I'll leave you two in here then. Heidi and Freda, your massage therapists, will be in in about fifteen minutes.'

'Massage therapists?'

I really don't want to be poked and prodded today.

'Uh-huh, Grant booked you in for a couple's massage. More special time.'

'Great,' I say, pretending to be happy with it.

I lie down on the bed wondering how I'm going to relax and the next thing I know I'm awake and there are two women with long blonde hair tied in matching ponytails standing over me.

'Hello, ready for your massage?'

I look over at Luke who's snoring beside me and I give him a nudge.

'Hey, what's going on?'

'Grant's arranged for us to have a massage.'

He looks up at the blonde women and immediately starts to smile. 'Work away, ladies,' he says, 'work away.'

My body starts to tense and I imagine I'm going to leave this massage more wound up than when I came in.

# Chapter 22

It takes me a while to find parking on Aidan's road, but I don't mind the little walk to his front door as it gives me time to get rid of some of my nervous energy. We're just going for a walk, two friends and a dog. I'm going to use today to prove to myself that it's possible for us to be just friends.

I find number 26, wedged in between all the other houses. It might be narrow, but it's freshly painted and neatly kept. I push open the tiny iron gate into the world's smallest front garden, which houses two tiny conifers in pots and two rubbish bins.

I ring the doorbell and a booming bark comes from the other side of the door. I always imagined Barney to be a cute, dopey Labrador but the noise makes him sound like a ferocious guard dog.

'Hey, you're bang on time,' says Aidan, opening the door a little and poking his head out. 'Are you ready to meet Barney? I should warn you he's going to be excited. The gate's shut, right?'

'Yes,' I say, turning my back for a second and when I turn back there's a 30 kilo Labrador jumping up at me. 'Oh, hello.'

'Down, Barney,' says Aidan in an authoritative voice.

Barney does what he's told and he stands in front of me wagging his tail furiously.

'It's OK,' I say, bending down to give him a proper cuddle.

'Look at you two, best of friends already.'

Aidan holds the door open for me to come in and I stand up and walk in.

'I know, best buddies,' I say, giving Barney another scratch. He lies down and rolls over and I start tickling his tummy.

'I'll leave you two to it, shall I?'

'Uh-huh,' I say as Barney starts to scratch his ears with his paws, looking incredibly cute in the process.

Aidan walks down the narrow corridor into the galley kitchen at the end and I follow him. It's not exactly a kitchen you'd lust over on Pinterest, but it's tastefully done and maximises the available space.

'So, this is nice,' I say.

'I don't know whether anyone's ever called it "nice" before. Functional, maybe,' he says, laughing.

'At least it's big enough for us to both to stand in,' I say politely.

'Yeah and Barney too.'

'How could I forget him?' I say, reaching down and scratching him behind the ear.

'So, we should go?' he asks.

'Sounds good to me.'

'I'll just grab my wellies.'

He unlocks the back door and disappears out. Barney rushes past and goes for a lap around the long and narrow garden.

Aidan comes back in with his boots a couple of minutes later.

'You've got a big garden.'

'I know, it's bigger than the house. It's why the rescue charity let me have Barney.'

'How old was he when you got him?'

'One. He didn't have a bad other life. He'd been living with an old man but he was too lively. I think it's quite common that someone has a dog for years, it dies and they get a new puppy, only they forget how much work it is and the guy's health started to fail.'

'That's really sad.'

He nods. 'I used to take Barney to see him at first, but he's got dementia and he can't always remember who we are. But luckily Barney went from him straight to me so he's never really had that whole abandonment thing going on.'

'That's good,' I say, making an extra fuss of him when he comes back in.

'Right then, let's go,' he says.

He picks up Barney's lead and I realise that Barney's excitement when I came to the door is nothing like his excitement to see the lead.

He tugs his way to the door and Aidan reaches out and grabs my hand to pull me along with them and I feel like I'm part of the gang. My heart surges in a way that it hasn't for a long, long time.

'Barney, no, Barney,' I say, trying to turn, but it's too late. Barney starts to shake and water droplets come flying out at an alarming speed and I'm soaked before I know it. Not that it matters. My jeans are covered in muddy paw prints from when I thought I'd get in on the ball-throwing action.

'Still glad you came?' says Aidan, laughing.

'Absolutely. I mean, this was the look I was going for.'

'Slightly muddy with a hint of wet,' he says, nodding. 'And I like your perfume too.'

'Soggy dog – I think it's going to catch on.'

'I'm sorry, I should have thought that everywhere would be saturated after all the rain we've been having,' he says.

'It's fine, really. Jeans can be washed. And look at him. He's having the time of his life.'

He really does look like he's the cat got that got the cream, trotting about with a stick in his mouth. It actually looks like he's smiling.

I start to shiver.

'You look cold,' says Aidan. 'I think it's time to go and warm up.'

'How about going to find somewhere to get a hot chocolate?' I say.

He looks over at Barney.

'I don't think anyone's going want him in their café.'

We watch as he rolls in yet another patch of sticky mud.

'I'm going to have to bath him,' he says, wincing. 'How about we head back to mine and I make us some hot chocolate? I can even run to the shop for marshmallows.'

'That sounds perfect,' I say, nodding. We're having such a lovely day I don't want it to end. I think we can do this platonic friends thing after all.

Half an hour later we're back at Aidan's house and I had no idea what a military operation it would be to get a wet dog into a bath. I had to wait outside holding Barney on the lead whilst Aidan lined the hallway with towels and then Barney was raced through at breakneck speed, not allowing him time to shake over the walls.

Aidan then lifted him up and plonked him in the bath where he cowered in the middle looking all sorry for himself. Now he's been hosed down he's about half his usual size. I've taken it upon myself to be the shampoo master and am having a great time washing him as it smells like bubble gum.

'Right, are you ready?' Aidan asks. 'I'm going to have to get him out. Can you grab those blue towels and make sure the door's shut?'

'Sure.'

I go over and push the door again to make sure it's secure. I hand Aidan one of the big towels that he'd got ready and I take one for myself.

'OK, so the shakes will be worse than in the park,' he says, grimacing.

I nod and shield myself behind a towel, and he lifts out Barney.

Barney's determined to escape the tiny bathroom and he shakes everywhere whilst searching for an exit. He starts to clamber over us as Aidan tries to cocoon him in a towel and by the time he swaddles him we're absolutely drenched.

'Always so relaxing going on a dog walk,' he says.

He rubs at Barney with a towel and when he's got the worst of it off, he opens the bathroom door and Barney bolts down the stairs.

We can hear him tearing up and down the wooden hallway and eventually it falls silent.

'He's probably found the blanket by the radiator in the lounge.'

'Ooh, that sounds nice,' I say, shivering.

'You must be freezing. How about we get you out of those wet clothes? Oh, I meant, I'll lend you some dry clothes. Not that I wanted to see what was underneath or…'

His cheeks look like they're going to catch on fire and I put him out of his misery.

'I knew exactly what you meant.'

He nods with relief.

'So, um, I'm guessing I won't have much that will fit you. Maybe some tracksuit bottoms or some pyjamas.'

'Because you're so much skinnier than me,' I say in mock offence.

'Oh, no, I meant that you know I've got long legs and my waist is—'

'—the same size as a small girl's. It's fine, I'm teasing. PJs are fine.'

'I can go and get them and you can wait here, or you can come with me and choose them.'

'I'll come with you, make sure you don't choose me anything too hideous.'

I follow him into his bedroom and Aidan starts digging through the chest of drawers. I take in the space, loving the fact that his bed is unmade, the blinds are still down and there are discarded clothes on the floor. I bet if Luke were having a woman to his house, his room would be hotel tidy with the assumption he'd get lucky.

'OK, so I've got these,' he says, turning round and holding out the clothes towards me when he catches me looking at the heap on his floor. 'Ah, sorry. I had a late night working and then I was up late and I thought I'd tidy the parts of the house that you were going to see. I'm not always this messy. Well, actually I kind of am, but I do try and make an effort.'

I start to laugh. I've never seen him so nervous and there's something incredibly sexy about it. The fact that he's not polished and he's shy and he's just him.

I go to take the clothes but when my hands make contact with his I feel a jolt of electricity. I immediately drop them as I fling my arms around his neck, kissing him with such force that he bumps into the chest of drawers. He doesn't seem to care and he kisses me back. His hands are in my hair and round my waist and suddenly they're tugging at my clothes.

I don't think I've ever wanted anyone as much as I want him right now. Our wet clothes drop to the floor and for the first time in a long time, nothing else seems to matter. Not my past heartbreak, not Luke and our fake relationship. The only thing that matters to me right now is Aidan.

# Chapter 23

It's been exactly twenty-four hours since I left Aidan's house and I don't think I've thought about anything else since. Goodness knows what I let slip through in the contracts today at work; I could have insured a mission to Mars for all I know, my mind was definitely not on the job.

I've barely made it through the door of my flat when I hear the intercom buzz.

'Hello,' I say, pressing the button to answer it.

'It's me, let me in,' says Marissa.

I just about have time to go into the kitchen and make a cup of tea for her before she knocks at the door.

'Blimey, look at that bump. It enters the room minutes before you.'

'I know, I ate quite a lot yesterday and it seems to have to have doubled in size.'

'Are you sure you've got your due date right and it's not about to pop out?'

I'm starting to panic; she's supposed to have another month to go. We're already cutting it fine with the surprise baby shower we've got planned in a few weeks as it is.

'Pretty sure. When you're married you only have sex once in a blue moon so it's easy to keep track of it.'

I laugh and we walk into the living room where she collapses into the sofa.

'You know, I didn't come all the way here to talk about my bump. You've got to put me out of my misery, tell me about you and Aidan.'

'What do you want to know?'

'Um, everything. Start at the beginning.'

I put her tea down for her on the coffee table and sit on the other end of the sofa.

'OK, we took Barney the dog for a walk at Basildon Park, you know the National Trust place?'

She shakes her head.

'It'll be a good place for you to go with the baby. It's got all this parkland with beautiful knotty trees. Barney absolutely loved it and he was tearing about in all the mud.'

'Got it, nature, mud, yes, yes, yes, but get to the good stuff. This baby could come at any second and then all I'd be left with is the bit about the leaves. I need to hear this, I may never have sex myself again, this is all I have left.'

'I'm pretty sure that other people have sex after they've had a baby. That's why people have siblings.'

'Yeah, but not for months after. Months!'

'OK,' I say, not wishing to induce early labour with her getting worked up. It's been a nightmare planning her baby shower as it is. 'So Barney, the dog, got really muddy.'

She throws me dagger eyes.

'There's a point to this part of the story.' I hold my hands up in defence. 'He got really muddy rolling in all these puddles, which meant he needed a bath and then we got even more wet. Which got us wet too and then we had to change.'

The look of anger subsides and a smile creeps over her face.

'And, you know, I was getting changed and then...'

'You suddenly had no need for clothes. Go on.'

'What! Marissa, I'm not going any further than that.'

'Come on, we all know where this story is heading and you've left out all the good bits.'

'And that's exactly the way it's going to stay.'

'So how was it?'

I close my eyes and I could almost be back there.

'It was lovely.'

'Ooh, lovely,' she says sarcastically. 'I bet he'd be well pleased to hear it described like that,' she says, picking up her hot tea and blowing on it.

'OK, it was sexy and hot and for a first time with someone, pretty damn good.'

'I guess pretty damn good is slightly better than lovely.'

'However I describe it, it'll sound lame and you know, it's actually private.'

Marissa has never been one for boundaries.

'Anyway, after that he lent me some PJs and his dressing gown and we sat on the sofa under a duvet for the rest of the afternoon and watched cheesy films.'

'That actually sounds cute,' she says and I see tears welling up in the corners of her eyes.

'Oh no, don't start crying,' I say.

'I'm not, I'm not,' she says, putting down her tea and rubbing at her eyes.

'You are, you're crying.'

'Ah, don't. It's these bloody hormones. They're raging. One minute I've got the horn, the next I'm crying. It's ridiculous.'

A key goes in the lock and I get back up to reboil the kettle.

'Hey,' says Becca as she walks through to the lounge unwrapping her scarf and pulling off her heavy wool coat. 'What did I miss?'

She sits down on one of the dining-table chairs and pulls off her boots.

'She didn't tell us any good bits,' says Marissa. 'She skipped right over them the minute the clothes came off in the story.'

Becca breaks into a smile. 'But the clothes came off and there is a story. So much for all this, "we're just friends".'

She and Marissa exchange knowing glances. I ignore them both.

'I knew there was more to your text than "let's have a girls' night in",' she says with a squeal.

Becca stayed at Gareth's house last night and I'd texted her and Marissa arranging tonight, not wanting to give too much away in a message.

'I can't believe that you've found someone you really like,' says Becca. 'So when are you going to end things with Luke?'

'I hadn't even thought about that,' says Marissa, curling her hands around her mug of tea once more. 'But of course you're going to have to stage your break-up. You can't risk anyone finding out you've got a real boyfriend.'

I sit back down on the sofa and the smile finally leaves my face.

'I don't know what I'm going to do yet. Things with Aidan might have been a one off. He's said to me before that he's not looking for a relationship and I don't know if I want one either. And then there's the whole timing thing – things are going so well with my Instagram account...'

'Izzy, are you just putting obstacles in the way?' asks Marissa. 'From the tiny snippets that you've told me it sounds like Aidan's well into you.'

Becca nods in agreement.

'I think you're just scared of getting hurt, but you've got to take a risk.'

'Easier said than done,' I say, sighing.

'Izzy, if I can get over what I did to start dating, so can you,' says Becca a little sternly and my hackles go up.

'Look,' I say, 'having someone you trust completely violate that trust – it makes you doubt everything.'

'Having someone who never stopped loving you wasn't exactly easy either,' she says.

'I wasn't comparing the situations!' I cry.

Becca and I never argue but I feel like we're teetering on the edge of something here and I don't know why.

'Look, Izzy,' says Marissa, weighing in. 'What Cameron did to you was shitty, but please don't let an arsehole like that get in the way of something really special. And as for the Instagram stuff, I know why it's been so important to you, but is it really worth choosing it over someone like Aidan?'

'I have been thinking about it,' I say honestly. 'Regardless of whether anything more happens with Aidan, I'm going to talk to Luke about ending things. It's time to see if I can make it as an influencer standing on my own two feet. We always knew we were going to have an endgame, it's time we set a date.'

'Set a date?' says Becca. 'That makes it sound like you're dragging it out.'

'Well, we've got a few sponsored posts for December and Luke's talking to Heart2Heart about a fundraiser; we can't really let people down.'

'And how's Aidan going to feel about you fake dating someone until you're finished?'

I bite my lip. 'I don't see why I'd need to tell him. He hates social media with a passion and explaining to him would make it seem worse than it is. It's not like I'm actually dating Luke.'

'Lying to him about something like that isn't really a great foundation for a relationship,' says Becca.

'Um, isn't that exactly what you've done with Gareth not telling him about Ben?' I snap.

'That's different and you know it.'

I take a deep breath to stop this from escalating.

'Look, there's no point in thinking about me and Aidan, as right now there isn't a me and Aidan. We're two friends that had sex. Lots of friends do it.'

'We've never done it,' says Marissa.

I pull a face.

'You know what I mean. People have sex all the time and it doesn't mean to say they're in a relationship. I'm just going to see what happens.'

'Life's too short, Izzy,' says Becca with an exasperated sigh. 'I think you're making a huge mistake.'

I'm taken aback by Becca. She's always been one to dole out sisterly advice but she's never done it with any judgement.

An awkward silence hangs in the air and Marissa starts to edge her way off the sofa.

'This baby's giving me gyp, she won't sit still,' she says.

'Are you OK?' I ask.

I'm not convinced that it's the baby making her feel uncomfortable.

'Yeah, fine. I think I'm going to go home and have a lukewarm bath. Do you mind?'

'Of course not.' I'm lying as I want her to stay and protect me from the wrath of Becca.

She prises herself off the sofa, rubbing her belly before she walks perfectly normally over to the front door, convincing me it was all an act to escape. 'I'll see you in the week.'

'Yes, of course.'

I give her a hug before she leaves and I wish I could go with her but I know I have to get to the bottom of what's really going on with Becca. I take a deep breath before I walk back towards the lounge.

Becca's taken Marissa's spot on the sofa and I can feel my body tensing. She looks up at me and her glare has been replaced by a weak smile.

'I'm sorry, I shouldn't have said any of that.'

I sit down and curl my legs up to my chest.

'You're probably right though.'

'I still shouldn't have said it. It's your life, you should be able to do what you want with it.'

Becca starts to cry and I lean over to comfort her.

'Hey, no, you were saying it because you care.'

'I do care,' she says, sniffing. 'But I was really mean.'

'I get it. You think Aidan's special like Ben was to you and you don't want me to lose him.'

She half laughs. 'Well, that is true,' she says, wiping a tear. 'I do know what it's like to lose someone, and so do you, but that's not why I snapped.'

'What is it? What's wrong?'

There has to be more to this than my love life.

'It's Gareth.'

I tilt my head, preparing to comfort her; a break-up would destroy her.

'What about him?' I say, fearing the worst.

'Last night he told me he loved me.'

I'm totally shocked and for a second I can't speak.

'And you feel the same way?' I say.

She rolls the sleeve of her cardigan over her hand before she wipes her face and nods.

'Oh, Bec.' I pull her into a hug. 'It's OK.'

She tries to laugh through her tears. 'It's ridiculous, isn't it? I'm upset that I'm in love with someone who loves me.'

'It's not ridiculous, it's understandable.'

Grief causes so many different emotions but the one that always catches me out is guilt. Some days I feel so guilty about all the times as kids that I said horrible things to Ben or about how I teased him that our parents loved me more. But most of all I feel guilty when I'm having fun instead of feeling sad that he's no longer here. I can't begin to fathom how much guilt Becca carries on her shoulders.

'I loved Ben so much and I thought I was going to spend the rest of my life with him. I know that we didn't take those vows, but we were engaged for so long that's exactly how I felt. And then Gareth... he's great. He's so different to Ben, but he's got the same generous spirit and I love him, I really do, but...'

'But?'

She takes a deep breath and the tears start flowing again.

'I can't help feeling like I'm cheating on Ben.'

I swallow back the lump in my throat. I find it difficult to imagine Becca with anyone other than my brother either, but she can't live her life in the past. She has to move forward.

'He would have wanted you to move on, you know that, don't you? He wanted nothing more than for you to be happy and he would have hated to think that he was stopping you.'

She nods quickly.

'I know, I know. If it was the other way round I'd want him to be meeting other people and moving on.'

'Then that's what you've got to keep in mind.'

'It doesn't make it any easier to do, though, does it?'

I give her another squeeze.

'I thought it would be years and years before I'd ever fall in love again. I didn't expect it to be so soon.'

'You can't measure these things. Only you know how you feel and if it's the right time. We all know how much you loved Ben and how you would still be with him now if he was here, but he's not and no one will blame you for moving on.'

'But your mum and dad, they've been so great to me over the years.'

'And they still will be. It doesn't change a thing. They just want you to be happy too.'

She rests her head on my shoulder, like she's done so many times since I moved in with her. It's the whole reason I moved in in the first place. I know that Ben would have wanted me to look after her just like I know he would want me to encourage her to be with Gareth now. But it doesn't make it any easier to deal with.

'Do you want me to put on *Gilmore Girls*?' I say.

'Yes, please.'

I find the remote and bring up Netflix; it's our go-to binge watch when we're upset. I've lost count of how many times we've watched all seven series.

My phone buzzes just as the opening segment starts and I see that I've got messages from both Aidan and Luke.

I look at Aidan's first. It's a picture of Barney looking at the camera with his sad eyes and it's captioned:

Aidan:
Barney wants to go on another walk sometime, are you up for it?

I desperately want to say yes until I read the message from Luke.

> Luke:
> Just got an email from Heart2Heart. They asked if they could offer dinner with us as an auction prize at the Valentine's Ball! I reckon we're going to get them loads of money!

In the heat of the moment with Aidan it felt like nothing else mattered. But other things do matter. There are so many people I'd let down if I suddenly stopped our showmance: Luke, our sponsors, the charity, Ben. I've never felt so torn between two worlds.

Life might be so much easier with a fake boyfriend, where there's absolutely no fear of having my heart broken, but it's stopping me from having a real life. I've got to decide what I really want and then I can work out how to get it without hurting anyone or letting anyone down.

# Chapter 24

I shut the car door and take a deep breath. I can do this. It's just ending a simple business transaction. I stand on the kerb, fussing at my hair and deep breathing until I finally pull myself together.

I ring the doorbell and Luke is standing there looking ridiculous wearing an apron and holding a wooden spoon in his hand.

'You're early,' he says, leaving me standing on the doorstep.

My teeth start chattering in the cold.

'I think I'm right on time. Are you going to ask me in, it's freezing out here.'

'Um, sure, why not.'

I follow him into the kitchen where there's all manner of activity going on. The extractor fan is whirring away, pans are bubbling and boiling over on the hob and he opens the oven and steam rushes out. And then there are the smells: garlic, lemon and rosemary; my nostrils kick into overdrive.

'You're going to a lot of trouble; I thought we were going to get a pizza?' I say, leaning over his shoulder to see what's on the hob. 'Don't tell me, you thought you'd snap some photos of us eating and then your real date is coming over. If that's the case you better have a doggy bag for me.'

'I cooked it all for you.'

I look over at the sauce he's mixing. He's really gone to a lot of effort, which is crazy since smashed avocado on toast is dead easy and dead Instagrammable.

'My stomach is very pleased. I've only just started to fancy food again, after, well you know.'

On the couple of occasions I've seen Luke since our weekend away, neither of us has been able to mention the food-poisoning incident. It's a wonder that we can still look each other in the eye after what we saw.

'Me too, I think that's why I got carried away. But you'll be pleased to know that everything is vegan. I figure you can't go too far wrong with plant-based food.'

'Very sensible. And very on trend. Great for the hashtags.'

'Absolutely. So I had an email back from Grant and he was really happy with how the campaign's been going. They've had good feedback on their new brochure too.'

'That's great.'

'He said that he'd really like to collaborate with us again in the future.'

'Oh, really?' I say, picking at my nails. Now would be the ideal time to tell him that I want out of our relationship.

'I also heard back from the Heart2Heart people. And they've already sold all the tickets for our table.'

'But they're charging £200 a ticket.'

'I know and they've already sold the eight available.'

'Wow, really?'

'Uh-huh, and of course they're still going to offer dinner with us as an auction prize. They hope we'll be auctioned off for thousands.'

My hands start to go clammy.

'Thousands?' I say, wondering both who would pay that and how I couldn't deny Heart2Heart that kind of money.

I think how many families like mine that could be spared the pain of losing someone close to them.

'So the dinner would be after Valentine's Day?'

'Yep. I'd imagine late February, early March.'

I nod. That's more time pretending. I think of Aidan; either I'll have to tell him the truth or I'll have to stop something before it starts with him. It's one thing to lie to strangers on the internet, it's quite another to lie to someone I really care for.

'So is the food nearly ready?' I need to change the subject and to stop myself from feeling sick.

'Almost,' he says, tasting the sauce on the hob with a little spoon before adding more pepper.

I sit down at the little kitchen table until he plates up the food. I'm waiting patiently for him to pop it down in front of me but he hovers with the plates in his hand.

'Shall we go through into the dining room?' he asks.

'The dining room,' I say in my best posh voice. 'Aren't we going to eat here?'

'Not tonight.'

I follow him out of the kitchen and I push open the door to the dining room as he's got his hands full – and I gasp. He's really gone to town for the Instagram photo. His trademark fairy lights have got another outing but it's the table that's the main focus with a silk runner down the middle, fancy-looking candles, as well as every piece of cutlery imaginable.

'Wow, you've been busy,' I say as he places the food down on the mats.

'Take a seat.'

I do as I'm told, taking the napkin from my place setting and put it on my lap, something I never do but this is so formal I feel like I should.

Luke sits down opposite me.

'Oh, I should pop the camera on to record this.'

'Definitely.'

He slides his phone into his selfie stick and holds it out whilst we pull suitably cheesy faces and point at the mouthwatering food.

'Got it,' he says, retrieving the phone and tapping away to post them.

'I had no idea you were such a good cook,' I say between mouthfuls. 'Were you not tempted to do the Great Office Bake Off?'

'God no, I can't bake. But I'm secretly hoping that they do an inter-office version of *Masterchef*.'

'Don't say that. I couldn't cope with another competition. Mrs Harris is a nervous wreck at the moment. Shouting at us one minute, bursting into tears the next.'

'She did really well to get into the final. Miles is intolerable.'

We discuss the highs and lows of the previous rounds and I shovel in the food until my plate is clear.

'That was delicious.'

I put my knife and fork down on my plate and rub my satisfied belly.

'There's more. I've made dessert.'

'Dessert? What type of dessert?'

'You'll see,' he says, picking up my plate and his and a small smile spreads over his face as he leaves.

'What a tease,' I mutter to myself.

He comes in carrying a tray with a plastic dish over the top.

'I thought we could do an Instagram Live.'

'For the dessert reveal? I like it.'

'OK,' he says, taking a deep breath. He's shaking, which is

weird as he doesn't usually get nervous. What on earth is under that plastic dish?

He does a thumbs up to let me know we're live and then he launches into character.

'So, Izzy and I are having a romantic meal in.'

'Luke just cooked the best meal, take a look at my Insta stories for pictures.'

'Thanks, honey, but the best is yet to come, here's the dessert.'

I do a drumroll on the table with my fingers and he lifts the lid to reveal it.

'Oh my God, is that chocolate cheesecake?' I say, my jaw dropping.

'Nutella cheesecake.'

'Ah, Luke, marry me right now,' I say, trying not to drool on camera.

'Funny you should say that,' he says, dropping to his knees.

I'm too busy staring at the cheesecake at first to process what is going on, but then something small and sparkly catches my eye and I notice that he's down beside me on one knee.

'Izzy Brown, will you marry me?'

I'm about to collapse into hysterics – he got me good there, that ring even looks like it's real, but then I see the phone and remember that he's recording.

'Well, sweetie,' he says, turning to talk to the screen. 'What's she going to say, folks, is it going to be a yes?'

He thrusts the ring box closer towards me and for the first time in my life I'm speechless. I'm hit by a plethora of emotions: surprise, horror, anger, confusion. What the bloody hell is he doing?

'Izzy,' he repeats again.

I don't have time to think about it. If I say no, I'll come across as a heartless bitch and shatter everyone's perception of the couple we are. I'll no longer be able to walk away with a shrug and an 'it didn't work out but I've got a best friend for life' spiel. I think of what a big deal the Heart2Heart event is and how much good we could do with the fame we're riding.

'Izzy?'

There's a hint of desperation and I look down at the ring one last time. It's not like if I say yes I have to go through with the whole wedding thing, is it? I mean, it would be better to say yes and then we break up behind closed doors?

'Yes,' I say, trying to feign enthusiasm and Luke leaps up and pulls me into a giant hug.

He kisses the top of my head and slips the ring on my finger before waving it in front of the camera.

'We're going to carry on our private celebrations now,' says Luke. 'But I am the happiest man on the planet at this moment in time. She said yes!'

He does a fist pump and then switches the live feed off before he turns back to me and sighs with relief.

'What the fuckety fuck were you doing? That wasn't part of the plan. We're supposed to date for a while and then break up.'

'Listen, don't get mad.'

'Don't get mad? Don't get mad? You just railroaded me into marrying you.'

'Hang on, we're only engaged, that's all. Just listen to what I have to say. Grant was telling me that if we were engaged he'd pay us to have the wedding there. We'd just have to go to their wedding fayre and sample their foods and—'

'And get married? This isn't some joke anymore, Luke. This is real life. I've got this great guy who I'm falling for, but I'm keeping him at arm's length.'

'A guy you're falling for? Izzy! What the fuck? You know you're not supposed to get involved with anyone. What if someone saw you?'

'Oh and like you haven't seen anyone since we started "dating",' I say, doing cringey air quotes. 'You bought Meredith on a flipping date with us.'

'That was different, firstly because you were there with us and secondly that was the last time I saw her.'

'I wonder why,' I say, thinking that it was hardly romantic.

'Because I'm not fucking stupid and I realised what I'd done wrong. Now is not the time to be gallivanting around with someone else.'

'Aidan and I have only been out as friends so far, but I can't help it, we just clicked and I want to see where it goes with him.'

'*We just clicked?* Fucking hell, Izzy. You know we're on the cusp here. We're influencers now. This isn't a dream anymore. It's a reality. This is the start of our new life.'

'But at what cost? The thing with Aidan, I think it could be something special, I can't jeopardise it for this. I mean, where does it end? We get engaged and then get married, and then what, we pop out a couple of kids?'

'Look, it's just an engagement and you've done the hard work now, you've said yes. Everyone is going to go crazy.'

I pick up my phone and already my last post has thousands of likes and hundreds of comments. Everyone is telling me how lucky I am and congratulating me on our engagement.

'Grant is offering us £10,000. Do you know what that means? It means that this is becoming financially viable. We could quit our jobs. We could—'

'Luke, you're not getting this. This isn't just a thing on Instagram anymore. It's our real lives.'

‘I know,’ he says, shouting. ‘This is real. That one sponsor is willing to pay half my annual basic salary. We can’t just walk away from this. Don’t tell me that you don’t need the money.’

I close my eyes. Of course I do. I’m struggling from pay cheque to pay cheque in a job that I know I don’t want to do forever. This would offer me an easy way out, but that doesn’t mean to say it’s the easy decision to make.

‘Will you at least think about it? Things haven’t changed between us, it’s just a ring you put on for our dates. We get more money. Job done.’

I think about Ben and why I wanted to be an influencer and about how many lives Heart2Heart could save with the money we might help them raise. I stare at the fake diamond and I feel myself dying a little more on the inside when I nod.

‘OK, I’ll do it. I’ll go through with this thing on the condition that this is *it*. We get engaged until just after the charity ball on Valentine’s Day, then we’re breaking up amicably, OK? Our follower numbers should be big enough by then for us to be influencers in our own right.’

‘OK.’

‘And I am categorically not going to try on any wedding dresses, do you hear?’

He nods. He’s got a small smile on his face and I can tell he’s trying to suppress an even bigger one.

‘Are you going to eat the cheesecake?’ he asks, cutting a slice.

‘I am so mad at you right now.’

‘So you don’t want a slice?’

‘Of course I bloody do, then I’m going.’

‘But we’ve got to plan and take a post-engagement photo.’

I glare at him as I take a bite. It’s to die for but I’m not going to show any signs of enjoyment.

'OK, so we can plan December's posts another time, but we've got to at least take a photo for our feeds. We can't waste this opportunity.'

I sigh loudly and put down my fork on the empty plate.

'If we take the photo I'm taking the rest of the cheesecake home.'

'Of course.'

'And it's definitely just until after Valentine's Day?'

'Just after the hype has calmed down, March at the latest.'

'End of February at the latest,' I say, gritting my teeth.

Three months. That doesn't seem that long. Aidan and I still haven't worked out what we are and I've still got to tell him about being an influencer. Maybe if I told him the whole truth, he'd understand. Either way it's only three months and then I can live my life without lies.

# Chapter 25

I'm pacing up and down by the front door, looking between my clipboard and my watch.

'How are we doing?' asks Becca, a panicked looked on her face.

'We're still missing Carla, and the mums.'

Becca nods. 'I'll phone Carla, and have you tried your mum?'

'Yes, but she won't answer the phone when she's driving, it's far too dangerous in her book.'

'Even with hands-free?'

'Don't get me started,' I say, taking a deep breath. 'Marissa's going to be here any minute.'

'Don't worry, I'm sure they'll make it on time.'

I look at my watch for the zillionth time.

'They better.'

Who knew planning a surprise baby shower would be so stressful? I thought it was bad enough co-ordinating everyone's diary to make sure Marissa's nearest and dearest would be able to attend before the baby graduated from university, but on top of nearly everyone running late, Marissa's been getting Braxton Hicks for the last few days and I've been terrified she was going to go into labour early and my hard work would be wasted.

I peer into the lounge; at least everyone is having a good time.

I'm looking forward to Marissa arriving so I can relax and start to mingle.

The door buzzes and I walk over to the intercom with trepidation.

'Hello,' I say, hoping that Marissa's not early.

'Hi, it's Carla.'

'Oh, thank God,' I say, sighing with relief. 'Come on up.'

I tick her off my list and circle mine and Marissa's mum's names. I'm starting to wish that I'd personally gone and collected them. Marissa's mum Karen is a little bit of a liability and is a terrible secret-keeper so I made Mum invite her out for coffee and offer to pick her up. But they were supposed to be here half an hour ago.

There's a knock at the door and I open it for Carla, who's one of our old school friends, and she wraps me in a warm hug.

'How are you?' she says, squeezing me tight.

'I'm OK,' I say, nodding. I know she's really asking how am I after Ben. It's what happens when I see someone for the first time in a while.

'Good,' she says, drifting off towards Becca to do the same.

The door buzzes again and I pray that it's my mum's voice that I hear.

'Hello, Izzy?' she says. Thank God.

'Come up quickly!'

I tick them off my list and I pop my clipboard down in the kitchen. I help myself to a couple of canapés, feeling relieved that I might just have pulled this off.

There's a knock at the door and I open it. Marissa's mum Karen waltzes straight through into the lounge and clasps her hands over her mouth when she sees the party.

'Oh my goodness, this is amazing. A baby shower, for us,' she says, turning to me and enveloping me in a big hug.

I want to point out that we're throwing Marissa a shower, but I bite my tongue. Karen's always had a bit of an issue with attention. Her mother-of-the-bride outfit was all white and looked suspiciously like a low-key wedding dress.

She pulls away from the hug and I notice that she's wearing a sparkly T-shirt that says KEEP CALM, I'M GOING TO BE A GRANDMA. Something tells me she might have had an inkling this was happening.

'It's such a surprise,' she says, turning to the room again. 'I had absolutely no idea. It's so wonderful you could all make it.'

The door buzzes again and it can only be one person.

'Right everyone, hush, hush, this will be her,' I say, thinking at least that it's temporarily stopped Karen from being the centre of attention. An excited hush falls over the room and all eyes are on me walking over to the intercom. 'Hello,' I say, trying to keep the nervous excitement out of my voice.

'Hi, Izzy? It's me, Aidan.'

There are a few murmurs round the room at the male voice.

'Oh, hi,' I say, wishing that the whole room wasn't listening to this. It's been two weeks since we slept together, which was also the last time I saw him. It's not that I haven't wanted to see him, it's just that I know if I do I'll have to tell him about Luke and I haven't been brave enough. So instead, much to the delight of my boss, Howard, I've been jumping at the chance of any overtime in the evenings and over the weekend, as an excuse not to see him.

'Can I come up? We need to talk.'

I take my finger off the intercom and sigh. We do need to talk but now is not the time. Marissa is due in five minutes and I've got a room full of women, not to mention my mother is here and no doubt she's hanging off every word.

'Now's not really a good time,' I say, turning and looking at Mum who's smiling like all her Christmases have come at once.

'It seems like it never is. But I really want to see you.'

'I want to see you too,' I say in a low whisper, not comfortable that everyone is hearing this. 'But now, really, really isn't a good time.'

'Right,' he says and I can hear that his patience is wearing thin. 'I guess I should have believed you when you said you weren't interested in a relationship. It was just that that sex was—'

'Come up!' I scream. I buzz open the door and keep huddled over the intercom panel, too embarrassed to make eye contact with the room.

'Izzy Brown, you've been keeping secrets,' says Mum, walking up to me with a huge smile on her face. I bet she's already planning her hat for the wedding.

'It's very early days,' I say to her.

'Doesn't sound like it's that early,' she says. 'I want to hear all about it.'

I look at all the other women who are still staring at me.

'Yes, Mum, and as I said to Aidan – now is not a good time.'

There's a knock at the door and I hurry over to open it.

Despite our audience, my heart swells as I see Aidan standing there.

'I'm sorry to drop in on you like this, but I had to see you,' he says.

'And I wanted to see you too,' I say, realising I've been a complete idiot putting my fake relationship with Luke first.

He leans over to kiss me and I hear a cough from behind.

Aidan breaks away and I watch a look of horror spreading over his face when he sees the room full of women.

'Ah, when you said it was a bad time…' he says, clocking the balloons and baby shower paraphernalia.

‘Yeah, I wasn’t lying. I do want to see you,’ I say, reaching out and squeezing his hand. ‘But it’s Marissa’s baby shower.’

‘Um-hmm, so I see.’

‘Did you want to stay?’

‘As much as I’ve always wanted to bob for dummies,’ he says, pointing at the big sign next to a big tub of water, ‘I think I’ll leave you to it. I’m actually on my way to my mate’s for the weekend in Southampton and I saw the signs for Basingstoke and I thought I’d come by on the off chance. Can we meet up one night in the week or next weekend?’

‘Come round again next weekend,’ I say, relieved that he doesn’t seem too mad at me. ‘That way we’ll have time to talk properly. I’ll call you.’

He raises an eyebrow.

‘I promise I will.’

He smiles and he turns to go when the intercom buzzes again.

‘Hello,’ I say, watching him go.

‘Hey, buzz me up, I’m busting for a wee and I might not make it,’ says Marissa.

I gasp, I’d momentarily forgotten all about her arrival and I press the button releasing the door. I turn to Aidan and notice he’s gone really pale.

‘Did everyone hear what I said?’ he says, whispering.

‘Yep, including Mum.’

He turns to look over his shoulder and she gives him a huge wave; she’s positively beaming and despite the fact I’m mortified, I realise how nice it is seeing her looking happy.

He gives her a little wave and tells us all to have a good time before he hurries out the door. But there’s no time to dwell on him now.

‘Right, everyone, *hide*,’ I shout. ‘She’ll be here any second.’

Some of the guests squeeze behind the sofa and others behind the dining table. Everyone's just in their place when Marissa knocks on the door.

She doesn't waste any time with pleasantries and barges straight to the loo.

'You would not believe the week I've been having,' shouts Marissa from behind the bathroom door. 'My mum is driving me bonkers. Did you know she wants to be there at the birth? Can you imagine? She'd be barging the midwife out the way and catching the baby as she pops out so that it would all be about her and how she single-handedly delivered the baby.'

I look over in horror at the direction of the standing lamp that Karen's feebly attempted to hide behind. She's pursing her brightly painted lips.

'I'm sure it would be lovely to have her with you. Offer that loving support,' I shout back. I can hear her washing her hands on the other side.

'Have you hit your head?' she says, walking out of the bathroom. 'We're talking about my mum, not yours. Do you know she's asked me not to have the baby the second week in December because she's got her work Christmas do and she doesn't want to miss it.'

'Surprise!' shouts Karen, jumping out into the middle of the room, forcing Marissa to turn and face the lounge. I didn't think anyone could look more shocked than Aidan did earlier.

Marissa's other friends and family belatedly jump out and shout half-hearted surprises at different times. It's not quite how I'd planned it.

Marissa's doing an awful lot of deep breathing and I'm starting to wonder if throwing a surprise party for a heavily pregnant woman was a good idea. What if she's gone into so much shock that the baby comes along right now?

'Oh my God,' says Marissa, staring at me. 'A baby shower. Wow. Aren't I the lucky one? Everyone I love in one room. And even my mother is here.'

She looks at everyone and then back at me with her eyebrow raised.

'Thanks, Izzy,' she leans over and hugs me and whispers in my ear. 'Shit, do you think my mum heard?'

'Yep,' I whisper back.

'Bollocks and I can't even drink.'

'None of us can,' I say, regretting that we'd made it a dry shower in solidarity of Marissa.

She puts a big, brave smile on her face and turns to face the room.

I watch her tense as her mum slips her arm around her daughter.

'Darling, isn't this wonderful, a baby shower for our little one?' says Karen.

'Yes, it's great,' she says, wriggling away and greeting everyone who has come up to fuss over her and her bump.

'So... Aidan seemed nice,' says Mum, sidling up to me.

'Yes, he is. Right, we've got a big schedule of games, we should really get started,' I say, grabbing my clipboard then flicking over the itinerary.

'Oh really, don't we get a little bit of time for a chat?'

'No, no, we've got to do the ice breaker. Right, everyone!' I shout over the excited chatter. 'Let's do the "guess the person from their baby picture" game.'

Everyone pushes towards the photos pegged to a line of string hanging along the length of the room and I stand back and catch my breath. It might not have gone to plan what with Aidan, late arrivals and Karen's attention-seeking, but I'm determined to get this back on track and give Marissa the baby shower she deserves.

Welcome to December
This_Izzy_Loves IGTV
No. followers: 20.3K

*Isn't Christmas truly the most magical time of the year? People are walking around happy and there are twinkling lights everywhere. Not to mention the Christmas music that I am blasting.*

*So let's do the monthly round-up. I don't think there's any escaping this blingy addition to my finger! After a totally romantic weekend away at Ingleford Manor Hotel where we spent the time cocooned in our amazing room and relaxing in their luxurious spa, and enjoying an eight-course tasting dinner (yes, eight!) I guess we fell even more for each other. Luke popped the question a few weeks later and I of course said, 'Yes!' I want to say a big, hearty thank you to everyone who has sent us a message to congratulate us and to the lovely companies that have gifted us products too. We're looking at a long engagement, but whatever happens, we'll take you along for the ride!*

# Chapter 26

Aidan rings my doorbell and this time I buzz him straight up, excited to see him. I pat down my curls and glance in the hall mirror to make sure I look OK. I feel like a jingly bag of nerves and can't quite settle until he knocks on the door.

'Hey, you,' I say, opening it.

He peers over my shoulder. 'No large pack of women hiding in your lounge today?'

Aidan takes a step closer to me and leans over and kisses me. My resolve of telling him the truth is weakening as he starts to run his hand down my back.

I eventually manage to prise myself away from him for long enough to drag him into the lounge; I've got to tell him the truth before anything happens.

'So, did you get your presents?' I ask. Aidan had stopped off to do some Christmas shopping in town before he came here.

'Yes, my mum will be very happy. She's difficult to buy for but there's a hand cream that she loves that's proved tricky to get hold of, and they had it here.'

I sit down on the couch and Aidan sits next to me. He rests his hand on my thigh and it feels so natural.

'Are you spending Christmas with your parents?' I ask.

'Yeah, my brother and his girlfriend are coming too, and my grandad.'

I'm jealous that he's going to have a big family Christmas; ours seem so quiet now it's just me, Mum and Dad.

'What are your Christmases like?' I ask.

'Mental. There are people everywhere. Mum has an open-door policy when it comes to Christmas, so all the neighbours will pop in at some point. Then my aunts and uncles and all my cousins come in the evening. We seem to have to eat and drink every time someone new comes in.'

'Sounds intense.'

'It is; we all just sit on the couch on Boxing Day ignoring each other, too busy recovering from the chaos. How about you, what are your Christmases like?'

I smile at first, until I remember. 'They used to be noisy and fun and—' I can feel myself choking up a little. 'The last couple have been…'

'Sorry,' says Aidan, reaching over and squeezing my hand. 'I didn't think.'

'No, it's OK. I almost didn't either. I still think of them as being Ben and me arguing over who gets the remote and us all arguing over *Trivial Pursuit*. The first year was awful. None of us could face spending it in the house, so Dad booked us a package holiday to Portugal. It was weird and warm and it didn't feel like Christmas. Then last year we stayed at the house but it was so quiet. It was just the three of us and we kept finding ourselves staring at the chair he should have been sitting in until Becca popped over in the afternoon.'

'Are you going away this year?'

I shake my head.

'No, my dad suggested it but I think we've realised that it's hard wherever we are. I'm dreading it but I'll focus on remembering the good times. Like how we have a star and an angel on the Christmas tree because Ben always said it had to be a star and I always said it had to be an angel. And he always bought something handmade like fudge or Christmas cookies. I have no idea when it started, it wasn't like him at all as he hated cooking, but he'd always do it.'

I don't even realise that I've started crying until Aidan pulls me into him.

'It's silly, isn't it, because it's not like I expected that we were going to spend every Christmas together forever more. He sometimes went to Becca's parents' house but we'd always see him at some point in the day.'

'Will you see Becca this year?'

'No, she's going to her parents' and then to see Gareth in the evening. I am happy that she's moving on and going to her new boyfriend's, but I'm going to miss her.' I wipe my tears and try and smile. 'So much for us getting in the Christmas spirit.'

'Yeah, how dare you put a dampener on the mood,' he says, stroking my hair. 'You know… I'm available on Christmas Day. I play a pretty mean game of Monopoly and I specialise in being awkward in television choices. *The Great Escape* versus *Mary Poppins*; *The Great Escape* wins every time.'

I wrinkle my nose and shake my head.

'*The Great Escape*? You know you've spent the last few months conning me into thinking that you've got the same awesome taste in movies as me, but come on. Seriously?'

'Oh yeah. It's right up there with *The Guns of Navarone*, *The Eagle Has Landed*.'

I scrunch up my face even further.

'I thought I knew you,' I say, laughing.

'Joking aside, I can come round for a bit. You know, make up the numbers for board games. If you don't think it's too weird.'

'Um, wouldn't your family miss you?'

'I'm sure with all the comings and goings they wouldn't notice if I snuck out for a couple of hours.'

'OK, but you know my parents are going to be there, right? And you'd have to meet them.'

He nods slowly.

'I've sort of met your mum already, and she seemed pleased to see me.'

'Yes, but if you met them properly then they'd like you and want to see you again.'

'Would that be so bad?' he says, raising an eyebrow.

'I guess not. Will you bring Barney?'

'Do you want me to?'

'Of course I do.'

Now he's the one that doesn't look so sure.

'You know he wreaks havoc wherever he goes.'

'That's exactly why you should bring him.'

'OK, but it's on your head.'

I laugh and he smiles back and I know this is the moment that I've got to be honest.

'You know, I've been meaning to talk to you about something.'

He's got the same contented happy smile that I seem to have been sporting a lot lately. I hope he's still looking like that after I tell him what I've got to say.

'Sounds ominous.'

'It doesn't have to be,' I say, taking a deep breath. 'It's just—'

My phone starts to ring and I stare at it vibrating across the table. I can't imagine how many times my phone has rung since the day that Ben died, but even after all this time I still get a wave of panic until I answer.

'It's Marissa, do you mind?' I ask, lifting it.

'Of course not.'

'Hiya.'

'Where are you? Are you home?' She sounds puffed out.

'I am. What's wrong?'

'It's started. I'm having the flipping baby and I can't get hold of Tim. He went to the bloody football and I told him to keep his phone on him, but he's not answering.'

'Calm down, calm down. It's going to be fine. I'm sure you've got plenty of time. How far apart are your contractions?'

'About twelve minutes. But they're so painful. I mean they're really fucking painful. And where's Tim? I'm supposed to be breaking his hands or shouting at him for getting me into this mess.'

'Do you need me to take you to hospital?'

'No, I've phoned them and they told me I can't go until the contractions are five minutes apart.'

'OK, OK, Tim has got time to get home. Look, I'm here with Aidan, we'll jump in the car and be with you in ten minutes. Hopefully you'll only have one more contraction before we get there. OK? I can even put you on hands-free so that I can stay on the line.'

'Just get here, don't worry about the hands-free, I want to phone Tim and leave him more abusive voicemails. Please come quickly, I don't want to do this by myself.'

'Of course,' I say, standing up and motioning for Aidan to come too.

I hang up the phone and clap my hands together with delight.

'Marissa's having the baby!'

'I got that,' says Aidan, 'and we're going? You know I haven't even met her yet? Do you think you should just go by yourself?'

'No, no, we need you. Or at least *I* need you. We'll probably need someone to make us cups of tea and to boil water and get the towels ready or whatever else you're supposed to do when someone gives birth.'

'She's not having it at home, is she?'

He looks terrified. I try and drag him out of my flat but he digs his heels in.

'No, at the hospital and it sounds like it isn't coming any time soon. We're just there to keep her company before Tim arrives.'

'Are you sure you don't want to go alone?'

'No, I really don't. Come on,' I say pulling him along. 'You might just be the distraction she needs to take her mind off her absent husband. In fact, she might be so pleased to see you that she forgets all about the contractions.'

I don't think either of us believe me, but at least he starts moving.

I drive as quick as I can to Marissa's and we've barely got up the driveway when the door flings open.

'Marissa, meet Aidan.'

'Aidan,' she says, beaming. He holds out his hand like a true gent and she takes it to shake it but the smile slides off her face and she grabs the doorframe and doubles over in pain.

'Holy shit,' mumbles Aidan. I realise that Marissa is still clutching his hand and now she's squeezing it hard. He doesn't try and move her, instead he tries to encourage her to breathe and she starts to do a bit of token exhaling.

I'm wondering if there's any point in going into the house or whether I should be bundling her into the car to take her to the hospital.

When the contraction stops she releases Aidan's hand and breathes out nosily.

'Bloody hell, those things. I'm so sorry, Aidan, is your hand OK?'

'I'm sure it will be,' he says, scrunching it up. It's bright red and probably burning with pain.

'I'm so glad you're here,' says Marissa, walking calmly down the hallway.

'How can you walk along normally after that?' I say in horror, both of us following her into the house. I've never witnessed anyone having a contraction in real life and it was two minutes of sheer terror.

She bats her hand in front of her face.

'They're like the most pain I've ever had in my life but then it goes and then it's fine again until the next one comes. Cup of tea?'

She breezes into the kitchen and I just stare at her.

'*Cup of tea?* Shouldn't we be getting you to the hospital? You were in so much pain.'

'I've got ages to go yet. I've got an app on my phone,' she says, waving it.

'Right, right. And Tim?'

'Still missing in action. But the good news is that it's almost full-time so hopefully he'll be checking his phone. It's so nice having you here. I was so scared by myself.'

She's welling up with tears and I go over and give her a hug. It's only been three minutes since her last contraction so I squeeze her back but make sure it doesn't go on for too long as I don't want to be squished like Aidan's hand.

'How about you two go and sit down in the lounge and I'll bring you some tea?' says Aidan. He bends down to give Marissa's dog Bowser a stroke. 'And I can take him out too if you like?'

'Oh, he'd love a little walk, to the park round the back of the estate? We're dropping him with my neighbour when we go to the hospital but I'm sure they'd appreciate it if he'd been out first.'

She fusses around getting his lead and poo bags ready, before searching for his ball which apparently is a must. I help Aidan find the mugs and the tea bags, and once he's all prepared for both the tea and the walk, he shoos us down the hall towards the lounge.

'What a sweetie,' says Marissa.

I nod because he is, but I'm also guessing he and his hands are trying to stay well clear of Marissa and her next contraction.

'I'm sorry for ruining your romantic afternoon,' she says.

'You didn't, we were just chatting.'

'Oh really, just chatting?' she says with a cackle.

'Actually we were. I was just going to tell him about Luke,' I say, keeping my voice down.

'You were what?' she shouts. I look over at the door, wincing in case he heard.

Marissa moves off the sofa and crawls onto the floor on all fours as the next contraction takes hold. I leap off too and start rubbing her back and moving her hair off her face. I'm really not too sure what I'm supposed to do now, but I've spent years doing the same when we've been drunk, so it seems like the natural thing to do.

'Bloody hell,' she says, walking on her knees to the coffee table before resting her head. 'These things are exhausting.'

'And getting closer. Have you checked your app?'

She looks down.

'Shit, that wasn't even ten minutes apart. Where the hell is Tim?'

She picks up her phone and dials again but it goes straight through to answerphone.

'Put your fucking phone on,' she screams and slams it down.

Aidan comes in with two steaming cups of tea.

'Everything all right?'

'Her contractions are getting stronger and longer,' I say.

'Ah, I'll get the dog out quick for ten minutes then,' he says, hurrying out the door.

'Have you got your bag all packed?' I ask.

'Uh-huh. It's in the kitchen.'

'Right, do you want me to phone your mum?'

'Um, no. I can't deal with her there. She'd drive me mental. I'd rather do it alone.'

'You won't be alone, I'll be with you.'

'Thank you,' she says, clutching onto me and I'm worried for a second until I realise it's only to give me a hug and not to squeeze the life out of me. 'I almost wish I could have you there instead of Tim. We've always been there for each other, haven't we?'

'We have.'

'And we always will be,' she says. 'Which is why I've got to tell you not to tell Aidan right now. The way he looks at you, Iz, I don't think Tim has ever looked at me like that in thirteen years.'

'That's why I want to tell him. Becca was right; I shouldn't keep secrets.'

'Iz, don't jeopardise a real relationship for a fake one. I think you'd be better off ending things with Luke than explaining it to Aidan. Imagine if you found out Aidan was staging photos of him looking all cosy with some other woman. Would you really believe that there wasn't more to it?'

Her phone vibrates across the table and she scoops it up.

'Hello,' she says, answering it. 'What the bloody hell do you mean you dropped your phone down the loo? Who the hell does that when their wife is in labour? Uh-huh, uh-huh, yes, I'm having the sodding baby. Now get your arse back here and get me to the hospital!'

She hangs up and looks at her phone.

'Did you hear him? He dropped it down the sodding loo. He went off to the Asian supermarket to find a giant bag of rice to put it in.'

Marissa starts to laugh and it sets me off too. It's not long before we're crying with laughter.

'Oh shit, here we go again,' she says, turning back round onto all fours.

'You've got this. You're a strong, independent woman,' I say, rubbing her back. 'You can do this.'

'Oh. Fuck. Off,' she says between deep breaths.

I give her a squeeze and I have to say I'm slightly relieved that Tim is on his way back as this is only going to get worse.

When the pain eases and she's recovered, she sits up.

'I'm actually having a baby, Iz. She's actually coming out.'

'I know, isn't it exciting?'

'I was going to say terrifying.'

'Terrifying in a good way.'

'What if I can't do it?'

'You can.'

'But what if I can't?'

'Then I'll be here and I'll help you.'

I wrap my arms around her and she clings onto me. And I think for the millionth time in the last two and a half years how lucky I am to have her in my life.

# Chapter 27

I glance at myself in the hotel room mirror and my sequinned dress catches the light. It's perfect Christmas party attire. I perhaps wouldn't have chosen to wear something so attention-seeking, but when a high street shop, whose clothes I often lust after but can't quite afford, sent it to me for free it felt like too good an opportunity to miss.

'That red really suits you,' says Luke, handing me a glass of champagne.

Luke's booked a room at the fancy hotel where we're having our work Christmas do. He suggested that I use it to get ready so that we can snap some photos for Instagram when we're done.

I'm jealous as the room's gorgeous and I wish I'd done the same. I'm getting a taxi back to Cleo's house with her at the end of the night where I'll be sleeping on an air mattress on her floor.

'Thanks, I feel like I look like Rudolph's shiny red nose.'

'It's Christmas, you're supposed to sparkle.'

'I can't believe it's Christmas next week,' I say with a tinge of sadness. The day seems to have crept up on me and I haven't quite prepared myself for it yet. At least this year Aidan will be coming over and hopefully that will lighten the mood.

We still haven't officially become a couple and I haven't told him the truth about my fake relationship. Keeping it a secret isn't any easier; it's eating me up inside. I don't entirely agree with Marissa about not telling him but every time I go to tell him, I think about Luke and the charity event and then I feel guilty that I'd be putting that in jeopardy. It's a lose-lose situation. The only saving grace is that time is racing by and it'll be Valentine's Day before I know it and all this will come to an end.

'I know. I've still got presents to buy. Including yours. What time do you want to come over on Saturday morning to do the big present swap?'

Luke and I want to spend Christmas Day with people we actually love so we're filming our present swapping in advance, to post on the day when we'll pretend we're spending it together.

'About 10?'

'Great, sounds good to me.'

Hopefully that will leave me plenty of time to go and see Aidan after and take Barney on another walk.

I take a sip of my drink, wondering if it's a great idea when I haven't had anything to eat since lunch. 'Ooh, that's good. That doesn't taste like a Lidl special.'

'It's a Taittinger special reserve. Sent by the compliments of Makayto to congratulate us on our engagement.'

'Well, cheers,' I say. The presents we've received have been amazing. We've got matching his and hers dressing gowns, a bespoke ring box that's probably worth more than my imitation ring, embossed stationery and enough champagne to throw a pool party in Marbella.

'They've offered to dress us for the wedding.'

'I guess that could be handy if we wanted a space-themed wedding. God, could you imagine? We'd be in matching outfits.'

Luke fills my glass up; I didn't even notice it was empty.

'We should take these photos soon,' he says, nudging me out of the way of the mirror so that he can pat his immovable hair.

'What's the rush?'

'We want to take them of us when we're still looking good and before you get sloppy drunk.'

'I do not get sloppy drunk,' I say, examining my glass that seems to be almost empty. 'When have I ever been drunk around you?'

'Um, the gin day? And the night we made gin cocktails.'

'Well, those were an exception. I can be around alcohol and not be drunk. Look at the weekend away we had last month. I barely drank a drop.'

'Because you knew it would have come straight back up. Come on, it's just a few photos.'

'Where should we pose?'

'On the bed?' he says, raising an eyebrow.

'Nice try. Why don't we go down to the lobby, we're ready anyway.'

'Fine,' says Luke, grabbing his tux jacket and slipping it on before we head out.

We arrive in the bar and it's a lot busier than it was an hour ago when I arrived to get ready. There's a few people milling about who I recognise from work.

I always find work parties so strange. Everyone's inhibitions fly out the window when they put on their swanky clothes. For those few hours everyone seems to forget that they've got to see these people again on Monday morning.

'Ring,' says Luke, pointing down at my finger. 'You've got to have it on for the photos as people will notice.'

'Really,' I say, sighing. 'Don't you think people have better things to do?'

'Not really. Haven't you ever read any of the forums on Tattle Life?'

'No,' I say, 'do they talk about us?'

'Probably, I haven't looked, but I've seen how they rip into everyone else.'

I shudder. I'm all for using the internet to connect with like-minded people but I hate the spitefulness that forums often breed.

I take the ring out of my purse and slip it on my finger.

'Did you want a drink whilst we're here?' asks Luke.

'No, I wouldn't want to get sloppy drunk,' I say with more of a slur than I'd intended. That champagne went right to my head.

He orders himself a beer and then carries it over to the corner where there's a mirror and a fancy chandelier hanging low. I'm sure he looks at the world through an Instagram lens as he's always sniffing out the perfect spots to stand.

He pulls his selfie stick out of his pocket, attaches the phone and extends it out. It's a sad state of affairs as I don't even bat an eyelid.

We've got the whole routine down now. We pose in slightly different positions about ten times and then we peruse them, work out what modifications to make and usually go again for another ten. We're like a well-oiled machine.

'OMG, it's you,' says a young blonde woman. She's dressed in a stunning aquamarine floor-length dress. 'Luke and Izzy. O-M-G. Can I get a selfie with you?'

I'm so stunned that I can't speak. Someone actually recognises us.

She pulls her iPhone out of her tiny clutch and plants herself in the middle of us. Luke proffers her his selfie stick which she gratefully accepts and she beams away.

'This is so cool, so are you here for the McKinley event?'

'Uh-huh,' says Luke, he's absolutely loving this.

'I can't believe they booked someone so cool. Are you

presenting the Bake Off awards or doing the after-dinner speaking slot? I heard rumours they were having Tim Peake, but you two would be so much better.'

'Well,' says Luke, coughing. 'Actually we turned down the speaking, thought it would be more fun just to take selfies with fans. You know.'

'Oh I do, I can't wait to post this,' she says, looking down at the photo. 'You've made my night.'

She totters back off to her friends and I look up at Luke.

'We weren't supposed to get recognised at work.'

'What do you mean, this is great. By the end of the night we could be tagged in all sorts of people's pictures. This is just the start.'

'But this is our work, Luke. I didn't want anyone to know about us – about the engagement,' I say, holding up my hand to illustrate the point. 'I can't take it off now in case that woman sees, and if I keep it on, all my work colleagues will wonder what's going on. This wasn't supposed to interfere with our day jobs.'

'It's not like it has. For anyone that doesn't recognise us we could just be a couple that met at work.'

'This has gone too far.'

The room is suddenly starting to spin and I don't think it's from the fizz we've been drinking. 'It's one thing to pretend online, but in real life, I'm seeing someone.'

'And didn't I tell you that you shouldn't?' he whispers. 'Look, I don't understand why you're getting so upset. Our plan's working so well that we'll soon be able to give up work. What does it matter?'

I can feel the knot in my belly growing. I'm looking around, paranoid who's going to see us. My arms are starting to tingle from the heat as anxiety whooshes round me.

'The important thing to do is relax. This is no big deal. Let me get you a drink,' he says, disappearing off to the bar.

I pull out my phone and instead of looking at Instagram I pull up my photos and find one that I took of Aidan holding Marissa's baby. Little Leah arrived twenty-four hours after Tim came home from the football and she is an absolute cutie.

Aidan was still at mine when she phoned to insist that we went to see her and something in me snapped when I saw Aidan holding the baby. Maybe I'd been brainwashed by the black-and-white Athena poster of the man with the baby in my formative years, or maybe it was my ovaries reminding me of their existence but something happened. I've accepted that Aidan and I are more than just 'a thing', I want him to be my boyfriend. After I sort out this mess with Luke of course.

Luke comes back and hands me a drink and I quickly put my phone back in my bag.

'Cheers, to us,' he says. 'This time next year we might not have to be at a cheesy work Christmas do.'

My stomach sinks. I'm being offered the chance to ditch my ordinary life and become a real-life influencer, which I've desired for so long, but now that it's happening, I can't help wondering if it's what I really want.

'Ooh, bird, cooee.' I hear Mrs Harris before I see her and I spin around and if she hadn't spoken I wouldn't have recognised her. She's dressed in a mid-length black dress that goes in and out in all the right places and makes her look fantastic. Her hair's got soft low-lights running it through it and it's been blowdried all flicky at the ends.

'Mrs Harris,' I say, wolf-whistling. 'You scrub up pretty well.'

'Easy there, tiger, you'll have to get in line. They're already queuing round the block for me. And who's this charming chap? I think he might jump to the head of the queue.'

'This is Luke, he works in Sales. Luke, this is Mrs Harris.'

Her smile drops into a more neutral expression.

'You don't work with Miles, do you?' she says, practically spitting his name out.

'Unfortunately I do, Mrs Harris.'

'There'll be no fraternising with the enemy, Izzy.'

'But haven't they already picked a winner – isn't this just the grand reveal?' says Luke.

Mrs Harris folds her arm over her chest and glares at him and he backs away slowly.

'I'll see you later on, Izzy. Good luck, Mrs Harris.'

She tuts and looks back at me.

'He's a bit dishy,' says Mrs Harris. She loops her arm through mine as we go to the dining room. 'You be careful, though. He looks pretty but he might only be after one thing.'

'Oh, don't worry, Mrs H, I'm in no danger of giving him that,' I say.

'I'm not talking about you. I'm talking about me. He might be trying to steal baking secrets for Miles.'

'Oh, OK, I'll prepare myself for that.'

'You better had. Just keep your ears open for any questions he asks about me and my baps, OK?'

'OK. Although you know your baps are often a talking point.'

'I know,' she says proudly. 'Now I need a drink. Do you want one?'

I shake my head and raise the glass I already have. She walks off and I look around to see if I can see anyone I know and I spot Cleo and Colin walking into the bar. I give them a wave and they weave their way across to me.

'Hello, hello,' says Cleo, giving me a hug and leaning on my shoulder.

'I take it the bar crawl went well,' I say, looking at Colin who's smiling away.

'Certainly did. I can't believe how busy it is out on a Tuesday night. Since when is Tuesday night a night to go out on?' he says.

'Tipsy Tuesday,' I say helpfully.

'It certainly is,' he says, giggling. It seems that the little bar crawl has allowed him to find his voice.

'Look at you, Mrs Harris,' he says as she glides back over with a cocktail.

'Don't think you can flatter your way back into my good books,' she says to him whilst trying to hide a little smile.

'Wasn't trying to,' he says. 'Bloody hell, Izzy, are you engaged?'

I look down at my hand.

'What, um, no, of course not,' I say, catching the eye of the women in the aquamarine dress.

'It's just how people wear them these days,' says Cleo, flashing her hand where she's switched one of her rings to her left hand.

I sigh with relief and give her a little smile of thanks.

'You know that's bad luck, don't you?' says Mrs Harris.

'Oh, come on. It's just another way that the patriarchy's been controlling us over the years,' says Cleo.

Mrs Harris gives a belly laugh. 'Now I've heard everything.'

'Who wants another drink?' asks Colin.

'Me,' says Mrs Harris, raising her half-empty glass.

'Don't you think you need to slow down?' I say, treading lightly; Mrs Harris doesn't usually like to be told what to do.

'Just calming my nerves.'

'OK, but remember you've got to climb up on the stage when they announce the winner and potentially make a speech if you win.'

'What do you mean *potentially*?' she says, outraged.

'Sorry, when you get up to make your speech.'

'I'm just settling my nerves. I'll be fine. Perhaps I'll just go and touch up my make-up. There'll be calling us in for the big announcement any minute now.'

It's probably a good thing that they're crowning the Great Office Bake Off champion before dinner as I'm pretty sure Mrs Harris would have polished off the whole table's wine allocation through nerves if it was after.

The dining-room doors are opened and there's a call to be seated. There's an excited chatter going round the room about who's going to be the victor and I realise that we're all going to miss the drama from the competition.

'Are you coming?' asks Cleo.

'I think I'm going to wait for Mrs Harris.'

'OK, see you in a minute,' she says, going in with Colin.

'Waiting for me?' says Luke, sidling up to me.

'In your dreams,' I say, laughing.

'If you only knew the starring role you've had in many of my dreams,' he says, winking.

'You two are just the cutest,' says the woman in the aquamarine dress, walking past us again. 'I can't wait to see your wedding pictures.'

She waltzes off and I look up to see Luke beaming. I know Luke always dreamt of being recognised but I never really imagined what it would be like. It feels weird having my virtual and real lives merging and to no longer have my phone to hide behind.

'You better go, Mrs Harris is coming,' I say, shoving Luke away.

He gives me a kiss on the lips as he goes and I'm left in shock.

'Mistletoe,' he says, pointing above my head at where I'm standing and I sidestep away from it and walk up to Mrs Harris.

'It's nearly time for the announcement,' I say, clapping my hands together. Finally the sodding Great Office Bake Off will be over.

She smooths down her dress before patting at her hair.

'Mrs H, are you OK?'

'Fine,' she says through deep breaths. 'Never been better.'

She doesn't look fine.

'It's just, what if I don't win? How will I ever show my face at work again?'

'Mrs Harris, it doesn't matter, does it? You've done so well to get this far. Out of the whole company.'

'Oh, Izzy. Don't be so naive. Of course it's about winning.'

For a minute I thought I was seeing a more vulnerable side of Mrs Harris.

'It's too late now,' I say, changing tack. 'You've done your final Bake Off and you can't change it. But look at you, you look fabulous. Just hold your head up high whatever happens.'

She gulps.

'You're right. Come on,' she says, looping her arm through mine.

We find our way to our table with Colin and Cleo and some others from our department and the Master of Ceremonies takes to the stage.

'And now, what you've all been waiting for,' says the MC. 'Please put your hands together for Paul Hollywood and Mary Berry.'

There are excited whispers round the room as everyone assumes there's been a great reunion, until we see a man and a woman walking across the stage with photo masks on their faces. There's a ripple of laughter as people realise it's our CEO and HR Director.

'Right,' says Roland, the CEO doing his best impression of

the baking judge. 'We're here to find out the winner of the Great Office Bake Off. Would the two final contestants join us on stage.'

I give Mrs Harris a quick hug before she totters up to the stage throwing dagger eyes at Miles.

'The winner of the Great Office Bake Off is…' says Mary, the director of HR.

I can see Mrs Harris holding her breath and I hope they put her out of her misery soon as I'm worried she's going to pass out.

'Petunia!'

It takes us a second to realise that they mean Mrs Harris, as we've never heard her first name before, and after a moment of stunned silence, our whole table stands on its feet and starts whooping and cheering.

The CEO hands over the trophy and Mrs Harris is so grateful that she almost kisses his face off, luckily for him he's still got his mask on.

Trophy in hand she staggers up to the microphone, her hands clasped to her mouth in surprise.

'I can't believe it; I can't believe I won. First, I'd like to say commiserations to my competition, you've been exceptional,' she says, turning to Miles. 'And then I'd like to thank my team in Contracts.'

We cheer so loud that anyone would think we'd won personally.

'I've always known I was exceptionally talented and it's been so lovely to finally be recognised for it, so thank you.'

She holds the trophy high over her head and I don't miss the little sneer she gives her rival Miles.

'Well, that competition certainly provided us with some highlights this year,' says the HR Director. 'Here, as they say on TV, are the best bits.'

A montage of photos showing the rounds of the competition is being shown on a big screen, and I feel all nostalgic. I can't help thinking what Luke said, that this could be my last work do and I can't help thinking how much I'd miss all my work colleagues. They may be bonkers, but I really do love them.

# Chapter 28

I used to love waking up on Christmas morning. I was always first out of bed. I'd sneak along to Ben's room and we'd mount an assault on our parents' bedroom, getting them out of bed well before dawn. Even when he lived with Becca ten minutes down the road, he'd still stay over on Christmas Eve so that we could carry on the tradition.

Now I wake up and it's light already. There's no excited scramble down to the presents. No one to argue with over the TV remote or who's eaten the last green triangle out of the Quality Street tin. Instead I lie in bed and post the pre-approved photos of Luke and me on Instagram.

I immediately get pings of notifications and once upon a time I'd have thought how sad it is that people are scrolling on their phone and commenting on Christmas morning, but now I'm grateful for the distraction.

I can hear Mum banging around in the kitchen and I know how hard today is for her too, so I get out of bed and slip on my dressing gown and head downstairs.

I walk into the kitchen and I'm struck by the amazing smell of cinnamon.

'Morning,' says Mum, opening the oven and pulling out cinnamon buns.

'Morning, this smells amazing. Sorry I slept so late; I should have come and helped.'

'Don't be silly. You know I like to cook to keep busy. Let me ice these and then you can have one.'

'They look amazing.'

'Yeah, I thought I'd try something new. Especially with Aidan coming.'

There's a smile on her face that's been missing for so long and I'm so glad that he said that he'd come to ours. It's not only my day he's going to brighten, but my parents' too.

'You know he's not coming until after lunch?'

'I know, I know. But I wasn't too sure what he'd like. So I've also baked gingerbread men, mince pies and a swiss roll.'

'Mum,' I say, laughing.

I know that she would have baked that much anyway, trying to take her mind off Ben, but I'm glad for once she's got a different reason to do it.

'Morning, love,' says my dad, strolling in with a bottle of champagne. 'Merry Christmas.'

'Oh, gosh, yes, Merry Christmas. When are we doing presents?' I say.

In the years since Ben died, we haven't really found our rhythm as a family of three. Where once we'd have opened them at the crack of dawn, the last couple of years we've put it off as it feels so wrong.

'Well, with Becca not coming over, there's no need to wait. I've only got Aidan a little present and I'm sure he wouldn't want to sit through us all opening things.'

'OK,' I say, getting up to my feet and taking the bottle of champagne out of Dad's hand. 'How about a glass of bubbles and we'll go through to the lounge.'

'Sounds good to me,' says Dad.

We get everything ready and take it all through to the lounge where we put the big tray of buns and the flutes of champagne on the coffee table.

Mum puts her Michael Bublé Christmas album on and we look at the pile of presents under the tree. It still doesn't feel right. I realise that I don't just miss Ben but Becca too. She's been such a part of our Christmas for years.

I watch Mum look over at the mantelpiece at the photo of us all together taken a few years ago during happier times. Despite the brave face we're putting on, I wonder if we're ever going to make our festive get togethers feel anything but sad.

I look over to the clock wishing that 3 p.m. and Aidan's arrival would come round quickly.

I try and move my belly but it's like a lead weight. I seem to have excelled myself with Christmas lunch, eating at least double my body weight. Mum overcompensated for the awkwardness of the day by making every side dish imaginable, and not wanting to appear rude, I sampled them all.

My phone's lit up on the coffee table and despite it only being a metre away, it takes me ages to lean forward and scoop it up. I collapse back on the sofa, exhausted from the effort.

Marissa has sent me a photo of Leah dressed up like a Christmas pudding. That baby is so adorable. I had no idea that I was going to be so smitten with her. Marissa's doing well – or as well as you can do when you've hardly slept in weeks. One minute she's crying happy tears and the next she's crying in frustration that motherhood is not as easy as it looks on Instagram.

Me:
My goddaughter is so cute xxxx

Despite there being no talk of an official christening, I've christened myself godmother as Marissa did suggest I was going to be when she found she was having a girl – that's pretty binding in my book.

Marissa:
Short-lived cuteness. She was like this for approx 30 seconds before she sicked milk all down it. Now I understand why people dress their babies in so many outfits – it's not just because they're showing off, it's because they're always pooping and sicking all over them. FML. PS. Merry Christmas – has Aidan popped over yet?

Me:
Hang on in there. People say it goes quick, she'll be 18 before you know it ;) And Merry Christmas to you all too – and no he hasn't come over yet, I'm a bit nervous!!!!

Marissa:
You'll be fine. Gotta run, her ladyship is wailing for food x

The doorbell goes and I forget the stone in my belly and I leap up.

'I'll get it,' I shout. My heart is pounding. I haven't introduced a man to my parents since Cameron and I forgot how utterly terrifying it is. I wish the worst I could fear would be my mum digging out naked baby photos or ones with awful fringes and teenage braces, but Mum always goes one better and digs out the home movies where I used to present my own TV shows.

They're all-singing, all-dancing monstrosities; I imagine this is her revenge for having to endure them live.

Mum and Dad hover in the doorway of the lounge trying to keep out of the way, whilst I open the door and I'm shocked to see Becca standing there.

'Merry Christmas,' she says, holding up her hands which are laden with bags of presents.

I don't move for a second as I can't quite believe it. A huge smile spreads over my face.

'Merry Christmas,' I say, leaning into a hug. 'What are you doing here?'

'It's tradition, I always come round,' she says, shrugging her shoulders as she pulls away. 'I was at Mum's and it didn't feel right. I needed to be here.'

I can feel tears prickle at my eyes.

'Becca,' says my mum, coming up the hallway. She hugs her and I notice that she's got tears in her eyes too. 'Are you staying for tea? I think we were going to play a game first and eat after.'

'Mum, more food?' I say, wondering how she could possibly think about eating after the massive lunch we just had. 'Aidan will have eaten too.'

'Oh, it's just some cold meats and some vol-au-vents before the cakes.'

'It's not Christmas in the Brown household without vol-au-vents,' says Becca, laughing. 'I'm sure I could eat a few.'

Dad gives her a hug too.

'I'll dig out the Baileys,' he says with a wink.

'I'm driving, Simon, but I'd love one of your special hot chocolates,' she calls to him.

'Righto. Izzy?'

'Baileys, please.'

Becca needn't have brought presents; I haven't seen my parents smile like this all day. I watch my mum fussing around and whisking her into the lounge.

I go to close the door and I hear a cough and I open it wider only to be jumped on by Barney.

'Hey, beautiful,' I say, bending down and he leaps up at me and licks my nose.

'Hey, that was my line,' says Aidan, leaning over and giving me a kiss and I stand upright.

'You need to be quicker,' I say. 'Come on in, it's freezing.'

I don't need to say anything to Barney as he's raced through already. The squeals from the lounge make me think that's he's found everyone. I hear a great thwack and Aidan closes his eyes.

'It's fine, it's fine,' I say, grabbing his hands and pulling him in.

'Is your mum still going to like me when he breaks an antique carriage clock?'

'Ha ha, she'll probably be thrilled, the only things like that she has were inherited from my grandma on my dad's side.'

He lets me drag him up the hallway and into the lounge.

Barney's lying on his back, legs akimbo, whilst Becca and Mum are rubbing his belly. His mouth is slightly open and from this angle he looks like he's smiling.

'I see you've met Barney.'

'We certainly have,' says Mum in a baby-talk voice. 'Oh, Aidan,' she says, standing upright. 'I'm Dawn.'

'Nice to meet you, I'm sorry if Barney broke something,' he says, surveying the room for damage.

'No, no, he just knocked over an old picture frame. He's fine. He's gorgeous. We're so happy you brought him. Oh, and that you came too.'

'I'm starting to get a complex. First Izzy, now you.'

'He's such a charmer,' says Becca, standing up to greet him.

'Aidan, this is Becca. She just popped in.'

'Ah, nice to meet you. Another person to play Monopoly,' says Aidan.

Mum and Becca splutter.

'Oh Aidan, you don't want to play Monopoly with Izzy,' says Mum.

He looks at me and I roll my eyes.

'I haven't cheated for years, OK?'

'What?' says Aidan, pulling a face. 'I could cope with you being ultra-competitive or perhaps a sore loser, but a cheater?'

'Once a cheater, always a cheater,' says Becca, before her eyes pop out of her head and she realises what she's implied and I shoot her a quick look. 'I mean, in board games, obviously.'

'I'll have you know, it's been at least twelve years since I cheated, in a board game.' I know I'm not actually cheating with Luke but I still turn purple with embarrassment.

'Um, really?' says Becca. 'What about the time we played Trivial Pursuit? That wasn't that long ago.'

'I was not cheating. I put the cards at the wrong end of the box. It was an innocent mistake. Honestly, Aidan, I'm fine to play Monopoly. I won't be the banker.'

'Hmm, I don't know,' says Aidan, laughing.

My dad comes in carrying a tray of drinks.

'Oh, hello,' he says, about to put the tray down on the coffee table and Aidan scoops it up.

'Barney's tail, nothing's safe.'

'Right,' he says, immediately bending over and giving him a rub behind the ear. I take the tray and pop it on the dining table at the end of the lounge.

'I'm Simon, by the way,' says Dad, standing up.

'Sorry, Dad, this is Aidan, Aidan this is my dad, Simon.'

'Nice to meet you.'

'And you,' Dad says, before he bends down to Barney once more. 'And you too. You're a lively one, aren't you?'

Barney is lapping up all the attention.

'Oh, I um, brought you both this,' Aidan says. 'It's a spiced sourdough loaf.'

He hands it to my mum and she stares at him and then beams back.

'Thank you, Aidan.'

'Did you make it?' I don't mean to furrow my brow but I'm surprised.

'Yeah, I have this thing about sourdough. I made a starter a few months ago and I'm kind of obsessed with feeding it. I thought it would be nice to bring something homemade.'

'It was really thoughtful. So Simon, we were just trying to decide whether to play Monopoly with Izzy or not,' says Mum.

Dad pulls a face. 'Wasn't it a lifetime ban?'

'Don't I get parole? I'm a reformed character.'

'That's what they all say,' says Aidan.

'Hey,' I say, playfully hitting him. 'You're supposed to be on my side.'

'Um, I thought you chose Barney.'

'Well…'

'How about we play Cluedo,' says Mum. 'I think it's still got all the bits.'

We all shrug. At least I can't get accused of cheating in Cluedo.

'OK, so I think it's Professor Plum, in the conservatory…' I pause longer than Dermot on *The X Factor* to create the dramatic tension, 'with the rope.'

I look around and wait for someone to show me one of the cards and no one does. I do a victory air punch before reaching over the wrinkly black envelope that contains the cards.

'Professor Plum, in the conservatory,' I say, peeling one card over at a time, 'with the rope,' I say, only for everyone to gasp.

'Um, lead piping,' corrects Becca, pointing at the card I've turned over.

'But no one has the rope,' I say, confused. 'I asked and no one showed me it.'

Everyone checks their cards again.

'Oh, perhaps it didn't have all the cards after all.'

'Mum, you checked!'

'Maybe I didn't count them right. Don't blame me, the menopause does all sorts of things to your memory.'

'Mum, you've been using that excuse for years.'

'One day you'll use it too,' she says. 'Anyone want to play again? This time we can all tick off the rope.'

'Um, perhaps we could play something else,' I say.

'Perhaps,' says Dad. 'What time are we having tea?'

I stare at him. I think I consumed enough calories at lunch to see me through a winter hibernation – how can he be hungry?

'Oh, yes, we've got loads. Shall I do a platter? Aidan, I'm sure you could eat, yes?'

'Um, something small. I had a pretty big lunch.'

'My mum doesn't know the meaning of the word small,' I say, watching her leave. 'Perhaps I should go and keep her under control.'

I'm walking out of the room when I spot a card on the floor.

'Look what I've found.' I hold up the offending rope card, it must have fallen out of the box.

'Dawn, look at this,' shouts Dad.

Mum comes in and I hold up the card.

'Where was that?'

'I found it on the floor.'

'That's funny, I didn't see it when I went out. Hmm, are you sure you didn't have it on you?'

'You weren't cheating again?' says Dad with a stern stare.

'Um, why on earth would I have it on me? I was the one that lost the game because the cards didn't match. Surely I'd have slipped it into the envelope if I was?'

'Oh, so you would, love.'

'I'm fed up of this, let's play Monopoly. I want to put this whole cheating thing to bed once and for all.'

I roll up my sleeves hoping that way no one will accuse me of hiding anything up there.

Aidan looks around the room. 'Has anyone seen Barney?'

'He came out into the kitchen with me when I was doing the food,' says Mum.

Aidan's face falls.

'And you left him in there alone? Was there any food out?'

'I was just pulling out the vol-au-vents from the fridge. I think I might have taken the meat out.'

He leaps up and runs through to the kitchen and we all follow. The whole thing happens in slow motion as he dives through the door, shouting an elongated 'Noooooo'. Barney's got two feet propped on the work surface and he's devouring the cold meat. At the sound of Aidan's voice he turns and leaps down and hangs his head in shame. His tail and bum are wiggling and his ears are pinned back to the side of his face. He looks absolutely adorable.

Aidan is white as a sheet and he looks mortified. Mum clasps her hand over her mouth and stares at the huge near-empty plate that once held the giant turkey and ham that could have fed the whole street, or evidently one hungry Labrador.

It's Dad who breaks the silence with a roar of laughter. He's properly going for it and it isn't long before tears appear in his eyes.

Barney looks delighted and creeps forward on his belly and nuzzles at his legs.

I look at my mum in horror, wondering if she's going to explode but she's looks like she's in shock.

'I'm so sorry,' says Aidan. 'I'm so, so sorry. Barney!'

He calls him in a stern voice and he's back to being a subdued dog as he sits at his master's feet.

'Don't be,' says my dad, clapping him on the back, tears rolling down his cheeks. 'That's the best laugh I've had in ages. Plus I'm not going to have to eat turkey for the next two weeks. Thank you, Barney.'

'I'll have you know that I had new recipes this year,' Mum says. 'A Mexican dish and a tagine.'

It only makes Dad laugh harder.

'I can buy you another turkey,' says Aidan. 'Or I can get the leftovers from my mum's; it was an organic one from Waitrose.'

'Don't worry about it, Aidan. Clearly my husband doesn't actually like turkey.'

I'm beginning to think Barney might have started World War Three, but then Mum starts to laugh too and Dad wraps an arm around her and pulls her in for a hug.

Aidan's cheeks are red. I give his hand a squeeze before I lean down and give Barney a cuddle.

'At least he didn't touch the vol-au-vents,' says Becca, picking up the plate that's still wrapped in foil.

'Now, that would have been disaster,' I say. 'So are we going to play Monopoly or what?'

'Yeah, come on,' says Dad.

'Perhaps I should take Barney and go home.'

'You're not going anywhere,' says Mum, 'you've got to make sure that Izzy doesn't cheat.' She gets another plate of food out of the fridge and walks out of the kitchen along with Becca who takes the vol-au-vents. 'Can you grab the bread sticks, Izzy.'

'OK,' I say, digging in the cupboard to find them.

'I feel so awful,' says Aidan. 'This is the type of thing that you're never going to forget. It's always going to be the Christmas where a dog ate your turkey.'

'And that's why it's so great,' says Dad. 'You've given us a proper Christmas memory, one that will make us laugh for years to come. I didn't think that was going to be possible after Ben to have Christmases that we'd look back on fondly.'

I can feel tears collecting behind my eyes. He's exactly right.

Dad walks out and I lean over and give Aidan a hug.

'Do you think that he means it, that he's never going to forget it? Bloody hell, I'm going to have to bake a bigger sourdough next year to make up for it.'

'Next year,' I say with a gulp. My heart might burst.

'Yeah, I'm hoping so,' he says, taking my hand. 'I hate to break it to you but I think we're a thing now.'

'Right,' I say, nodding. For once it doesn't feel scary. 'I wondered what this was and now I know it's a thing.'

He leans over and kisses me.

When we eventually pull away I realise how right it feels. And it's in that moment in the kitchen, with Aidan and Barney, whilst I'm holding the bread sticks, that I realise that I'm starting to fall in love.

# Chapter 29

'Sit up at the table, everyone,' I shout from the kitchen. I open the oven to pull the potatoes out, steaming my face in the process.

'Do you need any help?' asks Aidan, popping round the corner.

'You could take the wine over and open it? Bottle opener's in the top drawer.'

'Got it,' he says.

I try not to grin too much. We're acting like a proper couple hosting a dinner party.

The potatoes are the last thing to be dished up and I pop them on the plates then start taking them through to our dining table.

'This smells amazing,' says Marissa. She's seated at the table rocking the pram back and forth to keep baby Leah asleep.

'Let's hope it tastes as good as it looks.'

'I'm sure it will,' says Tim. 'So, Aidan, do you follow Reading in the football?'

'I'm more into rugby. I usually go and see London Irish a few times a season.'

Marissa gives me a little thumbs up and I wink back. I leave them discussing rugby whilst I get the other two plates of food.

I sit back down at the table and Marissa leans over to me.

'They're getting on well.'

'Aren't they?'

It's a bit of a shame that Becca and Gareth couldn't join us. She said that they had plans with his friends, but I wonder if it's because she still hasn't told him about Ben and she's worried that we'd let something slip.

Marissa carries on rocking the pram and Tim leans over her food and cuts it up, which she eats one-handed. They're like a well-oiled parenting machine, you'd never know that they'd only been doing it for a month.

'This is delicious,' says Tim.

'It is,' says Aidan. 'We should do a toast.'

He picks up his glass and everyone else does the same.

'To Izzy and her awesome cooking skills.'

'To Izzy,' everyone parrots back before we all chink and drink before we go back to eating.

'So, has anyone got any new year's resolutions?' asks Aidan.

'To get some sleep,' says Marissa, causing us all to smile.

'Mine too,' says Tim. 'How about you, Izzy?'

I have lots of resolutions, like to let myself fall in love in again, to stop lying to Aidan about Luke. None of them I can say publicly.

'Er, to go to the gym more.'

Marissa coughs loudly.

'Or to go at all.'

'Bloody hell, what happened to us?' groans Marissa. 'I remember when we used to make resolutions like to stay up and watch the sunset more.'

'To be fair we made those kind of resolutions,' says Tim. 'But we never went through with them.'

Marissa pulls a face and Aidan laughs at the gentle bickering that ensues.

'Let's all make a resolution as a group,' says Marissa. 'That we'll try and do this kind of thing more often.'

'I'd like that a lot,' says Aidan and I swoon. It means so much to me that he gets on with my friends.

We've almost finished eating when I hear a knock at the door and I look over, confused. It's rare for the door to knock without the intercom and I assume it's one of our neighbours.

I excuse myself from the table and wander over

I look through the spyhole and see Luke standing outside. What is he doing here?

My heart starts to hammer in my chest. The sound of chatter from the dinner table drifts over and I know it'll be fruitless to pretend to be not in.

I open the door a tiny bit.

'What are you doing here?' I whisper.

'Bad time?' says Luke, arching an eyebrow. He's got a small smile on his face. He knew I was having this lunch.

I hear someone walking up behind me and turn to see Aidan.

'I was just getting some water for Marissa,' he says, looking at Luke. 'Everything OK?'

'Aidan, this is my work colleague, Luke,' I say. 'Luke, this is Aidan.'

Luke pushes the door open wider and outstretches his hand for Aidan to shake it.

'I was just here to take photos of Izzy for our in-house magazine, but it seems I got the times wrong,' he says, holding up his large SLR camera.

'In-house magazine – are you going to be famous, Izzy?' says Aidan smiling.

'Ha ha,' I say. 'Not exactly. I'm sure it'll keep.'

'Actually, I was hoping to get them done as soon as possible,' says Luke.

'I don't see why the photos can't be taken at work,' I say, gritting my teeth.

'We've been over this. Mary likes the magazine to focus on people and their lives outside of the office. Makes people seem more real.' I'm wondering if he made up this pretend cover story before he got here or if he's thinking on his feet.

'Why don't you let him take them now, it seems a shame he's come all the way here,' says Aidan. 'I better get Marissa that water.'

He disappears into the kitchen and Luke gives me a wink. I want to throttle him but I know that Aidan will reappear at any second.

Luke gestures to the camera round his neck.

'Where are we going to take these photos?'

'What the hell is this all about?' I whisper with a hiss.

'Just thought that if you were cooking a big dinner party I could take a couple of photos for my feed, pretend I was there too.'

'This isn't fair, Luke. Aidan's here.'

'Funny, as that's the point, isn't it? He wasn't supposed to be. You weren't supposed to be dating anyone.'

'Izzy, are you still not letting him in?' says Aidan, walking past with the water.

'I haven't done my hair,' I say, patting it.

'I think you look gorgeous,' he says, kissing me on the top of the head as he walks past, making me feel even more terrible.

'He seems nice,' says Luke, raising an eyebrow. 'Now, are you going to let me in or am I going to have to stand out here and start talking very loudly about us?'

I sigh heavily and let him in.

We walk into the kitchen which is technically separate from the lounge, but the back wall has a large opening between the two rooms. I can hear the others chatting in the lounge and I'm mindful of how much sound travels in our little flat.

'So I got an email—' starts Luke.

'Ssh,' I say, pointing at the lounge. 'They'll hear.'

'OK,' he says in a quiet voice. 'I got an email from a soft drink company that wants us to take some photos in January. I know you said that you wanted to stop taking on new things, but the money is good.'

'I'm not interested.'

'He's really worth it then?'

I look out towards the lounge.

'He really is.'

Luke nods and I wonder if him seeing me with Aidan has made him realise that it really is time for this to end.

'Right, let's take these photos.'

'Are you actually serious?'

'It's going to be pretty fucking weird if I come round and then don't. How are you going to explain to lover boy that there's no clicking of the camera?'

I grunt and concentrate hard on the thought of all the money that we're earning for Heart2Heart as I pick up a wooden spoon. I pretend to stir dirty saucepans as he snaps away, desperate for him to finish and leave.

'Have you got them?' I say sarcastically after a few shots.

'Hmm, I could do with a few more,' he says, walking out of the kitchen and into the lounge. 'Hello, everyone, sorry to interrupt your meal.'

I quickly follow behind him and watch Marissa's eyes pop out of her head.

'I'm just taking a few photos of Izzy for our work magazine. Why don't I get one of you and your boyfriend – was it Andrew?'

'Aidan,' he says.

'Yes, Aidan. Why don't you two sit on the sofa?'

'I don't see why he needs to be in the photo,' I say.

‘Come on, this is supposed to be you at home,’ says Luke.

‘What about with her best friend instead?’ says Marissa.

‘I think boyfriend is a better angle.’

‘I don’t mind,’ says Aidan, shrugging.

He walks over to the sofa and sits down and I reluctantly follow suit. He slips his arm around me but I don’t sink into him like I usually would.

‘That’s lovely,’ says Luke, taking a couple of shots. ‘How about you give Izzy a kiss?’

I turn towards Aidan to tell him that we don’t have to and he leans over and gives me a quick kiss.

‘Wow, you two look great together,’ he says, putting down his camera. ‘Sorry again, Izzy, for getting the day wrong. And Aidan, thanks for all your help too. I’ll see you at work.’

‘Thanks,’ I mutter, still amazed of the gall of him to come and do this.

He gives Marissa and Tim a wave before he heads out the door and I sigh with relief.

‘I always expected from your stories that your work colleagues would be more fun,’ says Aidan.

‘They are. He’s not in our department.’

‘Izzy’s work colleagues are proper bonkers,’ says Marissa to Tim. ‘You should have heard the stories about their Great Office Bake Off. Has Mrs Harris calmed down after her win?’

‘Not yet. She keeps walking the trophy round the different floors just to rub it in.’

My heartbeat is slowing and I’m no longer sweating with nerves.

‘What are you going to do now that’s all over?’ asks Aidan.

‘Well, HR have decided to run another competition.’

‘Another Bake Off?’ asks Marissa.

'No, no. They wanted it to be more inclusive. So next year they're doing The Office Has Talent.'

'What's your act going to be, Izzy?' says Marissa, chuckling.

'Don't,' I say, groaning. 'Mrs Harris's trying to get us to enter with her. She wants to sing and have me and Cleo as her backing group.'

'Can she sing?'

'God only knows. We've all said no, but there's another month until the first round and she'll no doubt try and wear us all down.'

Everyone laughs a little too loudly and baby Leah starts to stir.

'Probably time for her next feed,' says Marissa, picking her up and settling with her on the sofa.

'I'll tidy up and get the dessert ready,' I say.

'I'll help,' says Aidan and we take the empty plates into the kitchen.

We load the dishwasher and when we're finished Aidan takes my hands.

'Thank you for this,' he says. 'I know that you want to take things slowly but it's nice to get to know your friends. They're as lovely as you are.'

I lean forward and give him a proper kiss, not like the forced one we had earlier in front of Luke.

I feel terrible lying to him, but it's only a few weeks until the charity ball and auction and then I can end things with Luke and concentrate solely on Aidan.

We eventually pull away and he sets about making coffee and I prepare the dessert. I hope that Luke seeing us together made him get the message, as the sooner I'm out of the fake relationship and concentrating on Aidan, the better.

Welcome to January
This_Izzy_Loves IGTV
No. followers: 21.4k

*Happy New Year, My Precious Little Poppets! This year is going to be a good year, I can feel it in my bones. Let's make it the best we can, huh? With a wedding coming up and a wedding dress to squeeze into you'd think that I'd be making all sorts of resolutions to diet and to exercise but my only resolution is to live my life the way I want to at the moment.*

*Now, for a quick recap on the month. Luke and I had a wonderful time at his Christmas do, there was dinner and dancing and dazzling lights. Then we made the pilgrimage to Winter Wonderland, where we got tipsy on mulled wine, glided on the ice (mostly on my bum) and tried every food on offer. On Christmas Day we spent the morning together eating croissants and drinking champagne, before we headed off to spend time with our families.*

*New Year's Eve went off with a bang. We had a small, intimate gathering of close friends. It made me realise how very blessed I am to have such lovely friends in real life as well as on here with all of you lovely followers! Love each and every one of you – big mwah!*

# Chapter 30

January is normally the worst month of the year: I'm usually broke, frazzled and my liver runs its own campaign for dry January. But this year, thanks to our #ad and #sponsored posts, I'm actually pretty flush and I even managed to pay my credit card off in full before the heart-stopping bill arrived in the post. It's the last weekend of the month and in previous years at this point I've been kissing the cash machines as my pay packet hits my account, but this year I haven't even bothered to check my balance to see if it's come in.

Luke was right – this really does have the potential to change our lives. But I've realised that, as appreciative as I am, although my balance now appears in black rather than red, it's not what I want anymore. Or at least I don't want it if I can only have it by being half of a Z-list celebrity couple. If it wasn't for the charity event I would have packed it all in ages ago. But that's only a couple of weeks away now and our amicable break-up that's going to follow is within touching distance.

It's not only the money that's made me beat the January blues; I have been spending more and more time with Aidan. I'm still trying to keep it low-key but today we're off on a big walk and then tonight he's taking me out to dinner.

My intercom buzzes and I'm excited knowing it'll be him.

'Hellooooo.'

'Hiya, are you ready?' says Aidan.

'Yeah, I'll be right down.'

'Great, and don't forget the swimming costume.'

I groan.

'I thought you were kidding.'

'Deadly serious – go and get it and I'll wait for you in the car, it's freezing.'

I'm trying not to let my mind run away too much, worrying about all the horrible things he might have planned which would explain why I need a swimming costume in January when we're going for a walk in the great outdoors. But I pick it up anyway and stuff it in my overnight bag and hurry down to the car.

'Hey, you,' he says as I climb into his Ford Focus.

'Hey, yourself.'

I lean over and give him a kiss before I turn to give Barney a pat through the dog guard but he's not there.

'Aren't we taking Barney?'

'Nope, he's with my parents.'

'Oh God,' I say, screwing my face up.

'I'm beginning to get a bit of a complex. Is it that bad that it's only me?'

'No, I just thought with Barney with us then we couldn't be doing anything too horrific like canyoning or caving.'

'In January?' he says, laughing. 'Are you mad?'

'But then why do I need a swimming costume?'

'I'm taking you away for a romantic night away. Just us.'

'Just us?'

'Yeah. We haven't really been out on many dates; we always seem to stay in or take Barney out for walks so I figured this was overdue.'

It's a really sweet sentiment and whilst I didn't really want to be out and about in public with Aidan properly until after I ended things with Luke, holed up in a hotel room ordering room service isn't the end of the world. In fact, it sounds pretty damn perfect.

'Let's do it,' I say, and Aidan grins and pulls away from the kerb.

Tears of laughter run down my face. Aidan's been telling me a story of taking Barney to the vet's for the past half hour.

'And you didn't tell him about the humping?' I say, wiping my cheeks.

'I didn't dare. Funny enough, we haven't been back to that vet's since.'

My ribs are aching from laughing so hard.

'I think we're nearly there,' says Aidan.

I look out of the window – I haven't been paying an awful lot of attention to the drive. We turned off the main road a long time ago and since then we've been driving through tree-lined countryside.

'Are you going to tell me where we are?'

'No,' says Aidan, staring straight ahead.

We turn down a road and we pass a cute chocolate-box cottage set back from the road. It looks familiar but I can't quite place where I've seen it before. The car rattles on and I see a thick wood. My skin starts to prickle as I hope that I'm wrong but this seems awfully like the route that Luke and I took to Ingleford Manor.

I'm starting to overheat and I unwrap the scarf from my neck.

'You OK?' asks Aidan, turning down the thermostat.

'Yes, fine. Just a hot flush, or something. Are we nearly there?' I ask, looking out of desperation for anywhere else we could be staying.

I see a sign for Ingleford Manor and I start to feel sick. We can't be. We just *can't*.

Aidan slows down and starts to indicate up the long drive.

'This is where we're staying?' I squeak. 'It looks really expensive – did you want to find somewhere cheaper?'

Aidan laughs.

'Not that it's about the money, but I managed to get an amazing deal on this place. I was talking to my brother about it and he'd seen it promoted online, so you don't have to worry that I'm bankrupting myself.'

I swallow hard and it hurts. My mouth's gone completely dry. I thought I felt sick last time I came here, but the churning that's going on in my stomach right now has nothing to do with food poisoning.

I can feel myself getting panicky. Surely someone's going to recognise me? The hotel are always featuring photos of us from our stay and Grant's always liking my posts and watching my stories.

Aidan winds the car round the turning circle and into the car park.

'Here we are,' he says, opening his door and climbing straight out.

I pull down the sun visor and flip open the mirror and inspect myself. Luckily I let my hair dry naturally this morning so it's big and curly and I didn't bother to put much make-up on, thinking we were just going for a casual walk.

'Are you coming?' he asks, opening my car door.

He's already unloaded our bags.

'Yes, of course,' I say, rewrapping my scarf tightly round my neck and trying to obscure as much of my face as possible. 'Hang on a sec.'

I dig into the front pouch of my suitcase and pull out a big woolly hat.

'There.'

'Weren't you just having a hot flush?'

'Yes and now I'm freezing. This is just what women have to deal with,' I say as we head towards the entrance.

We walk into the lobby and I spot the receptionist from my last stay looking earnestly at her computer whilst she helps a couple at the front desk. 'Do you want to check us in and I'll nip to the loo?'

'Sure,' he says.

I look around before pointing at the toilet as if I've just found it and I dash inside.

I hide in the safety of a cubicle, sighing with relief that I've made it over the threshold. I monitor Aidan's progress by opening the main door a sliver and when he's finished I come back out.

'Good timing,' he says. 'We're on the third floor.'

'Lead on,' I say, gesturing towards the stairs.

I see the back office door opening – the one where Grant usually springs from – and I start to hurry up the stairs two at a time, overtaking Aidan.

'What's the rush?'

'I'm excited to get in the room with you,' I purr over my shoulder.

Aidan gets a sudden spring in his step and we quickly find our room.

He flings open the door and he goes to kiss me but I turn and push him onto the bed which is right in front of us. Our room might be as tastefully decorated as the honeymoon suite but it's nowhere near the size. Typical: this weekend when I want to cocoon us in the room, it's barely big enough to swing a cat. But it does at least have a solid wall between the bedroom and the bathroom, thank goodness.

I start to walk towards Aidan, unbuttoning my coat whilst maintaining eye contact.

'I've arranged us a surprise for later on this afternoon, but we've got a little bit of time,' says Aidan.

'That's lucky, as I'm not in the mood to go fast.'

I slip my fleece over the top of my head, followed by my long-sleeved T-shirt, then I bend down and start unlacing my walking boots, that of course are stuck in a knot. I eventually pull them off and I start hopping on one leg, trying to tug at my woolly socks. By the time I slip off my vest and finally reveal my matching sexy undies, I'm worried that Aidan will have fallen asleep. Winter layers aren't really conducive for a sexy striptease.

He's clearly had enough and he leans forward and drags me onto the bed.

'When I said we had time, we don't have *that* much time,' he says, throwing me on my back.

Right now I'm not stressed about being recognised and I'm starting to enjoy myself, which means all I need to do is use all of my feminine charms to keep him in the room for the rest of our trip.

I move my head off Aidan's chest and reach over for a bottle of water on the desk.

He takes the opportunity to sit up.

'Hey, don't move. I'm coming back,' I say, having a quick drink.

'We can't stay here all day,' says Aidan.

'Can't we?'

Even if I wasn't trying to avoid all the hotel staff, I couldn't think of a better place to spend a Saturday afternoon.

'No, we could do this at home. I've got a surprise for us booked. We're off to the spa.'

'Sounds...' my heart starts to race until I calm myself thinking of all the places I can hide – steam room, sauna, under the big waterfall jets around the pool, 'lovely.'

'Come on, put your swimming costume on.'

A few minutes later we're dressed in matching fluffy hotel robes and heading towards the spa. Aidan's got his arm around me and when I hear Grant's larger-than-life voice echoing down the corridor I bury my head further into the crook of his arm. I'm practically nuzzling his armpits. He squeezes me tighter and despite feeling ridiculous, at least he doesn't seem to think my behaviour is strange.

We pass Grant and make it to the spa, but despite the chilled dolphin music I still can't relax. I've still got to avoid the rest of the staff.

'You look so tense,' says Aidan, rubbing at my arms. 'Which is why it's perfect I've booked us in for a mud session. It's what this hotel is famous for.'

I freeze.

'Mud session?'

My voice has gone all squeaky.

'Uh-huh, doesn't that sound good?'

He winks at me and pulls me towards the reception desk. The receptionist books us in and leads us through into the room where the therapist has her back to us. I sigh with relief when I see the long platinum white hair meaning it can't be Jacinda, until she turns round and I'm standing face to face with Heidi the Swedish masseuse.

'Hello, welcome to the mud experience. Have either of you done a mud bath before?'

'No,' says Aidan.

'No, never, uh-uh,' I say, shaking my head.

'OK,' says Heidi looking at me and I wonder if it's out of recognition or just because I'm acting strangely. She goes on to give the same spiel that Jacinda gave me in November. 'Have you got a hairband for your hair?'

'Oh no, I don't.'

She pulls one out of her pocket and hands it across to me before she smiles and leaves the room. Once she's gone I tie my hair up in a high bun.

I drop my robe and slip off my bikini. It's totally different being here with Aidan instead of Luke – the electricity is crackling between us as we get naked.

'How do you think we get in?' says Aidan.

'I think we just sit on the side and go for it,' I say, almost expertly demonstrating.

I slide into the soft oozy mud and this time I'm prepared for the odd sensation.

Aidan stumbles in and I have to jump up to try and steady him.

'Bloody hell, this stuff is weird,' he says.

I pop some mud on my face, hoping to disguise myself from Heidi for when she comes back.

'Bugger, I've got an itch on my nose. I'm worried I'm going to get mud in my eye. Will you scratch it?' says Aidan.

'Um, I've got just as much mud on my hands as you have.'

Aidan sits there fidgeting. It looks like neither of us are finding this to be the relaxing experience it should be.

'Shit, it's driving me crazy,' he says a couple of minutes later. 'Come closer, you can do it with your nose.'

'My nose? I don't think that's going to work.'

'Trust me, anything's better than the itch.'

I lean over and rub my nose gently against him just as Heidi walks in.

'Oh, um, shall I come back?' she says.

'No, it's not like that,' says Aidan, laughing. 'I had an itch, but I think Izzy got it.'

'Great, so I'm just going to put some mud on your face.'

'Thank you,' sighs Aidan.

'Oh, I see you've already done yours,' she says, turning to me.

'Couldn't resist,' I say.

'Right, I'll leave you in here for fifteen minutes then I'll come in with hot towels,' she says, walking out.

'My nose is itching again,' says Aidan, turning around.

'Oh really,' I say, turning and leaning closer with my nose. I give it the best rub I can before giving him a quick kiss.

'Now, are you starting to feel relaxed?' asks Aidan.

Now that Heidi is out of the way, I am.

'A little. Perhaps you can tell me another story about Barney and the vet's.'

'Oh, I've got plenty of those,' he says, launching into one.

Fifteen minutes later, Heidi comes in and places hot towels on our faces. 'Do you think you'll need me to help you out and into the showers?'

'I reckon we can get ourselves out,' says Aidan, much to my relief. 'I'm pretty much an expert with mud after dealing with my Labrador.'

'No problem,' she says. 'The showers are located just behind you and they're very straightforward to work. Then the nap room is on your right.'

'Great, thanks,' I say as she slips out again.

'I'm so ready to get out of here,' says Aidan, trying to slide himself free of the mud. He manages to get out and props himself up on the edge.

I surprise myself by making it too and I confidently turn

around and put my foot on the floor only to slide the moment I stand up.

Aidan goes to catch me but we're both so slippery that he practically has to rugby tackle me to keep me upright and we end up sliding back into the bath.

'That didn't go quite to plan,' I say, laughing.

He's got a lump of mud on the top of his head and I go to wipe it off but with my muddy hands I make it ten times worse.

'I think we're going to be stuck in here forever,' he says, leaning over and kissing me.

'Or at least until Heidi comes back. I thought you were an expert with mud?'

'I am. This mud will not beat me.'

He scrambles over the side and gingerly places his feet on the floor.

'I made it,' he says, before leaning over and holding onto me as I try and do the same.

'I feel like we're at Glastonbury,' I say, clinging onto him for dear life. We're slipping and sliding all over the mud floor we've created.

'Hurrah,' I say, punching the air in triumph when we reach the showers.

The cool water's a welcome relief after the hot mud and I notice that Aidan's showering with his back next to me.

'What's with you? Since when have you been shy?'

'Since you're all covered in mud and in a shower and we're naked. Do you have any idea how sexy that is?'

'And you're not looking because?'

'We're in a spa where Heidi could walk in on us at any moment.'

'Hmm,' I say, 'how about we ditch the relax room after and head straight back to our room?'

‘Sounds bloody marvellous,’ he says, shutting off the shower and we hastily put our robes back on.

It’s not long before Heidi knocks on the door and I feign a sore tummy and tell her we’re heading back out.

She gives me a small smile and wishes me well and we hurry out.

‘I’m so glad we took this trip,’ he says, sliding the key card into the door lock.

‘Me too,’ I say honestly.

‘And we’ve still got the fancy dinner in the restaurant tonight to go.’

I feel all the tension that I just got rid of in the mud come flooding back. The thought of sitting in a restaurant where Grant or one of the staff could recognise me at any moment terrifies me.

Not that I can think about that right now. No sooner has Aidan opened the door than he’s undone my robe and he’s guiding me to the shower. I think he might do his best to try and give my mind a temporary respite and make me forget about my other life.

# Chapter 31

When I wake up I roll over to find the bed empty.

'Hey, sleepyhead, I was just going to wake you so that we can go for breakfast,' says Aidan, slipping a T-shirt over his head. 'It's 10.30 so we better get a wriggle on. They only serve food until 11.'

He grabs my hands to help me out of bed and I instead pull him towards me.

'Hey, we can't be doing that,' he says, wriggling away. 'We'll start something that'll mean we'll miss the breakfast and I love hash browns.'

'Are you saying I can't compete with them?'

'It's a close call and on the average day you probably would win hands down, but not when it's an all-you-can-eat breakfast buffet which means unlimited hash browns.'

'Can't we order room service?' I say, sitting up to remind him I'm still naked.

'Breakfast is included in the room rate, so...'

'OK, I'll get dressed,' I say, sighing.

I climb out of bed and start to get ready. My curls are stuck up in every direction making it looks like I was electrocuted. Usually I'd scrape it right back into a tiny bun getting it as flat as I could, but the curls are my best disguise at the moment. I pull bits back from the sides and tie them up in a hairband. I look like I'm going to an Eighties party.

'Ready?' asks Aidan.

'I think so.'

We make it down to the dining room and it's busier than I thought it would be with only twenty minutes to go.

We sit down at an empty table and I've just caught the eye of a waitress to take our drinks order when I see Grant walking into the dining room with the head chef. The one that came out and met us personally after mine and Luke's tasting dinner. I shudder at the memory; the last thing I fancied after a severe bout of food poisoning was an eight-course gourmet tasting dinner.

'Are you OK?' asks Aidan.

'Yes, fine,' I say, picking up the drinks menu and burying my head in it. 'Just can't decide what to order.'

I try to pretend that I'm reading options. Luckily there are all different types of teas, coffees, juices and smoothies on offer so I can pretend until Grant and the chef leave the room.

'So what are you going for then?' asks Aidan.

'Coffee.'

'Wow, that was worth all that time studying.'

'Yes, well, for a minute there I thought I might go for a tutti-frutti smoothie but I think I'd prefer a caffeine fix. You kept me up pretty late last night.'

'It was worth it, though, wasn't it?'

'Absolutely,' I say, my cheeks flushing at the memory.

The waitress comes over and takes our drinks order and then we head up to the buffet. Aidan wasn't kidding about his love of hash browns. He's lined them round the edge of his plate like flower petals and dumped the rest of the breakfast items in the middle.

'What did you want to do for the rest of the day? Did you want to hang around here after we've checked out?' he asks.

'How about we leave and then stop somewhere for walk and maybe go for a cream tea?'

'That sounds like an excellent plan. But I should check you're not some heretic that puts the cream on your scones before jam, are you?'

'What do you mean? Oh no, you don't do jam then cream? You know, Aidan, it's been fun, but I think this might be the end of the line.'

He pulls a face.

'Perhaps we could cheat and get chocolate cake?'

I let out a dramatic deep breath. 'I guess there's always that. Although I don't share cake so we have to get one each.'

'Who shares cake?' he says, wrinkling his brow. He watches as a waiter walks over towards the hot plates. 'I better go and get some extra hash browns.'

When we eventually finish eating, or more accurately they take the food away, we head up to the room to get showered before we check out. Of course we showered together so we didn't check out quite as early as we'd planned. We walk back into the reception holding hands and I reflect on what a wonderful night away it's been.

I don't recognise the receptionist but I don't risk approaching him and instead head over to the leaflet desk whilst Aidan hands in our key. I've just found a flyer for a tearoom that isn't far away when I notice someone standing next to me.

I look up smiling, thinking it'll be Aidan back, but my face falls when I see that I'm standing face to face with Grant.

'I thought it was you,' he says, leaning forward and kissing me on both cheeks. I can feel my legs locking in place and heat spreading through my body. 'Izzy, how nice to see you.'

My heart is beating wildly and I try to work out what to say. I glance over my shoulder and Aidan looks like he's finished. He's going to be walking over any minute. I could pretend that Grant's got it wrong, that I'm not the woman he thinks I am, but my face says it all.

'Is Luke with you?'

'Um,' I say, still lost for words. Aidan walks up and puts his hand on the small of my back.

'Ready to go, Iz?' he says.

'Izzy?' says Grant, looking at Aidan.

I close my eyes. I know this is the moment that my life is going to come crashing down.

'Um, Grant, it's so nice to see you. Sorry I didn't tell you I was coming back here, it was all a bit of a surprise. Aidan here booked it.'

I wriggle away from his outstretched hand so that I'm standing alone. He looks at me in surprise.

'He booked it?' says Grant, looking at Aidan. 'And what does your fiancé Luke think about you coming away with another man?'

'Izzy,' says Aidan in a quiet voice. 'What's he talking about? Your fiancé?'

I know that I'm risking my Insta life but Aidan is more important. I'll deal with the fall-out with Luke later.

'I'm not engaged. Luke is a friend of mine, a fellow Instagrammer; we pretended to be together to get more brand sponsorship,' I say turning to Grant. 'But the truth is that we're not together. Aidan is my boyfriend.'

I shoot a look at Aidan hoping that's still true.

'But your romantic weekend? The pictures of you in the bath? You stayed in the honeymoon suite. You mud-bathed naked together,' he says, his voice growing higher and higher in pitch.

I can see Aidan's jaw clenching out of the corner of my eye.

'It was all fake. We staged it all.'

'But that invalidates our contracts. I'm going to have to ask you to leave,' he snarls.

'If you allow me to explain. . .'

'You'll be hearing from our lawyers,' says Grant, taking a step closer towards us and ushering us out of the hotel.

We find ourselves standing outside at the top of the staircase. Aidan is being painfully silent.

'Aidan… It all sounds so much worse than it is.'

He looks at me and my heart shatters into a million pieces.

'Luke was that guy who came to the flat to take photos. Is there even a work magazine or was that all lies too?'

'Let me explain,' I say, touching his arm but he snatches it away.

'Are you going to tell me you didn't come here and stay in the honeymoon suite and you didn't do a mud bath with him? Like the mud bath we did?' he says.

I think of our intimate session in the mud yesterday and a tear rolls down my face. How do I explain that mine and Luke's session was nothing like that?

He shakes his head and starts to walk towards his car.

'Aidan, please.'

He turns back to me and gives me a look of disappointment.

'I can't do this now, Izzy. I want to go home.'

'But I haven't even told you what happened.'

'I don't want to know. I don't know who you are anymore. You're just like Zoe.' He walks a few steps before he turns back and I breathe with relief that he's changed his mind. 'Are you going to be OK – will you be able to get a taxi?'

He might not have changed his mind but he's proved he's the

nicest person in the world for making sure that I'm going to get home OK. My heart burns in my chest.

I nod. The least I can do is to let him go when he needs to.

He turns and walks away and I stand there motionless. I watch him get in his car and speed off down the drive, leaving me in a wake of dust.

I can't go back into the hotel, Grant made that perfectly clear, so I start walking down the long driveway. Through the tears that are rolling thick and fast, I order a taxi and that's who I assume it is a few minutes later when my phone rings with a withheld number.

'Hello.'

'What the fuck have you done, Izzy?' screams Luke down the phone.

'I've fucked up my life,' I say and I close my eyes, trying to block out the angry tirade that follows.

Welcome to February
This_Izzy_Loves IGTV
No. followers: 22.2k

*Super quick one from me this time as this month is crazy busy unlike January that went on for an eternity, am I right? Luke and I had a relatively quiet month, because, again, January and everyone was broke. We didn't do #dryjanuary because we had too much lovely gin left over from our distillery visit and also from the lovely sponsors who sent us fizz for our engagement.*
*Apologies for us being a bit quiet over the last few days but we've been hiding away from the awful weather and having lots of snuggles on the sofa. Love you all.*

# Chapter 32

I've been staring at my computer screen for so long that the words on the page seem to be flying out at me and I'm wondering if the IT department have upgraded my PC to a 3D version without me noticing. Four days have passed since Aidan found out about me and Luke and I've been working on autopilot.

'Do you think Izzy can hear us?' asks Colin.

'I'm not entirely sure. Maybe if I talk about my buns loud enough she might. Or perhaps I can even give her a flash?… Nothing,' says Mrs Harris, almost disappointed. 'And I've got them here waiting.'

She takes the lid off the Tupperware and displays them proudly. 'What's the point of baking buns if no one's going to pick me up on using a *double entendre*? It's a complete waste of ingredients. Do you think I've been pushing The Office Has Talent act too much?'

'I don't think trying to persuade her to perform B*witched has left her in this state,' says Cleo. 'Izzy, do you want a cup of tea?'

I can hear them, but I feel removed from them like they're far away or I'm watching them through a TV screen. I couldn't face telling them all the full truth of what happened, but Cleo's guessed I've got trouble in both my love lives – real and virtual. I know I should talk back to them but I've gone into self-preservation mode where I've shut down everything but basic functions.

I did the same thing when Ben died. I never realised how break-ups could be so similar to grief. But I guess they are: again I've lost someone I loved in an instant.

The only difference is that unlike Ben's death, I was responsible for my break-up with Aidan. I've come to accept over the years that I couldn't have changed what happened to Ben. Unless I had a crystal ball and had got him to have his heart tested, there's no way I could have prevented what happened to him. But Aidan, that look on his face, is going to be burned on my memory forever as a reminder of exactly what I did to cause him pain.

I've called and texted multiple times over the last few days to try and explain to him but he doesn't respond. I've driven to his house but no matter when I go he's not there, and neither is Barney and his booming bark. I've even been to his café but Saskia told me to leave.

'Izzy,' says Cleo loudly whilst nudging me at the same time.

I turn my head and try and focus on her face.

'Izzy, do you want a cup of tea?' she asks. 'You've been working non-stop all morning.'

'I'm at work.'

The others splutter a laugh.

'But you haven't stopped; we're not that busy. If you don't take a break then you'll give us all a bad rep.'

I notice Mrs Harris's look of concern.

'I guess a coffee would be good,' I finally say.

I expect everyone to be pleased I've spoken but instead someone comes walking into our office, and they all look alarmed. Mrs Harris leaps out of her chair, motioning for Colin and Cleo to join her. They form a human chain around me and I look round to see what they're protecting me from.

'Izzy,' comes Luke's voice. 'You've got to speak to me eventually.

I know we can't talk here but if you won't answer your phone, you're leaving me with little choice. There's only so much firefighting that I can do alone.'

I bend under the arms of Colin and Cleo to look at him. He looks far from the composed and styled state that I'm used to seeing. He's got dark circles under his eyes, his skin's pale and his quiff is lopsided.

'I'll come and talk to you now,' I say.

'Izzy, you don't have to go anywhere,' says Mrs Harris. It's sweet of her to stick up for me even though she doesn't really know what's going on.

'You were just saying I needed a break. I need to talk to Luke.'

I stand up and they close ranks tighter around me.

'Really, I'll be fine.'

'I know where you sit, Sonny Jim,' says Mrs Harris, pointing a menacing finger at his chest.

If he's scared of her he doesn't show it; he clearly doesn't know her like I do.

I pick up my coat and follow him to the canteen.

'I've managed to calm Grant down and he's not going to say anything,' says Luke. We sit down at the table despite not ordering anything. 'We've fulfilled our obligation to him for the first contract so as long as we carry on as a couple on Instagram then he'll have no reason to tell anyone else. Obviously you're going to have to stop seeing Aidan. We can't risk that happening again. We've got the Valentine's Ball coming up and I know how much that means to you—'

'Luke, I'm not doing this anymore. I'm out.'

'What are you talking about? Grant isn't going to tell anyone. We can carry on with the plan.'

'Look, we were going to break up later this month anyway

– why can't we do it now? I can't pretend anymore, Luke, this is real life. People have got hurt.'

'More people are going to get hurt if we stop now. What about the charity?'

'I'll email them and explain that we've broken up. If it's an amicable break-up then we could still go through with the ball as friends.'

'Grant won't like that. I promised him we'd be a couple for another few months so that the advertising material he's got for the summer isn't obsolete.'

'Do you honestly think that I'm going to carry this on for him? What do you expect me to do – try on wedding dresses? This has gone too far, Luke. It's not a game anymore.'

'Is this about Aidan?'

'Of course it's about Aidan. I love him and now I've lost him. All for this stupid fantasy of becoming an influencer.'

'It's not a fantasy, it's real. We're so close, Izzy. So bloody close.'

I put my hands on my head and run my fingers through my hair. He's not listening to a word I'm saying.

'I've never stopped to think about what our actual life will look like. I've been too busy focusing on the short-term gain. The freebies, the money, the buzz of it all, but what's going to happen in the future? You keep moving the boundaries of our break-up and I'm stuck in a fake relationship with you forever. I want to have my own life, to get married, have kids.'

'I'd marry you.'

I slam my hands down on the table.

'For fuck's sake, Luke, listen to yourself. You want to marry me to get famous.'

'Maybe I'm in love with you,' he snaps.

I splutter a laugh. He looks serious but I know he can't be.

'Name one thing you love about me?' I say, exasperated. He opens his mouth before shutting it again.

'Shall I tell you what I love about Aidan?' I say in a calm voice, not believing that he had the audacity to say that. 'I love the way that he thinks about other people more than himself. I love the way that he talks to his dog like he's his best friend. I love how he always has time for the people closest in his life. I love that he would do anything to make sure a person was safe, even if it was breaking his heart. I love... absolutely everything about him.'

'And your point is?'

'You don't love me. You love the idea of the brand we represent. I was stupid to have gone along with this for as long as I did. But no more, Luke. We end this in the platonic way we always said we would. Why don't we meet after work and we can plan the details?'

I see the desperation in his eyes and I wonder if he's going to start pleading.

'You're going to be fine, Luke. Your star is rising and I don't think you need me at all.'

He looks right into my eyes before he nods.

'You're right. I don't need you. Fine, we end this.'

'Thank you,' I say, exhaling.

'No, Izzy, thank you for everything that you've done for me.'

I look down at my hands and they're shaking. I can't believe I did that and I made him listen. At least I know that I'm no longer living a lie.

I look up at the canteen staff who all jump apart and pretend to be busy. I get the impression they listened to every word.

'Can I get three flat whites and a skinny mocha?' I say, walking up to the counter. One of the women nods and goes to do the order. I smile to myself for the first time in days. I didn't realise how much I was worrying about a confrontation with Luke. I thank the woman as she places my coffees on a tray and after my scanning my pass to pay for them, I head back up to the office.

'Blimey,' says Mrs Harris. 'You look a bit happier.'

'Yes, I got things sorted.'

'Good. Here, he's not tried to poach you for an Office Has Got Talent act, has he? Miles would do anything to win.'

'No, and believe me no one would try and poach me. I keep trying to tell you I am supremely untalented.'

I hand out the coffees and I sit down at my desk. I pick up my phone in the silly hope that Aidan has sent a message or returned my calls in the few minutes I've been away, but of course he hasn't. The smile slides off my face. It doesn't matter that I've 'broken up' with Luke, I've still lost Aidan.

I open Instagram, wishing I'd never started using the bloody thing and I see that I've got loads of new notifications which is strange because I haven't posted anything for days. I click on the heart and see that they're comments, and not very nice ones either: 'Heartless Bitch', 'Evil Cow', 'Dirty Slag' being the most polite of the bunch. But it's not the comments that are disturbing, it's the photo that it's attached to. It's only a tiny preview but I can still see quite clearly that it's of me and Aidan kissing.

My hands start to shake and my blood runs cold when I click on it and see it. It's the photo Luke took at our fake photoshoot of us kissing. I quickly turn my attention to the caption, which is a heartbroken emoji and the caption: '**I can't believe Izzy did this to me.**' That bastard. He must have posted it the second he left the canteen. I bet he had it ready to go in his drafts. This was his Plan B and the reason why he left without a fuss.

Anger pulses through my veins and I storm away from my desk, not bothering to read the comments below. I barely register the calls of my colleagues over my shoulder; nothing's going to stop me now. I stomp down to Sales only to see Luke's chair is empty.

'Where's Luke?' I ask, my voice shaking with rage.

'He's gone. Can I help instead?' asks another guy.

'What do you mean *gone*?'

'He quit, first thing this morning.'

'What?'

'Evil Edward's not happy. He didn't even give any notice period. Just walked out.'

I shake my head. He had it all planned. He kept saying that he'd been saving up to be able to quit but I didn't realise he was close enough to whip away his security blanket.

I ring him but his phone's off. That bastard. I can't take that photo down as it's on his feed and I've got no way of stopping the hate that's coming my way. It's ironic that the picture that's ruined my Instagram career is the first truthful photo on Instagram that's been posted of me in months, if not years.

'Can I do anything for you?' asks the guy again. 'Evil Edward's watching and he's already on the warpath.'

'No, I'm fine, thanks,' I say through gritted teeth. I manage to hold it together long enough to make it back onto the stairwell. I lean on the banister and burst into tears. Just when I thought my life couldn't fall apart any more than it had; and what's worse is I've only got myself to blame.

# Chapter 33

I open the door and Mum's standing there clutching a big stack of travel brochures with a huge grin on her face. She stops smiling immediately when she sees my tear-stained face.

'Izzy, what's wrong?'

'It's Aidan, we broke up.'

She pulls me into a hug before she shuts the door and leads me through to the sofa.

'What happened? You were so happy.'

'We were. He took me away for a romantic night away and it was so wonderful and then…'

Mum takes off her coat and scarf whilst raising an eyebrow.

'And then?'

She leans forward and takes my hand.

'It ended,' I say, shrugging. I can't relive it again. My mum will be so disappointed in me.

'It was all my fault, Mum.'

'I'm sure it seems worse than it is. I'm sure if you talked to him—'

'I've tried but I can't get hold of him. He's not answering his phone and I keep going to his house but I don't think he's living there at the moment. His business partner won't tell me where he is. I don't know how else to get hold of him.'

'Oh, love. I'm sure he'll calm down. Everything seems better in time.'

'Does it?' I hope she's right. I think back to the weekend with Aidan and the feeling of utter bliss and utter contentment I'd had. I can't believe I'll never have that again.

I point at the brochures.

'Has Dad finally persuaded you to go away?'

'Yes, but we don't need to talk about that now.'

'Why do you two keep trying to hide the fact that you want to go away? What am I missing?'

'It's about where we're getting the money for the trip,' she says, pulling at the sleeve of her jumper.

Suddenly it all falls into place.

'You're selling the house? Aren't you?'

'We don't need to talk about it today.'

'Mum, it's OK.'

She takes a deep breath.

'We had an agent round to value it last week and we've decided it makes sense for us to downsize. We're thinking of getting somewhere small, close to town,' she says. 'Your dad's been trying to persuade me to travel before it's too late.'

'You're not that old.'

'No, we're not, but we've got to do the things whilst we're still fit and have the energy to do it. I fancy New Zealand and your dad wants to do Peru and we always said we'd go to Mauritius.'

'How long are you going for?' I say, thinking that I've got so used to having them round the corner.

'Don't worry, we're not going off indefinitely. We figured we'd go away a few weeks a year. That way we won't get travel fatigue.'

I try not to show my relief. I don't think I could have coped if they'd have gone away for a whole year.

'That sounds great, I'm happy for you.'

'You are?' she says, looking me in the eye. 'You're not too sad about us selling the house? I've been so worried.'

'Of course I am a little, but sometimes I find it hard to go and see you there. I can't imagine what it's like to actually live in it, with all the memories.'

'I hadn't thought about it until your dad started talking about selling and I started to realise that it had stopped feeling like home a long time ago,' Mum admits.

I open a brochure of tours in South America.

'I'm really glad you're moving on.'

'Yes, and I wish you would too. Have you thought about writing to Aidan?'

'Writing? No, I haven't. What happened with him… it's complicated.'

'Did you cheat on him?'

'Not in the conventional sense, but in some ways.'

She stands up from the sofa. 'I'm going to put the kettle on and you're going to tell me all about it. OK?'

I feel like I'm a little girl again and I don't dare disobey.

'OK, Mum,' I say, and when she comes back with the piping hot tea, I start to tell her all about it.

I come to the end of the story and there's a pause. My mum's facial expression is so neutral it's like she's advertising for Switzerland.

'Well,' she says. 'I wasn't expecting that. I knew that you were into the whole Instagram thing, but teaming up with Luke.'

'I know,' I say, wincing. 'I don't know how I let it get so out of control. I can't blame it all on Ben dying. Everyone else is doing well. Becca's getting serious with Gareth and you and Dad are selling the house and planning exciting adventures. It hasn't made you all implode.'

Mum puts her empty teacup down on the table.

'We're all struggling still, you know that, right?'

'I didn't mean to imply that you're not still grieving,' I say, feeling awful that I've caused offence.

'No, I meant the reason that we didn't implode is that we had you to look after us. On a bad day you were the one I'd phone and I know Becca was the same, that's why you moved in with her. Don't you see, you've been supporting us through our grief but we haven't been supporting you through yours. I don't know how I didn't see it, but you seemed so together.'

'I wasn't,' I say, realising how much I've been bottling up. 'I guess I just dealt with it in different ways.'

'Like creating a fantasy online life.'

'I sound like a nutter,' I say, laughing.

'I think you sound like a genius. I've wanted to escape so much from it over the last few years and you found a way to.'

'It didn't work very well, though, did it?'

'I think it might have got a bit out of hand.'

'A bit?'

'I wish you'd told us how you were feeling and what was going on. I always called you when I was low and I wish you'd done the same.'

'But it's different with you, isn't it? Everyone expects you to feel low. You're the mother, you lost your son. Becca lost her fiancé.'

'What is this, grief Top Trumps? I don't get extra points because I gave birth to him. He was your brother, Izzy, you spent your entire childhood with him. Maybe you spent more time with him than I did when you were both growing up.'

Tears start rolling down my face.

'You lost him too, Izzy, and perhaps we all need to be reminded of that.'

She leans over and hugs me again as I sob into her arms and I don't let her go.

'I've messed it all up,' I splutter.

'Nothing that can't be fixed. Come on, Izzy. You'll get through this. And if it doesn't work out I've still got Roger Davenport's phone number from that night at the ice hockey. I ran into his mum in the supermarket the other day and he's still single.'

'Mum,' I groan.

'Too soon to joke? Come on, you'll figure it out like you always do.'

'I don't know if I'm strong enough,' I whisper.

'Then we'll hold you up. You're going to get through this.'

I can only hope that she's right because I don't think I can cope with a broken heart for much longer.

Welcome to March
This_Izzy_Loves
No. Followers: 16.4k
Instagram post:

*I'm posting this on all my channels to say that I'm coming off social media due to the escalation of trolls. Instagram is somewhere that I've always felt safe and I've genuinely loved getting to know all my followers. I am so sorry if I've hurt or misled anyone, please know that that was never my intention. And don't believe everything you read or see: remember, there are always two sides to every story. I want to thank all my genuine and loyal followers. I've had an incredible journey but at this point in time I'm unsure if I'll ever come back on here. Thank you and I'm sorry, Izzy x x x*

April

Tattle Life Thread: Who misses This_Izzy_Loves???????

Karen1982DT:
Does anyone really miss Izzy? I used to love her stories and her lust for life. She was never up herself and I adored her shopping hauls. No one raids H&M like her. Please come back, Izzy, we miss you, hun!!!

GeriBestBath:
I miss her too. But still cross about what she did to Luke. I'd love her to explain herself though as maybe there was more to it? Either way I'd love to see her back on here. My feed's a duller place without her.

# Chapter 34

There's a knock at the door and I climb off the sofa. I used to be jumpy when the door buzzed or knocked thinking it was Aidan, but I've long since abandoned any hope that he will come. I sent him a long letter explaining everything and I've taken his silence as a sign that I should move on.

I'm expecting it to be Marissa. She and Leah are on their way over to spend the afternoon with Becca and me, and I'm guessing someone let her in.

I peer through the keyhole and take a step backwards in surprise.

'Hello,' I say, pulling open the door to find Gareth. 'I'm afraid Becca's not here, I thought she was with you.'

'She was, but it's you I wanted to see,' he says, leaning over and giving me a bear hug. 'I just want you to know that Becca told me about Ben.'

'Oh,' I say, pulling back. 'Is everything OK with you and her? Is she OK?'

'She's fine. She's in the car. I wanted to talk to you before she came up. Just us.'

'OK,' I say, ushering him inside to the lounge where we sit down at opposite ends of the sofa.

'You know that I've asked Becca to move in with me?'

I nod. She confided in me a few weeks ago that she didn't know what to do.

'Well, last night she finally told me that what's been holding her back was her need to tell me the truth. I was really bricking it, worrying about what she was going to say and then she told me about Ben. I was upset at first, more because I felt hurt that she didn't trust me to tell me, but then the more she talked the more I understood.

'And then she told me about you and what you've been doing for her since it happened. I think she's worried that if she moves out she'll lose you – so I wanted you to know that you'll always be welcome at our house. You might not be related by blood to Becca but you're family to her and I don't want to get in the way of that. Same for your parents, too, they'll always be welcome.'

My heart is bursting for Becca. She honestly couldn't have found a better man to fall in love with.

'Thank you, Gareth, that means a lot.'

'Good, and they're not just words. When we do move in together you're not to be a stranger. OK?'

'OK,' I say, nodding.

He leans over and gives me a hug again. He's not a natural hugger and it's quite stiff and awkward – much like my impression of him up until now – but I'm starting to see there's so much more to him.

'I'm going to go and let you have your girls' afternoon.'

I smile in thanks and he lets himself out.

A couple of minutes later the door opens again and Becca walks through cradling baby Leah.

'Look who I found on the doorstep.'

'She didn't literally find her on the doorstep before you question my mothering skills. I was holding her at the time,' says Marissa, strolling in behind.

I go over to Leah and give her a kiss on the head, before hugging both of the girls.

'Did your talk with Gareth go OK?' Becca asks. 'Sorry, he didn't give me any advance warning, he just pulled up and leapt out of the car.'

'Don't worry. It was lovely of him. I can totally appreciate what you see in him.'

She beams and spins Leah around.

'And you,' says Marissa, pointing at me. 'Look at you. You look great.'

I've got a sort of hybrid look going on. Apparently serums have moved on since my twenties and with a bit of experimenting I've managed to wrestle my curls under control.

'Thanks, I'm feeling a lot better this week.'

'What do we want to drink – tea or something stronger?' she asks, handing Leah to me.

'Perhaps a little bit of fizz. Celebrate the fact that I'm feeling a bit more like my old self.' I pull an exaggerated face at Leah. 'I can't believe how big she's getting.'

'I know – she's not a newborn anymore. Thank God. Don't get me wrong, it's not that I didn't enjoy it but it's just been one big sleep-deprived haze. And look – now she smiles and interacts with you.'

She starts cooing over my shoulder at her daughter before she sits down on the sofa.

'So how's she going down on Insta? How's her hashtag going?'

'Actually, I've made my account private and deleted loads of people.'

'What?' I startle Leah and I have to jiggle her a little more to make her happy again.

'Well, when she was born I suddenly didn't like people liking and commenting on her when I didn't know them. It made me question why I needed random strangers to validate my life, so I did a massive cull.'

'Wow,' I say, at a loss for words.

'I know. An end of an era, huh?'

We hear the pop of the Prosecco cork and Becca quickly walks through with a tray of glasses and hands them to us.

I struggle to hold both Leah and a flute so Marissa lifts her off me and handles them both effortlessly.

'Don't judge me. I've become the master of doing everything with one hand.'

'No judgement here,' I say, sipping my drink, 'only admiration.'

'So what's behind today's smiles?' asks Marissa.

I take another sip and let the bubbles fizz on my tongue.

'I had my appraisal at work a few days ago and it made me realise a few things.'

Becca raises an eyebrow in my direction. 'Like?'

'Like the fact that I love the working environment at McKinley's. And that you were right, Marissa, about employers looking favourably at my Instagram experience. After I chatted to my boss, Howard, he set up a meeting for me with the Marketing department, and whilst they don't have any openings at the moment, they've offered to mentor me and hopefully if something does come up I might be able to move across.'

'Wow, that's great,' says Marissa.

'Yes, and the best bit is, if I do move departments I'll still get to don my double denim for our B*witched act.'

'I can't believe you've been roped into that,' says Becca, sniggering.

'I know! So much for getting spare time back after Instagram.

Mrs Harris has organised us rehearsals with vocal coaches and choreographers nearly every night after work.'

'Has she heard you sing?' asks Becca.

'Not yet – you're going to have to give me lessons.'

'I'd be happy to,' says Becca. 'I'm really proud of you for getting yourself together in spite of everything.'

'I'm proud of me too. It feels like something is going right for me for the right reasons.'

'Plus I bet it helps not to see dick-face at work,' says Marissa.

I gulp down a bigger sip of my drink.

'That does help, a lot.'

'Do you know what he's up to now?' asks Becca.

'I don't. I deleted Instagram off my phone and I haven't heard from him since.'

Marissa looks sheepish.

'You know, don't you?'

'I might be posting less, but I still look at it a lot and I haven't stopped following Luke.'

'So what's he doing?'

'More of the same. He's doing a lot of photos with really obscure captions so you wonder what the tenuous link is until you get to the hashtag ad at the end.'

'I hate those ads. I know influencers have to make money, but I hate them shoehorning it in. At least this thing worked out well for someone.' I take a deep breath, disappointed in the karma of it all.

I finish the rest of my drink and go to top it up, offering to fill up the girls' only to see they've barely touched theirs.

'Let's have a look at his feed then,' I say, reaching over and picking up Marissa's phone.

'I don't think you should – look how good you were doing,' says Becca.

'Come on, I just want to see the odd picture,' I say. 'I promise I won't comment.'

'I wish you bloody would,' says Marissa. 'But from your phone, not mine. He shouldn't be getting away with what he did.'

I shrug my shoulders. 'He's quit his job, it's his livelihood now.'

'But he ruined your chances of being an influencer.'

'And probably did me a favour.'

I hold the phone in front of Marissa's face and she reluctantly taps in her key code. My fingers waste no time navigating to Instagram and I home straight in on his story.

He's standing in the gym doing weights and I don't care what he has to say. I click instead on his profile and scroll through the pictures of him. His photos look slicker and more polished but I guess he's a pro now and has more time to spend on them.

I scroll down far enough to be confronted with the photo of me and Aidan and I can't help clicking on it to see it again.

'Izzy, don't do it to yourself,' says Marissa, leaning over.

'Look how happy we were.' I turn the phone to show her and she gives me a look of pity.

It's then that I notice the little blue dot to indicate that there's another picture. I know I was angry when I saw the post originally, but how had I not seen that? I scroll across to find a different photo of Aidan and me – one that I've never seen before. Aidan's so close and it looks like we're about to kiss. It's beautiful and it shows so much love and I feel a tear rolling down my cheek.

'I love that photo,' says Marissa. 'You both look so in love. When did Luke take it?'

I stare harder at it before looking up at her. 'That's a very good question – when *did* he take it?'

I try and look for clues in what I'm wearing. It's the pale

jumper that I wore on the non-date to Ted's restaurant. My whole body tenses... he must have followed me.

'Oh my God,' I say, my heart starting to race. I put the phone down on the sofa and stand up, backing away from it slowly.

'What is it?' asks Marissa, picking up the phone and staring at the photo.

'That was taken the night I went for dinner with Aidan. Before we were a couple, before I'd even told Luke about us.'

'What? Are you serious?'

I nod and my brain starts to go into overdrive.

I thought Luke posting the original photo was spiteful but following me and taking photos months earlier, that's a whole different level of pre-meditation.

'What if he had this in mind the whole time?' I say, my blood boiling with anger. 'What if he wanted me to fall for someone else so he could break us up like this?'

'Surely Luke wouldn't have done that,' says Marissa.

'There's only one way to find out.'

I pick up my handbag and reach for my keys.

'You're not driving anywhere,' says Becca, snatching my keys away.

'I'll drive,' says Marissa. 'My car's got Leah's seat in it already.'

'You'd do that?' I ask.

'Of course. Someone has to back you up,' she says.

I smile with relief and we hurry down to the car.

Marissa straps Leah into her seat and she's asleep within minutes. We head out of the town centre and along the Reading road.

'What are you going to say to him?' asks Becca.

'I have no idea,' I say shaking, 'but we'll soon find out.'

*

I manage to persuade Becca and Marissa to stay in the car. They've kept the engine running, not for fear of a quick getaway but because Leah's still asleep and turning off the engine will apparently wake her.

'I feel like Charlie's Angels,' says Marissa as I climb out the car.

'I wish we were and then we could kick his arse,' says Becca. 'Which house is it? You know, in case you need back-up?'

'That one there, with the grey window frames.'

I stomp along the pavement and bang on his door until one of his housemates answers.

'Where's Luke?'

'Oh God, you didn't get it too, did you? He's had loads of visitors this week. FYI the clinic on Redlands Road is a good one if you want to be a bit more discreet than the hospital.'

'Where is he?' Not even the thought of Luke having an STI is making me any less mad.

'Luke,' he calls, watching me like a hawk. 'There's someone here to see you.'

He's halfway down the stairs when he sees me. He stops and clings onto the banister.

'What are you doing here? Come to beg for me back as you regret your Instagram exile?'

'Like I really give a shit about any of that. The whole time you were planning to post those photos. You used me all along.'

I see a flash of something in his eyes and I almost think he's enjoying this.

'What are you going to do about it?'

I go to launch up the stairs at him, but his housemate restrains me.

'Whoa, you don't want to be doing that. I'm a trainee barrister and you don't want assault on your record.'

I turn and glare at him.

'He's not worth it, whatever he's done,' he says.

I snap my head back to Luke, who's still looking down at me from the safety of the stairs.

'I wasn't always going to use it; I just thought I'd take out a little insurance policy in case it went wrong, which it did. I was planning for us to have the amicable break-up.'

'I don't believe you.'

He's got a smug smile on his face that I want to wipe off but I daren't as the trainee barrister is now filming everything – for evidence or maybe in the hope that I'll do something that'll go viral. Whatever the reason, I put my hand out to block the camera. I'm not giving him the satisfaction.

'You were playing with my and Aidan's lives.'

'And you were playing with mine too. You were never supposed to fall in love with someone. That wasn't part of the plan.'

'Well, one thing I've learnt in life is that it doesn't usually go to plan, Luke,' I snap before walking away. There are so many things I want to shout at him, but ultimately he's not worth it.

I storm back to the car as fast as my jelly legs will let me.

'Shit, Izzy, are you OK?' asks Marissa.

'No, just drive, please?'

She does as she's told and Leah opens her big blue eyes at me and smiles. I smile back at her before I start to sob and then she starts to sob too and the two of us wail in the back of the car.

We drive towards Basingstoke and it isn't long before we pass the turning to Aidan's house. I hadn't really connected that they lived so close together. For a second I'm tempted to go and try and talk to him, but what good would it do? He'd only tell me something I wouldn't want to hear. The best thing I can do is move on and put all this behind me.

Welcome to May
This_Izzy_Loves IGTV
No. followers: 15.2k

*Hey, everyone. I'm back to tell you my side of the story about what happened with Luke. I think it's time you knew the unfiltered version of what was going on outside the Instagram grid.*

*Luke and I were never a couple. Not a couple in the way that we pretended to be. Yes, we went on dates and cooked meals for each other but we were never more than friends – if we were ever even friends. We were work colleagues who shared the same dream. We both wanted to become influencers so that we could leave our jobs – and Luke had an idea of how we might get there. He suggested we fake a relationship to boost our profiles. The moment that he posted the photo of us and the likes racked up I was seduced by the possibility and I fully went along with the idea, for which I'm really sorry.*

*Our whole fairy-tale romance was a lie but to be honest I was lying on my Instagram feed long before that. Half the clothes I wore on my #OutfitOfTheDay were ones that I bought and took back because I couldn't afford to keep them. The stuff that designers sent me were often too big and I had to pin them at the back to keep them in place. I hate gin and I did a sponsorship deal with a gin company. I'm allergic to exercise and when I reviewed a fitness tracker I made my work colleagues wear it to get my impressive activity levels up. I don't own Louboutins and any time you saw me in them, they weren't actually my feet, they were my friends'. Most days I eat at the work canteen and I rarely cook for myself. Any home-cooked gourmet creation would have been a ready meal that I'd spent precious minutes arranging on my plate to make it look like I was a good cook. I have never uploaded an unfiltered photo of my face on Instagram. Not once. The ones I hashtagged as #nofilter were actually ones I'd doctored first in Photoshop.*

*So there you go, I'm a big fat liar. Or maybe I'm just an ordinary female social media user. I think we're all guilty of manipulating and filtering our lives to give them a gloss of perfection. Only I took it a step too far. To all the brands that we worked with, I am truly sorry. I have worked hard at my day job over the last couple of months, working overtime, and I will be contacting brands to ask if they would like products back or if I can donate them to charity. Likewise, any brands that paid me money: I will return it to you or make a charitable donation in your name.*

*I've also donated to the Heart2Heart charity, which I desperately didn't want to miss out on much-needed money after Luke and I pulled out of the charity ball. My best friends and I are going to run the Reading Half*

*Marathon to fundraise for them too – so for once I'm going to have to start the couch to 5k and not give up after the first session.*

*To all of the people that liked and commented on our story, I'm so sorry if you feel deceived. We hoped that we'd be a bit of light entertainment in a gloomy world – I know we were wrong.*

*I no longer want to be Insta famous because I don't like the person that Insta made me. I just want to get to know the real me again – the me without filters that doesn't need to have every moment of my life validated. The me that would never have dreamt of lying for personal gain.*

*Sending my very best wishes, this is This_Izzy_Loves signing off once and for all.*

# Chapter 35

I'm waiting for my computer to shut down when my phone beeps. It's a reminder from my Google calendar that I've booked a ticket to see *Ghostbusters* at the cult classic cinema club. Not that I would have forgotten. It's the first of the new season and I've been debating whether to go since I got the original email last month. Being in that cinema reminds me so much of Aidan. I booked a ticket, but I still haven't decided.

My computer finally goes silent and I sling my bag over my shoulder and wheel my chair under my desk.

'All right for some, swanning off in the middle of the day.'

'It's called flexi-time, Mrs Harris – you have it too, you just never seem to use it.'

'Hmmpf,' she splutters and goes back to her work.

'Have a lovely weekend, everyone,' I call.

'You too,' calls Cleo and I get a wave from Colin who's on the phone.

I don't know why I haven't made better use of my flexi before, but now that I'm having therapy sessions on a Friday afternoon I've been enjoying working a four-and-a-half day week. I don't seem to notice that the other days are longer.

I hurry down the stairs with a spring in my step. Posting the truth on Instagram has been liberating. Yes, I got stick for it.

There were a lot of angry and upset people when they realised that Luke and I had been fake, but there were also loads of lovely people that applauded my honesty.

If anything I hope it makes people think a bit more carefully about who they follow. The lines are so blurred now between advertiser and the man in the street, it's hard to know what's real and what's not. Of course, Luke and I took it to the extreme but it worries me how easy it was to do.

I'm still thinking of him as I turn the corner and walk down the steps down to his old floor. The doors open and I see him walking out – for a second I wonder if I'm hallucinating, but I'm not, he's there right in front of me.

I stop in my tracks. I haven't seen him since that day at his house. I'd been half expecting to hear from him after I posted on Instagram about the true nature of our relationship.

'Luke,' I say, keeping my position halfway up the stairwell. 'What are you doing here?'

He takes a step towards my staircase and narrows his eyes.

'Do you have any idea what you did with your little stunt?'

There's an unpleasant lilt to his voice and I almost wish we had his barrister friend still with us.

'Little stunt?' I say, trying to sound calm.

'Yeah, do you know how many followers I've lost since your post? Brands have dropped me. You know that I do this fulltime now, don't you – it's my job.'

He runs his fingers through his hair, sending his quiff lopsided.

'You should never have posted those photos of me and Aidan. All I did was try and set the record straight.'

'Well, thanks, Izzy. Thanks a lot.'

He gives me a cold hard stare and I can hear my heart thundering in my chest.

He turns and stomps down the stairs towards the entrance. I clutch the handrail tight and take some deep breaths, waiting for my quivering legs to be steady enough to move. The odd person brushes past me as they go on their lunch break and eventually I compose myself. I pass the Sales floor and the doors fly open and Luke's colleague that I spoke to after he quit walks out. He smiles at me and I try and smile back and we walk down the stairs together.

'Hey, did I see Luke back in the building today?'

'Yeah, would you believe he came in to ask for his old job back?'

My chest grows tighter. I couldn't imagine potentially running into him every day.

'Did he get it?'

'Did he hell! My boss is fuming that he quit without notice – he'll only give him a basic reference too.'

'Oh dear.'

'Yeah, I would feel sorry for him, but he landed us all extra work until he was replaced.'

'Any idea what he's going to do now?'

'I think he said he was going to try the old estate agent's he worked for.'

I can't suppress a grin as this is the best thing I've heard in ages. Obviously I'd never want to ruin someone's career but after what he did to me I can't help feeling the tiniest bit vindicated that he got what he deserved.

I'm pleased that that part of my life has got the closure it needed – now I just need to sort out the other loose ends.

*

'I know I should have come here a long time ago,' I say, taking a deep breath, thinking that I've become a cliché. A cool breeze blows around my shoulders and I wish I'd worn a coat. I got lulled into thinking it was spring when I'd seen the blue skies and sunshine overhead. 'You know, I've started to go to therapy because of you. To be honest I should have done it a long time ago. It's nice talking about yourself to a stranger. I mean, talking the truth about what's really going on in my head to a stranger, not like the lies I used to tell on Instagram stories.

'I miss you. I really fucking miss you and it hurts like hell. Every day. And I never ever told you that I loved you, and I did. You knew that, right?'

Tears sting in my eyes and I take a deep breath. I promised myself that I wouldn't cry. That isn't what this was about.

'Everything around me is changing. Mum and Dad have accepted an offer on their house, Becca's agreed to move in with Gareth and I'm going to get an unknown flatmate. Life is going on and it's changing and I've got to stop being scared. I can't be frozen in a moment anymore. I can't live wishing that I could turn back time. I would do anything to turn back the clock, but I can't. So I have to move forward and I'm going to do it and I'm going to make you proud. I've realised that it doesn't have to be with Instagram. I know you'd be proud of whatever I was doing as long as I was proud of myself.

'I love you, Ben, and I always will.'

It feels so weird to tell him I love him out loud but at the same time it feels like a huge weight has been lifted off my shoulders. I put the bunch of daffodils that I brought with me and lay them next to the tree and look out at the view over the park. He'd always loved this spot when we were kids. We'd spend hours under this very tree having picnics, trying to climb it, acting out

*The Princess Bride* from sticks that had fallen from its branches. I don't know why I hadn't thought of coming here before.

I sit down and rest my back against the trunk and I watch the world going by. Mothers pushing prams around. Dog walkers getting their arms pulled off by their dogs. It's so full of life here and I can't think of a better spot to remember Ben.

I'm slowly learning to accept that I might not be OK for a long time but that eventually, whilst I won't ever forget him and I won't ever miss him less, I'll learn to live with the empty feeling. But finding ways to be closer to him help.

A big yellow Labrador bounds across the park and for a minute I hold my breath until I see a woman walking behind it. I try to hide my disappointment that it's not Barney.

I pull a book out of my bag to distract myself. I'm halfway through it and I'm loving it. Since I quit social media I have so much free time and I'd forgotten how much I loved reading. It's the perfect thing to do in a bid to be kind to myself after an emotionally exhausting therapy session.

'Are you sure you don't want us to come with you?' asks Becca.

I look at her and Gareth curled up on the sofa.

'Nah, I'll be fine. I can't imagine it's going to be your thing. Plus it's a sell-out.'

'See you later on then,' she says. 'Call us if you need us.'

'Thanks, see you later.'

I shut the door and head downstairs towards my car. I'd booked the ticket on autopilot, pleased that it was the original *Ghostbusters*, another one of mine and Ben's childhood classics. But since I booked the ticket I've thought more and more about Aidan. It's so much our place but I've decided that there's only one way to get over that and that's to go. I've already become the new and improved me and I've realised I'm strong enough to do most things and I certainly ain't afraid of no ghosts: ex-boyfriend or ectoplasmic.

By the time I walk through the door into the cinema my bravery is waning. The smell of popcorn drifts over to me and I can't help but be hit by the memories of last summer.

I grit my teeth, buy some chocolates and head on into the screening room. It's already quite busy and I head towards the back, trying to keep my head down so that the not so friendly usher doesn't clock me.

I flinch as the doors open and more people walk in but none of them are Aidan. The lights finally go down and the trailers start to play and I stop watching the door and try to get lost in the movie, which is surprisingly easy to do.

The end credits roll and I'm pleased with myself that I managed to make it through a film here. I take my empty chocolate box and head out past the usher who glares at me. I want to tell him that I haven't even got my phone on me – it's in the car – but he still scares me so I hurry into the lobby instead.

'Izzy?'

I turn and see Aidan holding a stripy white-and-blue bag of pic 'n' mix.

'You weren't in the middle, so I thought you weren't here,' he says.

'Thought it was time for a change.'

He smiles and my heart melts.

'You're looking well,' he says.

'So are you. Have you been away somewhere?'

'Yeah, I've been up in Scotland. I developed an app for a museum up there, and whilst I didn't need to be there, I thought a change of scene for a couple of months would do me good. Everything that happened with us… it reminded me of how things ended with Zoe and it put me back in a bad place.'

The lobby is thinning out around us and the usher walks over to us.

'You two again. Don't you have homes to go to?' he says, putting his hands on his hips.

'I guess I should be going,' says Aidan.

'Me too.'

I follow him out onto the street and we linger on the pavement.

'I'm sorry about how things worked out,' I say. It's a woefully inadequate start to an apology. 'If it makes it any better, you did know me. Everything between us was real.'

I expect him to look angry or hurt, but he simply nods his head.

'We don't have to do this, you know. I got your letter and you explained it all there.'

'You got it?' I say, feeling gutted that I'd poured my heart into it and it had gone unanswered.

'I did, but not until I got back a couple of weeks ago. I thought about coming to see you and then I thought I'd come here and I sort of hoped I'd run into you. Look, I bought you something.'

He pulls out a paperback from his hoodie pocket and hands it to me.

It's a well-worn copy of *The Princess Bride*. I open it up and look inside.

'It was mine. I found it in a box of books in my parents' loft.'

I read the little looped writing on the title page. '*Dear Aidan, Happy 12th Birthday, love Mum and Dad.*'

'I thought you might want to read it.'

He hands it to me and my eyes prickle with tears. Even after everything that's happened, he's still doing nice gestures.

'I'm sorry, Aidan. I shouldn't have got involved with you when I did. I couldn't help it, you were too easy to fall in love with.'

Shit. Of all the times to start telling the truth.

'You fell in love with me?' He looks up in surprise.

I'm aware that there are other people milling about around us, but I don't care.

He takes a step closer to me and my heart starts to pound.

'I looked up your Instagram, I read your post with the truth. People were pretty mean to you,' he says with a wince.

'I deserved it.'

'A little,' he says. 'But it was still harsh.'

'Maybe. I don't care anymore. I've left that part of my life behind.'

He holds my gaze and then he steps back.

'So,' he says, pointing to the film poster on the wall. '*Jaws*, next month?'

I wrinkle my face up. 'I've never seen it.'

'What? How could you not have seen it?'

I shrug my shoulders.

'Too busy watching *The Princess Bride*, probably.'

He laughs and it makes my heart ache, I've missed his laugh so much.

'Maybe I'll see you here?' he says in a way that makes me feel like I might not have lost him completely. Perhaps we can salvage a friendship at the very least.

'I'd like that,' I say, smiling.

He smiles back before he turns and walks away.

I watch him go and I hate myself. It's not a friendship I want. Why can't I call out and tell him how I really feel? Why am I still so scared to even try?

I drag my feet towards the car park before I stop; I'm stronger than this. I can't keep running away from things in life that might cause me pain. What's the worst that could happen? I'm heartbroken already as it is.

He's got quite the head start on me and I only just catch sight of him as we reach the train station car park. I call out to him a couple of times, but I can see he's wearing giant headphones that I bet are noise-cancelling. Of course he is, he's not going to make this easy for me.

I reach the station and watch him go through the ticket barriers all the while shouting at him but he can't hear me. I run to follow him but I'm blocked by the barriers.

'Excuse me, miss, you need a ticket to get on the platform,' says the guard.

'I don't need one. I'm not getting on a train, I just need to tell that man I love him.'

The guard looks over his shoulder at Aidan.

'Right, but I can't let you onto the platform without a valid ticket.'

'But I don't want to go anywhere.'

I bite my lip and try to keep calm. I look up at the board, there's two minutes until his train.

'Could you make a station announcement and get him to come back?'

'That's not what I'm employed to do. Now, if you don't want to buy a ticket…'

'Buy a ticket! That's exactly what I'll do. One adult to Reading,' I say, pulling out my wallet.

'OK, then. Are you sure you don't want a return?'

'No,' I say as an automated announcement plays out.

*'The train now approaching Platform 3 is the 22:39 service to Reading. This is a stopping service calling at…'*

I ignore the rattled-out list of stations hoping the guard will hurry up.

'That'll be £6.70, then, please.'

I hand over my card.

'Um, we don't accept Tesco's Clubcard.'

'What?' I fumble through my wallet to find the right card.

'Do you want to do contactless or pin?'

I can hear the train pulling into the station.

'Contactless,' I shriek.

He nods and after placing it on the card reader hands it back to me. The ticket prints automatically and I snatch it out of his hands, not caring about my receipt, and shove it in the barrier.

I rush onto the platform and spin around looking for Platform 3. Right now it seems harder to reach than Platform 9¾. I run towards the footbridge and then back down, searching when I hear the whistle blowing behind me.

I'm too late.

My heart sinks and I stagger backwards and I hang my head in my hands as the train pulls away.

'Izzy?'

I look up and see Aidan standing in front of me.

'What are you doing here?' I say.

'I decided not to get on my train,' he says.

'But why?'

'Because I was sitting on the train and I saw you spinning round in circles on the platform and I figured, or at least I hoped, you were looking for me. Were you?'

'Maybe,' I say, taking a deep breath.

'Good, because I hadn't meant to walk off when I did.'

'You didn't?' I say, confused. It looked pretty deliberate to me.

'No, I'd had other things to say, about the letter, about what happened, and then you said… what you said.'

'Ah, yes, I told the truth for once.'

He smiles and nods.

'And of course it freaked me out.'

'I bet it did.'

'So why did you come to the station?' he asks.

'Huh? Oh.' He's looking at me intently and I take a deep breath. It seemed like such a good idea in my head, but now I'm a bag of nerves and I quickly blurt out, 'You know that thing we were having before it all went wrong? I wondered if you wanted to try again?'

'No, I don't want to just have a thing anymore,' he says with a slight shake of his head.

I feel like I've been punched in the gut. What an idiot I was for thinking he would.

'A thing isn't good enough. This time I want to be all-in.'

'All-in?' I say, my heart starting to beat even faster as I desperately hope he means what I think he does.

'Uh-huh,' he says.

'OK,' I say, taking another deep breath, my hands starting to shake. 'You want to be my boyfriend?'

I hold my breath waiting for his answer. I can't quite believe he could possibly say yes.

'Yeah,' he says, grinning. 'I actually do.'

'An actual boyfriend,' I say and it doesn't seem scary in the slightest. I take hold of his hands and I go to pull him in for a kiss when the guard tuts loudly.

'Public displays of affection are not tolerated on the platform,' he says before he turns his back and we both laugh.

'Did you mean what you said earlier about falling in love with me?' he says, causing my cheeks to burn.

'I didn't mean to blurt it out like that. I know that we hadn't been together that long, but I haven't felt like that for a long time and um, sometimes you just know.'

His face breaks out into a huge smile.

'Sometimes you do,' he says, pulling me towards him a little. 'I love you too.'

'You do?'

He nods.

Not even a grumpy ticket inspector is going to stop me grabbing him, only he gets to me first and cups my face before kissing me with so much force that he almost knocks me over.

'Half an hour until another train,' he says when we finally break apart.

'You know I've got my car in the car park? We could be back at yours in half an hour, no train journey, no waiting.'

Aidan takes my hand and we walk towards the ticket barrier and then he stops.

'You know if we go back to mine, Barney's going to be all over you and it's going to be ages until I get to have you all to myself.'

'And? You know Barney's the real reason that I wanted to get back together with you, don't you?'

'Damn it, I should have known,' he says, shaking his head.

'Come on, the sooner I give him a cuddle, the sooner we can—'

I don't have time to finish the sentence as Aidan's whisked us through the barrier and we're running up the road.

'Stop, stop,' I say, needing to catch my breath. I reach forward and give him a kiss as if that's the real reason I needed to stop and not that my calves were killing me from all the running I've already done in pursuit of him tonight.

'Come on, or else we'll never make it.'

He takes my hand and starts pulling me along and I can't stop laughing.

When Ben died I didn't think I'd ever truly be happy again, let alone be happier than I've ever been in my life, which is how I feel now. I certainly haven't been this in love before. It's terrifying, and exhilarating, and amazing, and that's what makes it real. I might have accidentally fallen in love with him and we might not have got off to the best start but something tells me that this is only just the beginning.

# Acknowledgements

Thank you first and foremost to you – lovely reader – for reading this book. I really hope you enjoyed it! I wouldn't get to be here without you, so thank you for keeping me in a job that I mostly adore (all except that point in the first draft between 40–60,000 words where I would usually rather eat my own arm than write). Also sending big book love if you leave a review for it too – it makes such a huge difference to a book's visibility, so thank you! To all the book reviewers and bloggers, thanks for picking my book off your ever-increasing TBR piles and taking the time to review it – you are all superstars.

To my agent Hannah Ferguson, thank you for always being there to bounce ideas off and for general cheerleading when times get tough (cough, that dreaded 40–60k). Also, to the rest of the team at Hardman and Swainson – Jo, Caroline, Thérèse and Nicole for all they do for my books.

I'm also delighted to have found a home at HQ. Thank you to my editor Emily Kitchin for making me dig deeper and for really helping to bring Izzy's story to life. Thank you also to the rest of the team at HQ who I'm looking forward to getting to know better! And to Jon Appleton for the copy-edit and the kind words about it.

A big thank you to Julia and Frederike at Droemer Knaur for their continued support, and their enthusiasm for *We Just Clicked*.

This book was such a joy to write in so many places. I took my Instagram research very seriously and all those times when my husband told me off for scrolling, I could tell him I was actually working – and not faffing about on Insta. In some places it was also heartbreaking to write and I could only imagine the pain of losing a sibling. Whilst the Heart2Heart charity is fictitious, there are charities such as The British Heart Foundation and CRY (Cardiac Risk in the Young) that offer support and information about Sudden Arrhythmic Death Syndrome (SADS).

I absolutely loved writing the scenes based in McKinley's Insurance. The company was based on a big organisation that I spent many a happy summer temping at during my university years and, whilst they never had an office bake off, they did keep coming up with kooky ideas to make work 'fun'. The real Mrs Harris, who still scares me a little, asked me to put her into a book and so I did. I hope that it made you smile. Thanks also to my friend Kaf, who gave me as much of an insight as she could remember about working in insurance – any errors are all mine.

Thanks to my friends for keeping me sane during writing: Ken and Janine Nicholson, Jon and Deb Stoelker, Heather Mason, fellow rom-com writer Lorraine Wilson, Marie Amsler, Catherine de Courcy and (much missed) Diane Barcelli. Also to my far-flung friends that support me wherever they are: Christie, Sarah, Sonia, Ali, Laura, Kaf, Hannah, Jo, Sam, Ross and Zeenat.

To my family as ever, thank you for putting up with me whilst I wrote this – Evan and Jess – sorry I spend so much time hiding away behind my keyboard. To John and Mum, Heather and Harold and Jane – thanks for being so supportive. Finally thanks to my husband Steve for always being there and providing me with much needed Baileys/gin/chocolate buttons.